Varón ushered Kara back toward the SUV, his touch shooting through her body like electricity.

It was possessive, commandeering, and so charged with energy, Kara knew she wouldn't be able to sever it until *he* decided to turn it off.

"You don't have to have your hands on me," she said. "Where do you think I'm going to go?"

"Nowhere," he said, but didn't drop his hand. "You're not that stupid."

Kara sank back into the leather seat and studied him. Classic, chiseled jaw and nearly black hair, suntan, deep-set eyes that showed nothing more and nothing less than he meant them to.

Varón shook his head, a faint smile growing on his lips. "We're an unlikely partnership, aren't we? A month ago, you were pushing me toward Death Row and now I'm your cohort in crime."

"And what happens when I run out of useful information about this killer?" she asked. "What orders will you give to your minions if I cross you?"

"Don't," he said darkly.

Acclaim for Kate Brady's Novels

"Kate Brady writes remarkable prose, providing a stunning visual of each scene...Brady pulled me into this story from the opening paragraph and kept me riveted through its violent, frightening conclusion. If you enjoy a dark, pulse-pounding thriller Where Angels Rest is a highly recommended read." —*USA Today*'s Happy Ever After blog

"Spine-tingling...With its quick-paced plot, nonstop action, and sizzling romance, this read will keep you on the edge of your seat." —*RT Book Reviews*

"Has everything a good suspense novel should...Full of surprises and on-the-edge-of-your-seat scenes that were action-packed and exciting...an amazing, unforgettable story that had me hanging on every word until the very end. —NightOwlReviews.com

"It has been awhile since I stayed up late to finish a book but *Where Angels Rest* kept me glued from the first page until I finished the last page...I will be getting the rest of the series and eagerly look forward to [the next book]." —NovelReaction.com

Last to Die

"A winning combination of complex characters and an intricately woven plot." —*Publishers Weekly*

"The author seems to have an innate talent for creating gripping suspense with witty and determined characters. *Last to Die* is a roller-coaster ride, full of ups and downs, twists and turns. Hold on tight!" —*RT Book Reviews*

One Scream Away

WHERE EVIL WAITS

Also by Kate Brady

One Scream Away
Last to Die
Where Angels Rest

WHERE EVIL WAITS

KATE BRADY

FOREVER

NEW YORK   BOSTON

Copyright © 2014 by Kate Brady

Excerpt from *Where Danger Hides* copyright © 2014 by Kate Brady

All rights reserved. In accordance with the U.S. Copyright Act of 1976, the scanning, uploading, and electronic sharing of any part of this book without the permission of the publisher is unlawful piracy and theft of the author's intellectual property. If you would like to use material from the book (other than for review purposes), prior written permission must be obtained by contacting the publisher at permissions@hbgusa.com. Thank you for your support of the author's rights.

Forever
Hachette Book Group
237 Park Avenue
New York, NY 10017

www.HachetteBookGroup.com

Printed in the United States of America

OPM

First edition: February 2014

10 9 8 7 6 5 4 3 2 1

Forever is an imprint of Grand Central Publishing.
The Forever name and logo are trademarks of Hachette Book Group, Inc.

The Hachette Speakers Bureau provides a wide range of authors for speaking events. To find out more, go to www.hachettespeakersbureau.com or call (866) 376-6591.

The publisher is not responsible for websites (or their content) that are not owned by the publisher.

For Brady, my true love;
For my parents, who taught me
how to recognize true love;
For my children, who are the gifts of true love.

ACKNOWLEDGMENTS

I offer sincere gratitude to my editor, Selina McLemore, for her ever-wise counsel on this manuscript, and my great appreciation to Alex Logan for taking the ball across the finish line.

I continue to exist in a state of astonishment at my good fortune in having caught the eye of agent Jenny Bent, and thank her from the bottom of my heart for hanging in there with both advice and encouragement at every turn.

Anyone who has read this section of my books knows they will see the names Carol Whitescarver and Elaine Sims as two fellow writers to whom I owe much; this manuscript is no different. Those lengthy conversations over Sunday salad bars and late-night reviews have inspired me too many times to count.

I extend my deepest appreciation to Joyce Lamb—author extraordinaire, editor extraordinaire, blogger extraordinaire; personal humorist, cheerleader, and industry consultant. Devoted friend.

I am indebted to my niece, Shannon Dean, who will be in NYC when this book comes out, living in the real world of editing and publishing. Thanks for honing your skills on this manuscript.

Finally, I thank my wonderful family for letting me spend so much time in a pretend world with pretend people, for listening to me talk about what happens while I'm there, and for loving me anyway.

PROLOGUE

"TRUTH."

Sasha Rodin heard the word and stopped behind the gate of the riding arena. He peeked between the slats to watch. Seven teenagers crowded into a circle a few feet away, excluding Andrew Chandler, who had spat the word like the arrogant prick he was.

Sasha sneered, his fingers curling and uncurling on the riding crop in hand. So this was the group he'd been slaving over—stuck-up girls and Chandler-lookalikes who had nothing better to do with their time than take horseback rides and play stupid games, while minions like Sasha catered to their every desire.

"I have an idea," one of the girls said. Her name was Jessica. Yesterday, while hanging nameplates on the stalls to assign each party guest to a horse, he'd tried to imagine what a 'Jessica' looked like: prissy, pale-skinned, and blond, with an air of superiority clinging to her like perfume. Of course, the same could be said for all the guests. Kara

Montgomery, the birthday girl, didn't know any other type.

Not that it mattered who had come to Kara's party. The only person she would notice was Andrew Chandler. She'd been pining over him for years, since before she even had boobs. Had never even noticed Sasha.

The circle of kids broke. "Okay, Andrew," Jessica said. "Truth. Which of the girls in this circle do you want to fuck?"

Andrew smiled. No doubt who he'd pick: the pretty heiress to Montgomery Manor. Sweet fifteen and never been fucked? Sasha doubted it. Even so, this was Kara's lucky day. She was about to get a confession from a boy as rich as she—

"Evie," Andrew said, and the circle gasped. Evie stood and did a little victory dance, and Kara's cheeks turned bright red. Sasha smiled. Served the bitch right.

"Your turn, Kara," a boy named Matthew said. "Truth or dare?"

Kara's chin went up. This should be good.

"Dare," she said.

"Go, girl," Jessica said, and again, the circle gathered tight. A moment later they all moved back out, eyes twinkling mischief. A skinny guy named Anthony looked at Kara.

"You know that guy saddling the horses?" he asked. "That Russian dude?"

"Sasha," Evie said. "I heard someone call him."

Sasha stiffened. What the—

" 'Sasha?' " one of the other kids asked. "That's a girl's name."

"Not for a Russian dude, I guess," Evie said. "Besides, have you looked at the way he's built? Trust me, he's no girl."

"So, Kara," Anthony continued. "Go invite him into the tack room. Your dare is to play Seven Minutes of Heaven with him."

Kara's cheeks paled. Play around with the son of an immigrant stable hand and an immigrant housemaid? Sasha could see the panic on her face. "He's old," she hedged, squirming. "Like, twenty or something."

"You scared?"

Sasha looked at her. Not scared, he realized. Disgusted was more like it.

"Come on, Kara," Matthew said. "I heard he was a big, famous baseball player."

The kids giggled and a red spot of rage came into Sasha's vision. They were mocking him. He wasn't a big, famous baseball player, but he should have been. He'd gotten drafted to play ball in the Minor League right out of high school. Had finally made it out of this pit and found a way across the Great Social Divide.

Then one bar fight ended it. Turned out the other player was the grandson of a steel tycoon out of Pittsburgh. Before Sasha knew it, there were lawyers and media, and the League ended his contract.

Dream gone, just like that.

Of course, Sasha hadn't let it rest. He'd gotten a ski mask and met the tycoon's grandson in a dark alley one night, pulled a Tonya Harding on him. The man never walked straight again.

After that, though, it was back to Virginia. Back to stringing barbed wire and cleaning up horse shit for Willis Montgomery, whose daughter hadn't even noticed he'd left. The only thing different now was that during the two years Sasha was gone, Kara Montgomery had grown up.

And she'd grown up nice. Fifteen today, and her father throwing a weekend-long party. He'd fawn all over her, give her a Ferrari or maybe a blooded Arabian. He wouldn't give her a hug, though. Everyone knew Willis Montgomery preferred a good gelding to his daughter.

Not Sasha. He hated horses. Liked girls just fine. Liked them a lot.

Seven minutes with Kara Montgomery? His mouth went dry. Do it, bitch. I dare you to, too.

She stood and straightened her spine, started toward the gate. Sasha blinked. Jesus, she was coming to find him. Heat surged between his legs and his heartbeat picked up. Seven whole minutes with Kara Montgomery and everybody was going to know what he did to her. They'd expect it, even.

She passed through the circle of her friends, not looking at Andrew. Her cheeks were flushed and knuckles white, but Sasha was most rapt by the way her nipples tightened to tiny little buds beneath her tank top. Her friends giggled—except Andrew, whose humor had faded. They cheered her on as she pushed the arena doors wide.

"Sasha?" she called.

His cock strained against the zipper of his jeans and he didn't question his luck any further. If Kara Montgomery wanted seven minutes with him, he wasn't going to deny her. It was her birthday, after all. And this was the Land of Opportunity.

He stepped out. Kara stopped in her tracks. Sasha smiled, his fingers stroking the crop and his gaze skimming her young curves, telling her in no uncertain terms that he knew exactly why she was looking for him.

And he had seven minutes.

CHAPTER
1

Seventeen years later...
Thursday, June 20, 7:03 p.m.
Atlanta, Georgia

L OUIE!"
Kara Montgomery Chandler shouted from deep in her gut but Louie didn't hear her. Damn it. She wasn't far away but the space between them churned with noisy fans, security guards, and vendors selling everything from chili dogs to stuffed tomahawks. Streams of humanity poured toward the gates at Turner Field, with Louie and the boys sucked into the current trying to make it to their seats before the first batter came up.

Seven minutes from now.

Kara's heart beat faster. Dear God, she had to stop them. She had to stop the killing. That thought washed over her in a wave of horror. Nausea rose to her throat and her fingers clenched her cell phone—the keeper of gruesome, inconceivable horrors. She swallowed back bile, struggling to wrap her mind around what was happening. After a year of weird mysteries, a shocking reality had emerged: Her husband had been murdered. Others were dying. All because of her.

Look what you've done.

She closed her eyes, willing it to be a dream. *Please, let me wake up. Let it not be happening.*

Someone bumped into her and she stumbled. "Sorry, lady," the offender said, grabbing her arms. Kara looked down, checking her hand. Her phone was still there, clamped in white knuckles. No, it wasn't a dream, it was real.

So catch Louie. Hurry.

She bullied down the panic and pushed to higher ground, scanning the veins of people flowing toward the turnstiles. A flash of red hair bobbed in the crowd.

"Aidan!" she shouted. He stopped and turned, fans edging past him as he searched out the voice. His shoulders slumped and a minute later he and his friend Seth separated from the crowd and moved upstream toward her.

"Mom," Aidan groaned. Fourteen years old, and out with the guys. The last person he wanted to see was his mother. "What are you doing here?"

She forced a smile. Keep calm; don't scare him. "I need to talk to your uncle Louie."

Louie came up between his own son and Aidan. "Wait here, boys." He took Kara's arm and walked her several yards out, where the crowd had thinned. "I told you we'd talk later. I can't bail on Seth and Aidan. They did chores for weeks to buy these tickets."

"I know," Kara said. She'd paid them exorbitantly to wash her car and weed the front garden, re-organize a closet that didn't need it. Then, when Father's Day came around and they still didn't have enough for the tickets, she and Louie's wife threw in the last fifty bucks themselves. She didn't want them to miss this game, either.

But things had changed. People were dying. She had to make Louie believe her.

"I got another message," she said, her throat knotting with tension. "I have to show it to you."

"Not here."

"Louie—"

"Damn it, Kara, I told you I'd look into it. I pulled the file on Andrew's accident this afternoon and talked to the chief. I also stuck my nose into the Penny Wolff investigation since you're so worried about her. There's a good team working it, but they don't know where she is. She just vanished."

"She's dead."

"You don't know that."

"I *do*. That's what I'm trying to tell you. I have proof now." She held up her cell phone. "Right here."

Louie frowned, then ran his hand over his face, as if he could wipe away everything she'd told him. He glanced at the boys. "Hold on," he said, digging the tickets from his pocket. He threaded back through the few straggling fans and sent the boys off to find their seats. When they were on their way, he started back to Kara. She turned on her phone to call up the grisly messa—

Crack. A shot split the sky. Louie dropped.

Kara's heart went still. She stared and the screams started. One person, then another, and soon people scattered like billiard balls. Some dropped to the ground; others ran for cover. Louie was the only one who didn't move.

No. Kara forced her feet into action. She staggered toward Louie, dodging a handful of fans who had hit the ground. They came up as it registered that no second shot had sounded—and by the time she got close to Louie, others were there, too.

She fell to her knees beside him. A bright red stain bloomed on his shirt.

"Dad?" Seth's voice. He and Aidan pushed through a growing wall of onlookers. Someone's hand appeared on Louie's chest and pressed down, and Louie gagged on his breath. A trickle of blood formed at the corner of his mouth.

"Dad," Seth cried, sinking to the ground. Aidan crouched beside him and they clung to one another as Louie's eyes rolled, searching for focus. They stopped on Kara, glazed and wide, and his lips moved through a bubble of blood.

She bent down to listen. Only one word touched her ear.

"Run."

Sasha took Louie Guilford out with the first shot. Good light, powerful scope, no wind, and Guilford made it easy by separating himself from the crowd. One squeeze of the trigger and people scattered like droplets of water on a hot skillet.

And right in the center of it: Kara Chandler.

Fuck. She shouldn't have been here.

A knot of rage tightened in the back of Sasha's skull. He lowered the rifle and looked. Without the scope, the scene was like ants scrambling after someone kicked their mound, but he could still make out Kara. She'd shown up just seconds before he fired. Bitch. This was the second time she'd interfered with his plan. First, a couple of days ago with Penny Wolff. Then, with Louie Guilford.

He took a deep breath, started to count to ten to cool off but stopped at five. Okay: Didn't matter. Wolff was dead and Guilford—if he wasn't dead by the time he hit the sidewalk—would be soon. Problems solved, even though Kara was doing her best to fuck things up. She wouldn't succeed. And he'd make damn sure she understood that she was the reason people were dying.

She was the reason for everything. And soon, she would know what that meant. She would learn the truth.

Sasha took out his earplugs and unscrewed the scope, his mood lifting as the pain in his head let up. He didn't like guns—his own brand of killing was much more *personal*—but now he was glad he'd spent time learning to shoot. His father had always said that practice led to perfection. Wouldn't he be impressed with *this*?

He loaded up the gun, anxious to show off tonight's handiwork. He wouldn't be able to get in close and take a nice gory photograph like he had with Penny Wolff but Louie Guilford was a cop and he'd just been shot down outside a Braves game at Turner Field. This would make tonight's news. The Atlanta PD would go nuts. Maybe Ted Turner would even speak.

Yes, there would be plenty of publicity to share between father and son.

And Kara? He'd have to think about her later. Right now, he needed to get out of here. He was situated on an overpass six hundred yards away—a safe enough distance for a while, but there was no sense in lingering. Authorities were too busy clearing people from sight and moving Louie Guilford to safety to analyze the trajectory of the bullet just yet, but it wouldn't take long before they did. Within minutes, they'd have choppers in the air and roadblocks surrounding this whole area of the city.

Wouldn't matter. Within minutes, Sasha would be gone.

Too bad. He'd love to stay and watch Kara suffer.

He shook his head. Patience. Her birthday was right around the corner and now that Penny Wolff and Louie Guilford were out of the way, Sasha could get back to preparations. It was a scheme more than a year in the making, one that had cost hundreds of thousands of dollars and taken him all over the country. A plan so Machiavellian it had left even his father slack-jawed.

Only one kill left now—a girl named Megan. Sasha would bring her home tomorrow night. Then all would be ready, just in time for Kara's big day.

He smiled and tossed one more glance toward Turner Field. Poor Kara. She must be horrified by now, but it was about to get worse. His reign of terror was just beginning and he'd seen to it that there was no one she could turn to for help. Nothing she could do to stop him from making this the party of a lifetime.

Three more days. Happy Birthday, Kara.

CHAPTER
2

Friday, June 21, 11:56 p.m.
Atlanta, Georgia

I T WAS AN ODD place to find Kara Chandler, at an odd time: a squalid alley in the armpit of Atlanta, nearly midnight. The air sweltered—code orange, said the news, with dramatic warnings for asthma sufferers and the elderly to stay inside—and here, in an alley off Vine Street, the odors of urine and smog and rotten trash clung to every surface like a film.

Luke Varón inched to his left, peering past a Dumpster to the sidewalk. An odd place indeed for Kara Chandler, yet there she was, looking nothing like he'd expected. The heels were gone, her normally businesslike bun now falling in gold waves over her shoulders. In place of the usual classic suit, she wore jeans and a short-sleeved blouse, and instead of a fashionable purse, a shapeless macramé sack hung over one shoulder with her right hand buried deep inside.

Gun.

Luke held to the shadows. Two aluminum-caged security bulbs studded the eaves behind him but he'd broken the nearest one, forcing what was left of the sickly light toward the street. Kara Chandler paused, then took a few steps to go peek into a culvert that wasn't visible from the alley's entrance. Luke's hackles lifted: Ms. Chandler had been here before.

"Mr. Varón?"

Her voice stroked the night and every fiber of Luke's body tightened. Damn, he shouldn't be here. In two days, eight and a half tons of cocaine cut with levamisole would arrive off the Georgia coast, and with the shipment, Frank Collado. Luke had spent the last week securing the route from Colombia. He'd returned to the States a few hours ago, longing only for a clean bed and about sixteen hours to languish in it.

What he'd found was a message from Kara Chandler: Assistant District Attorney for Fulton County and Andrew Chandler's wife. As either identity, she could threaten the security of the shipment. As both, she was downright dangerous.

"Mr. Varón?" she said again.

Luke strung the silence out another inch, then said, "Here."

She whirled, a bulge forming in the canvas of her bag. "Where? Come out, damn it."

"So you can shoot me through a wall of macramé?"

"I didn't ask you here so I could shoot you. You're not worth the effort."

"Flattery," Luke drawled. "There's a saying about where that will get you."

"I need to talk to you. Come out."

He did, leading with a G18. Her gaze dropped and he

watched the details of the weapon register in her eyes: a lightweight, 9mm shooter with a threaded barrel to accommodate a silencer, and just now sporting an extra magazine that held thirty-three rounds. Tonight, he'd added the extra clip just for show, but in fully-automatic mode, the G18 could fire all thirty-three bullets in less than two seconds. It was legal only among law enforcement and the military.

Luke Varón was neither.

He didn't know what she was carrying, but it didn't take her long to determine she was outclassed. The bulge in the bag slackened.

Luke tipped the Glock skyward. "Your turn," he said, but Kara Chandler didn't move. "Lady, pull your fucking hand out. I'd hate to fill you with bullets and then learn you were going for lipstick."

An inch at a time, she withdrew her hand—empty. Luke lifted the edge of his Armani suit coat and tucked his gun in the holster. He took two steps to his left so when she angled to keep her eyes on him, the frail light caught her face. Not that he needed any reminders of what she looked like: hair the color of sunlight, bottle-green eyes dulled by tragedy, two teasing little tucks in her cheeks that flashed like lightning when she was angry and perhaps—Luke could only speculate here—when she smiled. Without her heels, she stood only a few inches above five feet, but she carried herself as if meeting him eye to eye.

On her turf—in a courtroom trying to convict him of murder, for example—Kara Chandler was the definition of cold control. Out here, she was wired so tight Luke thought she might snap if she so much as took a deep breath.

"You called?" Luke asked.

"Yes," she said, but beneath the steel nerves, Luke caught a quaver in her voice. "I have a proposition for you."

Luke feigned delight. "Now, what could a faithful public servant like you want with a common criminal like me?"

"This has nothing to do with the DA's office. It's personal."

"Even better," he said, and let his gaze run down her figure and back again. Christ, Andrew Chandler had been one lucky son of a bitch. Except, of course, that he was dead. He'd been killed by a drunk driver while walking across a street, along with the woman on his arm.

Elisa.

"I want to hire you," she said, and he almost blinked. He caught himself and arched a dark brow instead.

"I'm not a stockbroker or private chef, Ms. Chandler."

"I know what you are. You're a drug cartel hit man, an arsonist, and a cold-blooded killer. So this job should be right up your alley. I want you to blow up a boat and make sure its owners die in the fire."

Luke was flabbergasted. Christ.

"I'll pay you," she said. "I want it done tonight, as soon as possible..."

She rattled off details, speaking right past him as if she'd rehearsed a script. His skepticism climbed to the surface. He'd already checked the area. There were no electronics and no surveillance. The thought passed that Chandler could be wearing a wire, but she was an unlikely choice for a sting.

Besides, this didn't have the feel of a scam. District Attorney Ben Archer hiring Luke Varón to commit multiple murder? No way.

"It should be done at least two hours before sunris—"

"Why me?" he asked.

She stopped, startled. "Because you can get away with it. You proved that when you walked out of court a month ago. You can get away with anything."

"More flattery," he said. "But you must know dozens of good criminals."

Her gaze might have melted steel. "Besides you, the criminals I know are behind bars."

"Ah, yes," Luke said, letting the hint of a smile show. "You aren't accustomed to a checkmark in the LOSS column. I'm sorry I tarnished your record."

She took a step toward him. "It wasn't a loss, it was a mistrial. And you were guilty. You know it and I know it. You killed a man in that warehouse fire—some unidentified soul who went to an unmarked grave. You should be in prison for the rest of your life."

"Lucky for you I'm not. Who would you call to commit *your* felonies?"

She gritted her teeth. "I don't know how the evidence against you disappeared but I know there was enough to put you away for life, at the very least. The fact that you're a goon for Gene Montiel and have access to his resources is just proof that he's as dirty as the DA thinks."

"And as powerful?" Luke suggested. Kara Chandler wasn't a gracious loser. Apparently, that was especially true when the freed defendant—Luke—worked security for a multi-millionaire land developer who owned a good portion of Atlanta's businesses, police, and justice department. A man the DA claimed had ties to a major drug cartel.

The DA was right: Gene Montiel *did* have a tie to a major drug cartel—Luke. But that didn't have anything to do with Kara Chandler.

"I appreciate the *film noir* character of this little

charade, Ms. Chandler," Luke said. "But is District Attorney Archer really so desperate to nail Gene Montiel that he's sending you into dark alleys to entrap Montiel's...goon?"

"This isn't a charade. I told you, this is personal."

"Prove it."

"Excuse me?"

He skimmed down her blouse buttons. "Show me you aren't wearing a wire."

Her eyes blazed, but Luke could see that she was thinking about it. Considering stripping her clothes in a lonely, dark alley with a hit man for the Rojàs cartel, just to prove she wasn't wired. Proof enough, Luke thought, and couldn't quite believe his eyes when her fingers slipped the first disk through the hole. Jesus, she was going to do it. He felt like a twelve-year-old who'd just stumbled on a *Playboy* magazine under a mattress, watching her cleavage and the upper swells of her breasts come into view, her flat, pale belly revealed an inch at a time. His blood drained from his brain as she slid the blouse from her arms and let it drop to the pavement with her bag.

You don't have to do this. The words rose to mind but didn't make it past his lips. She unzipped her jeans and shimmied the denim over her hips—an unconsciously seductive move from any woman in any circumstance, and almost unbearably so in the heat of night with a woman of Kara Chandler's lithe curves and unexpected mystique. Luke's mouth went dry as she stepped from the jeans, then straightened and squared her shoulders.

The notion of sixteen hours in bed took an unexpected turn. Luke swallowed and took his time looking. Long, slender limbs and gently flaring hips, lace-edged underwear cut high enough and low enough to accentuate soft curves usually encased in power suits. Her breasts strained against pale satin cups, and Luke's fingers curled into fists with the desire to trade the bra for his hands.

"Satisfied?" she asked.

"Hardly," Luke said with more honesty than he intended. He stepped toward her, noting a trickle of perspiration between her breasts even as a shiver drew her nipples tight. "You and I both know transmission devices can be almost imperceptible, except upon close inspection." He circled around her, stopping at her back to brush a hand beneath her hair and lift it from her shoulders, fanning his fingers through the waves. A sweet scent rose to his nostrils from the pulse point on her throat, an incongruous touch of elegance in the fetid alley.

But there were no electronics. If she was wearing a wire, it was installed someplace that would require exploration to find. That thought sent a surge of blood against his zipper, but a wave of anger flowed right behind it. Kara Chandler was no blushing virgin. She was a widow and a mother, an Assistant District Attorney in a major metropolis, a woman who'd taken Luke to court once for murder and whose boss was committed to destroying Gene Montiel.

And she was playing a game. Luke didn't like games when he didn't know the rules.

He coiled the mass of gold around his hand and tightened the slack, tipping her head back to expose a pale stretch of throat. "You think it's a good idea, presenting yourself to me like this? Perhaps you don't know what I'm capable of."

"I know exactly what you're capable of," she said through clenched teeth. "It's the reason I called you. And it's the reason I wrote a letter that identifies who I'm meeting, when, and where. It also contains the DA's evidence against Montiel."

Luke was careful not to react, but his gut tightened. If Kara Chandler had hijacked evidence and let it leak before the shipment arrived, the whole operation could collapse. Eight and a half tons of levamisole-laced cocaine would never make it to shore.

Neither would Frank Collado.

Luke brushed the backs of his knuckles over the warm flesh on Kara Chandler's neck. "You're lying," he said against her ear, but he was afraid she wasn't.

A breath shuddered between her lips. "I'm fully aware that you have Gene Montiel's resources at your disposal, and that you can disappear on a moment's notice to a nation without extradition. But understand that if I am murdered here tonight, nothing short of that will keep you from being arrested."

Luke tightened his grip on her hair, pulling her nearly naked frame against him. "Murder wasn't what I had in mind," he whispered. A bit of bald truth in a tangle of lies. He waited for a shiver of fear, but instead she jerked away and spun on him, teeth bared.

"Do it, then."

Luke stared.

"You think I don't know what kind of man you are? That I didn't know before I came here what you might demand?" Her voice vibrated with anger, maybe even with disgust, but at the same time, tears bloomed in her eyes. "Your mistake is in thinking I care," she shot. "If sex is the currency you want, then get it over with. It's hot out here and it stinks."

Luke was stunned. Assistant District Attorney Kara Chandler stood in front of him with nothing but scant inches of silk and lace between them, so desperate for his cooperation that she had stolen evidence from the DA's office, contacted a hit man, and offered him money—and more—to kill someone.

Warning bells went off. *Walk away.* In two more days, Collado would be his. A tumble with Kara Chandler wasn't worth losing him.

Walk away.

Luke stepped back, scooped her clothes from the ground, and fired them at her chest. "Count yourself lucky that I'm partial to brunettes," he said, but didn't bother turning away while she hurried back into her clothes. He tried not to notice the sense of loss in his gut as she covered herself, tried not to wonder what—besides a setup— would drive a woman of the law to such extremes as to try to hire a hit.

That thought was more than Luke could ignore. She bent down to pick up her bag and just before she would have walked away, he stopped her with his voice. "Ms. Chandler," he said, "you never told me: Whose boat and whose death?"

She looked him straight in the eyes. "Mine."

CHAPTER
3

Kara turned to leave but Varón's hand clamped on to her arm.

Yes, she thought, with a thump in her chest. *Please.*

"Yours?" He sounded incredulous.

"And my son's," she said. "We need to fake our deaths. We need to disappear."

He looked as if he couldn't decide whether to curse or laugh. In the end, he simply said, "I'm listening."

His hand burned her arm like a brand. He was too close again, the heat of a summer night intensified by the heat rolling off his body. And the strength. For a moment, Kara was certain she had done the right thing. Luke Varón was sheer power. In retrospect, she knew that his calm arrogance when she'd prosecuted him for murder had been born of utter certainty the charges would never hold up. The man had strings to places she couldn't begin to reach, a network of gorillas to do anything he asked, and was capable of acts of deceit she could only imagine.

"Let go of me," she said. "I won't be manhandled."

His lashes dipped to her throat, where she had buttoned her blouse all the way to the top. "Sex is okay, but no manhandling?"

"I said, let go of me."

He dropped his hand. Instantly, Kara found it easier to breathe.

Do it. Tell him enough to get him on board. "I believe my son and I are in danger," she said. "I want you to fake our deaths, then provide us with the protection and the resources I need to find out who's responsible."

Varón cocked his head. "I think you have me confused with the police, Ms. Chandler."

"I already talked to a detective."

"And?"

And within hours, he was dead. Just like Penny Wolff. Both of them gone right after Kara had spoken to them.

A wave of conscience hit and she glanced around the alley, wondering if the killer was out there this very moment, targeting Varón next. She tamped back a pang of guilt. For God's sake, Varón was cold and evil and lethal. A month ago, she'd led the charge to put him on Death Row.

Besides, he was untouchable. He was the last person she should worry about.

"The police can't help me," she said. "For God's sake, do you think I would choose to deal with the likes of you if I had any other option?"

"You really need to work on your flattery."

"One week, Mr. Varón. Take us underground and give me seven days."

He crossed his arms. "What makes you think I can do what the police couldn't?"

"Don't toy with me," she snapped, taking a step toward him. "You work with a network that's better organized, better trained, better financed, and better armed than any

police department in this country. You can find out anything about anybody, and you can cover your tracks doing
it. I know how to run an investigation. All I need from
you is—"

"A goon?" He crossed his arms. "The way I remember it, your husband's firm went bankrupt, left you with
a heap of bills to pay. I doubt you can afford my services,
Ms. Chandler."

Kara powered down a sneer of revulsion. "I can afford
you," she said. "Name your price."

His brows went up and it was all Kara could do not to
back up a step. "Well, I'll have to think about that, now,
won't I?" he asked. "But what if I say yes and at the end of
the week, you're still in danger?"

"Then my son and I will take our new identities and
disappear. By then, I'll wager I will have committed a
number of crimes—this being one of them. I won't be in
much of a position to prosecute you for yours."

He thought about it for a long moment and Kara found
herself holding her breath. Dear God, she needed him.
She needed him to stand between Aidan and her, and a
murderer. She needed him because he was capable and
strong and invulnerable, and wouldn't be hindered by
obeying the law.

But he wasn't buying it. He shook his head and did the
one thing she'd been afraid of: He laughed.

Kara's heart plunged to her belly. The bastard. She'd
risked everything coming to him. "Answer me, damn
you. Yes or no?"

He stopped laughing, then reached out to smooth a
lock of hair behind her ear. "No," he said. "In fact, not just
no, but *fuck* no."

Kara felt as if she'd been kicked in the chest. He couldn't

be doing this. Andrew's killer was out there. He'd killed Penny Wolff and Louie. She and Aidan had to get away.

But not with any help from Varón. He'd made that perfectly clear.

She stepped back, her knees unsteady, swallowing the panic that rose to the back of her throat. She turned and forced her legs to move, spine straight and chin high, leaving Varón in the alley behind her. Dread congealed in her chest, growing thicker with every step, and she picked up speed to put distance between her and the crazy ruse that had brought her to that alley and Luke Varón. By the time she hiked back to where she'd left her car, she was shaking with emotion. Fury, grief, fear.

Mostly, fear.

"Damn him," she said, swinging out into the street. Not even just *No*, but *Fuck, no*. The bastard.

She drove out of town and headed north. All right, so Varón was out of it. But she still had to move. On to Plan B. It had even less to recommend it than Plan A—Varón—but people were dying everywhere she turned.

So screw Varón. For all his arrogance, he was right about one thing: He wasn't the only criminal she knew.

She found an all-night Walmart, bought a ready-to-use phone, and punched in Jay Kemp's number. Kemp was a bouncer who had acted as an informant on a case a couple of years ago, in exchange for a plea in his own case. He was an asshole, and greedy. He would be capable of the boat explosion. Beyond that, she would be on her own. He didn't have the resources Varón did to keep her and Aidan safe or give them new identities.

Still, he was the only choice left.

The call lasted thirty seconds. Yes, Kemp was interested. Yes, he would meet her. The bar where he worked closed at two. Three o'clock, then, in the parking lot of a boarded-up bowling alley on Hawkins Store Road. Empty lot, abandoned. No cameras.

Enough time to check on Aidan.

Kara drove out of her way and rolled past a trash can, dumping the phone from Walmart. She parked and, using her iPhone, called Sally Guilford. It was almost one in the morning, but she knew Sally would be up.

Sally was planning Louie's funeral.

Seth answered. "Aunt Kara. Mom and I were just talking about you. We decided you wouldn't be up this late."

"I couldn't sleep," Kara lied. So many lies, now. She wondered if she would ever keep them straight.

"We're going through pictures of Dad," Seth said, his voice thin. "We just found a bunch from that time at Stone Mountain when you and Uncle Andr—" He stopped, and Kara closed her eyes.

"I remember," she said. "Andrew got stung by a bee."

"Yeah," Seth said, and Kara fought to keep the tears from her voice. No teenage boy should have to watch his father die. And no teenage boy should lose his best friend.

That's what would happen if she went through with her plan to disappear with Aidan. Seth and Sally would think they were dead, right on the heels of losing Louie. How could she do this to them?

Reality gripped her. How could she not?

She smothered a stab of guilt and forced herself to speak. "Is Aidan asleep?"

A strange silence came over the phone. Kara heard Seth whisper something, then he said, "Here's Mom."

Sally came on. The back of Kara's neck prickled.

"Kara, aren't you at home?" Sally asked.

"Uh, no. Did Aidan fall asleep?"

Sally hesitated and Kara's heart skipped a beat. "He said he wanted to go home and be with you tonight. I took him over to your house after dinner. He said you'd be home soon."

Oh-God-oh-God-oh-God. The trembling started. It was all Kara could do to speak. "Okay. I'm on my way there now. Let me call him. Thanks."

She couldn't disconnect fast enough. Her fingers shook on the phone and as she dialed she peeled out of the parking lot, gunning toward her house. She listened through the rings, her heart thumping faster with every passing second. Aidan's answering message picked up.

No.

She fumbled with the phone and dialed again, wheeling around a corner. Again, no answer. Oh, God.

Aidan.

CHAPTER
4

LUKE STAYED WITH KARA Chandler for five miles, then passed her surveillance off to an agent named Garrett and drove to an all-night Kwik-Mart on Chase Street. He stuck the gas nozzle in the tank of his car—a loaded Porsche Carrera that had been waiting for him at Customs when he'd returned to the U.S. a little over a year ago— and ducked into the store. He headed for the second stall of the restroom, removed his suit coat and rolled up his sleeve, then lifted the lid of the toilet tank and withdrew a small, waterproof box. He pocketed the cell phone from inside the box, washed his hands and restored his clothing, and paid for the gas in cash.

A mile later, he pulled over and punched POWER on the phone, noticed a message, and dialed Vince Knutson. "What did you find out about Andrew Chandler's widow?"

"Check the phone. I already sent it."

Luke's gut loosened a fraction. Knutson was on it. In his late fifties, Knutson had a genius for computers and access to virtually everything the FBI had. The DEA was a different matter. Turf wars.

"What did she want?" Knutson asked.

"She wants me to explode her boat and make it look like she and her kid die in the fire."

"Ah, Christ," Knutson said. "She's running."

"From what?"

"I don't know. Best I can tell is she may be running from a sniper."

"What?"

"Yesterday afternoon, Kara Chandler went to see a detective in the Atlanta Police Department—a buddy of her late husband's named Louie Guilford. After they spoke, Guilford pulled the file on her husband's accident, started poking around."

Luke frowned. Her husband had been dead for a year. "I've been through Andrew Chandler's killing a hundred times. There's nothing there. Guilford couldn't have found anything."

"We'll never know," Knutson said. "Last night, when you were en route to Savannah, Louie Guilford got picked off by a seven-millimeter Remington Magnum before a Braves game, walking to the gate with his son. Kara Chandler was there. He died in her arms."

The police can't help me. Something tugged in Luke's chest. No wonder she was willing to do anything to get out of sight. She was one scared lady.

But she was also a lady who could send Collado into hiding. Luke clenched his fists, as if trying to hang on to everything they'd put in place over the past year. "She says she has evidence against Montiel."

Knutson cursed. "I thought we'd put a lid on that. We've almost got this thing in the bag, Luke. Between us and the DEA we've got agents at every location, ready to pull the plug. But if Kara Chandler leaks something about

Montiel beforehand, it's all over. We'll never see those drugs except through the autopsies of kids they kill."

I'll never see Collado.

"Did Mrs. Chandler seem determined to carry this thing through?" Knutson asked.

Luke recalled her slender fingers on the buttons, her pale breasts glowing like half moons, while a man she believed to be beyond redemption looked on. *Name your price.*

"Pretty determined, I'd say."

"Then she's onto something. And if it's big enough to make her threaten Montiel with evidence the DA's office has been ordered to sit on, she'll find someone else to do what she wants. We're just lucky you're the first place she turned."

"Second," Luke said darkly. "Louie Guilford was the first."

"So watch your back." A phone rang on Knutson's end. "Hold on."

Luke tried to jostle pieces into place: Andrew Chandler had been dead for a year, because of a random drunk driver, and now his wife was picking up the scent of murder when Luke had never picked up the scent of anything. The cop she'd confided in was dead. And Kara herself was scared enough to try to hire a known criminal to help her disappear, and ballsy enough to harbor evidence against Montiel as insurance to pull it off.

But she was in over her head.

Knutson came back. "That was Garrett. Kara Chandler just hit a Walmart near Eaton and bought a prepaid cell phone. He watched her pull over and make a call, then peel out."

Luke swore. He hadn't expected her to move so

quickly. "So, who's Public Enemy Number Two? Since I refused her job, who would she go to next?"

"I don't know. Garrett picked up the phone she dumped, so we'll find out. But meanwhile, she's moving, and everywhere she turns, she's tripping wires. You gotta stop her."

Luke bullied his brow with his fingers. "Rig her boat and stash the detonator. Get her some papers and IDs, and send me someone to make them over. Call me when you're ready."

"What are you going to do?"

"I'm gonna break into her house, find out what the hell is going on."

"Better hurry. Garrett says that woman is *moving*."

Kara raced toward Buckhead, dialing Aidan again and again. Terror clouded her vision.

Look what you've done.

She got to the intersection just outside her neighborhood and saw blue lights. God, God, God. A car blocked the street, and two police cruisers. A tow truck was working on the car.

No. She pounded the steering wheel, her heart lodged in her throat. "Go," she said through clenched teeth, and kept dialing Aidan. She thought about backing out and going another direction but there wasn't another quick route, thought about pleading with one of the officers to go on to her house in front of her, but couldn't get past the memory of Louie in her arms, drawing his last breath. She thought about why Aidan might not be answering his phone and let the tears flow, more helpless than she had ever been in her life, and then, suddenly, the stalled car was out of the way, the cruisers pulled to the side, and an officer waved her through.

She raced into her neighborhood and swung into the driveway. She ran to the porch, fumbling the key into the lock and slamming the door closed behind her. She started to dash upstairs to Aidan's bedroom, then veered to the great room first, hardly able to think. If anything had happened to Aid—

She stopped. Relief poured into her lungs.

He was there, sprawled on the couch in plaid pajama bottoms, his chest rising and falling in even motions. His phone sat on the end table showing her missed calls, and a set of headphones was strung to his ears. He was asleep, music playing.

Kara closed her eyes. She wanted to reach out and touch him, brush the rusty lock of hair back from his forehead like she had when he was little. But she didn't. Don't wake him yet. The time would come soon enough. With or without Luke Varón, the Chandlers were going to disappear tonight.

She went back to the foyer and sank against the wall, looking around at the welcoming entrance hall, cozy living room, homey great room. Sorrow welled up inside. For most of her life, from the rolling hills of Virginia horse country to high-class boarding schools in England to chalets in the north of France, she'd never felt at home. Her father had showered her with gifts but little else and her young adult years had been spent following Andrew around, mothering Aidan, and picking up her education one or two courses at a time. Finally, they'd settled in Atlanta and *this* house was hers. It hadn't been Andrew's choice—it wasn't big enough, elegant enough, showy enough. But Kara liked the simplicity and wanted Aidan to grow up in a normal home with a normal mother and father, not with maids and cooks and gardeners. This home had become her haven.

After tonight, she might never see it again.

She drew a deep breath and looked at her watch. An hour and a half before she had to meet Jay Kemp. She pushed from the wall and climbed the stairs to her bedroom. Tears stung the backs of her eyes and she dumped out the macramé bag on her bed. Her gun, a .38 Glock Andrew had insisted she carry after her first contentious case in the DA's office. Cash, the thick roll she'd collected as payment for Varón. Her wallet and the standard IDs—driver's license, credit cards, courthouse pass. She wouldn't need them anymore, but it would look strange to investigators for her to have left home without them. Her iPhone.

She stopped, clutching the damnable phone. She didn't want to take it. She wanted to throw it against the fireplace or crush it beneath her heel. But she couldn't. She was too much a prosecutor to destroy evidence. And this phone contained evidence of the most horrific kin—

Fwsshhh.

A whisper of sound brushed behind her. Every nerve turned to steel. She listened, afraid to turn, straining to hear past the sudden drumming in her temples.

The pistol lay on the bed and she inched her hand toward it, hardly daring to breathe. Behind her, the air went dead silent and the thought passed that maybe she was just hearing thi—

Fwsshhh A soft brush of satin. The drapes.

Dear God, someone was there. Aidan? No, he moved through the house like a bull. Besides, he was downstairs sleeping.

Please, Aidan, don't wake up.

Kara curled her hand around the pistol grip, slid her finger over the trigger. She took a deep breath and whirled.

"Freeze," she said. "Don't move."

CHAPTER
5

SASHA HAD TO MOVE. Big night tonight: the final kill. Kara had certainly done her best this week to throw a couple of wrenches into his plans but both of those complications were dealt with now. In the end, all she'd really done was provide a way for him to add an extra dose of horror to her life.

He smiled. She must be scared shitless now, after her front-row seat for Louie Guilford's murder. For a year, Sasha had been watching her, controlling her, killing for her, and she hadn't even known it. But now, he wanted her to know. He was almost ready for her; he wanted her to be ready for him, too. Only two more days.

He shook off the daydream and looked at the clock. Time to move. He had a message for Kara and wanted to show it to his father before he sent it. It was late; the staff at the nursing home would give him a hard time, but they'd let him in. They had to, anytime he wanted. He'd already gone around that mulberry bush a few months ago with a crotchety old nurse, presented her with a copy of the Nursing Home Reform Act of 1987, and came back in the middle of the night for the next three visits just to watch the biddy turn red with anger.

Tonight, he didn't have time to argue with the staff. He just wanted to see his father.

So much to share.

He pulled into the parking lot in his 2013 Lexus sports coupe, bleeped the key fob to lock the car, and strolled into the lobby, hands in his pockets. He started out whistling, then stopped himself: too much. He sauntered past the front reception desk as if it were perfectly normal to visit at this hour, keeping an eye out for Nurse Ratched and inwardly daring someone to stop him.

No one did.

He headed down the hall and around the corner to Room 144, pressed the door open. The smell of this place always sickened him: The lobby smelled like cold metal and antiseptic; the room smelled of feces and urine and stale bedsheets, festering beneath a thick layer of Hawaiian Breeze air freshener.

The weak rasp of a snore touched his ears. His father lay in bed sleeping, the skeletal leftovers of a man once hardy and brilliant. Now, he was little more than a vegetable.

Sasha had made him that way. It was one of his fondest memories.

"Hello, *nana*," he said, and though he'd barely spoken, the rasp changed. His father knew he was there. And couldn't do a damn thing about it.

"Wake up, I don't have much time. I have something to show you."

The skeleton shifted and Sasha turned on the bedside lamp. His father blinked, glancing past Sasha to the door.

"No, no one will come. They wouldn't intrude on a touching visit between father and son."

His father's mouth began to work, like a hungry carp. His hands came to his chest, fingers curved inward with palsy, breathing labored, eyes still keen and intelligent. What a waste: an IQ of 165 and a terminal degree in mathematics, and yet he'd spent his life mucking stalls and waiting on Willis Montgomery's family, hoarding stacks of Russian mathematics magazines to feed his brain at night and tutor his sons. One of his sons, anyway. Sasha's gifts were in challenges of the body, not the brain. Once, his dad had lowered himself enough to come to one of Sasha's baseball games. Sat in the stadium with a rod up his ass and something on his face that might have been shame. He couldn't comprehend that a child spawned of the great minds of Dmitri and Darya Rodin would choose baseball over scholarly pursuits. That wasn't why they'd moved to America.

No, they'd moved to America for Stefan. Stefan, of the brilliant mind. The crown jewel of the Rodin family.

Sasha looked down at his father, whose eyes were glazed with worry. A thin layer of drool dribbled down his chin. Deliberately, Sasha picked up the stack of logic puzzles on the nightstand and moved it two inches, just to remind his father they were there. A little remembrance that a great mind had been deprived of oxygen just long enough to turn his body to Jell-O. And while everyone else thought Dmitri's mind had gone the same route as his body, Sasha knew better. His father understood everything.

Everything.

"I have something to show you, *nana*," he said, pulling out his phone. Dmitri's panic spiked. His body made a series of little twitches. They'd done this before, with every kill. Just a few days ago, Sasha had brought in a picture of Penny Wolff, strangled and propped up against the wheel well of his old beater Dodge van. He'd driven all night to dump Penny's body out of the way, in a cornfield in Mississippi. But before he'd sent Kara the picture, he'd brought it in to the nursing home. He knew how his father liked to share in his accomplishments.

Now, he called up the message he would soon send to Kara. Enlarged the screen so his father could make out the details. It was right off the front page of today's newspaper: ATLANTA DETECTIVE GUNNED DOWN AT BRAVES GAME.

"Did you see this on the news last night? I hope you knew it was my work. I couldn't get in for a close-up on this one, but I think you'll still be impressed. I'll bet you had no idea I could shoot like that, did you?" he said, putting the phone in front of his father's face. "I've been practicing."

Dmitri's eyes closed.

"*Nyet*," Sasha said, and slapped him hard. "Read it."

His father did, the genius eyes staring, the carp-mouth working, the limbs twitching. A small groan came from his throat.

"I know," Sasha said, deliberately misinterpreting his father's horror. "He was a surprise to me, too. Kara forced me to make a change in plans. It's okay, though. The girl I told you was next—Megan?—well, don't worry. I'm on my way to get her now." He looked at his watch and feigned surprise. "Oh, my, I'd better get going. She'll be getting off work soon."

His father's breathing hitched. His head rolled back and forth.

"Oh, don't be upset, *nana*. I'll come back and show you Megan when I'm finished with her. I know how much you like to share in my accompli—"

A knock sounded. Sasha pocketed the phone and the door pressed open.

"Mr. Rodin?"

A nurse's aide peeked in. Sasha stood, a finger of anger pressing on the back of his neck.

"I was just leaving," he said. He tried to sound casual but the finger began tapping. He studied the girl. She was thin, with brown hair pulled into a ponytail, wearing the requisite smock and sensible shoes. Couldn't be more than twenty years old. He glanced at the plastic tag pinned to her pocket: Sarah Fogt.

"I was checking on Mr. Rodin," she said. Sasha glared at her and she took an involuntary step back. "He had a cough today, so I just wanted—"

"If he had a cough, why wasn't I notified?"

She swallowed. "Well, it wasn't that bad, but—"

"You're new here, aren't you?" Sasha asked, bearing down on her a bit.

"Y-yes," she said, her gaze darting back and forth between him and the bed. His father's breaths came quick and shallow. Sarah looked concerned.

"Well, let me introduce myself," he said, turning on the charm. Sasha wasn't bad looking and had a physique that impressed women. He could play the games. "I'm Sasha. Dmitri is my father." He held out his hand and she gave him a limp-wristed shake. "I didn't mean to snap at you, but a cough—that sounds bad. He developed pneumonia once."

She withdrew her hand and started back-pedaling. "It wasn't too bad...I've just been checking on him every once in a while, that's all."

A black spot appeared in Sasha's vision. *Liar.* His body went tight. Sarah Fogt was a lying little bitch.

But he couldn't do anything about that now. He closed his eyes on the black spot and forced himself to breathe. It was more important to send his message to Kara than to worry about some nurse's aide here.

So leave Sarah be. She wasn't worth the trouble.

He patted the phone in his pocket and glanced back at his father. "Well, if he hasn't been feeling well, I'd better not keep him up. I just hadn't been here for a couple of days, that's all. I know it's late."

He bent over his father to kiss both cheeks the way Russians did. *"Do svidaniya, papa,"* he said aloud, but when he touched the second cheek, he lowered his voice to a whisper: *"Ya vernus."*

I'll be back.

He held the girl's pale eyes as he walked past her, memorizing them. Sarah Fogt, his mind repeated, making sure to remember. *Don't get in my way.*

CHAPTER
6

KARA TIGHTENED BOTH HANDS on the gun. "Freeze," she said again.

The intruder didn't, but slipped from behind the drapes. Tall and heavy-shouldered, with jet hair and eyes the color of black coffee.

"You," Kara breathed. "Damn you," she said, but at the same time, relief shivered through her limbs. She bent her elbows and then chided herself for that bit of foolishness. Relief was illogical. Luke Varón was a criminal. He'd broken into her home. Aidan was here.

She leveled her aim. "What are you doing here?"

"I had second thoughts so I came to discuss the terms of your offer," he said, and his gaze dipped to the gun. "But this isn't a good way to foster a trusting employer-employee relationship."

"As opposed to breaking into my home and hiding like a criminal?"

"I *am* a criminal. I thought you were counting on that. And because of that, I thought it wise not to be seen ringing your front doorbell."

Her fingers tightened on the gun, so hard cramps screamed up the tendons in her arms.

"Ms. Chandler," he said, his voice stern, "I'm getting a little tired of having to talk you down from a gun. The way you're shaking, you're going to shoot me by accident."

"It won't be by accident. And I didn't think I was unclear when I explained the job to you," she said, keeping her voice down for Aidan's sake. "I want people to think we're dead—my son and I. I want the news to report it and show footage. You've proved that you have the means to make something like that happen. Without going to jail," she added with poor sportsmanship.

"I do," Varón agreed. "But the price has to be right. Do I recall that you told me to name it?"

Kara's courage faltered. Despite her bravado in the alley, here in her bedroom, with her son downstairs and not another soul within shouting distance, a shiver rippled across her breasts.

Varón's gaze dipped. "I wasn't thinking about *that*," he said. "Well, in the spirit of honesty, I'll admit it does cross my mind. After all, here I am, alone with you for the second time in one night, the first time with you nearly naked and now, with you backed up against a bed and your limbs already quivering."

"My son is here. Even you aren't so vile as to try to rape me in front of my son."

A dark brow lifted. "You credit me with a conscience, Ms. Chandler? In my business, it would be a weighty thing to lug around."

"I credit you for not wanting to be shot dead."

The ghost of a smile crossed his lips. "There is that. But no matter. I prefer my women willing and eager." His eyes smoldered. "I'll wait."

A frisson of sensation shuddered through Kara's limbs. It came from nowhere and curled low in her belly, while Varón strolled around the room, dragging a finger across her dresser, picking up and setting down a hairbrush, a mirror—laying claim to the space. Kara half expected him to open a drawer and fondle a pair of underwear just to show that he could. And would.

Bastard.

But she needed him. Dear God, she needed him to help her put an end to this madness.

He propped his hip against the dresser and crossed his arms. In the mirror behind him, Kara saw the seams of his designer suit pull across his upper back and a tremor of fear rattled in her chest. He was six-three and outweighed her by probably a hundred pounds—every ounce muscle. She hadn't seen a gun this time, but knew it was there.

Then again, he'd had his opportunity to rape her in the alley and instead, he'd lobbed her clothes at her and sent her on her way. There was something else he wanted.

"I won't give you the evidence against Montiel until you deliver your part of the bargain," she said. "Don't ask."

"I wasn't going to."

"What, then? If not Montiel's safety, not money, and not sex, what do you want?"

Varón looked her straight in the eyes. "I want to know *why*."

"Excuse me?"

"Contrary to what you may believe, I generally require a good reason to commit a felony. I want to know what happened to make you think your husband's death wasn't an accident, and why you're running now."

She blinked. She hadn't told him anything about Andrew's death. "I don't know what you're talking about."

"Bullshit. You went to Louie Guilford yesterday and asked him to re-examine your husband's death. You weren't crying 'murder' a year ago. What changed your mind?"

Her brain stalled. Louie wouldn't have told anyone about their conversation. "How do you know about that?" But a second later, an answer jammed in her throat. "You?"

Varón cursed. "Christ, I didn't shoot a man down in front of his kid. As soon as your prosecutor's mind starts working, you'll find I was out of the country until this afternoon."

She eyed him, surprised that he seemed genuinely insulted by the idea. She studied the hard features of his face, the depth of his eyes, and for a second couldn't help wondering what he might be if he weren't a drug cartel's henchman. If his jaw had been less angular, his gaze less intense, his smile less cold.

But none of that was the case. He was a murderer, with a well-documented history of hits. If Ben Archer was right, the only reason Varón had surfaced in Atlanta was to help Gene Montiel launder money for a surviving splinter of the defunct Rojàs cartel. And while the billionaire developer Montiel stayed clean through savvy politics and by sponsoring a share of well-publicized programs for the downtrodden, Varón had no such redeeming qualities. He was just a well-dressed thug, and as far as Kara could tell from her unsuccessful case against him, he was as untouchable as he was ruthless. An entire Federal murder case had toppled like a house of cards.

So she shouldn't give a damn that talking to him now might put him in danger.

"I believe that whoever killed Louie also killed a

woman earlier this week and murdered my husband a year ago," she said. "And maybe others."

Varón blinked. For a split second, his face registered something that might have been shock, but in the next heartbeat his expression showed nothing. "The man who killed your husband was John Wolff. He confessed."

"But he was innocent."

Varón looked at her, his eyes like a glacier. "Convince me."

Kara took a deep breath. She had to do it. "A year ago, on the day of my husband's funeral, I received a message on my phone. It was a picture of Andrew in his coffin and it said, 'Look what you've done.' I didn't know who it was from and no one answered when I called the number back. After a while, I chalked it up to a vindictive defendant or maybe a lover of Andrew's."

"Lover?"

"There were several," she said, trying to sound matter-of-fact. "A month later, after John Wolff had confessed to running Andrew down while drunk, Wolff was transferred from jail to a minimum security prison to await trial. He was killed in a riot the next day. I received another text. It had a picture of Wolff from the newspaper and the message said, 'Look what you've done.'" She swallowed. She'd had no love for the man who accidentally killed Andrew and had every intention of seeing him prosecuted. But she hadn't wished him dead. Wolff had taken a shank to the throat in the melée at the prison.

"And the phone number?"

"I had deleted the first one a month earlier, so I don't know if the second was the same. But I had the police check this one. It was a prepaid cell. I got no more text messages like that until this week." She paused. "After I went to see John Wolff's wife, Penny."

Varón looked at her like she was crazy. "Why would you do that?"

Kara knew it made no sense. She went to a drawer and pulled out a pair of sunglasses. "For the past year, since Andrew died, I've been receiving strange gifts and notes. Anonymously. On Monday, the anniversary of Andrew's death, I received these." Her voice dropped. "They were his."

Varón stepped closer, apparently unconcerned that she still had a gun in her hand. "Just because someone was in possession of your husband's sunglasses doesn't mean he killed him. John Wolff confessed to that."

"John Wolff lied." Kara felt like a child trying to get an adult to believe there really were monsters under the bed. "It had never seemed right, about John Wolff driving drunk and killing Andrew. Wolff wasn't a drinker. He worked hard; he had a newborn baby daughter with cerebral palsy."

"He *confessed*."

"As part of a deal," Kara insisted, still half in shock herself. "Penny Wolff told me. John sold out for money and took the blame for killing Andrew."

Varón was incredulous. "A payoff in exchange for a double murder rap?"

"Not murder and not double. Not at first, anyway. It was second-degree Homicide by Vehicle. In the state of Georgia, that carries as little as three years and at the time, Elisa Moran—the woman walking with Andrew when he was hit—was still alive. So Wolff turned himself in, two days after the accident. He was contrite and remorseful, and had no history, not even a parking ticket. If Elisa Moran hadn't later died of her injuries, he would have gotten three years, or five at the most. It must have seemed like a good deal for what he would get in return."

"Which was what?"

"Ten thousand dollars a month, for the duration of his prison sentence. Enough to get their baby the medical care she needed."

Varón's tension was a palpable thing. "Who? Who would offer him a deal like that?"

"His wife didn't know. John gave the first payment to Penny the morning he turned himself in to the police. But then, a few days later, Elisa Moran died. Additional charges were filed, and Wolff was held, then transferred to prison. He was killed right after he got there. Penny Wolff never got a second payment."

"And she just came clean with you about this?" Varón sounded skeptical. More than skeptical. Astonished. "After all this time, you want me to believe that all you did was walk in and ask for the truth about your husband, and Penny Wolff spilled a year's worth of lies?"

Not quite, Kara acknowledged, with a twist in her belly. She'd walked in with Andrew's sunglasses and the certainty that whoever killed him was coming back, fired a salvo of accusations and threatened Penny Wolff with prosecution—including complicity in Andrew's death. She'd told Penny she'd be separated from her daughter, and intimidated her as thoroughly as she would have intimidated a lying defendant on the stand.

She might as well have painted a target on Penny's back. *Look what you've done.*

"Ms. Chandler?" Varón touched her arm. She snapped back as if she'd been scalded. "If this is true, why didn't Penny Wolff come forward before now?"

"Because she was afraid of the man who struck the

deal with her husband." She looked up at Varón. "And she was right to be." Kara went back to the drawer. With shaking fingers, she withdrew a purple striped scarf and spread it on the bed. "Penny was wearing this on Tuesday night when we talked. The next morning, my son Aidan found it tied to his bike handles."

Varón's brows drew together and he picked up the scarf. Tiny holes pierced the fabric, with a dark stain around each.

"Blood," he said.

"Yes. She's dead."

"How do you know?"

Bile rose to her throat and she pulled out her iPhone. "A few hours after Aidan found this scarf, I received a text message." She showed him the message. And the picture that came with it. It was the one Louie hadn't lived to see.

"Jesus Christ," Varón said, looking at the picture. It was Penny Wolff, dead. The purple scarf sat on her lap, along with what looked like a wire garrote. The text message said, "Look what you've done."

"You got this on Wednesday?" he asked.

"Yes. The day after I'd spoken with her. I didn't know what to do. I realized that I was probably the last person to have seen Penny. I was scared. I called in an anonymous tip and the police found Penny's front door broken in. Her living room was ransacked. Her toddler was in a playpen where Penny had put her while we talked. They didn't find Penny."

"So you went to Louie Guilford. You told him about the sunglasses and your conversation with Penny Wolff, about the scarf. Everything you just told me?"

Tears bloomed in her eyes. "Almost. He died before he

saw it all." She looked up at him, the talons of fear clawing at her heart. Varón didn't deserve her concern. He was a criminal through and through and had broken in here demanding the truth. Still, the idea that tomorrow she might get a picture of him on her cell phone, dead, stuck in her mind like a tick.

Varón took two steps away, then spun back to her. "So you decided to disappear?" His voice was harsh. "Change your identities, get some fake IDs, and hire yourself a thug to double as a bodyguard and babysitter. Is that it?"

She steeled her spine. Yes, that was about the size of it.

"That's crazy," he went on. "You're not a cop. Even with your background, what makes you think you can track someone like this down—especially from underground, when you can't talk to anyone?"

"That's why I need you." She paused, feeling as if every slim chance she had of finding this killer was tied up in Luke Varón's cooperation. He was right: She couldn't do this alone. "Your part in this is strictly grunt labor, Mr. Varón. The rest has nothing to do with you."

"The hell it doesn't," he growled, then looked at the pistol, seeming to have forgotten it for a while. "And for the last time, put that fucking gun away. You aren't going to shoot me."

A new voice came from the doorway. "But *I* might."

CHAPTER
7

LUKE TURNED TO THE voice. *Ah, Christ.*

Aidan Chandler stood at the door to the hallway, bare-chested and wearing green plaid pajama bottoms, holding a .22 caliber rifle in his hands. Pillow lines creased his cheek.

"Aidan," his mother gasped, and the fear in her voice only made the boy tighten his grip. It was a featherweight Winchester 70 from the gun case downstairs, a collector's piece from the early 1960s. Luke had taken inventory when he entered the house.

"Who are you?" the boy asked.

Luke showed both palms. "I'm the man your mother hired to help you out of a bad situation. But I'm going to reconsider if the two of you keep pointing guns at me." He slid some steel into his voice. "Put the rifle down, son."

"Mom?"

Ms. Chandler's face had lost all color. She knew Luke Varón. She had to know that if he chose to take on an impulsive fourteen-year-old—even an armed one—there was little doubt about the outcome.

"Put the gun down, Aidan." Her voice quavered. "There's nothing to be afraid of."

"Then why are *you* holding a gun?"

"I'm not." For the first time since Luke had entered, she laid the pistol down. "He scared me when he first came in, but that's all. We're just talking now."

"I heard," the kid said, and Luke noticed a sheen of moisture on both cheeks. Christ, he'd been listening. *Whoever killed Louie Guilford yesterday also killed my husband a year ago.* If Kara Chandler was right—if Andrew Chandler's killer was still out there now—the implications were huge. It meant Chandler's death hadn't come from inside the cartel.

It meant Elisa Moran had died for nothing.

"Is it true, Mom? Someone murdered Dad?" Aidan asked. He was shaking.

He *had* heard. "I think so," his mother said. "It's the same person who's been sending those weird gifts I get. On Monday, he sent me your father's sunglasses."

"What?" Aidan said.

"Aidan, we have to get away. I went to Louie and the killer knew. That's why he killed him. And he killed a woman I went to talk to on Tuesday and he's not just watching me. He's watching you, too. The scarf on your bike came from him."

"Oh, God."

"Mr. Varón can help us go underground. He can make it look like we're dead."

"Varón," Aidan said, and scowled. "You're the bastard who got away with that murder in the warehouse."

"And I can get away with making it look like you and your mom are dead," Luke said. "Get you out of sight."

"Forever?" The boy swallowed and looked at his mom. "Are we going to hide forever?"

"Of course not," she said, but her voice rang with

uncertainty. "Just until we figure out what's going on and it's safe again."

Aidan looked back at Luke. He had the same clear green eyes as his mother. Haunted, probing, distrusting. His hair was tinted red like his dad's. "I don't want to go anywhere with him," he said, jerking the rifle toward Luke.

Luke glared at him. "This would be a good time to listen to your mother, kid. And a bad time to shoot the man who's going to help you."

"How?"

Luke glanced at the clock, making sure Knutson had had enough time to get everything in place, then checked his phone. Yes, Knutson was done. He'd sent Luke a tracker to the detonator. "Your boat is rigged to blow," he said. He started with the truth, then let the prevarications roll out. "We'll lay your tracks to the water and set off the explosion, then I'll take you both underground and give you protection. One week, while your mom tries to figure out what the hell is going on. After that—" He shrugged. His best *none of-my-business* gesture.

But it *was* his business. More so than they could ever imagine.

"And you're doing this for money?" Aidan asked.

"Why else?" he asked. He conjured up a leer and let it touch Kara Chandler. "Though I might have taken something more from your mom if you hadn't come busting in with a rifle."

Aidan Chandler actually hissed. He was a millimeter away from pulling the trigger.

Good kid.

Luke looked at Kara. "The other gifts you received— where are they?"

She opened the bottom drawer of the dresser. "Here."

"Bring them. Don't leave any behind. I need a bag for these things—a grocery bag or something. Aidan, go put on a shirt—long-sleeved so you don't get scratched up in the woods. And tennis shoes. Don't bring anything else. No iPod, no cell phone. Nothing."

Mother and son both stared.

"Unless you weren't serious," Luke said.

Kara Chandler looked at her son. "Go, Aidan. Do what he says."

"And leave the rifle here," Luke said.

Aidan scowled at him, then tossed the rifle onto the pillows. "Wasn't loaded anyway."

"I know," Luke said. "I collected the bullets."

Aidan scoffed, then hurried out, and Luke found Kara Chandler studying him as if she didn't understand. "A bag for those things," he reminded her, and she went into the closet, came back with a pillowcase. Luke watched her gather up the macramé bag she'd brought into the alley, then stuff the items from the dresser drawer into the pillowcase—a pen, a necklace, a watch—several greeting cards. He cringed at how many fingerprints had probably been compromised. Still, better to take them. He'd want to get a good look at each item.

"You need something small and personal," Luke said, "something it would be easy to drop and that someone will recognize as yours." He skimmed her hair. "Your hair is usually up. Bring a hair clip."

She fingered through a box on the dresser and came up with a clip, followed Luke out the bedroom door. Then she pulled up short.

"Oh, God," she said. Carrying the damnable pistol again, she used her free hand to dig into the pocket of her jeans. She pulled out her iPhone. Luke hadn't heard it but now noticed it was vibrating. He came to look over her shoulder.

She slid a finger across the screen. A text message, from a number with no name.

"No," she whispered, and Luke took her arm. She began to tremble.

"Open it," he said, and she touched the screen of her phone. A picture came up.

Ah, Christ.

It was a photograph of Louie Guilford from today's paper. And a message that said, "How is Aidan?"

Ms. Chandler's knees gave out. "Whoa," Luke said, propping her up against the wall. Aidan came from his bedroom, took one look at his mother being manhandled, and lunged.

"Back off, stud," Luke said, strong-arming him.

Aidan realized his mom wasn't fighting and grabbed the phone. He went white, then read the text message. "Oh, God."

Luke took back the phone and closed the message, spent five seconds in her privacy settings disabling all location services, and blew out a breath. What the fuck was going on? He didn't know, but one thing was damn sure: Kara Chandler was coming with him.

"Come on," he said, and herded her to the stairs, leaving Aidan to follow. Halfway down, though, he pulled up short. Headlights swung in the driveway.

Fuck.

"We have to go," Kara said, as Luke peeked out through the blinds. He recognized the shape of the car.

"Too late," he said. "Police."

MESSAGE SENT 1:58 a.m.
Sasha stood on a bridge over the Chattahoochee River

and looked at the phone in his hand. A wave of satisfaction washed over him. It was late, but that was by design. Showing his dad the photo of Louie Guilford had been worth the time, and he liked the idea of Kara receiving the picture in a moment when she was alone and vulnerable.

And how had he done? Was she awake now and pacing the floors? Was she crying over Louie Guilford or still worrying about Penny-of-the-Purple-Scarf? Had she been sleeping, perhaps, and awakened by the soft *ping* of her phone with Guilford's photo, or would she not see the message until tomorrow, and receive his picture along with her morning coffee?

It didn't matter. All that mattered was that she realize Sasha wasn't finished yet. He still had more gifts for her. He was saving the biggest one for her birthday.

He turned off the phone and took out the battery. It was a cheap prepaid phone that he bought by the dozen and never used more than once. But even the cheap prepaid phones might have GPSes, so he accounted for that. He always disposed of them somewhere out of the way, the minute he was finished sending Kara a message.

This time, he hadn't gone as far as usual: He still had to catch Megan tonight and time was ticking. But this would do—a secluded old bridge in Sandy Springs. It would be the first time a message had been sent from the Atlanta area, but even if Kara did have a way of tracking it, which was doubtful, it wouldn't do her any good. The phone would be in pieces at the bottom of the river and Sasha would be long gone.

Besides, Kara wouldn't go to the police now. Not after what happened to Louie Guilford. And not after he'd made it clear that Aidan was in his sights, too.

Sasha dropped the battery and the cell phone onto the pavement, crushed both with the heel of his shoe, and tossed them over the bridge and into the river. He wiped off his palms and hurried back to his van.

Megan was waiting.

CHAPTER
8

Police? Kara's breath stopped. She stepped down two more stairs to look out the window with Varón, but the doorbell rang. Oh, God.

"What do they want?" Aidan asked in a whisper.

"I don't know," said Varón.

"They found Penny Wolff," Kara said. "They must have. They must know I was there."

"You don't know that." Varón cupped both her shoulders, turning her square to him. "Listen to me—last chance. Do you still want to go underground?" he asked, and Kara could hardly think. Too many images in her mind...Penny Wolff, with the scarf piled on her lap and a coil of wire, her throat marked and her eyes bulging... Louie, lying on the sidewalk bleeding with the boys looking on...And the picture of him on her phone: *How is Aidan?*

Varón's fingers bit into her upper arms. "Kara," he said, and her first name coming from his lips startled her into looking up at him. "Do you want to go through with this?"

Reality rolled back into grasp. "Yes," she said, taking

Aidan's hand. He seemed taller and older than he'd been just yesterday. And yet, still a child. "Can you do this, Aidan?"

"We have to," he said, "before he kills someone else." *Me.* He didn't say it, but Kara knew the thought was there.

Varón took the pillowcase and handed it to Aidan, along with the macramé bag. "Take these," he said in a hush, then turned back to Kara. "Aidan and I will go down the back stairs and wait in the dining room. You find out what the police want. Don't offer any information about Penny Wolff."

"I have to tell them—"

"She's dead, Kara, there's nothing you can do to change that. Listen to me. You've always had reason to hate Penny Wolff. You went to her house and were probably the last one to see her alive. Your son is carrying her bloody neck scarf in that bag."

Kara closed her eyes. He was right. "What if they're here to arrest me?"

"They aren't. There's only one car and no lights or sirens."

Yes. The arrest of an Assistant District Attorney would be a bigger deal than that.

Varón's hands came to her face. He rubbed his thumbs over her brows, then drew them down over her lashes and cheeks, hard. "Easy," he said when she tried to pull away. He ruffled her hair. "It's the middle of the night. You need to look like you fell asleep in your clothes."

Oh. Yes, of course. She wasn't thinking clearly. The world was spinning and her one source of stability was Luke Varón.

The doorbell rang again. Varón held his hand open in front of her and for a second she didn't understand. Then it dawned on her that she still held her pistol. This one was loaded, but up to now, he'd never made a move to take it from her.

So this was the moment: Trust Varón or not. She turned and looked at Aidan holding a bag of disguises she'd already gathered and a pillowcase filled with bizarre evidence of some terrifying murder scheme, and knew there was no choice.

She gave the gun to Varón.

He pocketed it but didn't gloat. Instead, he braced a knuckle beneath her chin. "You can do it," he said.

Yes, she could. She had to.

Varón and Aidan headed down the back stairs through the kitchen and into the dining room. From there, Kara knew he would be able to hear her conversation. She went down the front stairwell in a strange fog that made her feel only partly in control. Varón appeared to be doing what she'd asked him to. But with the smallest tilt of thought, his actions could just as easily be interpreted as holding her son hostage at gunpoint while listening to make sure she followed his instructions with the police. She tamped that thought down—*she* had contacted *him*—and headed toward the front door. She started to straighten her blouse, then thought better of it: Damn Varón, but he was right. If she hadn't been in the midst of planning a felony with a known criminal, she'd have been asleep. She should look like it.

The doorbell rang a third time. Kara gathered her poise and opened the door.

Two uniformed officers stood on the stoop and, God help her, she recognized both of them. One was Drew Connelly, a twenty-something patrolman who had once been assigned as her escort during three days of a particularly high-profile trial. He had developed something of a crush on her. The other was Paul Langford, a near-retirement beat cop.

Langford stepped forward. "Counselor," he said, "we're sorry for disturbing you at this hour. But we're doing some legwork on a missing-persons case."

Missing person? Not murder. Then they didn't know yet that Penny Wolff was dead.

Kara worked to keep her heart from pounding through her chest. She was Kara Chandler, Assistant District Attorney. Not Kara Chandler, accomplice to hit man Luke Varón and perpetrator of fraud and a dozen other soon-to-be-committed crimes. She rubbed her forehead. "What's going on?"

Langford said, "A woman named Penny Wolff has disappeared. You remember her?"

They knew she did. They knew a helluva lot more than that. Otherwise, they wouldn't be here.

Kara touched her stomach. It seemed to be liquid. *You can do it.*

She tried to recall what she *shouldn't* cover up. The name Penny Wolff would be familiar to her. Penny's husband had confessed to killing Kara's. And it would be crazy to deny that she'd seen Penny, especially since she'd made no effort to cover her trac—

"Investigators found your phone number in some of her things."

"My number?" That's why they were here. Kara had written it down and told Penny to call her if she remembered anything else. She summoned her poise. "Oh. Well, that's because I went to talk to her. Tuesday night."

The two officers looked at one another. "What time?"

"About seven thirty."

Langford scratched his head. "Why?"

Kara straightened. "This week is the anniversary of my husband's death," she said, and Langford nodded. "Penny lost her husband in the ordeal, too. It just seemed..." She lowered her head. "John Wolff never meant any harm to my husband. It seemed time to acknowledge that."

"Huh," said Langford. "So you two...er...talked for a little bit?"

"Yes. And I gave her my number. Are you telling me that she's missing now, Officer?"

"She is. Her living room was all torn up and her kid left behind. You haven't heard that? It's been on the news."

He was suspicious. Stay the course. "I've been a little distracted this week. No, I hadn't heard. Is her child all right?"

"Yeah. She's with a relative now. How were things when you left her?"

"I was only there a few minutes. Penny was fine. Her living room was fine and she said the baby was in a playpen. Penny showed me out the front door when we finished."

Connelly jotted that into a notepad. Langford said, "Was your conversation with her...er...hostile?"

"Not especially," Kara lied, and clamped her jaw shut. Say no more.

"Was there anything she was worried about? Anything strange going on with her?"

"If there was, she didn't say anything to me about it."

"Do you know whether she had any plans for the rest of that evening?" Connelly asked.

"We didn't talk about that."

There was an awkward pause while the two cops glanced at each other, apparently deciding whether or not what she was saying was worth bringing her in to talk to the detectives. They didn't know Penny was dead yet; that much was certain. Otherwise, they wouldn't be following leads in the middle of the night.

Connelly licked the tip of his pencil. "What was she wearing when you saw her?"

The question always asked of the last person to have seen a missing person alive. Kara closed her eyes. "A dark gray skirt and light blouse. Cream. And she had a scarf—"

"Ms. Chandler?" Connelly said. "Are you all right?"

No. She wasn't all right. She drew a deep breath, the room filling with secrets and lies, pressing down on her from every angle. She could almost feel Varón listening in.

You can do it.

"She was wearing a purple scarf with stripes," she said. "I hope she's all right. She's been through enough."

Langford nodded. "You both have. Tough week, huh?" Everyone knew that Kara had been with Louie Guilford when he died last night. Her family's friendship with the Guilfords was well known. The boys had always called the adults "aunt" and "uncle," and Seth and Aidan were more like brothers than friends.

"Yes," she said. "Tough week."

"Let us know if you think of anything that might help us, okay?"

"I will. Of course." Relief hovered just out of reach as they moved toward the door. Almost there. Then Langford turned around.

"Ms. Chandler, I was wondering…Where have you been tonight? I didn't expect you to be dressed at this hour."

She strung out a little indignation. "I spent most of the day with Sally and Seth Guilford. It was draining. I guess I fell asleep on the couch."

"Sure," Langford said, and backed off. "Okay. Good night, then."

She shut the door behind them and tipped her forehead against it. Langford was no idiot. He was going to call the lead detective on Penny Wolff's case right now, and by morning—if not before—Kara would be called in for questioning.

She forced herself to take a deep breath, feeling as if she was aboard a runaway train. She didn't know where it was going or why she was on it. She only knew it was running too fast to make sense of the twists and turns, and that with every curve it picked up speed.

Now, the train was headed for a gorge, with Luke Varón driving.

"Let's go."

Varón's voice. She turned and looked at him, a known murderer with his suit coat hooked slightly on a gun holster, as if he'd had his hand on it the whole time she was talking to Langford and Connelly—and her son standing right next to him. The reality of that threatened to steal what little strength she had left in her limbs. She wanted to close her eyes and open them again and have Varón disappear, along with this whole insane idea about trying to take Aidan into hiding.

But when she closed her eyes, she saw Penny Wolff. And Louie Guilford.

And Andrew.

Varón watched the cruiser pull away. He turned around. "We're going down to the dock. You two walk on the path to leave tracks; I'll head through the woods."

Kara took Aidan's hand and they followed him through the house toward the back door, Varón showing knowledge of the floor plan that took Kara by surprise. *I know. I collected the bullets.* He must have come straight to the house after they'd spoken in the alley. Rigged the boat—or had one of his minions do it—found his way inside, and made himself at home waiting for her.

Very efficient. If she weren't so scared, she'd be impressed.

She locked the back door, leaving things as she would have had she not expected to die in an explosion. There was no doubt that police would question her taking the boat out in the middle of the night, especially since she'd just spoken to two of them, but whatever reasons they suspected for her actions wouldn't matter.

She'd be dead.

She and Aidan kept to a path with railroad tie steps, a hundred yards down a hill to the dock, while Varón skirted into the dark of the woods. The air smelled of damp pine straw, the temperature such that beads of perspiration collected along on the back of her neck. They got to the edge of the dock and stopped, looking for Varón.

He emerged from the black spread of trees a few minutes later, a wraith, holding something in his hand. A wedge of moon turned his face into dark planes and angles.

"Get your hair clip," he said. "The two of you walk to your boat and unhook the line. Drop the hair clip on the dock, then get in the boat and start the engine. Once the boat is ready to go, take off your shoes and set them on the dock upside down. Climb out and push off the boat. Then pick up your shoes and come back here in your socks."

Kara tilted her head. "You've got it all planned out, don't you?"

"That's why you hired me."

Yes. Yes, it was.

Heart pounding, Kara did as instructed, Aidan following close behind. A moment later they stood in the woods beside Varón with their tennis shoes in hand and watched the boat float out into the water. It seemed as if it took forever, but finally Varón said, "Good enough." He turned to them. "Put your shoes on. We're going to need to move."

Apprehension rippled through Kara's bones. This was crazy. But they put on their shoes and Aidan picked up the pillowcase. Kara took the macramé purse containing the whole of their identities and slung it over her shoulder. Varón pointed his hand at the boat.

"Good-bye, Chandlers," he said, then pressed a button. *Fffrumph.*

CHAPTER
9

"Bye, Kara," one of the kids said, giggling. "Have fun."

Sasha wasn't sure who had spoken and didn't care. All he could think about was Kara Montgomery and the flush of color in her cheeks. Her eyes fell the length of his body, snagged for a split second on his erection, and the color in her cheeks deepened. Andrew Chandler called her name and it was then she moved, stepping through the open door of the tack room in sheer defiance.

Sasha licked his lips.

"Kara," Chandler said again. "We were just kidding. You don't have to take the dare."

You don't have to let this lowlife touch you.

Sasha stepped forward. Hatred seeped from every pore. Once, when they were both younger, he and Andrew had stood together at the rail of the mating pen, watching one of the Montgomery stallions fuck a Chandler mare. In a sick sort of way, it was a turn-on to watch such an elemental act of sex—the stallion sniffing the mare and getting agitated, doing the dance and mounting her, sinking his teeth into her neck. This was a big-money mating, *so when the stallion's cock finally came out of the mare oozing a thick stream of semen, the handlers whooped and cheered, and Andrew high-fived Sasha. For one moment in time, they'd been equals.*

But not now. You fucked up, rich boy, *Sasha thought.* Now she's mine.

Andrew moved but Sasha stepped into his path. "Stop treating her like a baby. She's fifteen. She knows what she's doing."

"Kara?" Andrew said.

She drew herself even taller. "Seven minutes. But no longer."

Sasha's blood sang through his veins. Seven Minutes of Heaven with the princess of Montgomery Manor. Wonder what her old man would say to that. Wonder what his old man would say to that, come to think of it.

No, he didn't need to wonder about his old man. Sasha knew exactly what he'd say. "She is not the one for you." *In other words*: You're not good enough.

He brushed that thought away. He'd learned early on that he couldn't live up to his father's dreams for a son. Only Stefan could do that and Stefan was gone.

So, fuck you, Dad.

Sasha came to the door, feeling Andrew's eyes on his back. Kara stood in the center of the room, probably counting down the seconds. Cabinets and shelves lined the walls, all stashed with riding equipment. In one corner a bunch of saddles were lined up on pegs, and in the other, a ring of barbed wire the size of a tractor wheel lay in a coil on the floor.

He turned to close the door and Andrew's voice stopped him.

"Hey, lose the crop, asshole," he said, and Sasha

looked at his hands. He'd forgotten he was carrying anything.

He chuckled. Stupid shit. If he wanted to use a crop on her, there were a half dozen more hanging on the wall three feet away. But he tossed the crop toward Kara and watched it land at her feet. He smiled and turned to Andrew. "In case she wants to take a ride."

He shut the door in Andrew's face, turned to Kara.

Six minutes left.

The explosion knocked Kara back a step.

"Let's go," Varón said. He had Kara's arm before her heartbeat evened out. He pulled her up the bank and into the woods, not quite running, but moving with fast, long strides that had Kara jogging to keep up on the uneven terrain. Aidan skirted through the woods beside them and they moved parallel to the lakefront, fifty feet above the bank and about seventy-five yards from the backs of homes that lined the water. The sound of raging flames trailed into the night behind them, the scent of gasoline tingeing her nostrils. Lights came on in windows along the way and minutes after the fireball exploded, the sirens started, wailing past them on the road above.

They kept up the pace for what seemed like miles, Varón's gait growing uneven, as if he had a cut or splinter in his foot. Still, he kept them moving and finally they came to a spot where the lake narrowed and a bridge spanned the banks. Kara stopped, her lungs heaving.

"Mom?" Aidan said.

A stitch cramped her side. "I'm fine. But we need to cross the lake."

Varón rubbed his thigh. "We don't need to cross—"

"Listen to me," she said, panting. She was in okay shape

for a thirty-something mom, but the sprint along the lake bed had taken it out of her. She turned to Aidan. "Uncle Louie's fishing cabin. It's only a few miles from here, but it's on the other side of the lake. We can stay there." Even in the darkness, she could see Aidan cringe. "Honey, he'd want us to use it. He'd want us to be safe. Damn it, Aidan, he'd want us to find out who killed him and your father."

She started toward the bridge but Varón said, "No."

"This is what I planned, Mr. Varón. You don't have a say."

"The hell I don't. You hired me to keep you safe. I'm not doing it in some fishing cabin I've never seen before."

"No one ever uses it. We'll be out of sight."

Nearby, too nearby, something caught her ear. It was the low hum of an engine. She glanced around but it was too dark to see anything.

"We'll do this my way," Varón said, and pulled her back into stride.

"Hey," Aidan said.

A spear of alarm got Kara in the chest. She tried to pull away but Varón's hand tightened on her wrist. Suddenly, it didn't feel like they were being helped anymore. It felt more like they were being kidnapped.

"Let me go," she said, but he didn't. He ducked beneath a tree limb, then snapped the next one off in his hand, limping, but moving fast, dragging Kara.

Aidan sprang, landing on Varón's back, and the pillowcase fell into the pine straw.

"Let her go," Aidan roared, on him like a bronco.

Varón bucked him off and gave Kara a jerk. Her back hit his chest, her right arm wrenched behind her in a V. One big hand fell over her mouth and the position alone held Aidan back in shock.

"Enough," Varón snapped. "I don't want to hurt your mother, but if you force me, I will."

Stars danced before Kara's eyes. She hung her weight on the forearm across her chest but it was like hanging on a tree limb. He crushed half her face beneath his hand, barely letting in air, and in the back of her mind she realized he could snap her neck in two seconds flat. Right in front of Aidan.

"Let her go," Aidan said, and Kara could hear the terror in his voice. He would be brave, he would try to take on Luke Varón. But he was just a boy. He'd lose.

She went still. Dear God, don't let this bastard hurt Aidan.

"For Christ's sake," Varón said, his heart thudding against her back. "I could have killed either one of you ten times over tonight if that's what I wanted. I'm not going to hurt you. I'm just doing the job you hired me to do."

Somewhere in a distant corner of her mind, she heard the engine again, as if it had been waiting. "Pick up that bag," Varón said to Aidan, then hauled Kara another thirty yards, this time up the incline of the bank, straight to a car waiting in the darkness. Aidan followed. He would be on good behavior as long as Varón threatened Kara. The son of a bitch knew how to keep a kid in line.

A second man got out of the car. He came around and opened both passenger-side doors. Varón said to Aidan, "Get in front." Aidan balked and the second man pulled out a gun.

"Mmm—" Kara cried.

"Tell your son to do as he's told," Varón growled against her ear.

She managed a nod to Aidan and he climbed in. Varón pushed Kara into the backseat, loosening his grip only enough to let her move and piling in after her. The other man slammed the front door on Aidan and jogged around to the driver's side while Varón reached below the seat. He grabbed her wrist and hit it hard, then hit his own.

Handcuffs.

Aidan locked eyes with Varón, then glanced at the handcuffs. A ribbon of terror unfurled in Kara's belly. The irony of trying to escape a killer by being kidnapped by Luke Varón was too great to contemplate. She tugged on her wrist, but he was ready for it. There was no give.

"When you settle down, I'll take them off," he said without looking at her. He kept his eyes on Aidan. The second man put the car in gear and began inching through the woods with no headlights, and Kara tried to think enough to note details. Fifty-ish, wearing a black ski cap and dark jacket, even though it was the dead of summer. His face was smudged with black and he wore long sleeves and dark gloves. She didn't recognize him.

The car engine revved and they bumped out of the woods. Varón shut his eyes, as if the ordeal had been hard on him as well. The bastard. She commanded herself to think. *I could have killed you ten times over already.* That much was true, she realized. If he'd wanted to harm her, he'd had plenty of opportunity before now. In the alley or in her bedroom. Not to mention that he'd been in the house alone with Aidan before she got there. He might have easily killed him in his sleep while she was out buying a phone to line up a meeting with Jay Kemp or stuck behind a tow truck in her neighborhood.

I'm just doing the job you hired me to do. Pray, God, it was the truth. She watched the darkness go by, trying to imagine why he was taking her request to such extremes.

He was supposed to be grunt labor. Besides a payoff, he had no stake in her actions.

I want to know why, he'd said. It was all he'd demanded.

A terrifying hunch took root in her brain. "Are you part of it?" she asked.

"*You* called *me*, remember?"

"But this is beyond what you were hired to do. You must have a reason."

She could barely see his face in the darkness. "It's not what I intended, either," he said, seeming surprised by his own admission. "I give you my word, neither of you is in danger from me. Your husband's death is of interest to me, that's all."

"What do you mean?"

He glanced at Aidan and lowered his voice. "Not now."

"Now," Aidan said. He turned around in his seat, facing Varón. "Damn you, why do you care about my father?"

"My mother used to tell me not to ask questions unless you're sure you want the answers."

Aidan scoffed. "You don't have a mother. You were raised by wolves."

That got a faint smile from Varón. "Her name is Katrin. And she would tell you to respect your elders."

Aidan wasn't distracted. "What is it you don't want me to hear about my father? That his company was corrupt? I knew that already. Everybody in Atlanta knows that. That he cheated on Mom? That's old news, too."

"Aidan," Kara said, but he went on.

"I want an answer: What was my father to you?"

Varón took a deep breath. "A hit," he said. "I was hired to kill him."

CHAPTER
10

LUKE WATCHED HIS WORDS sink in. Kara and Aidan were speechless.

Fine. Luke needed time to think, too. Things were happening too fast. His head pounded and his thigh hurt like a son of a bitch. After nothing more than a few minutes of conversation with Kara Chandler, everything he thought he'd known was in doubt. The man who'd killed Andrew Chandler and Elisa Moran wasn't dead.

That changed everything.

Kara Chandler's eyes drilled into Luke. "You didn't kill Andrew. You couldn't have. You were in custody when he was killed."

"That's right," Luke said. At least, that was the story. "Custody" had actually been the FBI field office.

"How do you know that, Mom?" Aidan asked.

"Because when I was preparing the case against him, I tracked his movements. He entered the U.S. nearly a month before your dad died and was taken into custody three weeks later. He was in jail when your dad was killed."

"The lady did her homework," Luke said, and looked

at Aidan. "I was hired to kill your father, but I didn't get the chance. I want to know who did."

"Don't like the competition?" Aidan jeered. Luke might have chuckled if the stakes weren't so high. If Andrew's death wasn't the result of a drunk driver, then the operation with Collado could have holes they'd never suspected. "I want to find your dad's killer and so do you. That puts us on the same team."

"On the same team where?" Kara asked. "Where are you taking us?"

"Not to some fishing cabin," he said. "Out of the way. Where no one can find you."

They drove north, into the foothills of Appalachia and onto narrow mountain roads. After a few minutes on a winding, gravel lane, lights came into view and then the house itself. It was an angular, three-story lodge-style building with cedar siding and deep decks surrounding the upper two stories. It had windows everywhere, floor-to-ceiling, with skylights all across the front. Luke had insisted on the big windows and the skylights.

Knutson hit a button and the garage door opened. He pulled in and nested the car next to the Carerra someone had driven back earlier, then went around to get Aidan.

"What are you going to do with us?" Kara asked, and Luke saw true fear in her eyes. He wished he could say something to make it go away. But a cartel hit man wouldn't bother.

"Come on," he said, and tugged on the handcuffs to pull her out of the car. Knutson nudged Aidan up the stairs and Luke sent Kara up behind them, climbing the stairs at her back. At the top, the door opened and kitchen light flooded the top of the stairwell. A dark head bobbed past the doorway.

Maddie. Ah, Jesus, they'd sent Maddie.

They walked into the kitchen and Luke kicked the door closed behind him. Knutson tugged off his black cap and tossed it on a desk, revealing a shock of thick white hair. Kara pulled back, eyeing Knutson with distrust and probably scouring through everything she knew about Luke Varón to try to place Knutson as one of his associates. She wouldn't be able to. Luke's identity was what the FBI referred to as deep cover: No matter how far authorities dug, they would only find the history the Bureau had created for him.

He started across the kitchen, pulling Kara to a bar stool at the island. He could think of a scenario or two in which he wouldn't mind having Kara Chandler and a pair of handcuffs in the same room. This wasn't one of them.

Luke produced a key from his pocket and Kara lifted their wrists so he could unlock the cuffs. He didn't.

"Aidan," he said, not taking his eyes off Kara, "explain to your mother this wouldn't be a good time to turn stupid."

"Mom—"

"Are you threatening me, Mr. Varón?" she snapped.

"I'm stating a fact. When I threaten you, *querida*, you'll know it."

She held his eyes but a swallow convulsed in the hollow of her throat. A slender throat, pale and smooth, and leading to things beneath her blouse Luke had already seen. That ought to be the farthest thing from mind, but standing this close, catching the same sweet whiff of perfume that had captivated him in the alley just a few hours earlier, he found it difficult keeping his mind on the reason she was here.

Maddie had no such issues. She shot him a perturbed glare, then slipped around behind him, carrying a large canvas bag. *"Señor?"*

"Estoy listo para tú," he said. "I was just making sure my guests don't get any wild ideas." He tossed a glance to Aidan. He was ninety percent sure his actions with Kara had been harsh enough that the boy wasn't going to do something stupid. Ten percent not.

He stuck the key in the lock of the handcuffs. Kara rubbed her wrist.

"Comienza con el niño," Luke said to Maddie.

"Start *what* with the boy?" Kara snapped, and Maddie unzipped her bag. Glasses, a comb, and a couple pairs of scissors.

"Darken him up and cut his hair," Luke said. "Give him a tattoo. You ever wanted a piercing, kid?"

Aidan looked dumbstruck. Luke picked up Kara's macramé bag and dug inside. "Madelena will give you both a new look. It's what you paid me for, right?" he said, coming up with the stack of bills. Twenty thousand dollars. She'd been ready. He went back into the bag and found a wig and makeup. She wasn't completely unprepared, just mostly. He gave the wig a once-over and dropped it in the trash can. "Madelena can do better. You're first, Aidan. There's a bathroom back there."

Aidan looked at his mother, who nodded. "It's what we were going to do anyway."

He didn't like it, but followed Maddie to the back. Luke waited until they were out of sight, then picked up the pillowcase. Andrew's sunglasses, Penny's scarf, and what else? She said she'd been getting anonymous gifts for a year, and cards.

He emptied the pillowcase onto the granite island. Knutson came within earshot and positioned himself so he could see.

"Tell me about these things," Luke said. But he wasn't sure he wanted to know.

Kara stood and placed the items in a certain order, lining up one of the greeting cards with each. She picked up a pearl necklace on the far left. "This was the first thing I got. It came two months after Andrew died—there are dates on all the cards. I found it wrapped in gift paper and left on my front porch."

Luke looked. A standard greeting card, like those that would come in a box of stationery. The picture on the outside was a pastoral watercolor of a horse grazing in a field with wildflowers at its feet. On the inside, just a single word hand-printed in angular, black capitals: TRUTH.

" 'Truth?' " he asked.

"I don't know. I didn't understand, either, but after a while I let it go. Then, a few weeks later, same thing—a box on my doorstep. It was this, a woman's watch." She pushed it toward Varón, then handed him the card. It was like the first, except the horse was a different color and he nipped at grass growing beneath a split-rail fence. It had still probably come from the same box. Inside, the card read, TRUTH.

Luke frowned and picked up the next three cards, one after another, examining each gift. A pair of leather gloves and a similar card, with the same handwritten word. A man's tiger-eye ring and another card. An engraved ink pen and card. All of them: TRUTH.

"And you have no idea who is leaving them or what the message means," he said.

"No. Aidan always thought it was a secret admirer confessing his crush—*truth*. And he laughed and called him cheap because none of these gifts is new," she said, pointing to the black gloves. Luke had noticed: They were leather, but worn at the edges. The pearl necklace was broken; someone had tied a knot in the string to keep the beads from falling off. The pen even had a message engraved on it. *All my love, Gina.*

"Weird gifts to get from a secret admirer," Luke said.

"Weird, yes. But until I received Andrew's sunglasses, I didn't consider the possibility that their owners were dead."

"Were they all delivered to your front door?" Knutson asked.

She blinked, as though she'd forgotten he was there. "I found the sunglasses and card on my car at the grocery store. On Monday."

"What store?"

"Harry's, on Powers Ferry."

Knutson would find out if there was video of that parking lot.

"And Penny's scarf was tied to Aidan's bike handles. He and Seth were at Seth's neighborhood pool."

Christ. Whoever was leaving the gifts had been keeping an eye on both of them.

"And you never noticed anyone following you, calling you at strange hours, like that?" Luke asked.

"Only the gifts and the text messages."

Maddie came out of the bathroom, looking for Kara.

"Okay," Luke said, and pushed the tokens and cards back into the bag. "Go get your new look. The last thing I want is to blow up a boat and arrange for your bodies to be found, only to have the two of you re-surface somewhere."

She looked at him, a dubious tilt to her head. "You're very thorough, Mr. Varón."

"That's why you hired me," Luke said, but knew Kara

Chandler was too familiar with cops to be snowed too easily. He'd have to remind her that he was, as she put it, a resourceful thug and not a Federal agent suddenly scrambling to save an undercover operation.

He'd have to make sure she stayed wary of him.

He went to Maddie's stash and sifted through the boxes of hair color.

"Use this," he said to Maddie, reading the box. "E-twenty-three, 'dark chocolate.'" He shot a wink at Kara. "I told you: I'm partial to brunettes."

Luke left Maddie to handle Kara, a job that was certainly within her capabilities despite the meek demeanor she'd presented. He picked up the pillowcase and Knutson followed him down half a flight of stairs to a study with windows from floor to ceiling. He poured himself a deep shot of tequila, drained it and poured another, then opened the French doors to the wraparound deck. He rubbed his thigh.

"The leg okay?" Knutson asked, joining him on the balcony.

"It's fine," Luke said, though they both knew he was lying. A chunk of bone had come out with the bullet, but another chunk hadn't. Most of the time, it didn't show in his movements, even when it hurt like hell. But a sprint through the uneven terrain of the riverbank had got it going.

"You're scaring that poor woman to death," Knutson said.

"She needs to be scared. She doesn't know what she's into."

"Do you?"

"No," Luke said honestly. "But I know more than I did

when you rigged the boat. The man who killed Andrew Chandler and Elisa Moran is still alive. He's the one sending those gifts to Kara and he's probably the one who killed Louie Guilford. John Wolff was part of it— he copped that guilty plea in exchange for money—and Wolff's wife is missing. Dead."

Knutson went to stone. "I think you'd better catch me up."

Luke did, as much as he knew, from Kara's receiving the sunglasses to going to Penny Wolff and then Louie Guilford, and to the text message she'd received threatening Aidan just a couple hours ago.

"How is Aidan?" Knutson repeated, and Luke turned on Kara's cell phone. He forwarded her messages to his computer, while Knutson called headquarters. This was going to require resources outside what they had in place for Collado.

Luke booted up a desktop and put in the security and clearance codes, then stuck in a flash drive. A moment later, the computer gave a series of dings as the messages from Kara's cell phone arrived. Knutson came up behind him and Luke opened up the files. "The first message came via text a year ago, on the day of her husband's funeral," he said. "It was a picture of Chandler in his coffin."

"Someone at the funeral, then." Knutson made himself a note on a piece of paper from his wallet. There would have been hundreds at the funeral of Andrew Chandler. They were a well-known family. But they'd check everyone. "Pretty doubtful he signed the guest list, though."

"Kara deleted that message, but maybe the tech guys can recover it from the phone," Luke said. "She said she didn't recognize the number and got no answer when she called it. After a while, she wrote it off as someone being vindictive."

Knutson hummed a note and Luke opened the first of the text messages Kara hadn't deleted, the one that came eleven months ago, right after John Wolff's death. It was a photo from the newspaper, *The Atlanta Journal-Constitution,* from an article about the riot at Floyd Correctional Institute. "When this picture came and had the same text message as the first—*Look what you've done*—she got suspicious and held on to it, but still had no idea who'd sent it."

He clicked to the next message, the one from tonight with the picture of Louie Guilford. *How is Aidan?*

"It's more than just a guilt trip now," Knutson said. "He's upped the ante to threatening her kid."

"Find out what the APD knows about Guilford's shooting. It was a long-range shot with a hunting rifle so they're probably running competition rosters and shooting clubs. Gotta be someone with training."

Luke moved on to the picture of Penny Wolff. He took the photo he'd seen on the tiny iPhone screen to the eighteen-inch monitor.

"Mother of God," Knutson said.

Penny Wolff had been propped up against the wheel of a vehicle—a van, maybe—her head pulled back to expose ligature marks on her throat, her eyes bulging. The scarf appeared to have been dropped on her lap, and the wire itself—presumably that which had strangled her—lay on top.

"She didn't fall this way," Luke said, stricken. "It's an exhibition. He took her body, drove her somewhere, then put her on display before he took the picture."

Luke zoomed in, first on Penny's throat where the ligature had dug into her skin and left dribbles of blood every few inches, then on the wood at the end of the wire—a handle—and finally on the wire itself, which lay across Penny's scarf and was—

"Holy fuck." Luke stared, his stomach turning. "It's barbed wire."

CHAPTER
11

SASHA TOOK THE WIRE garrote out of its satchel, wrapped his fingers around the carved wooden handles, and crouched behind an empty truck in an alley off Ackley Street. The alley backed up to the club where the girl named Megan worked as a waitress. He'd watched her before and knew the drill: Shortly after three a.m., Megan would come out the back door, like she always did, and head down the alley for three blocks, like she always did. She'd cut over to Main Street where she would have left her car, like she always did.

And pass right by the van Sasha had waiting.

He drew a deep breath, uneasy with the plan even though he had it down to a science. Megan had been a problem from the very beginning. He'd checked phone directories, listened for hours for names to be called at busy delis, looked up church memberships, and had even gone into funeral homes and checked the names in the sign-in books. He did all the things he'd done to locate the others, but hadn't been able to find a Megan. He'd racked his brain to think of places where he might hear it come up, and eventually had a brainstorm: college classes. He didn't even have to enroll. He'd just sauntered into classes at the nearest couple of universities for the first few days of the summer semester, stayed seated in the lecture hall long enough for each professor to call roll on the first day, and listened. He attended twelve different classes over the course of four days and in the end, in a class called "Technology and Social Change," the professor read the name Megan Kessler and a young woman raised her hand. "Here," she said.

Yes, *here*. He'd found her.

And gotten lucky. The Megan he'd found was young, a bit overweight, and socially inactive. She lived in an apartment complex a few blocks from campus. One of her classes met at night, on Mondays and Wednesdays, but she always walked home using a well-lit path, and there were always people around.

That wouldn't work.

However, on weekends, Megan waitressed at a club in Canton. Late. Alone.

Sasha looked at his watch—four twenty. Past closing time for a Friday night. *Come on, Megan.* Time was ticking. After all the diversions he'd already had with Penny Wolff and Louie Guilford this week, Sasha couldn't afford to wait any longer for Megan. Kara's birthday was only two days away.

The back door opened and Megan stepped out. Sasha's pulse picked up. His fingers tightened on the handles of the garrote. Megan carried a plastic bag over to a pile of trash, then paused to fasten a barrette in her hair. She looped her purse over her shoulder and started walking, nearer, nearer. Sasha's blood began to pound and everything started. The rage climbed on top of him and with it, pain. He tried to count—*one, two, three*—but despite what the prison shrink had preached, deep breathing was a crock of shit. The pain started anyway, a pulse point at the back of his skull, and he knew too well what was coming. The grinding jaw, the black spots in his eyes. The nosebleed and shortness of breath, the stretching in his groin that sent white-hot shards of pain through his vitals.

And finally, the orgasm. It would shatter the rage and let him up again.

In the old days, he'd hated it—being held in the talons of that mystical beast Dr. Lyons called rage. It had spurred him to an impulse that cost him fifteen years in prison. But now, he cherished it. He groomed it. He even *fed* it, when necessary.

Tonight, the beast was hungry. It wanted Megan.

He tied a bandanna over his nose, watched her come near and pass him by, close enough that he could smell the odors of cigarette smoke and beer and French fries even through the bandanna. His groin tightened more, and spikes of pain stabbed between his legs. This was the stage when he was still supposed to be able to control it: *Name it, claim it, aim it,* preached Lyons, and Sasha had learned just what the bastard wanted to hear.

Name it: I have jealousy toward my brother.

Claim it: My anger is legitimate and it is mine to feel.

Aim it: I will channel my anger in healthy, productive ways.

Sasha snapped the wire tight, feeling it vibrate all the way to his shoulders. Yes, he'd known what to say to make the prison shrinks happy. But he also knew the truth.

Name it: Kara Montgomery Chandler.

Claim it: Kara, you're mine.

Aim it: Kara, you're dead.

He blinked but the black spots were in his eyes and

barbs of pain jabbed at his groin. He let Megan get five paces ahead, then came out from behind the truck. He didn't sneak, didn't duck walk or tiptoe. He walked with swift, deliberate strides, holding the handles of the garrote in each hand with the wire hanging in a circle at his knees, thinking only of the moment of release to come.

Megan turned, let out a squeak, then spun around to run. He caught her with the wire from behind, a lasso around the throat, and she stumbled back. She grabbed at the wire, her fingertips ripping open, and Sasha pulled harder, harder, until the wire rang tight and his head and groin nearly exploded with pain. He gritted his teeth and suspended her in the air, an animal growl rumbling in his throat. Her hands flailed in useless circles that caught nothing, and a gurgle rose in her throat.

Her legs gave out. Sasha wanted to howl. The pain in his groin gave way to orgasm, the red curtain of rage exploding into a thousand pinpoints of light. He let Megan sink to her knees, some visceral instinct keeping his arms out and the wire tight for several more seconds, then finally bent his elbows and let the weight of her body sink to the cement.

He dropped the handles and stood over the heap that was Megan Kessler. Moisture soaked his crotch and for several seconds, he sucked in air, waiting for the pain to ease. He scrubbed his sleeve across his upper lip— nosebleed—then pressed his hand against his chest to keep his heart from pounding through his rib cage. One heartbeat at a time, his senses crept back into grasp.

Sasha smiled. What would Dr. Lyons think of *that*? He'd learned to channel his rage, all right. Right into the wire garrote.

Thanks, doc.

He pulled off the bandanna and wiped the blood from his nose, then reached down to Megan Kessler. She may not be dead yet, but as long as he'd crushed the windpipe... He grabbed a fistful of her hair and stretched out her throat to look. The wire was lodged deep. No chance she was still alive.

He looked around to make sure they were still alone, then plucked the garrote from her throat. His van was only twenty feet away—an old white Dodge with no windows. He'd worried a little that if authorities ever got a hold of the photo he'd sent of Penny Wolff, with her propped up against the wheel well in a cornfield in Mississippi, they might be able to figure out what he was driving. But he didn't think it would matter. He'd bought this van off a guy with cash, never transferred the title. And usually he drove the Lexus. This was strictly a work vehicle.

He carried Megan Kessler's body over and shoved her through the side door. Slammed it closed and backtracked to the abandoned truck where he'd hidden to wait for her. There, he collected his satchel. Coiled up the lovely wire and tucked it back in the case.

Okay, Kara. Last one.
It's time.

Luke's throat went dry. He couldn't believe what he was seeing. "Barbed wire," he said. "That garrote is fucking barbed wire."

Knutson picked up the purple scarf and shook it loose. The holes took on new meaning and the dark stains around each began to make some sort of sick sense. He looped it in a loose circle twice around his arm, with the ends dangling in the way a woman might wear it around her neck. The bloody holes lined up.

"Jesus Christ," Luke said, and Knutson unwound the scarf. Luke had seen a lot of weapons in his day. South American cartels were notorious for creative killings.

But he'd never seen anything like this.

On the computer, he zoomed in on one of the handles of the garrote, enlarging it. The hairs on the back of his neck stood up. "These are turned wood. Like, hand-crafted. This garrote was *designed*."

"That's a scary amount of forethought," Knutson said.

That's a scary amount of sick.

"We know what happened to Andrew Chandler and Penny Wolff," Luke said. "But what about all the others in between? The people who owned the gifts Kara received and that represent some *truth* to the killer. Are they all dead?"

Knutson made a noncommittal gesture. There was no way to know, but it was a good bet. "The bigger question now is, who's next?"

How is Aidan?

Luke rubbed a hand over his head. "We need to hole up the kid."

"We can put him in the safe house you used when you were supposedly in custody. It's not far."

Luke nodded. Didn't want to think about how he was going to get Kara to let him—a cartel hit man—take Aidan away from her. He doubted that was what she had in mind when she'd hired him.

Knutson said, "I'll call Quantico and do some history. See if I can find any bodies that were missing something personal when they were found."

"Check the ink pen," Luke said. "I saw an engraving."

Knutson pulled it from the pillowcase using a handker-chief, and spun the silver into the light. " 'All my love, Gina.' "

Someplace to start, anyway.

Luke closed his eyes, almost disbelieving all that had changed in a few short hours. To have Andrew Chandler's death come back to haunt him now...It was crazy. He thought he'd put that behind him.

"I was talking to Chandler an hour before he died," he said.

"Wasn't your fault, man."

"I'm the one who put Elisa with him."

"Wasn't your fault."

"But it wasn't John Wolff's, either," Luke said. "That much is clear now."

Knutson advanced on him. "You've got a job to finish, Luke: Eight and a half tons of cocaine. You can't let some psycho with his dick in his hand and a thing for Kara Chandler throw you out of the game."

Luke knew that. "My part in that is already finished. I'm waiting right now, that's all. If you take the kid off my hands, I can figure out what's going on with Kara. It won't stretch my cover to do it." He shut down the computer, ejected the thumb drive, and pocketed Kara's cell phone.

Knutson looked wary. "Remember who you're dealing with, Luke. She's a prosecutor. She'll smell bullshit a mile away. Don't forget who you are."

"I won't forget who I am," Luke promised, and added another vow that only he could hear: *And I won't forget what I have to do.*

CHAPTER
12

K ARA SAW THE CHUNKS of gold hair hit the floor, felt her head grow strangely light, and didn't know whether to be relieved or terrified. This was what she wanted: She wanted Kara Chandler to disappear. She *needed* it. But feeling it happen—and knowing it was happening according to Luke Varón's plan rather than her own—added a layer of the unknown to something already inconceivable.

What was Andrew Chandler to you?

A hit. I was hired to kill him.

She closed her eyes, hardly able to wrap her mind around it, as the woman named Madelena worked. She whacked Kara's hair into a pixie cut and brushed on dye that looked almost black, then proceeded to apply makeup with a heavy hand. Kara would have done much the same, but Varón was right: Madelena did it better.

When Madelena was finished, she plucked at Kara's sassy haircut with her fingers and hit it with a hair dryer for all of a minute. Kara shook her head and felt five pounds lighter. Madelena handed her a mirror.

Kara swallowed. She wouldn't have recognized herself.

Playful waves the color of dark chestnut and mussed, feathery bangs that made her cheekbones stand out. Her eyes were smoky with shadow and dark mascara, the green of her irises popping like emeralds. Her lips were lined and painted the color of candy apples.

"Now the clothes," Madelena said, and pushed a bag into her hands. She pointed at a door off the kitchen. "In there."

Kara slipped into the bathroom and put on the clothes. A short denim skirt and lacy white tank, with a second black tank over it. Beaded sandals. Dangling mesh earrings that almost brushed her bare collarbones. She could have been a hooker on Spring Street.

She walked back into the kitchen at the same moment Luke Varón reappeared. He stopped and his gaze took her in one inch at a time. Surprise tinged his features. Surprise, and something else that made everything below her waist seem to loosen.

"Jesus." Aidan stepped up behind Varón. "Mom, you—you look like a stripper."

Kara gathered up a dose of indignation, aimed it at Varón. "A fine observation for a child to make about his mother."

Madelena hurried to hand Kara a pair of eyeglasses. "Here, *senora*," she said, and Kara took them. They had narrow black frames, the size of gum sticks.

"Now you look like a graduate student," Aidan said, "who works nights as a stripper."

Varón cocked his head. "Excellent job, Madelena," he said, and shifted his attention to Aidan. Also a brunette now, his hair was shaved short to expose a tattoo climbing up the back of his neck—an abstraction of a dragon with a dagger and flames. Permanent ink, Kara had been informed, but not injected. It would wear off over a few weeks' time. Kara had watched Aidan's transformation occur one step at a time, but the final product still jarred her. The tough-kid, street look had aged him, made his neck look thicker and his shoulders broader. She thought he might be getting a perverse kick out of the image.

"The pajama bottoms aren't working for you, stud," Varón said. To Madelena: "You brought him clothes?"

"There," she said, nodding to a stack on the seat of a stool. "He wouldn't leave me alone with his mother to go change."

Varón's brows hiked up. "Good man," he said to Aidan. "You're going to need that sense of protectiveness from here on out. Fine, then. It's just as well you stay in pajamas for now, anyway. That way you can catch a few Zs while I talk to your mom."

A scowl crossed Aidan's features. Kara seethed. Aidan was a smart kid, and savvy. But he was no match for the manipulative mind games Luke Varón played.

Aidan picked up the clothes. "I'll be back, Mom."

When he was gone, Kara turned on Varón. "You know just how to pull his strings, don't you? Making him feel like you want him to protect me, and like he'll miss something important if he doesn't go do what you want."

"Just stating the facts."

Madelena turned to them. "Mr. Varón?" She adjusted the volume at a small TV mounted beneath the kitchen cabinets and stepped aside. "You see?"

Varón took two steps closer, peered at the television. The morning news was just signing on. Kara tuned in and her heart took a tumble.

She was dead. Reports claimed that both she and Aidan were feared dead in a tragic explosion that had rocked the night. A boat belonging to the late Andrew Chandler had gone up in flames at a little after two in the morning, and while there was as yet no sign of Assistant District Attorney Kara Chandler or her fourteen-year-old son, authorities were saying the Chandlers were believed to have been aboard the boat at the time of the explosion. The cameras showed streams of workers pouring in, preparing for a search as threads of daylight brightened the sky.

Saturday morning. She and Aidan had ceased to exist.

A picture of Andrew filled the screen and snippets of the ubiquitous tale floated past Kara's ears... *well-known builder... associated with Montiel Enterprises... killed with Elisa Moran in a hit-and-run accident... drunk driver confessed to leaving the scene...*

Kara closed her eyes. Poor Sally and Seth, to lose her and Aidan a day after Louie.

Look what you've done.

Madelena gathered up her supplies, packing them all back into a large bag. The man who had driven the car reappeared as well, seemingly unconcerned with the news reports, helping Madelena pack up. He picked up the dark layers of clothing and hat he'd discarded, and threw them into her bag while Varón crossed his arms and listened to the television. He seemed impervious to the presence of the driver and Madelena: They were minions who milled around him doing their prescribed jobs while he reigned over the castle.

Varón clicked off the TV and pulled a small stack of cards from his pocket. He held them out to her. "Your name is now Krista Carter. You live at Sixteen Twenty-five Campbell Street, Apartment Five-E. You were born at Our Lady of the Saints Hospital in Lexington, Kentucky. Since you grew up with horses, I picked Bluegrass territory for your background."

He thumbed through the cards as he spoke: driver's license, credit cards, social security card. Costco membership, voter registration card, even a birth certificate. Of the latter, there were two: one for Krista Carter, born in Lexington, Kentucky, in 1980, and one for Austin Carter, born in Hamilton County, Ohio, in 1999.

Kara marveled at the documents. They looked completely legit.

"For a couple of days, the news will report that you and Aidan are suspected dead in the explosion," Varón said. "After that, they'll find bits and pieces of your bodies—enough to positively identify both of you."

"Bits and piec—" She couldn't finish.

Varón met her eyes with utter solemnity. "I'm sending Vince to search through my stash of dead bodies and plant limbs in places authorities will find in a couple days." He cocked his head. "You want it to look real, don't you?"

The inanity of that registered by droplets. Jerk. She looked up at him and saw the faint humor in his eyes, then cursed, forcing herself to relax: There were no bits and pieces of bodies to be strewn in the lake.

Still, another thought prickled her skin: Varón may not be able to produce bits and pieces of body parts containing Chandler DNA, but he *could* produce false police reports about it. No surprise there. She'd already suspected he had an in somewhere in the police department.

Or in the DA's office? Kara hadn't lied about having new evidence against Montiel. What she hadn't told Varón was that for some reason she didn't understand, Ben Archer had suddenly put a halt on the indictments they'd been preparing. Briefly, Kara had wondered if there was something going on deeper than she knew—Had Montiel paid off the DA? But she knew it was more likely that Montiel's position as a respected billionaire and generous philanthropist was more to blame. One of his biggest projects was *pro bono*—a nationwide program called *HomeAid* to construct low-income housing. Ask any person on the streets about Montiel and *HomeAid* was sure to come up. Campaigns to keep it going after Andrew's stake in it fell apart had been a source of wide public support.

Varón, on the other hand—Gene Montiel's "chief security advisor"—had no philanthropic side. He did what he was paid to do, even when it was murder. End of story.

"Fine," she said with a petulant lift of her chin. "I don't care how you get it done."

The man he'd referred to as "Vince" picked up Madelena's bag and leaned toward Varón. "We're outta here, Luke. I'll call you."

Kara's pulse skittered under the surface of her skin. They were leaving—leaving her and Aidan alone with Varón. She didn't know why that should scare her; Vince Knutson and Madelena were on Varón's side.

But she was scared.

She bolstered her courage and when Madelena and the other man left, Kara glared at Varón. "I'm going to check on Aidan. When I come back, I'll need my phone back."

"Your phone is out of commission for a little while. While I pull the text messages and see what else is there."

She frowned. Thorough, indeed. "A computer, then. I want to see what I can find out about the investigation into Louie's murder."

"When you come back," Varón said, "I'll have some things to talk about, as well."

A warning? Kara wondered, but shook it off and went to the back room. She rapped her knuckle against the door. "Aidan?" No answer. She pressed the door open.

He lay on the sofa, with short dark hair and the tattoo on his neck, wearing jeans that would no doubt sag to his knees and a DMX t-shirt Kara had never seen before. He'd traded in his favorite Nike sneakers for a pair of two-hundred-dollar BIOMs supplied by Varón. He didn't look like Aidan, and it took that first instant of shock to register that the form on the sofa was indeed her son and that he was indeed, sleeping.

Okay. Kara forced herself to take a couple of deep breaths. It was just as well that he get some sleep. It was time to face off with Varón.

CHAPTER
13

SASHA BROUGHT MEGAN HOME; he was glowing on the inside. So close now.

He propped Megan's body in the corner of her stall, snapped a couple of pictures of her to send to Kara later, then fell onto the cot in the tack room. He woke in what seemed like a blink of the eye, patted the floor for his iPhone, and lit the screen: 7:32. Less than three hours of sleep, but that was okay. The hardest work was done. Now it was just a matter of burying Megan before she got hard to handle, before she went stiff or started crawling with insects or smelling.

He rolled off the mattress and opened the door, letting the sun pour in, then crossed the lobby of the stable to use the bathroom. When he came out he looked around. It never got old, seeing what he'd built: The arena, equipped with jumps and clean-raked footing that even Willis Montgomery would have admired, all of it climate-controlled. A restroom off the lobby area, tiled and decorated like one found in a nice restaurant, except that it also had a shower. A tack room the size of a motel suite, which, in fact, Sasha had taken over as his bedroom ever since the structure was completed.

And eight stalls, each with rough-hewn pine for the walls and the finest flooring money could buy: a deep layer of gravel covered by a thick stall skin, topped off with eight inches of coarse sawdust for the horses' bedding.

Of course, there were no horses in these stalls. There was something much better.

He closed his eyes, imagining the look on Kara's face when he brought her here. How many nights had he lulled himself to sleep thinking about retribution? How many years had he been locked in prison with nothing but dreams of showing the mighty Kara Montgomery just what he was capable of? Of fucking her and punishing her and killing her for all that she'd cost him? And yet, ironically, it was during those same years that he had discovered something much better than a good fuck to give her.

He'd discovered the truth and it had set him free.

It would kill Kara.

He showered, rummaged through a box in the tack room for a granola bar to keep him going until breakfast, and switched on a TV in the corner. He didn't expect anyone to know that Megan Kessler was missing yet; it had only been a few hours. But he liked following the news about Penny Wolff and Louie Guil—

Assistant District Attorney Kara Chandler, presumed dead overnight in a tragic boat explosion...

Sasha spun toward the television. He blinked, dread clutching at his throat.

This wasn't possible. He listened harder, trying to replay the words already passed and at the same time make sense of the new ones coming from the reporter's mouth. Explosion. Missing. Boat. Presumed dead.

But Kara couldn't be dead. He wasn't finished with her. When Kara Chandler died, it would be by Sasha's hand.

He had the weapon. He had the practice. He'd set everything up. He would reveal the truth, watch it knock the light from Kara's eyes, then choke the life from her lungs with the barbed wire garrote he'd fashioned in her honor. It would be his retribution. His glory.

The story ended. Panic took hold and he grabbed the remote, frantically clicking through channels. He found a repeat of the same story on another station, watched it, then found a third.

No way. *No fucking way.* She couldn't have done this to him. Bitch.

Beads of perspiration popped up from his flesh. He paced, the television newscasters summarily unconcerned that he wanted to hear more, *needed* to hear more. On every channel, they moved on—showed a few shots of authorities picking up pieces of the boat and dragging the river, a photo of Kara and her kid, and gave a brief biography of who she was. And then, as if there were anything else in the world that mattered, they moved on.

Fuck them all.

His breaths came short. This was impossible. He'd sent her a text message of Louie Guilford just hours ago from the bridge. She'd received it—he knew she had. He'd *felt* it . . . lying there on a mattress in a stable he'd built for her, he'd sensed that she got the text, and he'd drifted to sleep with her horror filling his dreams. She had to be terrified. She had to have figured it out by now. After her husband's sunglasses and Guilford's death and all those gifts . . . After his threats to her son and the picture of Penny Wolff. She had to have been smart enough to realize he had something planned for *her*—

Sasha stopped, a thought pinging in the back of his mind. Wait, that was it. She *did* have to know. He'd taken care to be cryptic early on, keeping his distance while doing what was necessary to build this precious stable and prepare for her arrival. But by now, she had to know.

And just when she caught on, she and her kid went missing in a boat explosion? Dead?

I don't think so.

A sneer rose up and Sasha moved through a few more channels, caught the end of one last local report. No bodies. No plans. No explanation. She and the kid were just gone.

Sanity squeezed in, one drop at a time. That bitch. How dare she try to hide from him? This was *his* plan. She had no right trying to change the outcome.

Rage threatened, but arrogance won out. Kara may be smart, but not as smart as Sasha. She couldn't defy him. She couldn't elude him.

He calmed and got out the iPhone—the one dedicated for his business with Kara. He resisted the urge to turn it on here and jumped in the Lexus. He drove, not sure where he was going, only certain that he didn't dare let the GPS he was about to use start at the stable. He got into Atlanta where there would be plenty of towers, smiled at himself, and headed for a parking lot at Turner Field. He liked the irony of that.

When he was parked, he got out the phone and turned it on, then re-enabled the GPS.

Kara's phone had a tracking program—he'd installed it himself. He'd been tracking her for months, and she had no idea, and her kid, too. All he'd needed was to have the phones in his hands for a few minutes to install the programs, and he managed that one afternoon at a Memorial Day party. No problem at all.

He waited while the phone found service, clicked

on the device he wanted to find, and watched the little bars light up as the satellite searched for Kara's phone. Nothing.

His jaw clenched. What? He tried again. Nothing.

Fury rose in his gut, and he switched over to access Aidan's tracker. A signal came up. His heart started beating again. Aidan's phone was still alive, somewhere north of the city, near Blue Ridge. In the middle of fucking nowhere.

He frowned. It didn't make sense that Kara's phone wasn't working but Aidan's was, especially if they'd both been blown up in a boat explosion. He'd known she was smart, he'd known she was resourceful. But he hadn't expected her to try to escape him by making people believe she was dead.

He set the phone on the dashboard where he could see the map. *Very good, Kara. Nice move, indeed.*

But now it's my turn.

CHAPTER
14

Luke watched Kara come back into the kitchen. He didn't react, but it was a damn close thing: golden tresses gone the way of dark pixie-punk, makeup that only exaggerated the jewel-tones of green and gold in her eyes, clothes that covered too little and yet left plenty to his imagination—and memory.

Christ, he couldn't remember the last time he'd been intrigued by a woman. Attracted, yes, but *intrigued*? Women were plentiful creatures, entertaining enough in their own way, and he was gentleman enough to always lay down the ground rules of getting involved: no strings, no families, no investment. Easy come, easy go.

For the most part, it worked. The occasional woman had gotten her feelings hurt when the inevitable end rolled around, and once or twice he'd even been sorry himself. But he'd long ago accepted the fact that Luke Varón wasn't the sort of man a woman took to meet Mom and Dad. He was dark and callous, driven by demons and immersed so deep in the life of the cartel that he'd occasionally, after some particularly heinous act, found himself with his back against an alley wall, panting, whispering his true identity over and over again in a panic: *Lukas Mann, thirty-eight, Hopewell, Ohio. Mann. Luke Mann. Two wholesome parents in a wholesome town, a passel of siblings and a white picket fence…*

The momentary reminder had never mattered. In a decade, he hadn't seen his family for more than a couple weeks total—he hadn't even made it home when his father died. There had been a few days last year when he was between the fall of the Rojàs cartel in Colombia and the rise of Collado's takeover in Atlanta…a handful of short days when he'd gone back home, thinking he was finished with the underworld, used his own name and spent some time helping his brother, a sheriff, clean up a string of murders in their little hometown. He'd watched Nick let go of a grudge that had existed between the two of them for years, watched him fall in love, and he'd wondered, just for a moment, if he'd ever be in those shoes.

Then came the news: Collado had slipped through the cracks of the Rojàs takedown. How quickly Luke had been sucked back into the life, and spent the next several months setting up house in Atlanta—under Montiel's wing. "Security," they called him, a title that meant nothing and gave him access to everything.

He was Luke Varón this time. Hit man, breaker of legs, and murderer of dissidents. Terrorizer of young women and teenage boys.

Then again, he thought, looking at the young woman walking toward him just now, this one didn't frighten all that easily. She came at him with her shoulders square and steel in her eyes.

"Here," he said, pouring her a mug of coffee. He topped off his own from the same pot, slanting a grin. "So you won't think I'm trying to poison you."

She peered at him as if that's exactly what she'd thought, then took the mug. "Why didn't you kill him?" she asked. "Andrew."

Luke met her eyes. He wanted to tell her that he wasn't a cold-blooded killer, that he wouldn't have hurt Andrew deliberately. But he was Luke Varón.

"I was incarcerated," he said. "You knew that."

She looked at him as if she'd hoped for a better answer, and for the first time he could remember, he regretted the ruse. The disappointment in her eyes cut into his soul.

Nothing he could do about that. He had to play on—at least until Collado was in custody. Maybe later…

Stop it.

Her shoulders drooped and Luke's heart went out to her. She was scared. She was hurting. She was exhausted. She was going to miss Louie Guilford's funeral tomorrow, leaving a whole bunch of people in shock, grieving for her and Aidan. Her friend, Sally—Guilford's wife—had been calling her phone since early morning. Luke wasn't looking forward to telling her that.

"Is Austin sleeping?" he asked.

"Aust—" she started to ask, then closed her eyes as if she'd tasted something bitter.

"You should start using the name. And you are Krista. Get used to it."

She lifted her chin, a gesture that reminded him of the gritty blonde he'd first met at the courthouse, not the jittery brunette who now stood holding a coffee mug so tight her knuckles were bloodless. She met his eyes with an unyielding gaze.

"What was my husband to you? Why would you go to all this trouble to find his killer?"

"Twenty thousand dollars."

"Bullshit."

He treated himself to a slow appraisal of her new look. "You look good as a brunette. Not that you didn't look good as a bl—"

"Stop it."

His gaze snagged on her breasts and he canted his head. "You should lose the bra. It doesn't fit the new image."

"Damn you. What do you know about Andrew?"

Luke leaned back against the counter. "Ben Archer thinks I'm here to head up a splinter of the Rojàs cartel."

"Aren't you?"

He ignored that. "Has it occurred to either of you: Why Atlanta?"

"Excuse me?"

"Why Atlanta? There are no Rojàs relatives here. It's land-bound. It's a major metropolitan area with a top-notch police force and a significant DEA-FBI presence. It's not an easy headquarters."

"Unless you have a front," she suggested. "Say, something like Montiel Enterprises."

He smiled. "I see Ben Archer has gotten you on board."

"You came here only a year ago, on Montiel's payroll. 'Security specialist.' And yet, you aren't responsible for any of Montiel's obvious security issues. You aren't designing locks or camera systems, you aren't a software guru, you aren't even a bodyguard."

"Perhaps I'm just so good at my job the police can't see me doing it. Stealth Security."

She wasn't amused. "You can't blame Ben for suspecting the worst. It's what your history suggests."

"Not to mention that busting up a drug ring headed up by a man everyone else thinks is a humanitarian would put Archer in any elected seat he wants. But you still haven't answered the original question: Why Atlanta? Gene Montiel wasn't enough. There had to be someone else."

She glared at him with eyes of steel, but her voice came out frayed. "Who?"

"Your husband."

Gene Montiel watched *Good Day, Atlanta* with only half an eye, more interested in the sports section of the paper than in the human-interest stories that passed for television news these days. But all that changed when the name Andrew Chandler caught his ear.

His heart dropped and he set down his coffee mug, aiming the remote at an eighteen-inch television and bumping up the volume. The news was startling: Kara Chandler and her son, dead in a boat explosion.

He watched the report and his gut hollowed out. He didn't know what it meant, but every instinct crackled along his nerves like a current. Collado was due to arrive within a day or two. The shipment was scheduled to be distributed within hours of its arrival near Savannah. And at the same time, Andrew Chandler's family had suddenly been involved in a tragic accident?

Montiel rubbed a hand over his face. He'd come too far to let anything ruin this delivery now. Everything he'd worked for in life, everything that meant anything to him, was wrapped up in this deal with Collado. His businesses, his charity work, his reputation, his family. Even with Ben Archer breathing down his neck and threatening to ruin him, Montiel had so far managed to hang on. In only a few more days, he would be crowned the kingpin of one of the country's most lucrative cocaine rings.

He couldn't let anything stop that.

He shoved away from the table and opened his brief-case, pulling out a dedicated phone. He dialed, making contact with the only person he dared, even though he knew he shouldn't be doing it.

"Goddamn it, why would you risk calling me like this?" the man snapped.

Montiel swallowed. He wasn't accustomed to being the one who *took* orders, but knew that in this case, he needed to stay with the plan. "Have you seen the news this morning? About Andrew Chandler's wife?"

"I'm watching it now," he said. "Tragic."

"That's it? Tragic?"

"Well, what else would it be? You think I had something to do with it?"

"Tell me everything's still all right. Everything is a go."

"Everything's still all right. Everything is a go."

Montiel cursed. He didn't like deals where he had to rely on others; he liked to handle details himself. That's how he'd gotten as far in life as he had.

But for this, that wasn't possible.

He blew out a breath. "You'd better not be jerking me around. This is too important."

"I know how fucking important it is," the man shot. "So, Gene—" His voice grew dark. "Don't call me again."

CHAPTER
15

K ARA BLANCHED. "My *husband*?" she asked. She was shocked, Luke thought, but within seconds, anger seeped in. He was about to accuse Andrew Chandler of something awful. He wouldn't be the first. "Andrew didn't play in those circles," she shot.

"Forgive me, Ms. Chandler, but I don't think you always knew just where your husband was playing."

That hurt—Luke could see it in her eyes, along with a truth he imagined she didn't want to acknowledge. A sliver of guilt slid under his skin but he flicked it away. He needed for her to be willing to share Andrew's secrets with him, her knowledge and her suspicions. Even their pillow talk.

He could think of a pretty good place to do that. There was a giant Jacuzzi in the master bedroom upstairs and a big king bed that had been calling his name even before he met up with Kara Chandler. It wouldn't stretch Luke's ethics too far to use the circumstance of a post-orgasmic glow to find out what she knew.

"Get to the point, Mr. Varón."

"Your husband's firm built Montiel's low-income

housing. Andrew entered into a ten-year contract with HomeAid just before he died."

"He was a general contractor. It was his business to enter into contracts with developers."

Luke studied her. He wished Andrew Chandler was still alive so he could put a fist in the man's face. His wife didn't deserve this. She was a good woman—strong, intelligent, principled. And as captivating as an edgy brunette as she'd been as a sophisticated blonde.

He tamped back that last observation and reminded himself that a tumble with Kara Chandler was out of the question. Aside from the fact that she'd sooner shoot him than kiss him, there was a fatherless fourteen-year-old boy involved. Fatherless, in part, because of Luke. The thought passed that Lukas Mann might have been a big enough man to handle that, but Lukas Mann wasn't here. Luke Varón was. Mann had gone under long ago, and only rarely surfaced for air.

Luke traded his mug for a set of papers in a hutch. Kara followed him into the great room and he sat down on the sofa, opening the file on the coffee table.

"Do you recognize this sub-contract?" Luke asked, handing her a contract between Chandler Enterprises and a company called MHA out of Savannah: Macy's Heating and Air.

"Lining up sub-contractors was part of Andrew's job. Why would this one be special?"

"Because this one is a contract for distributing cocaine, nationwide. Everywhere HomeAid needs a furnace."

She went rigid. It wasn't the first time someone had suggested that her husband had secrets. But it might have been the first time someone had laid clear, hard evidence at her feet.

"What are you talking about?"

"Macy's transports cocaine. Close to five pounds per unit. That's what they found was the optimum amount in the test runs."

"You're out of your mind."

"Like this," he said, and pointed at a diagram of the heating unit. "The cocaine comes in from sea. Divers move it from fishing boats offshore to the bottom of tourist boats around Jekyll Island. From there, it's taken right down the road to Macy's, where they fill each blower chamber with close to two pounds of powdered cocaine. The combustion chamber holds the rest. They ship it to regional distribution centers for HomeAid, empty the chambers, then the drugs hit the streets while the units get installed into houses."

Hate filled her eyes. *"They?"*

Luke was ready for that. *"We,"* he said.

Kara stood and stepped away from him, the air around her vibrating with tension. He could see her mind spinning.

"Bet you wish you hadn't died last night, huh?" he asked. "Ben Archer would promote you to God for information like this."

She wrapped her arms around her torso. Hate rolled off her in waves. But she didn't deny her husband's involvement. That was what struck Luke as most odd.

"You knew," he said, and a sliver of disappointment slipped under his skin.

"I knew he had secrets. But I didn't know it was…" She shook her head, her hands clenching into fists even as a tear rolled down her cheek. Fury versus pain. Always a brutal battle. "I thought it was just women."

"Just women?"

Her eyes went hollow. "We married young. I was used to it."

And that was the sum of that marriage, Luke thought. If he'd been cut from a different sort of cloth, he might have wondered how long it had been since a man had handled her well, or made her feel loved. But he wasn't, so he pushed that thought away and said, "I think it would take me longer to lose interest."

She blinked, apparently uncertain whether he'd complimented her, and Luke shrugged. "I'm just sayin'."

He forced himself to move on. "You were explaining—"

"No. I wasn't explaining anything because I don't know anything. I don't know what Andrew was doing. I only know he—" She stopped.

"What?"

"Nothing."

"Damn it, I can't help you if you don't come clean with me."

"It was nothing." She grew wistful. "Just something he promised me once, that's all."

She closed up and a knot of disappointment tightened in Luke's gut. If she was telling the truth—and she was pretty damned convincing—she truly might not know much about Andrew's activities. She might not be able to help him.

But he had to try. He owed it to Elisa, not to mention that he now had Kara Chandler and a fourteen-year-old kid in his care. But whatever he did, he would have to do it in the persona of Luke Varón. He couldn't risk it any other way.

Luke gave her a look that was at once dark and hungry. "Here's the deal," he said, his voice clipped. "I want to find the man who killed your husband and is now stalking you and your son. Not because I care about the two of you, mind you, but because I can't afford to have any loose ends out there right now." He smirked. "How's that for irony? I help you find your stalker and you help me run the cartel."

She glared at him. He went on; this was the hard part. "Part of that is getting your son out of the way."

The color drained from her face. "No," she breathed.

"You hired me to do a job. I need to be able to do it."

She closed the distance between them, visibly fighting to keep her voice low. "You can't take my son."

"I give you my word he'll be safe."

She jerked back. "Your *word*? You're a killer yourself."

"I don't hurt kids," Luke growled. "And I haven't gotten to the top of one of the most secure organizations in the world without learning something. You know that, too, that's why you called me. I can keep him safe. He'll be unreachable. I'll let you know where he is. You can talk to him anytime you want. I'll make sure he's comfortable. I promise you all that."

She stared. He wasn't sure whether fury or fear would win out. "I'm not leaving my son."

"You don't have a choice, Counselor."

"Oh, really?" she asked. She advanced on him again, fury rising to the top. "It seems to me that you're the one with no choice, Mr. Varón. Have you forgotten about the letter I wrote about Montiel? It will surface before your precious shipment does unless I do something to stop it. And right now, I don't think I'm in the mood."

Luke went still. Ben Archer wouldn't go through with the case no matter what he thought he had in the way of indictments—the FBI had made sure of that. But in the meantime, if Kara had absconded with some of the DA's intel, she could single-handedly spook Collado.

"You're a reckless woman, Ms. Chandler," Luke said. "Brave, but reckless."

"I'm past caring about bravery or recklessness, Mr. Varón. I would think my contacting you in the first place proved that."

Luke eyed her. "You don't think very much of my character, do you?"

"I don't think very much of your character. Your only saving grace is that I do think a lot of your skill set. But all deals are off without my son by my side."

Luke shook his head. A parent's love for a child—it was the most powerful force on earth. Luke had been one of the lucky ones. The Mann kids knew about parental love and support. Even the one who'd gone to work for a drug cartel.

"All right," Luke said, and let his eyes trek down Kara's body. He'd let her have this round. In the end, he'd win. "With one condition."

"You're hardly in a position to demand conditions, Mr. Varón."

"You're hardly in a position to decline, Ms. *Carter*."

She quailed a fraction, then lifted her chin.

"Lose the bra," he said.

"You're out of your mind." She started to turn away, but he caught her arm and spun her around. Luke tried not to notice how much he liked feeling his hand on her bare skin. Like having lightning at his fingertips.

Kissing her would be even more explosive.

Christ. Stop it.

"You can't resemble Kara Chandler," he said, keeping his voice rough at the edges. "That means more than just changing your hair and the outer layer of clothing. It means you change your walk, your attitude, the way you speak. It means: Lose the bra."

She swallowed, as if not knowing whether to believe he was genuinely concerned about her ability to stay *incognito* or whether he was just feeding his own lasciviousness. So it was with both astonishment and admiration that he watched her twist her hands beneath the back of her shirt, unsnap her bra, and tug the straps down over her elbows in that way a woman can. Two seconds later, the satin came out from beneath the tank top and she slammed it into his chest. He caught it against his shirt by sheer reflex.

"Your turn," she snarled. "Find Andrew's killer."

CHAPTER
16

SASHA KICKED THE DOOR *shut behind him. Who'd have ever thought Kara Montgomery would come in here like this, putting on a show? Seven Minutes of Sin, from her perspective—playing with the bad boy while the love interest stands outside waiting. Andrew wouldn't interrupt. Neither would the other kids. That's not how it was done.*

So: Sasha had six minutes.

He stepped toward Kara and she grew an inch taller. "Don't even think about it," she snarled.

He stopped. Felt like she'd slapped him across the face. Tease. Bitch. *He'd known she was just using him to make Rich Boy jealous, but goddamn it, he didn't care. She was his now, just for a little while.*

"You chose the dare," he said. Heat coursed through his veins. He'd gotten hard as a rock just waiting for her, and now all that heat boiled into anger. "What's the matter? If I were your pretty Andrew, you'd have your panties around your ankles already."

Her cheeks darkened. "This is just a game. I don't even know you."

Sasha scoffed. That was the fucking truth, if ever he'd

heard it. Christ, he'd been around for almost all her life and she barely knew he existed. He even remembered when she'd first arrived here and all the hype that surrounded her adoption. He was five and Stefan was sick, and their mother had worked extra hours in the big house for weeks getting ready, and when the day finally came, Sasha stood behind a door and watched a crowd of rich folks fawn over her and wondered what a stupid baby could have done to deserve all the fuss.

Nothing, that's what.

He advanced on her. "I'm Sasha. My parents have both worked here since before I was born. I'll bet you don't know them, either, though, because we're all invisible. All the people who make your food and keep your stable clean and make special name cards for the kids at your fucking birthday part—"

"That's not true," she said, and he was within arm's reach now. His blood was on fire. He was alone with Kara Montgomery and had free rein, but the rich girl was all talk. Didn't want to be soiled.

"You think you're so much better than the rest of us," he snarled. "You aren't even a real Montgomery. The only reason you have anything at all is because your old man thinks it makes him look good to spend money on you. You were probably born in the streets, lower than me. Did you ever think of that, rich girl?"

She stared him down but Sasha could see he'd struck a nerve. Standing this close to her, he could feel the tension vibrating from her frame. A scent rose around him—something sweet but with an edge of spice to it. Not the simple scent of his mother's honeysuckle perfume or some cheap body wash; this had layers of aromas that tickled his nostrils.

It was the smell of privilege. Privilege she didn't deserve.

"You're just luckier than me, that's all. Lucky little rich bitch."

She winced, as if she'd never been spoken to so harshly before. Sasha unfastened his buckle.

"Stop it," *she said, backing up.* "I'll tell my dad and he'll throw your whole family off this farm."

"Really? You're going to tell your daddy that you agreed to come in the tack room and suck off the likes of me?"

"This was just a game."

"I like games." *Sasha dropped his pants, freeing himself. He was ready. Jesus fucking Christ. He was so ready.*

She winced and turned her head. Holy shit, maybe a virgin after all. He wasn't fool enough to think he could fuck her and get away with it, but he sure as hell was gonna enjoy that mouth.

She glanced at the door behind him. Sasha laughed. "What're you gonna do, call for Andrew? Is that the same Andrew who just said he wants to fuck Evie?"

The insult hit its mark. Her chin went up.

Sasha pushed his advantage. "Show him, Kara. Show him what he's not getting. He doesn't really want you anyway. I heard him talking to his dad. He's just making time with you to get his dad a special deal on that stallion's sperm. It's all business."

The barbs brought tears to her eyes. They glistened like water on emeralds. Sasha reached out and threaded his fingers into her hair. Careful, don't grab yet. Just a little pressure.

She sank to her knees, her hands bracing herself on the plank floor. Sasha almost lost it. "That's it, baby. Do it."

He clutched her hair, guiding her forward.
Seven Minutes of Heaven, down to five, now.
It was all he'd need.

Kara watched Varón turn the bra over in his hands. She shivered, bracing herself for him to notice the panels she'd hastily sewn inside—emptied of cash now—but he only crossed the room and dropped the garment into the trash can. Announced that he needed a couple of hours to pull together some leads and suggested she go lie down with *Austin* for a while.

Kara didn't argue with him. Aidan needed the sleep; *she* needed the sleep. She hadn't slept much all week and whatever was going to happen with Varón, she would need to be clearheaded. Already, she could feel the exhaustion taking its toll on both her actions and her judgment. She felt as if she couldn't trust her own thinking right now.

I fucked up, baby, but tonight will change everything. I'm making it right.

Oh, Andrew. What did you do? The night he died, he'd seemed so upbeat. He'd acted as if some great weight had been lifted from his shoulders. *Tonight will change everything,* he'd promised.

It certainly had.

She stretched out on a daybed in the room where Aidan slept, her mind going in circles, her heart aching for Andrew and Louie and the Wolffs and the man someone named Gina loved, whose pen was among the collection of gifts from people who were almost certainly dead. She thought about Sally hearing the news of the boat explosion and Seth—who'd just lost his father—losing Aidan as well, and wondered if Varón's compulsion to keep the drug ring intact would prove enough reason to keep Aidan safe. A host of invidious thoughts followed her into sleep and she snapped back when a knuckle rapped at the door.

"Krista." Varón's voice. He tapped again. Kara rolled off the couch and looked at the clock. It was noon, on the first day of her nonexistence.

Aidan stirred as she opened the door. She ran her fingers through her hair, winced at the short spikes, and looked up at Varón in the doorway. "What?" she snapped.

"Ooh," he said with a disarming smile. "Not a morning person." He looked past her at Aidan, who pushed to the edge of the sofa, getting oriented. "We need to move. Come on out and I'll catch you up."

Catch you up. Kara blinked. She'd slept while Varón had carried on. He'd changed out of the sleek suit and now wore jeans and a loose Oxford shirt in an unlikely shade of pink. The collar was open and his sleeves were rolled into folds on his forearms, accentuating deeply tanned muscles. He hadn't shaved and a blanket of stubble darkened his cheeks, but his hair was damp as if he'd just showered.

"Mom?" Aidan said. Kara shut the door on Varón. Aidan frowned at her new look, then ran a hand over his own head. Remembered.

"God," he said, and got up and walked to a mirror. Kara swallowed, realizing she looked as out of character as he did. Miniskirt, spiky hair, no bra. She wasn't a busty woman, but she had some curves. Enough that she didn't generally go without a bra.

Aidan turned from the mirror and said, "I can't believe this. Why is this happening? I don't get it."

Kara wrapped her arms around him, laid her head on his shoulder. When had he gotten tall enough for her to do that?

"I don't know," she whispered. "But we'll figure it out.

The important thing is to stay strong now. And stay out of sight."

He stepped back and looked at her, a frown marring his forehead. "You should've told me. Why didn't you tell me?"

"I didn't understand it myself." Kara squeezed his hand. "But we'll figure it out. Come on. The first step is to find out what Varón has in mind."

"You trust him?" Aidan asked, looking skeptical. "He was supposed to kill Dad."

"No, I don't trust him, not as far as I can throw him. But the bottom line is, he wants to know who killed your father as much as we do."

Aidan was too sharp to let that slide. "Why does he care about Dad in the first place?"

And there it was, that knife in the chest. Kara tamped back the impulse to offer platitudes: Aidan deserved to know the truth about his father. "Honey," she said, and saw his hackles lift, "it looks like your dad was into something bad before he died. Varón showed me evidence of... Your father was part of Varón's cocaine ring."

Aidan blanched. Every sinew grew tight. "No."

"I think so," she said, though even as she said it, she knew she was hedging. In her heart, she was sure Varón was right. "I only know that whoever killed your father is still out there, and he's hurting people and trying to scare me and Varón is going to help us find him."

Aidan backed up a few steps, as if the suggestion had come as a physical blow. "That's bullshit," he spat. "Dad didn't do cocaine. He didn't buy it, he didn't sell it. It's that son of a bitch, Varón. He has you believing lies."

He trembled with emotion, his face nearly bloodless. Kara's heart went soft. It was awful to realize your father wasn't a saint. She remembered that well. Except it had happened at a much younger age for her than for Aidan.

She went to him and ran her hand across his head, feeling the strange carpet of silky spikes of eighth-inch long hair. "Luke Varón is a criminal, yes. But he's smart and resourceful and he wants the same thing we want. And he's all we've got."

"We've got new identities. Let's just go. Start over someplace."

And have Varón searching for us, too? She didn't want to admit that part—the part that made her feel as if Varón was their captor. "Aidan, I know about men like Luke Varón. If the delivery of his cargo is at risk because your father's killer isn't dead, trust me, he'll find him. We'd be crazy not to use him."

Aidan rubbed the heels of his hands in his eyes. "How?" he asked after a long moment.

"We've waited long enough," she said. "Let's go figure that out."

CHAPTER
17

MORRIS SLEDGE WAITED. Sat on the open gate of his pickup truck, spit tobacco juice at rocks in the dirt, and felt the sun beat down. He'd called the Panola County Sheriff's office forty minutes ago. Wished the assholes would hurry, but knew they wouldn't. They never took him serious. Didn't believe him when teenagers had been hidin' out smokin' pot in his barn. Didn't believe him when Newt Fulton set up a telescope on his porch and watched Morris's house every hour of the day. Didn't believe him when the aliens crunched paths in the cornfields like them crop circles he'd seen on TV. Fuck, they'd even brought charges against *him* for that one. Claimed he was disturbin' the peace shootin' at his own corn.

Here he was a good citizen who actually went to the local high school on Election Day and cast his vote for sheriff and all them county commissioners, and then when he called, they took their sweet old time coming out and hardly believed a word he said. They probably expected not to find anything this time, either.

Well, wouldn't they be surprised?

Ten more minutes passed before Morris saw the

white Ford heading his way. He climbed off his truck and stepped out of the drive, moving to the center of the road to wave them down. Gus Flaherty was driving, and some young kid with a deputy's star was in the passenger seat. Morris couldn't remember the kid's name; kin of the Cahill family, he thought.

"Morris," Gus said, getting out of the car. He didn't even bother putting on his flashers. "Dispatch says you found somethin' in your corn. It better be interesting, you makin' us come all this way out here."

"It's interesting," Morris said, and started past his truck. He stopped and pointed at the chain that usually blocked off the drive. "I seen a bunch a vultures circlin', figured I'd come out an' have a look."

Gus looked at the kid-deputy. "You called us out here to see some deer carcass or something?"

Morris spit out the chaw. "Somethin'," he answered, and walked past the nose of his truck. He went about twenty more feet and the deputies followed, the corn-stalks making a wall on either side of the drive. Then he stopped and waited for them to come up beside him.

Morris bent down to the edge of the blanket he'd thrown over the heap. He hadn't liked the way the woman looked at him, her throat all marked up and her eyes ate out by bugs. He snatched off the blanket.

Both deputies staggered back.

"Holy Jesus," Gus said, and threw up in the corn.

Aidan shored up his courage. The thought of talking to Luke Varón made him sick to his stomach. But he couldn't let the bastard keep jerking his mom around.

And he couldn't tell his mom the truth.

He came out of the bedroom and went straight to

Varón. "You son of a bitch," he said. "Where do you get off telling my mom that Dad did cocaine? He didn't. He *didn't.*"

Varón set down the plate he held—a pile of bagels and bananas and big bunches of grapes. He pushed it across the granite island as if offering it. Aidan felt his mom come up behind him.

"No, he didn't," Varón said. "Your dad was the dealer, not the user."

Aidan's hands fisted. *No way. Oh, God.*

The shame nearly smothered him. *I've taken care of it, Aidan,* Dad had said. *Just keep your mouth shut and forget it ever happened.*

The memory nearly buckled Aidan's knees. *Jeez, Dad, what did you do?*

Aidan caught his mother's piercing gaze, looking as if she was about to start cross-examining him, prying for the truth. Damn it, he had to be careful. He'd promised. It was the last conversation he'd had with his dad.

He'd promised.

"You're lying," he said to Varón. An easy target for his anger.

"I'm not, but it doesn't matter. The point is, you and I are on the same team now. We all want to find your father's killer."

Aidan studied him, feeling as if he was being played, but not sure how. He didn't like Varón. He wanted to tell him to fuck off, then he wanted to walk away without looking back. But Varón was like a car wreck on the highway. Aidan couldn't seem to drag his eyes away. He remembered his mom's case against him a few weeks ago. She'd talked about him as the worst type of criminal, the lowest thing society had to offer, and Aidan had conjured up an image of someone stout and old, with a pock-marked face and thick nose that hissed when he breathed. Someone who couldn't string two sentences together without sounding like a thug.

In reality, Varón was nothing like that. Last night, he'd looked like a man who made his living on Wall Street and had season tickets to the symphony, a guy who might try to buy drinks for his mom. Today, he looked like a star athlete on his day off. Another guy who might try to buy drinks for his mom.

Aidan glanced back at his mom. She was looking at Varón the way she might look at something she found crawling under the sink.

Okay. No worries there.

He said to Varón, "What are you planning to do with us?"

"A valid question," Varón answered. "First, I was going to give you breakfast. Or, lunch, rather. Bagel?"

"Screw breakfast. Answer my question."

Varón picked up a small tablet and a pen, pulled a stool up to the island. "Second, I want you to talk me through the murders. Everything you can think of, starting with your dad's."

Aidan frowned and looked at his mom. Her appearance took him by surprise. Jeez, she could almost be an older girl at his school, the way she was dressed. Except for the worry in her eyes. That still looked like Mom.

"Mom," he said. "Don't trust him. We need to get out of here."

But she'd made up her mind—he could tell. She was going to talk to this man who'd kidnapped them, a man who knew too much about Aidan's dad and yet who knew nothing. She was going to tell him everything she knew.

She came to the island. "Have something to eat, Aidan," she said, then turned to Varón. "What do you want to know?"

Sasha shifted, circling his foot to keep his leg from falling asleep. The house had been quiet for the past couple hours, but now there was movement. A light here, a shadow there.

Kara.

My, my, he really *had* frightened her. So much that she'd faked her own death and taken refuge in this big, isolated house, tucked away in acres and acres of forest. Even with the beacon on Aidan's cell phone showing him the way, it had been tough to find.

But he had.

Rich bitch. You think you can hide from me after all these years?

He'd left the Lexus off a beaten path a couple of miles down the mountain, hiked through the woods with the GPS, then scouted out a vantage point. Not too many choices. The forest was untamed and the thick summer foliage made it hard to see very far, but the flip side to that was that he could get pretty close without being seen himself. He had a couple of close-but-no-cigar calls in deciding on a good location, but eventually found a tree that worked. Sasha looped the strap of the rifle over his shoulder, hoisted himself up, and climbed high enough to see, positioning himself with his back against the tree trunk. With one leg hanging over the branch, he could cock his other knee and actually brace it against another branch. Not quite comfortable and he had to keep working the pins and needles from his leg. But steady enough for decent shooting.

He unwound the strap from his shoulder and sighted the big house through the trees. Just the way the folks at the gun club had taught him. Sasha had practiced. He'd gotten good. Good enough that with the right gun and the right scope, he'd offed Louie Guilford from six hundred yards out. Of course, that was with a perfectly clear sight-line, not in a fucking forest where you could hardly see thirty yards for the trees. But he didn't need to be a sharpshooter today. He didn't want Kara dead yet. He only wanted to let her know that he was here. And still calling the shots, so to speak.

He smiled at that, rested the butt of the rifle against his thigh, and peered through the trees at the house. Patience, now. He was good at patience; the years in prison had made him an expert at that. Staying back, keeping under the radar. Waiting your turn so you don't become someone's prison pet.

It had worked for a while. Until someone caught a glimpse of him in the shower.

He gritted his teeth, the memories only making him more angry at Kara. Her fault, all of it. Rich, haughty bitch. She'd taken everything from him, and never even batted an eye.

Well, turnabout's fair play. Kara Montgomery Chandler was about to learn that. She thought she'd gotten herself to safety, with her little boat ploy and this hidden house. But sooner or later, she and that brat kid would have to come out.

And when they did, Sasha would be waiting.

CHAPTER
18

I ALWAYS THOUGHT YOUR FATHER'S accident was too coincidental to make sense," Varón said. He aimed the conversation as much at Aidan as at Kara, as if trying to make Aidan feel included. He really was skilled at playing people, Kara noted. She'd be wise to remember that.

"Why?" Aidan asked.

"Because I knew there was a hit out on him, remember?"

Aidan sneered. His hands closed into fists.

"But this shit you told me about," Varón said, "it's different. This is personal. So, start by racking your brain. Is there anyone, *anyone,* who might have a grudge to pick with you?"

"Of course there is," Kara said. "I make my living among people who hate me."

"Then it will be a long list. But make it anyway. Chances are good he'll be on it."

"You keep saying 'he,'" Aidan said. "Maybe it's not even a man. Did you ever think about that?"

"We won't rule it out," Varón said, "but strangulation is hard; it takes muscle. Not to mention that Penny Wolff told your mom her husband had struck a deal with a man. And," he started to say something else but paused, looking at Kara. "The type of murder weapon used on Penny Wolff suggests a man."

Kara frowned. Penny Wolff had been strangled. "Type?"

He hesitated and Kara had the feeling this was something he didn't want to say. He blew out a breath. "She was strangled with barbed wire."

"Barbed wire?" Aidan's face went white. Kara felt as if a gale-force wind whipped over her.

"Does that have any significance to you?" Varón asked. "Can either of you come up with a reason someone might relate barbed wire to you?"

Kara couldn't come up with a reason; she was too busy trying to keep the contents of her stomach where it belonged. *Barbed wire.* She closed her eyes and remembered the picture of Penny Wolff. The details hadn't been clear on the phone image. But the scarf... "Dear God, the holes in the scarf—"

"Yes. And Knutson and I transferred the photo from your text message to a larger screen. There's no doubt: It's barbed wire."

Kara got up and crossed her arms over her midriff, pacing. She couldn't wrap her mind around it. Who could hate her enough to kill other people and try to make her feel responsible? *Look what you've done. TRUTH.* And who could be so angry that he would do his killing with barbed wire?

The answer came in a flood of horror: There were several. A defendant she'd put in jail over the course of her career. A family member of a defendant. She could even think of a lawyer or two she'd beaten who were marginally psychopathic.

"Kara," Varón said, "is there anyone you've sent to Death Row who's actually been put to death?"

"No. Not yet."

"But you have put people on Death Row."

"Two. Levar Townsend. He raped and killed two women in 2005. He's been through several appeals, but hasn't won any."

Varón wrote down his name. "Keep going."

"Wyland Sellars. He shot and killed his wife and her parents in a hostage standoff with his two kids, then killed a bailiff trying to break from court."

"I remember that," Aidan said. "That's when Dad bought you a gun."

"Yes. But Sellars has years of appeals ahead of him." She thought of something. "Where's my phone?"

Varón said, "I have it. I'd rather you not use it right now."

"I need Internet."

Varón strode to a desk and opened a briefcase. He came back with an iPad and Kara Googled a list of her cases over the years, picking out the ones that had the potential for a killing spree of vengeance. There were five. In addition to Townsend and Sellars, there was a cat burglar who'd nearly killed a woman who awakened during a break-in and who had been paroled after serving three years. A pair of brothers who'd owned a package store they set on fire for the insurance money, killing an employee. They were still in jail but there was a third brother who'd threatened to kill Kara in a rage, right in front of God and everybody. And there was a heroin addict who'd shot his dealer to get a hit when he didn't have enough money to buy it. He, too, was still in jail, but Kara had always suspected that his father—an "elder" in some fanatic religious organization—was crazy enough to try to kill her.

"His name is Elijah Grooms," Kara told Varón. "He's a crackpot and his son is in jail."

"Okay," Varón said, and added the name to his list. "Did any of these cases have any association with barbed wire? With cattle or farms or anything like that?"

Kara was clueless.

"You were raised on a horse farm, right?"

She shrugged. "That was ages ago. My mother died when I was six, and my father died four years ago. His will stipulated that Montgomery Manor be sold and it sold to a developer. It's not a horse farm anymore. It's the reason I still have some money after Andrew's busi—" She stopped and Aidan rolled his eyes.

"Geesh, Mom, it's not like I don't know."

Right. "After Andrew's business went bankrupt. Most of my father's estate was a lump-sum donation to an undisclosed recipient. A charity, I guess. But the rest came to me."

"Dad wanted to start breeding horses here," Aidan injected, "but Mom didn't want to."

Varón's brow hiked up in question.

"I didn't love that life," she explained. "I mean, I liked the horses, but it was a life that was—cold. Maids and private chefs and stable hands. I didn't want Aidan to grow up in that world."

Varón tilted his head, then said, "Okay," and moved on. They spent twenty more minutes talking through possibilities, Aidan standing soberly in the corner with his arms crossed over his chest. Eventually, they came around to the night Andrew had been killed.

"He'd been out," Kara said, feeling the sting of both

anger and embarrassment. "He had a standing appointment on Thursday evenings. I don't know with whom, but this night, he was apparently with that woman, Elisa Moran. I got a call that he'd been hit while crossing the street. Elisa Moran was taken to the hospital, but Andrew was pronounced dead at the scene."

"And there was never a lead on the driver," Varón said. It wasn't a question. He knew the details. Kara supposed he was just trying to get them from her perspective.

"A few leads," she said. "But two days later, John Wolff walked into a police station and turned himself in. He was charged with first degree homicide by vehicle and leaving the scene, but he cooperated fully and showed remorse and claimed he didn't remember the accident—that he was shocked at the condition of his car. He probably would have received the minimum sentence of three years, with some time suspended, but then Elisa Moran died, too. He was killed two days after he was transferred to prison."

"The question," Varón said, "is what happened during those two days?"

"Which two days?" Aidan asked. "The ones after the accident or the ones after Wolff went to prison?"

"I know what his wife told me about the two days after the accident," Kara said. "She said her husband was scared. Crazy scared and she didn't know why. He wouldn't talk to her. He'd left his car somewhere—he said it had broken down—but then it turned out to have been the car that hit Andrew and Elisa Moran."

"Penny didn't know about the hit-and-run?" Varón asked.

"Not until John left to go to the police station and confess. She knew he hadn't done it. He never drank and wasn't out that night. She tried to convince him not to go but he told her he'd made a deal with the devil and had to pay, but that the money would be worth it."

Aidan looked shocked. "Why would anyone agree to that?"

"The killer got to him," Varón said, but Aidan frowned. He didn't seem to be able to wrap his mind around what he was hearing. "Think about it," Varón said. "The killer comes to you with a deal: Take the fall for an honest accident, which probably won't carry much jail time. For your trouble, your wife and sick baby girl receive ten thousand dollars every month you're in jail."

"That's bullshit," Aidan said.

"I'm not finished. Then the killer says, 'By the way, have you looked at the front end of your car this morning?' And when you do, you find the victims' blood all over it, dents and clothing fibers on the bumper. My guess is the killer had scouted John Wolff out and chose him because he was someone whose car he knew he could steal, who had an Achilles' heel and who wouldn't have an alibi—"

"God," Kara said. It was starting to fall into place. "Penny Wolff said her husband worked a four a.m. to noon shift at a shipping depot. He was in bed every night by eight. That's why she was sure he hadn't gone down to Atlanta the night Andrew died."

Varón nodded. "The killer probably had the whole story laid out. If Wolff turned himself in and confessed, he'd be out of jail before his daughter got out of grammar school and his wife would have all the money she needed to take care of her while he was gone. If he didn't, he would still go to jail, but for a lot longer."

Kara was dumbfounded. The entire course of events had unraveled in his mind. "How do you know all that?"

"Because that's what I would've done," he said.

A chill slithered down her spine. Kara closed her eyes. It made sense—the way Varón spelled it out. Penny Wolff had held her silence until Kara walked into her home almost a year later and unleashed her own set of threats. Then, within hours, she'd been killed.

And that was on Kara. *Look what you've done.*

"You couldn't have known," Varón said, and the fact that he had read her mind unnerved her further. She pressed the heels of her hands against her eyes.

"Mom?" Aidan was at her side.

Dear God, she couldn't fall apart. Not now.

Varón looked at her. "We need to talk about the deal I offered, Kara. I don't need a kid getting in my way."

"Deal? What deal?" Aidan asked.

Varón was calling up something on his cell phone. He found it and held out the phone to Aidan. "I want you out of the way, someplace safe. This is a picture of the place you'd go. It's a nice place; you'll like i—"

Aidan batted the cell phone from his hand. It clattered to the floor. "Fuck you."

"Aidan," Kara was mortified, but knew Aidan was just scared. "I said no to that deal," she explained. "Do you think I would send you away on Varón's word? He's the devil's spawn. I know that."

"Right here," Varón injected. "Listening."

"Shut up," she shot. "We have to work with him, Aidan. This is our chance to get out from under this killer's nose. We are *dead,* so this killer can't torment us anymore. That's thanks to Varón's help."

"It has nothing to do with Varón wanting to *help*, Mom. It only has to do with what *he* gets out of it."

Varón stepped around the island and came to Aidan,

looking down at him like a giant bird of prey. "You're right, kid. I don't much care what happens to the two of you. But you need to wake up and realize that I have sufficient motivation to babysit both of you until I get the answers I need. There's eight and a half tons of cocaine riding on this."

Ice water washed through Kara's veins.

"And what about afterward?" Aidan asked.

"Afterward, I'll send you on your merry ways."

"I don't believe you," Aidan said. "We know too much. When you're finished using us, what's to keep you from killing us?"

"Nothing," Varón acknowledged. "But you won't be going back to life as the Chandlers, so I have faith you'll get out of Dodge. It would certainly be the wisest course of action." He turned a leering grin to Kara. "Unless, of course, your mother decides she wants to find a way to repay me for my efforts."

Aidan sprang; Varón put him on the floor with one shove of his hand. Aidan clambered up and started for him again.

Kara grabbed him. "No," she said, but could hardly see through the tears in her eyes. "I can't watch anyone else die, Aidan. Especially not you." She shook his shoulders. *"We have to do this."*

Aidan gaped at her. His eyes filled with despair and he jerked back from her hands. "I guess you two have it all figured out." He shot a look at Varón, then a glare at his mother. "Let's hope he's as good as you think he is."

CHAPTER
19

AIDAN STORMED FROM THE room. They thought he was giving in and would go along. No way, though. No way was he going to hang here and let Luke Varón tear apart his father. *Your father was part of a cocaine ring.* A wave of emotion washed in and while he wasn't sure what it was, it felt as dark and heavy as when his dad died. He hadn't known how to shake it off then, either. He'd been powerless.

And he'd be that way again if he let Varón take charge. Varón was evil. And he had it wrong about his dad. Dad wasn't the one dealing coke.

Aidan was.

Jesus God. *Please don't let that be why Dad died.*

Aidan made giant loops around the room for two minutes, then knew what he had to do. He couldn't let his mom learn the truth—he'd promised. Besides, he had some contacts, too—people who were part of Varón's precious drug ring. Hell, that's how he'd gotten into this mess in the first place. Aidan hadn't talked to Raul Valesquez in over a year but he knew where to find him. Knew that if anyone might be able to tell him who was pulling the strings, it would be Raul.

He stopped, hesitating to leave his mom behind. But hadn't she taught him to act when you were in trouble? She didn't know about Valesquez. And she dealt with low-lifes like Varón all the time; she could handle herself until Aidan found help.

From who? Uncle Louie? His dad?

For a moment, the sense of loss was so overwhelming Aidan almost sank back onto the bed, but then he thought of Varón and his accusations. He had to go, and the sooner he left the sooner he'd find help. Seth would help him. Tomorrow was his dad's funeral and he'd died because of what he knew. Together, they'd figure something out and find Raul.

So, go. Get out of here. Varón didn't think Aidan had brought his cell phone, but he had. Now, he could use the GPS to get through these woods and back to Atlanta. The way he looked, no one would spot him as Aidan Chandler. Hell, he barely recognized himself when he looked in a mirror.

Aidan headed back to the spare room where he'd changed his clothes and napped. He padded his pocket to make sure he had the phone and its charger, then walked through to the other side of the bath and out into a hall, down a half flight of stairs. Saw a triple set of French doors out to one of the decks and swallowed a giant knot in his throat.

He had to go. He had to find Seth and Raul.

He pushed open the door before he could reconsider, whispering words behind him: *Bye, Mom. I love you.*

Kara watched Aidan leave the room. Her heart was in pieces. He had to be scared out of his mind and here she was on the verge of letting Luke Varón call the shots.

Varón had better reason to protect her and Aidan than she'd ever suspected and she needed him. She needed him to kill this bastard for her. Was that the same as hiring him as a hit man herself? Maybe. But so be it. This killer had murdered Andrew and Louie, Penny and John. And maybe all the other people whose personal items had come to Kara in little boxes.

So go ahead, Varón, she thought to herself. *Kill the son of a bitch for me. Protect your goddamned drug ring. Just keep my son safe.*

She picked up the cell phone Aidan had knocked from Varón's hands and looked at the photo of the safe house. A rec room in a chic, modern condo. Pool table, widescreen TV, foosball. She thumbed through a few more photos, then slid the phone onto the island. "How far away is this pla—"

"Shh," Varón said. He cocked his head, listening, then groaned. "Goddamn it," he said. He started from the room and Kara saw his hand touch the small of his back. For the first time, she realized there was a gun beneath the loose tail of his shirt.

Her heartbeat kicked up. She followed Varón down the hall and into the spare room where she and Aidan had slept, then out the other door and down a half flight of stairs. At the other end of a room, a set of French doors stood open.

No.

"Aidan!" Kara screamed, but Varón was already outside, on the deck. He threw a long leg over the rail and dropped to the pine straw a story below, rolling and coming back up, and starting to run. Kara caught a glimpse of Aidan in the woods. He, too, had gone over the railing. He was running, humped over, dashing into the trees.

Oh, God.

"Stay there," Varón yelled behind him. "I'll get him."

Kara searched the trees. Aidan had disappeared. Panic seized her heart. She couldn't just stand here, but going over the railing would be crazy. She couldn't move as fast as either of them. "Damn you, Aidan," she shouted through tears in her throat. She couldn't catch her breath. Dear God, Aidan had run off and a hit man was chasing after him while another killer had scared them into faking their deaths and—

A gunshot pierced the air.

CHAPTER
20

LUKE DROPPED. *Rifle.* Jesus Christ. A rifle—a big one. Not a *pop* but a *boom*, and from the west.

Louie Guilford got picked off by a 7mm Rem Mag before a Braves game.

Luke yanked the gun from the back of his belt and picked up his head, listened. Caught the end of Kara's scream of horror from the deck, then a rustling in the woods just a few yards away.

Aidan. He wanted to yell to him but couldn't risk giving his location to the shooter. Christ, the kid probably thought Luke was the one shooting at him. He'd run like hell.

Anger burned in Luke's chest. A shooter—here. But how? The answer came to him on a wave of self-hatred: *stupid, stupid, stupid.* But there was no time for that now. The shooter had been waiting. Could have been perched in a tree for a while now, content to wait until they came out of the house.

The bushes rustled twenty yards away. Aidan was scrambling, zig-zagging like a disoriented animal.

Another rifle shot exploded through the sky.

Luke's heartbeat slowed. *No way, fucker.* Varón, the hit man, surfaced and Luke wanted to hunt the bastard down and take him out with his bare hands. But he couldn't leave Aidan out here, and couldn't leave Kara. He checked the pistol—a .45 G.A.P.—and glanced back to the house. Kara was gone. A microsecond of terror flashed in his brain but then he saw that she wasn't lying on the deck, hit by a rifle bullet, and he spared a thought to be grateful she had sense enough to run back inside and hide. Turned his attention back to Aidan.

Stay down, kid. Stay still and stay down.

He listened; the forest had gone silent. Birds, insects, ground creatures—everything utterly still in the aftermath of the rifle shots. If the shooter had seen Aidan, he'd probably seen Luke, too, and with a good rifle he could have a range of a thousand yards. In the forest, though, a bullet would only go as far as the closest trees, and the view was limited to what you could see through the foliage.

Which only meant the shooter was a helluva lot closer than a thousand yards. Not far at all, given the blast.

Luke shifted, moving slowly, cursing the light pink shirt. He tried to recall what Aidan had on: black t-shirt, jeans. Better than Luke, then.

He took small steps, staying low, putting the weight on the outside of his soles. Wished for a breeze to obscure the sound of his movements but the air was staid and silent. A creek gurgled about thirty yards away; if Aidan had any brains at all, he'd flatten himself into it, using the rise of the bank on either side as cover. If that's where he was, the water would be in his ears and he wouldn't hear the shrubs rustling over the gurgle of the creek. Good if your bodyguard is trying to sneak up on you; bad if it's your killer.

But the killer wasn't *that* close. The sound of the shot assured that. He was close enough to risk taking a shot through foliage, but not close enough to walk right up on a kid hiding in the creek bed, even if he'd started moving after that last shot.

Luke moved low and slow. Broad daylight, but the forest was uncut. Near enough to noon that the few shadows that did cut through came straight down, giving nothing away. Only his movement would draw fire.

The sound of the creek became audible; Luke inched closer and looked. Sure enough, Aidan had hunkered down in the water, head covered, but his eyes on Luke. He looked horrified.

"Get away from me—"

Luke shushed him with a hand. "I'm not the one who fired at you," he said beneath a whisper. "Stay down and get behind me."

Aidan blinked, glanced at the gun in Luke's hand, and began shaking his head. He was a kid. A confused, terrified kid looking at the man who was supposed to have killed his father.

Luke pointed his gun to the ground and moved toward him. "Someone is shooting at you with a rifle," he snapped. "For God's sake, did it *sound* like it came from this pistol? Get behind me."

Aidan frowned. A bullet smashed into a tree twenty feet away.

"God," he said, and Luke hit the ground on top of him. Felt Aidan's whole body trembling beneath him. But not fighting him.

"Stay. Stay," Luke said in a hush. "He can't see us unless we move. Too many trees."

That much was true, Luke assured himself: too many

trees. The shot had been wild. The asshole was taking potshots now, just aiming in the general direction Aidan had run. Because he couldn't see them or because he was having some fun? The answer brought a chill. This bastard had used one shot to take out Louie Guilford in a crowd of people. He was trained.

He was having fun.

Luke shifted, just enough for Aidan to breathe.

"Where's my mom?" Aidan asked, panting. "Where's Mom?"

"At the house," Luke said, speaking right against Aidan's ear. Now or never. There wouldn't be a better moment to make an impression on the kid. "She's probably getting ready to run out here into the fray to save your sorry ass. Is that what you want? To get your mom killed?"

Aidan opened his mouth but Luke cut him off. Spoke fast and low. "That's what you're doing. Your little escapade delivering cocaine for Raul Valesquez will get you both killed if you don't let me handle it."

Aidan made a strangled sound. "How di—"

"It doesn't matt—" *Shit*.

Another shot. Luke hunkered down over Aidan. The rifle fired several shots, then paused, then started up again. Probably had ten bullets: The shooter had stopped to reload.

None of the bullets was close, but Aidan trembled in fear beneath him. Luke was pretty sure it was more than just the bullets scaring him at this point. The mention of Raul Valesquez had shaken him up even further.

Luke didn't move, but continued speaking against the back of Aidan's head. "It doesn't matter how I know. What does matter is that your mother can help me catch the bastard who's out there taking potshots at us right now, but she can't think straight when you're not safe. You want me to get rid of him, before he kills both of you? I need your mom to do it."

Aidan's breaths came as short, half sobs. "It's my fault. I shouldn't've—"

"But you did," Luke said, knowing it was cruel. "How do you think your mom will feel when she finds out how this all started?"

"No. God, don't tell her. Don't—"

Ten more shots. Luke cursed. The bastard had a shit-load of bullets. The rifle didn't sound like it was coming any closer and they were protected by the creek bank, but they had to get out of here before the shooter got bored with the game and came after them for real. Luke had run out of the house with only the thirteen rounds already chambered in his gun. A sniper lying in wait could have hundreds.

"Give me your phone," he said, and Aidan jerked.

"I don't hav—"

"Don't lie to me. How do you think this bastard found us? Give me your phone. I want to call your mom."

Aidan squirmed, already dialing. Luke snatched it from his hand.

"Aidan?" Kara's voice came on. Panicked, breathless.

"He's okay," Luke said. "I'm okay, too, thanks for asking. Listen to me. There's a gun case downstairs in the stud—"

"I know. I found it. I have the Ruger in my hands already."

He should have known.

"I just loaded it," she said. "I'm looking for a place to fire. I'll cover you."

"Upstairs. There's a window in the loft bedroom." He

could hear her dashing through the house, puffing. "You know how to shoot?"

"Shut up. Where are you? Where's Aidan?"

"I've got him. First thing is this: Go to the kitchen door by the stairs and push the garage door opener, and grab my phone off the island. Then go upstairs to the loft."

He heard her footsteps and her breathing, could almost hear her heart beating like a wild thing.

Keep her calm. The only thing worse than seeing her kid get shot by a psycho would be for *her* to fire the bullet that killed him.

He heard her running up the stairs, then a pause. "Go to the window but stay to the left. Use the barrel of the gun to split the blinds."

"Yes." She was panting.

"Can you see outside?"

"Yes. But I don't see you. Where's Aidan?"

"We're through the trees at eight o'clock. Past the fire pit."

"Okay."

"We're not far. The shots came from the west. On my cue, start firing through the window toward two o'clock. Leave the blinds down so you don't get glass in your face. Keep firing, every two seconds. You have fifteen shots."

"That's only thirty seconds. Can you make it back in thirty seconds?"

"I'll pick up firing after you stop, and cover us the rest of the way." He looked at Aidan, who nodded. Back to Kara. "Listen to me. As soon as you run out of bullets, get down to the garage. Get in the Porsche. I have the keys."

"Okay."

He shifted, getting his feet beneath him and waiting until Aidan had done the same. Ready.

"Kara," he said, wondering just how much poise she was capable of under the circumstances. "We're gonna run like hell. Can you do this?"

"Yes. Damn it, yes. Say when."

Luke tossed Aidan's phone to the ground ten feet away, gave Aidan a nod.

"When," he said.

CHAPTER
21

THE RUGER LIT UP from the loft window. They ran. Aidan was quick like a rabbit; Luke took long, ground-eating strides that sent spikes of pain into his right thigh-bone. They sprinted through the trees to the sound of bullets popping from the Ruger in the loft every two seconds and when they were close enough that Luke knew Kara would be out of ammunition, he stretched out his arm and fired toward the west, still running, sideways, keeping the shooter pinned with a shot-per-second until Aidan dashed into the garage. Luke fired his last bullet and followed him.

"Jump in," he shouted, lunging for the car. The top was down.

Aidan did, head-first, crunching into a ball to fit in the tiny space behind the front seats. Kara wrangled with the front door and fell into the passenger seat, clutching Luke's cell phone in hand. He turned the ignition and the tires screamed, and the car lurched backward and fishtailed into the turnaround. Narrow mountain roads; he would save no time trying to go out backward, even in daylight.

"In the glove box," he shouted over the roar of the engine, "there's a nine-millimeter."

She jostled the latch and found the gun, while Luke threw the Porsche in gear and gunned the gas. Aidan grunted. Not much of a seat back there. A rifle shot soared overhead. Luke ducked and swerved, and Kara cursed. A second later, she opened up with the 9mm.

"Keep firing but get down, for God's sake," Luke shouted. "Get your head down."

She did, and the car tumbled down the long drive, Kara sticking her arm out and firing behind them.

Three minutes after it had started, it was over.

Luke slowed, then pushed a button that brought the roof of the Porsche up over them. "That's it," he said. "We're out of range. You're okay. Put the gun down."

Kara's hands fell to her lap and Luke closed his hand over them. He wrenched the 9-millimeter from her hand and dropped it on the floor beside her feet, driving more reasonably now, sharing in the flood of adrenaline. Her breaths were shaky, her fingers clammy and trembling.

"Aidan?" she said.

"I'm okay," he said. In the rearview mirror, Luke saw him trying to unfold his limbs. He couldn't. The seat was too small. "God, what was that?" he asked.

It was a good question. Kara and Aidan had disappeared in a boat explosion and been reported by the local news as missing but presumed dead. Ten hours later, the killer knew exactly where they were.

Kara's phone was disabled. Knutson was transferring everything on it to Bureau computers. "Do you have iCloud enabled on your phone, Aidan?" he asked.

"Uh, yeah. I guess so. I mean, it came free with the phone, right?"

Luke gritted his teeth. Christ, he should have checked that. Should have known a kid wouldn't part with his precious phone. "The bastard's probably been tracking both of you just like a navigation system would."

"Then he can still track mine."

"No. Yours is disabled. I didn't know Aidan brought his," he snarled.

"How do we know he didn't follow us just now from the house?" Aidan asked.

"He was on foot. There's no other way up to that house but this road. He'll have to hike to wherever he left a vehicle before he can start after us. Even if he has a motorcycle, it would have had to be far enough away that we have a good head start."

"I can't believe it," Aidan said. "I never thought about some stranger tracking my phone."

"Maybe not," Luke said. "But someone did."

Sasha watched them scatter. For three seconds after his first shot, it was like playing pinball: The kid rolled into the creek bank, the man shot after him, the woman— Kara?—bounced off the deck railing and ricocheted inside. Open season, Sasha thought, and was starting to enjoy himself.

But he hadn't prepared for the gunfire that opened up from the top floor of the house. Just when the kid and man started running for the garage, gunfire came from inside. Controlled and consistent: a shot, then a couple seconds— just enough to tempt Sasha into taking aim again. Then another shot, another pause, and so on. Over and over until the man and boy had gotten close to the house.

The bitch. She'd ruined his day at the arcade. And she *was* Kara—there was no doubt about it. Her hair was dark now and cut close to her head, and she'd been dressed more like a nightclub bartender than an attorney. But it was Kara. He'd been watching her for too long not to recognize her gait, her actions, the flow of her movements. Those traits hadn't changed since she was a child.

The pinballs rolled into the garage, while Sasha remained treed by gunfire. Nothing came close—she was just keeping him cornered long enough to give the others a chance to get inside, but it still pissed him off. In his imagination, he'd had her cowering on the floor in a heap of terror, acknowledging his superiority. Not fighting back.

Nontheless, it didn't matter. He was still in charge and he'd succeeded in sending her a message. *Your ruse didn't work, Kara. I know you're alive.*

A little sports car—Porsche, he thought—launched from the garage. Sasha sent a few rifle shots after it and Kara fired back as they pulled away. Not the same gun this time; the sound was different. He'd have to find out who the man was. Whoever he was, he was well-armed.

The car vanished and Sasha let out a sneer. So, she'd found herself a bodyguard. Faked her own death, disguised her appearance, and hired an armed bodyguard. He should have known. Just as soon as he'd learned she had probably faked their deaths, he should have figured she had help. She lived in the justice system. She was acquainted with all sorts of cops and lawyers and even rabble.

An unexpected turn to the game, Sasha thought, with a pinch of admiration. He'd have to think about this.

He climbed down from the tree and neared the house. Hesitated. Would anyone else be in there?

He thought about it, remembered the way the kid had sneaked out and how a single gunman—Kara—had kept Sasha at bay from the third-story window while the bodyguard rescued the boy. No, there wasn't anyone else in the house. If there was, it would have been all hands on deck to get Kara's son back to safety.

So. Time to have a look at the man Kara had helping her.

He went in through the garage. Functional, but not much used. Upstairs. The kitchen was extravagant—big, with gourmet perks. A man who liked to cook. Or maybe he had a woman living here, too. Sasha kept going, through a great room furnished with cushy neutral furniture, with skylights and soaring windows, then through a dining room and three bedrooms. In one bedroom sat a daybed and a sofa, both of which appeared to have been slept *on* but not *in,* as if the users of the room were only visiting. He stuck his head in the adjoining bathroom and found two bags of clothes—women's clothes in one and a boy's in the other.

Sasha smiled. These were the clothes Kara and her son Aidan had discarded, in favor of the ones they were wearing now.

Very smart, Kara.

He thought about it, checked the bathroom wastebasket and looked in the shower and toilet. Nothing. He went back to the big kitchen and looked in the trash can beneath the counter.

And there it was: locks of wavy blond hair. Kara's hair, all cut off now.

He smiled and collected a handful of yellow silk, pocketed it, then dug a bit farther. Found a discarded wig, some boxes of hair color, permanent ink markers, and a pattern for a tattoo—all the evidence of the Chandlers' transformation. He laughed aloud, sheer glee overwhelming him.

Such drastic measures. She must be scared out of her mind.

And the man...Now, there was a mystery. Sasha continued through the house, finding his way to the master bedroom and closet, going through every drawer and article of clothing. Nice suits—*really* nice suits—and general clothing, basic toiletries and linens, a few electronics. But nothing else.

Sasha looked around, frowning. The place was housekeeper-clean, generically decorated, and comfortably furnished. But it wasn't lived in. The pictures on the walls were art, not family photos. The knickknacks on the shelves appeared store-bought rather than collected. There were no plants or personal items lying around or little piles of paperclips and loose change. No little bowls on the shelves where life's detritus had gathered.

He headed up to the third floor and found the window where Kara had taken even, carefully strategized shots in his direction. The blinds were bent al! to hell, and a couple of shards of glass still jutted out at the bottom of the window frame, having snagged there. Shell casings littered the floor.

He frowned. Shell casings. Where had the gun come from?

He went back downstairs, past the bedrooms and the great room, and found one more level of living space, six steps down a landing. A sunroom sprawled off the back of the house, with three sets of French doors opening onto a massive deck.

He smiled. This was the man's office. A huge desk, a computer, a phone, a fax machine, a printer-copier, the works. And on the opposite wall, a gun cabinet with broken glass. Sasha closed his eyes and could see it: Kara coming out on the deck and realizing that her son was on the run, seeing the man go after him, then hearing shots and racing back into the house, terrified, running to grab the first gun she could find, breaking the glass to get to it . . .

She must have been panicked. The thought made him smile.

He went to the desk, booted up the desktop. Not much on it, and he didn't recognize any of the icons, not even for the operating system. That wasn't unusual—fifteen years in prison had left him behind the technological curve—but still . . . He clicked on one of the icons. A security block came up. Clicked on another one, same thing. He managed to get into one, but it was encrypted.

Sasha frowned. This dude had some serious issues with paranoia. Either that or he had some serious secrets.

Or he was someone a lot bigger than Sasha had considered.

His pulse picked up speed and a tide of anger rose: another curve ball thrown by Kara. Who the fuck was this guy? He had to think.

And had to hurry. It had been fifteen minutes since the shooting had started. This house wasn't an easy place to get to, but if this dude was connected to authorities, they may have made a call the minute they got out of gun range. He shouldn't spend any more time here.

But he couldn't leave without sending a message. He had to show Kara what she'd done now.

He fingered the hair in his pocket and pulled some out. What would she think if she got a photograph of her own hair, and realized how close he'd been?

He shook his head. There was something creepy about that, given the circumstances, but creepy wasn't good enough. He wanted her terrified. Feeling responsible. Feeling guilt for pretending to be something she wasn't.

Feeling his power.

He rubbed his forehead, thinking, his pulse pounding in his temples. The noon news had reported that enough evidence had been found to presume both Aidan and Kara Chandler dead from the boat explosion. They meant body parts. Which, of course, wasn't true, since Sasha had just seen their body parts all in good form, running like hell. She was good—good enough to get the police to report utter lies. Good enough to write her own rules for the game. Good enough to get someone smart and strong and capable working with her.

His nose itched and he reached up. Blood. Goddamn it, his nose was bleeding. Blood pressure rising. He swiped his sleeve across it. He had to get out of here.

He walked back through the house, keeping his sleeve against his nose, looking for inspiration. He found it in the garage.

The perfect way to turn up the heat.

CHAPTER
22

EVEN FIFTEEN MINUTES AFTER their escape, Kara still felt out of breath. She could hardly fathom what had happened.

Varón pulled onto the broken-up parking lot of a gas station that appeared to have been abandoned decades ago. "Let me have my phone," he said, and Kara handed it to him. She'd grabbed it off the kitchen island before she ran out of the house to meet them in the garage, just as he had told her to. Even trapped by a volley of rifle-fire, he'd been able to think clearly.

It was more than Kara could say for herself.

He killed the engine and climbed out of the Porsche. He stepped a few paces out of earshot and began talking into his phone.

Kara sank back against the seat and watched him. None of it made sense. Least of all, Varón.

"Are you sure you're not hurt?" she asked Aidan. "You were humped over."

"Jeez, Mom. I just outran a guy shooting a rifle at me. I don't think a side-cramp is a big deal." He plucked at his wet, muddy clothes and blew out a breath. He frowned, but clearly had something more to say. He shook his head. "You know, back there in the woods—"

Kara waited but he didn't finish. "What?" she pressed.

"He kept me from getting shot. Varón did. He threw his body over me when the shooting started."

Kara closed her eyes.

"I mean it, Mom. If a bullet had come my way, it would have hit him first. He protected me."

A rush of gratitude surged in but collided with a wall of uncertainty. Luke Varón, drug lord and hit man. Hired by her as a glorified bodyguard, and now saving her child's life.

Kara stroked Aidan's face—he didn't pull back the way he usually did—and the sensation that her entire universe sat beneath her fingertips eked in. If anything happened to Aidan...She swallowed back the thought. She couldn't dare to finish it.

She looked at Varón. He spoke into his phone a few feet from the car, fury vibrating around him like heat waves off the pavement. The cuffs of his sleeves hung loose and his shirt was dark with mud and water. His hair stuck up from where he'd raked his fingers through it. For a man accustomed to utter and complete command of his world, the fact that a sniper had encroached on his property seemed to have knocked him for a loop.

He disconnected and stood for a minute, his hands low on his hips and his face turned skyward. Formulating a plan, for sure.

"Stay here," she said to Aidan, and got out. She walked over to where Varón was standing. He turned a determined, dark glare on her.

"He shouldn't be with us," he said, his voice so low Kara had to strain to hear it. He tipped his head toward Aidan.

"I know," she said, and he let out a breath. He seemed relieved.

But Kara was hanging on to control by a fragile thread. *Look what you've done*. She'd put her own son in the path of a killer. Two killers: the shooter and Varón. Which one was more dangerous?

Varón spoke quietly. "Knutson will take him. He had a son once. You can trust him."

He took Kara's arm and headed back to the car. Aidan was silent as they got back in but Varón caught Aidan's eyes in the rearview mirror.

"I'm taking you to meet Knutson," he said. "You're going to a condo. Police would call it a safe house; my people will treat it that way and keep it secure. So long as you do what you're told, you won't get hurt."

Kara felt Aidan's rising panic. "Mom, please," and she turned on him.

"Damn it, Aidan, do you know how frightened I was back there? Do you?" Tears began to flow. "I have to know you're safe. I'm not doing this to hurt you, Aidan. I'm doing it to keep you alive."

"And what about you?" Aidan asked. "What's going to keep you alive?"

"I am," Varón said. Then his voice went chilly. "My shipment, remember? I need her."

Varón turned the key and the engine snarled to life.

Kara closed her eyes. She was usually so in control, so self-assured. But the horror and exhaustion of the past week had shaken her in ways she couldn't even identify. All she knew was that people were dying and her son had been shot at, and that Varón was the one person involved who seemed to know what steps to take.

Aidan curled into the backseat. Kara wondered about

his acquiescence and thought that deep down inside, he might be relieved. He was trying to be so mature and so strong, but he was still a child. He'd lost his uncle and learned that his father's death had been a murder. He'd learned that someone had threatened him and left behind everything to go on the run with a stranger. He'd gone outside for two minutes and been shot at. He had to be terrified.

They drove for forty minutes, northeast, then pulled into a mall parking lot where Varón got out. He left the keys in the ignition.

"Come on," he said. "We're leaving this car."

Kara and Aidan climbed out. Kara watched as Varón dug her iPhone back out of his pocket, turned on the power, and dropped it in the ashtray of the Porsche.

"Wait—" she said, but he held up a hand.

"All the information that was on your phone except for the location system has been moved. Nothing's lost."

Aidan understood before Kara did. He looked at Varón, and despite that he'd never admit it, he looked impressed. "You're gonna let him hunt down that phone, right? Follow his own tracker?"

"Don't get your hopes up," Varón said. "If he's got any brains, he won't follow it. He'll know we're waiting for him."

"Still," Aidan said. "Send it to Timbuktu."

They followed Varón to a silver Escalade parked about fifty yards away. It was unlocked, with keys inside.

Kara looked at him. "You're very efficient, Mr. Varón."

"Resources. I believe they're the reason you hired me."

Yes. But his ability to snap his fingers and have people jump to obey his every command was as frightening as it was convenient.

She tried not to think about that, climbed into the Escalade, and they left the Porsche in the parking lot of the mall. They drove the Escalade up 400, out of the metropolitan area, then doubled back and took small roads back to I-75. An hour later, they pulled into a state rest area on the highway.

Knutson was there, his face set in a scowl.

Varón stiffened. "What's the matter?"

Knutson glanced at Kara and Aidan, then apparently decided to speak in front of them.

"I didn't want to tell you over the phone. I sent someone to your house to scout around right after you called and said you'd bailed. But before they got there, nine-one-one got a call. Your house is on fire."

CHAPTER
23

S ASHA STAYED TO WATCH the flames, a sense of victory coursing through his veins. He knew he should go; sooner or later, even in this remote area, someone would see the fire and call it in. Even more likely, Kara's new bodyguard would come back, hoping to find clues to who had shot at them.

But he couldn't drag himself away. The roar of the flames, the crackles. The blinding light and searing heat. The smell of a giant bonfire.

The power.

He got out the phone and snapped a picture, then another, then another, trying for the perfect shot. Every time he took one, he'd look up and find a better one—bigger flames, wider angle, something. So he kept waiting, backing up, taking pictures of his handiwork. Finally, he had the ultimate picture: the broken window on the third floor, giant flames licking at the exact spot where Kara had stood.

He laughed out loud. Oh, that was perfect.

He punched in Kara's cell phone number. He hesitated to use this phone—he'd been so careful not to ever use it for anything but tracking Kara, and he'd never done that from the stable. But now that they knew he'd found her, they would disable her GPS settings. Then they'd retrace his steps and locate this phone, anyway.

So he might as well make it easy for them.

He typed in the message, attached the new *wonderful* picture. Hit SEND and felt a surge of glee wash over him. *Take that, Kara, with your new identity and your new bodyguard. See what good all your efforts we—*

A movement caught the corner of his eye. Sasha froze. He blinked, squinting through the trees at the narrow lane to the house. A car? He waited a few seconds and watched, the foliage blocking most of the view and the fire too much in his ears to hear anything. But sure enough, a moment later, the nose of a car came into view.

A cruiser.

Shit. Police.

"My house is on fire?" Varón repeated. He clenched his teeth. Kara thought his jaw might snap.

"I'm sorry, man," Knutson said.

A snarl came from Varón's throat, something rabid. His hands balled into fists. "Fucker burned up my house?" He looped a few steps, as if looking for something to hit. He stopped in front of Knutson. "Did it start in the garage?"

"Looks that way. It's still going, but they're trying to get it out. Not an easy place to get to with fire trucks. A couple of our men are there, too."

"There was gasoline in the garage," Varón said. "He didn't plan this. He just took the opportunity when he saw it. Goddamn that bastard."

Kara reached for Aidan's hand. He squeezed it back, tight. Shock painted his face.

And fear. What if they hadn't gotten out?

Varón raked his hand through his hair. After a moment, he shook his head and visibly pulled himself together.

"You know what to do," he said to Knutson, and Kara realized there would be nothing else said as long as Kara and Aidan were standing there. "Let's move on."

Knutson nodded. He held out both hands, one each to Kara and Aidan. "Take these. Clean phones so you can contact each other. Don't use them to call anyone else."

Kara took the phone, surprised to feel her fingers shaking. *Let's move on.* The fire at Varón's house hadn't changed anything. They were still here to deliver Aidan to Vince Knutson.

She almost choked on the tears clogging her throat. With every fiber of her being she searched for a reason not to split up from her son, but couldn't find one. This wasn't going to end just because she'd faked her death. The killer had found her and shot at Aidan, and the place where they'd taken refuge had been torched. Even Varón was being targeted now.

Kara looked at Knutson. *He had a son once.* She had no way of knowing how much of what Varón said was true, but couldn't shake the feeling that Vince Knutson might be Aidan's best bet. If Varón had been interested in tracking down the killer before, he was doubly committed after the house fire and the quickest way to end this madness was to help him figure out who the hell was doing this. And make sure Aidan stayed out of sight until they did.

He threw his body over me. And now, Knutson arrived with dedicated phones so they could stay in contact with one another. It seemed an unlikely bit of sensitivity for outlaws—almost as if they didn't want her to be worried.

Of course they didn't, she reminded herself. They needed her to focus on the killer.

"It's what I promised," Varón said. "You can contact each other anytime."

She looked at the new phone, going to CONTACTS. There were three. She dialed the first, and the phone in Aidan's hand rang. She disconnected and dialed the next. Knutson's phone chimed. All right, now the third. She had a feeling she knew whose number this was.

Varón. He reached to his belt and cut off the call.

"Satisfied?" he asked, and closed in on her. "Damn it, I just ran through gunfire and dropped a Porsche. Now my house is in ashes. I want this killer as much as you do."

Not possible, Kara thought, but then she looked at him. He looked like he wanted to kill the next ten people he saw. *All because he was worried about his shipment of drugs?*

She didn't have time to think about that right now. She was leaving her son.

Tears welled up and she looked at Aidan. He was oddly compliant—she hadn't expected that. Maybe she'd over-estimated his maturity. He was still a child. Literally running for his life.

And for him, she had to be strong. If she let on that she was even more terrified than he was, it would only scare him more. "It will be okay," she said, taking his hand. "Go with Knutson. Do what he says. As soon as it's safe, I'll come for you." She looked at Varón with a silent, icy promise: *If he's not okay, I'll make you sorry you ever lived.*

Varón dipped his head in a nod.

Kara fought back the tears and hugged Aidan, the fiercest hug she'd gotten from him since he was little. "I love you," she whispered, and in a very small voice, he said, "I love you more."

They separated and Aidan gave Varón a strange look—almost sheepish—then followed Knutson to the same car that had kidnapped them from the riverbank some fourteen hours earlier. Fourteen hours. It seemed impossible to imagine how much their lives had changed in so little time.

Kara watched them drive away, her chin quivering with pent-up emotion. When Knutson's car was out of sight, Varón touched her arm. "We need to move. Let's hit the restrooms," he said, and pulled two bags from the backseat of the new SUV. He handed one to her. "New clothes. Go change."

Kara took the bag, wondered about it, but was too drained to argue with him. He walked her to the women's room entrance and she held herself together until she got inside, then sank against the wall and cried. Fear and regret and uncertainty welled up. Emotion overflowed in huge, hot tears and gut-deep sobs, and a hundred terrible scenarios ran through her mind about what Knutson might have in store for Aidan.

Eventually, the tears ran out as sheer exhaustion settled in and reason clawed to the surface. She'd done the right thing: She'd gotten Aidan out of the line of fire. Nothing Knutson was planning could be worse than being shot or strangled with barbed wire.

She dried her cheeks. Reaching into the bag, she found a dark green dress, slipped into it without much thought, and donned a pair of strappy sandals. She stepped back out to the mirror and looked.

Whoa.

The dress was a slinky halter with an open back and

a deep vee neckline. At the vee, a large brooch collected the ruching from across both breasts, which fell in elegant drapes of fabric to the hem in the middle of her thighs. The shoes added three inches and the sassy hair looked the same as it had before she'd slept on it or outrun a shooter.

She found a supply of makeup in the bag and touched herself up from the tears as best she could. Heavier than she was accustomed to but not quite what Madelena had done.

Whatever it was Varón had planned, she had to follow through. He had Aidan.

She came out and found Varón standing where she'd left him, clean-shaven and wearing a new set of clothes. Dark slacks and loafers, crisp butter-yellow shirt with a Ralph Lauren logo and the sleeves folded up over muscular forearms. She knew the strength of those arms now, and the skill. Both were frightening.

His gaze trekked down the bodice of the dress and to her legs with sheer male admiration, but when his dark eyes found hers, they were soft. "Are you all right?" His voice was so gentle it was almost her undoing. Damn him. She didn't think she could handle tenderness just now, especially from him.

She took refuge in sarcasm and gestured to the dress she was wearing. "Why wouldn't I be? Knutson is quite the manservant. I don't suppose I should wonder how he got the sizes right."

"He'd be insulted that you're surprised."

She smoothed a hand down her body, tugging the short dress a little lower. The problem was this: Varón was right. She didn't dare wear the conservative garb she normally did. The change in just hair and makeup wouldn't be sufficient to conceal her identity should she run into someone who knew her. She would have to play the role assigned.

Varón took her bag of discarded clothes in one hand, and the other hand slid to the small of her back. He ushered her back toward the SUV, his touch shooting through her body like electricity. It was possessive, commandeering, and so charged with energy Kara knew she wouldn't be able to sever the current until *he* decided to turn it off.

"You don't have to have your hands on me," she complained. "You have my son, damn it. Where do you think I'm going to go?"

"Nowhere," he said. "You're not that stupid."

He maintained the contact all the way back to the Escalade. Once inside the car, he opened the skylight and handed her yet another new phone he pulled from the glove compartment. This was an iPhone, like the one they'd left in the Porsche.

"This has the same number and all the information from your old phone," Varón told her, starting the engine. "Sans the tracking capabilities."

Kara frowned, but got it: Like it or not, they didn't want to eliminate the killer's preferred choice of communication. But the idea that she was expected to hear from him again brought a chill. So did the realization that Varón had managed to have a new phone programmed with her original number in a matter of hours, and then delivered to a new vehicle.

"Is there any place you *can't* reach?" she asked.

"Phones are easy. A ten-year-old could have programmed a new phone with your number and transferred the info from the old one."

"But a ten-year-old didn't. Someone in the phone company did."

"Someone with the skill set of a ten-year-old, who appreciated a little bonus in his pocket. That kind of person isn't hard to find."

"Or someone who valued both his kneecaps?" she asked.

"You've been watching too much TV. Kneecaps are pretty rare."

Kara sank back into the leather seat and studied him. Classic, chiseled jaw and nearly-black hair, suntan, deepset eyes that showed nothing more and nothing less than he meant for them to. In depositions and on the stand in a courtroom, he'd never displayed a hint of anything beyond insolent thug. He'd barely said ten words, letting his lawyer speak for him and subjecting Kara to insolent male regard at every turn. But more recently, traces of human being had occasionally surfaced. *Stay back from the window so you don't get cut . . . He threw his body over me . . . That fucker burned up my house.*

Kara looked down. "I'm sorry about your house," she said. The words came out unplanned.

"It's just a building."

"It was a building that was your home. I know that's hard to lose."

"For you, maybe. I'm different."

"No shit," Kara said.

Varón shook his head, a faint smile growing on his lips. "We're an unlikely partnership, aren't we? A month ago, you were pushing me toward Death Row and now I'm not only your cohort in crime, but your son's babysitter."

"If anything happens to him, you won't have to worry about Death Row," she said. "I'll kill you myself, faster than you can blink."

"So noted," he said, settling back against the seat.

The tension that had seized him when Knutson gave him the news about the fire seemed to loosen its grip a touch. He dropped his wrist atop the steering wheel and pushed the cruise control button.

"How did Knutson lose a son?" she asked.

His Adam's apple bobbed. "Leukemia. He was ten." He glanced at her. "He'll take care of Aidan."

She let out a deep breath. "I know he will—so long as you tell him to. But if you were to give a different order, he'd carry that one out, too, wouldn't he?"

"Obedience is one of his more valuable traits."

"And what happens when I run out of useful information about this killer? What orders will you give to your minions if I become a burden or cross you?"

"Don't," he said darkly.

Right. Kara touched her stomach. Every conversation with him was a roller coaster. The turns were so sharp she felt queasy.

"You need to eat," Varón said. "You haven't had anything since yesterday afternoon."

She frowned, and her nerves rippled. She should have known. "You watched me before we met?"

"Only for a few hours. I'd only been back in the States that long." He slanted her a look. "You can't be surprised that getting a message from you raised an eyebrow."

"*You*, suspicious of *me*," she mused aloud. "There's a reversal of roles."

"I'm versatile that way."

He took an exit ramp just north of Atlanta and Kara was just about to ask him where he was going when the new phone bleeped. Her heart jumped and Varón frowned, then pulled off the road and stopped the car along a curb. It wasn't the phone Aidan would use. It was the iPhone like hers they had used to keep the lines of communication open with the killer.

"Look at it," Varón said, and Kara touched the screen to life. There was a text message.

"Oh, no," she said. Her heart dropped to her stomach. "God, no."

He took the phone from her hands, holding it above the console between them so she could see. He touched the keys.

A picture came up: his house, flames. And a message: *Nice move, Kara. But now look what you've done.*

CHAPTER
24

POLICE WERE ALL OVER. Sasha cursed. Emergency vehicles began to pile up, including tankers filled with water, and the firefighters struggled to get hooked up and save what they could of the house. Soon, though, their strategy turned to wetting down the surrounding area—a sign of defeat in a secluded forest with no fire hydrants.

The destruction pleased Sasha. He ducked back into the woods so he could watch from out of sight and something caught his eye on the ground. He snatched it up—an iPhone. The kid's, he realized.

He smiled. Wasn't sure how he might use the boy's phone but disabled iCloud and all the location services, just in case. Pulled out the battery, too, then pocketed the phone and moved deeper into the forest. From there, the view was pretty good and he watched the commotion with almost giddy delight. The forest was full of the sounds of his doing. Flames and waterfalls and sirens and shouts. Even more people arriving.

Among them, a couple of men in suits. That was strange. Sasha couldn't see what vehicle they had driven; most were parked a good distance away. But they walked around talking to the police and any firefighter who would spare a moment, then started circling the still-smoking house.

Investigators of some sort. Arson specialists? Plain-clothes detectives? Insurance guys? They'd sure gotten here in a hurry.

They split up, one of them heading in Sasha's direction. Shit. This guy was scouring the ground, looking for something, widening his path.

Getting too close.

The lizard part of Sasha's brain kicked in. *Go.* But careful.

Moving slowly, he shifted, trying not to rustle the bushes. He extracted himself from his hideout, looked down at his shirt, and cursed. Light gray. He hadn't realized when he followed the GPS that he was coming to a forest; he hadn't dressed for camouflage.

Still, he was pretty far away and the man was nearer to the house, which had quickly become a skeleton of soaked black char. If Sasha made a run for it, he could get deep into the trees and over the ridge before they caught sight of him. Plus, these were suits, while Sasha was an athlete. And he knew right where he was going.

He inched backward, eyeing the suit, then eyeing his path, and back and forth so he didn't trip, moving like molasses. If he just made another twenty yards, he could drop down over a ridge, then into the creek bed, and he'd be out of sight until the suit crested the same ridge. By then, he'd be too far away to be seen.

The man in the suit began moving in the opposite direction, eyes downcast, and Sasha breathed relief. He turned—still a good idea to get the hell out of here—and just as he took his first full step, a nearer voice rang out.

"Freeze. FBI."

Sasha lunged, sprinting through the forest. *FBI?* The voice came again, repeating the same command, and as he ran out of earshot from the hoses, he began to hear the rustle of pine straw and sticks. Shit. The guy was coming. The second suit? Sasha cursed himself for that carelessness even as he ran, twigs clawing at his shirt and fallen trees rising like hurdles. His heart raced as if he were running the Triple Crown, his lungs dragging in air.

"FBI. Freeze."

The voice again, but it was more distant now. The man had lost ground. Sasha made it over the ridge and ran low on his haunches; here he could run and not be seen, depending on how far back the pursuer was.

FBI. What the fuck?

He tried not to think about it, concentrating instead on getting to the copse where he'd hidden his car. He used every ounce of athleticism dodging limbs and hurdling fallen trees, and after six or eight minutes of a sprint, he slowed to a jog, sucking in air. He chanced a look behind himself, and relief came in a deluge of laughter. The suit was long gone. He'd made it.

Beautiful.

He hustled anyway—alternately jogging or hiking fast—until he got to the nest he'd made for his car. He pulled off the limbs and branches that would have concealed it from a passing eye, thinking hard about what he'd heard.

FBI. Really? Incredible.

His lungs worked overtime, his pulse pounding a spot in both temples like a hammer, but he barely noticed the discomfort. FBI. That's who the man was. A barely lived-in house. Computers and equipment. Encoded files.

A Porsche? He wasn't so sure of that, but why else would Federal agents in suits be dispatched to some isolated house fire in the woods within an hour of the flames starting? And the boat explosion, the news reports that body parts had been found. That wasn't something just any two-bit criminal could make happen, even for Kara. That was the kind of thing that required strings. Resources.

Oh, Kara. Surprise heated his cheeks, and the sprint, and yes, anger. She'd found an FBI agent to take her under wing. Every time he turned around, the bitch pulled one over on him again. He'd have to think about this. Had he been careful enough about DNA? Yes, he was scrupulous about rubber gloves or wiping away prints. His hair was shaved almost to his scalp. He always wore long sleeves just in case someone might notice the tattoo of barbed wire that climbed up his arm, and when the rage-beast had hold of him, he covered his face. He knew he might end up with a nosebleed because even with all that prison therapy, he never had managed to learn to keep that beast at bay.

That was okay. He was saving it to unleash on Kara.

It was that thought that brought sanity back within his grasp. No way would he let some jackass FBI agent ruin a party he'd spent years planning. He *would* have a second crack at Kara Chandler. He *would* bring her to her knees. And he *would* kill her in the end.

This just made the challenge a little greater. A game requiring more cunning than any logic game his father had ever tried to press him into playing.

Fuck you and your puzzles, Dad. I'm going to best the FBI. And take Kara as my prize.

The gnawing anger fell off to a nibble, his heart rate easing back to normal. Sasha sat back against the driver's seat. Think, *think*. First, get this car out of here. If the house he'd just torched belonged to an FBI agent, they wouldn't be satisfied poking around within a small radius of the fire. An agent was among The Important Ones. They'd search until they found the car's nest, even if it took them a week of scouring this mountain. And depending on how soon he'd shaken the agent following him just now, it might not take them much time at all. They'd call in twenty people, maybe a team of dogs. Choppers and infrareds. They'd *hunt*.

He drove the car about fifty feet out of its nest, then remembered the phone he'd used to send the picture of the burning house, just moments ago. Now, the FBI was involved. They had offices filled with techno-geeks who could find anything from a phone. It was the perfect time to get rid of it, and he would do so with a flourish. One last message, but this one he wouldn't send. He'd let the fuckers *find* it.

He threw the car into park and accessed a notepad on the phone, typed in a message to Kara's new friend and set the message up as wallpaper. He got out, smiling at his own cunning. Using his shirttail, he wiped all traces of fingerprints from the phone, then carefully scooped out a trench of dirt and stood the phone vertical in it.

Then he reached into his pocket and pulled out a lock of Kara's blond hair, rubbed it between his thumb and fingers, and let it rain down onto the phone.

Come on, then, Mister Federal Agent. Game on.

CHAPTER
25

LUKE STARED AT THE photo of his house—flames lapping at the very window where Kara had stood. He ground his jaw. It wasn't enough for the motherfucker to kill the people she came in contact with or to drive her into hiding, or even to shoot at her son. He had to use Luke to terrorize her even more. Luke didn't really care about the property; he didn't even care if some asshole wanted to jerk *him* around.

But he did care that this bastard had killed Elisa and Andrew Chandler. And against his better judgment, he cared about the woman sitting next to him, a woman whose slender frame had just turned to blown glass. She looked as if she might shatter.

Luke pulled the phone from her hands, forwarded the text to Knutson, and took a call back from him two minutes later.

"Can I talk?" Knutson asked, sounding harried.

Luke glanced at Kara. She would hear only one end of the conversation. "Yes," he said.

"I just got a call from one of the agents at your house.

This asshole is still there, somewhere. At least, some-one is."

Luke felt something shift inside. His hands fisted. *Careful.* Don't react.

"The agent chased him into the woods but never got a good look. They're widening the search now. Gonna take that mountain apart."

Luke let out a slow breath. He wanted to be there. Wanted to be the one to hunt the bastard down himself.

But that wasn't going to happen. The shooter was gone. Those woods were dense enough to hide a bear, especially if you'd come through them once on foot and knew where you were going. If the agent on foot had already lost him, he wasn't going to find him again now.

They'd find *evidence* of him, though. One thing the FBI was good at: analyzing trails.

"Go on," Luke said, trying to clear out the emotion so he could focus on facts.

"The bad news is this: The agent issued a halt com-mand. *'Freeze. FBI.'* Twice, he said."

"Ah, Christ."

"Would he have found anything to ID you in the house?" Knutson asked.

"No," Luke said. He was careful, even there. But still, *Freeze, FBI.* Damn it. The FBI didn't get called to house fires.

"Look, it may be time to bring you out. Your part with Collado is done, anyway. You can't risk being seen by him. He thinks you're dead."

"I was looking forward to correcting him," Luke said darkly. And it was the understatement of the decade. Luke *lived* for the moment Collado learned the truth.

"Your cover is compromised, Luke. Say your farewells

to Collado's men now. Get out of the way and let the rest of the team pick up those pieces."

Luke rubbed a hand over his head. "What else?" he asked.

"It's going to take a while to have a formal report about the fire, but unofficially, it smelled of gasoline and you were right that it started in the garage. They found his perch. A tree about sixty-five yards into the woods."

"At two o'clock from the south-facing window in the loft," Luke said.

"Right. After they processed it, one of our guys climbed up. Found one narrow alley of unobstructed view, right into the clearing around the back deck Aidan went over. But in any other direction—toward the creek, for example—he couldn't see shit for the trees."

"So he wasn't trying to kill anyone. Not this time."

"Maybe."

Luke cursed. "The shooter made Louie Guilford with a single shot in a crowd. This time, he had a direct shot at Aidan and me in close range, but missed? No way. It's a game. The fucker's playing with us."

"Did you have a seven-millimeter rifle in the house?"

"No. Why?"

"Because they found one, pretty burnt up."

A souvenir. Luke wondered what else they would find.

"He must've stashed a vehicle somewhere," Knutson said. "Maybe we'll get a tire track. Something that matches the one Penny Wolff was leaning against."

A waiting game, then. Waiting to find a trail, waiting for the killer to make a mistake. Luke wasn't good at waiting.

"Listen," Knutson said. "From Kara's phone we found that a tracking system was installed last Memorial Day. More than a year ago."

Luke ran a hand over the back of his neck. He wasn't a man who was easily spooked but thinking about that—imagining someone following Kara's every move for that long, keeping tabs on her any time he wanted to—that gave even Luke the creeps.

He told kara, then asked Knutson, "Where's it coming from?"

"All over the damn place. It looks like he never accessed the tracking system from the same location. With time, the techs might be able to triangulate a probable vicinity, but it's gonna take an investigator with some mathematical savvy and a lot of time on his hands."

"Then find one."

"That's the plan," Knutson said.

"All right," Luke said. "We're gonna stop and get some food, put out some feelers. Let me know when you find somothing."

Luke disconnected and Kara looked at him. "So, do you have another ten-year-old who can trace phone trackers backward?"

"Sure," Luke said. "But your stalker accounted for that. He made sure not to access it from any one location."

She turned away, her features hard as marble. She'd just been shot at and her son whisked away, and a killer who had created some twisted, deadly game had just demonstrated a disturbing willingness to be flexible. Her desperate ploy to disappear hadn't helped at all.

Except now she had Luke on her side. He gave in to impulse and laid a hand over hers. Mistake. Even in the heat she was clammy and cool, and the undercurrent of a tremor vibrated deep in her bones. Adrenaline was like that. After the rush wore off, it could be a real bitch.

An unexpected urge rose up. Luke wanted to tell her it

was okay, that he was one of the good guys. He wanted to tell her he was sorry about her husband, even if his death turned out to be the result of some freak with a vendetta instead of an error on Luke's part. He wanted to tell her that she was in safe hands—his—and that she didn't need to be afraid of him.

But those weren't things Luke Varón would do. Lukas Mann, maybe, but not Luke Varón. And while Luke Varón might well be the kind of man to use encouraging words and comfort for the purpose of getting in her pants, he wasn't a man who would let emotion make him lose sight of the prize while he did. He had to keep his head. He still wanted Collado. A fuck with Kara Chandler along the way would be a distraction he couldn't afford.

Besides, Kara Chandler wouldn't be the kind of woman who fucked. She would make love, passionately and ardently, with a hundred deep emotions wrapped up in the act.

Luke fucked.

He lifted his hand from hers, allowing his head to clear. "Don't worry," he said, "I'll find him. I have—"

"Eight and a half tons of cocaine at stake." She scoffed, but it lacked edge. After a minute, she looked up. "Aidan told me you put yourself between him and the bullets."

Luke winced. His oversight with Aidan's phone might just as easily have gotten the kid killed. "I ducked just like him, that's all."

"That's not how he saw it."

"Whatever," Luke snarled. Luke Varón was no hero. Just ask Elisa.

"Well," Kara said, her voice almost a whisper, "thank you."

Luke blew that off and pulled back onto the street, events of the past eighteen hours running through his mind like a hamster on a wheel, getting him nowhere. He tried not to spare energy on the matter of losing the house. It belonged to the U.S. government and even the clothes and few personal belongings he'd had there weren't particularly valuable to him. Everything on the computer was stored in digital safes. He only used that house occasionally. His Luke Varón persona owned a condo in midtown Atlanta, in one of Montiel's buildings.

So, the house was no great loss. No reason at all for any emotion.

Except there *was* emotion, and Luke didn't know what to do with it. A flashback hit him...Standing outside his brother's home, the emergency vehicles all lined up and the living room a charred, drenched mess. Nick had a home. A meaningful one, with loved ones inside and his own handiwork in the design and labor. Luke had nothing so valuable.

But still: The fucker had burned up his house.

He got back into Atlanta and swung into a paved driveway that disappeared behind a twelve-foot stone wall. For a hundred yards, he rolled between two columns of gnarled pecan trees that stood along the lane like sentries, then slowed at the wrought iron gate.

"Mr. Varón," a uniformed guard said. Luke glanced at the badge for his name.

"Rodgers. How are you?"

"Happy to see you back." Rodgers leaned forward and saw Kara in the passenger seat, gave Luke an approving salute, and opened the gate. Luke pulled through, wove another couple hundred yards through more pecan tree soldiers, and slowed in front of an enormous plantation house that had somehow survived Sherman's march through Atlanta a hundred and fifty years ago. It wasn't alone; there were a few dozen such relics in the area. But to Luke's knowledge, this was the only one that was now an exclusive gentlemen's club.

A valet came forward.

"No thanks," Luke said, waving him off. "I'll put it away."

He drove to a parking area off to the side.

"What is this place?" Kara asked.

"It's called The Parthenon," Luke said. He pointed out the high plantation pillars across the front and sides. They held up a twenty-foot deep porch. "It's a club."

"The Parthenon. I've heard of it. But I never knew where it was."

"They don't advertise."

"And you're a member?" She gave a little snort. "I was under the impression they were exclusive about their clientele."

"Very exclusive. And yes, I am."

Kara narrowed her eyes at him. "You weren't a member a month ago, when I was pulling together a case against you."

Luke formed his most innocent half grin. "Yes, I was."

She stared, then rubbed her hands up and down her arms as if she'd felt a chill. Starting to realize just how ineffectual her office had been in taking him to court.

"It's not your investigator's fault for not finding out," he said. "There's a code of ethics here: What goes on in The Parthenon stays in The Parthenon. How would Atlanta's elite conduct the shadier side of business and politics if places like this went around giving out names every time some Federal judge got curious? Of course, a fair number of Federal judges are members."

Her cheeks went white. "Then I can't go in there. I'll be recognized."

"Probably. I'd almost take a bet you'll see someone in there you know. Time to take your disguise seriously, *Krista*."

He got out of the car, then came around and opened the passenger side door. She climbed out and stood in the vee between the open door and the seat, primping, and he ran his gaze down her new look. She was nervous about the disguise, but a man would be hard-pressed to associate the businesslike Kara Chandler with the hot little number on Luke's arm tonight. The dress was sexy as hell and the soft, spiky hairstyle was far removed from the DA's office. She certainly didn't look like a woman with a teenage son. Her breasts, sans bra, were cupped perfectly by the fitted bodice of the dress. Her legs were long and slender, the hem just short enough to assure that every man inside would lock eyes on her ass and pray for her to bend over. And her eyes, well, they were startling green windows to a soul divided: half on a rampage to find the son of a bitch who had killed her husband and terrorized her and her son. The other half-petrified.

"It's been a while since I've brought a woman here," he said, and she looked up at him.

"So now I'm your hooker."

"I don't pay for sex. You're my girlfriend."

"I can't be your cousin?"

An unexpected grin rose to his lips. Part of this, he just might enjoy. The part that made it acceptable to put his hands on her. He stepped in and bent his head, smoothing his left hand down the side of her rib cage. "It would be a little awkward to touch my cousin like this."

Kara stiffened. "You don't need to touch me at all."

He locked his elbow just enough that she couldn't slip out. "There are only two reasons women are permitted inside this place. One is if they work here. You don't. The other is if they are the special guest of a member."

The look on her face was one of pure disgust.

"Play it," Luke said. "Be timid, but not coy. Don't flirt or give anyone a reason to think you're up for grabs. Sharing is common here—almost expected—and I'm not in the mood. Don't show confidence. Be quiet and be subservient."

"Just the way you like your women?" she sniped.

Not at all. I like them smart and strong and passionate, and dressed in power suits I can peel off one layer at a time. "Yes," Luke said. "Just the way I like my women."

He walked her through the parking lot. When they got closer to the entrance, Luke released her arm and laid his hand on the small of her back. Wanted to make sure everyone understood. He felt her reaction to his touch and bent his head. "Women here are accessories and nothing more," he murmured. "But it makes you useful. Play your cards right and they'll talk around you as if you aren't there."

"What makes you think there's anything here worth hearing?"

Luke stopped, frowning at her. She really didn't get it yet. "Andrew was a regular here, every Thursday," he said. "This is where he was the night he died."

CHAPTER
26

A CHILL WASHED THROUGH KARA. Andrew, a member of The Parthenon? She couldn't even identify the emotion seeping into her veins...fury, indignation, shame.

Maybe plain old pain.

Anger willed out and Varón's fingers brushed down her spine. "Easy, lover," he said, piloting her up the cobbled walkway. "You're supposed to enjoy being with me."

Kara couldn't even muster a smart-ass response. She was too deep in the surreal experience of walking into an exclusive *club* where her late husband had committed acts of felony with a drug cartel. And here she was, posing as Luke Varón's escort while police searched the lake behind her house for her body and no doubt tried to connect her to Penny Wolff's disappearance.

She could hardly think past the insanity of it all.

Varón escorted her through the front entrance, tipping greetings to staff, and Kara looked around. The foyer was straight from *Gone with the Wind*. She skimmed the crown molding, expecting surveillance cameras, but didn't see any. She glanced at the giant ferns sprawling on pedestal stands and imagined tiny microphones in the foliage.

Varón bent his head. "There aren't any," he said, reading her mind. "That's one of the rules."

Of course it was. *What happens at The Parthenon...* Kara's skin pulled into a spread of goose bumps. It must be the blast of air-conditioning hitting her bare shoulders after coming inside from a sultry evening, that's all. It wasn't the bizarre setting, it wasn't that Varón seemed to sense every thought as if it were printed on her forehead, it wasn't the brush of his breath across her ear. And it certainly wasn't the possessive hand on her spine.

A man in a dress suit approached, his collar open. He wore a shiny gold chain around his neck, the swirls of a tattoo peeking out at his collarbone.

"Welcome, Mr. Varón," he said, his face splitting into a smile. Kara noticed a light accent. Eastern Europe, she thought. "Will you be dining? Chef Grayson has pan-seared duck with blueberry-cardamom chutney or pork medallions drizzled with balsamic-maple glaze—"

"I'll tell you what," Varón interrupted, smoothing a big hand over his stomach, "I think I'll start with a nice cold beer first."

"Of course." The man smiled. "To the bar, then. Follow me."

Kara said nothing. They passed a lounge where a man sat at a grand piano playing easy jazz, and a few other men relaxed and talked in deep-cushioned armchairs. They passed a couple of closed doors and walked to the back of the house, where a sports bar materialized.

It was busy. Flat-screens adorned every wall and the air smelled of wine and sautéed mushrooms and grilled steak. A large patio opened out the back, then farther to a pool oasis with stone waterfalls. Inside, baseball blasted overhead, the chatter like that of any other sports bar on a Saturday evening. Occasionally, a group groaned or cheered as games and races played overhead.

Varón walked Kara to a table along a back wall, sat down across from her, and crooked a finger at a waitress. She was dressed in a bikini top that barely sufficed as a bra, with a skirt clinging to her hips a good six inches beneath a belly button ring. Kara caught herself looking away, instinctively worried that the skirt might slip, only to notice that all of the wait staff was female, and all dressed the same.

Andrew. How many nights had he dragged in late? How many had he spent here?

Varón placed an order but Kara didn't hear; she was too busy scanning the clientele for Federal judges or other people who shouldn't find her here. Varón leaned forward onto his forearms. "You look skittish. Stop it." He picked up her hand, lacing his fingers into hers and lifting both of their arms up onto their elbows, holding hands over the table. A lover's gesture.

"Why did you bring me here?" Kara asked.

"We need to put out some feelers for your husband's killer—without alerting the world that the killer is still alive."

"The world," she echoed. "You mean the people bringing in your shipment."

"My colleagues would be as concerned about this new development as I am. The people here know how to be discreet."

As he spoke, he gave a nod toward the bar, where two men broke from a ball game and approached the table. Kara took them in. One had a bleached-blond crew cut and a neck the size of a redwood tree, with a Celtic cross tattooed on either side. A second was model-gorgeous—as tall as Varón, with light chocolate skin and ice-blue eyes, and dreadlocks collected in a tail at the back of his head. Both were dressed in knit shirts with sport coats over them. Kara was pretty sure why they wore jackets even in the summer heat.

These were Luke Varón's hands and eyes and ears. Armed, trained, obedient. Ben Archer would have shit a brick knowing she was in their inner circle just now.

The model locked eyes with Kara and Varón's fingers tightened on hers. The blond gave her a not-so-subtle once-over, and Kara knew she'd been thoroughly judged: Luke Varón's whore for the night.

He tugged on her hand. "Scoot over here, honey. Make room."

He hooked an extra chair with his toe and dragged it beside his. Kara bit back the insult and rose, moving around to sit beside him while letting his goons have the other two chairs. The half-naked waitress came back with a beer for Varón and a glass of white wine for Kara.

Varón barely acknowledged her to his men, except to say, "This is Krista."

"Nice," the bleached blond said, and the model said, "She got a sister?"

Varón's lip actually curled. "Keep it in your pants, Burke," he snarled, and Kara could feel his frame tighten. "Krista, this is Jared Beckett and Keith Burke. We work together."

Which was as much as Luke Varón would say to his girlfriend *du jour*, Kara thought. She bit her tongue and played the part. Showed more interest in her manicure than in whatever the men were about to discuss but felt the blue gaze of the model—Burke—like a flame.

Varón pulled her hand to his lap, staking his claim. Illogically, Kara was thankful.

He leaned in over the table. "You may have heard about an explosion last night in Buckhead," he said. "It killed an assistant DA and her kid."

"Chandler," said Bleach. "It's all over the news. Strange time of night for a woman to take a boat out, so APD is looking at foul play."

Varón nodded. "Cops will turn the Chandlers inside out, including looking at Andrew Chandler's affairs again. Gonna get dicey, with a dead kid and all."

Kara looked up and Varón squeezed her hand. *Easy*, said his touch. *Don't show interest*.

But they were talking about her child and husband. These men had all known Andrew. They probably knew more about him than she did.

"Bad time for an investigation," said the model. "Collado spooks easy."

"Then we need to make sure he knows there's nothing to worry about," Varón said. His hand was heavy and warm on Kara's hand. "You may also know that John Wolff's wife has gone missing. It turns out Mrs. Chandler paid her a visit the night she disappeared."

"Whoa," said Bleach.

Varón paused to let a cheer die down at the next table. "Which explains the ADA's middle-of-the-night boat ride. I'm thinking Kara Chandler had it in for Penny Wolff. She'd just passed the one-year-mark without her husband, maybe been nursing a grudge against Wolff all that time..." He shrugged, letting the others finish the thought for themselves.

It took every ounce of energy for Kara to keep still. He was starting rumors about her.

Bleach scowled. "Kara Chandler blames Wolff's *wife* for her husband dying? That doesn't make sense."

"When was the last time a woman scorned made sense?" Varón asked. "All I know is the cops went to question Ms. Chandler about Penny Wolff in the middle of the night, and less than an hour later, her boat blew up and search teams are dragging the lake. Sounds to me like a woman who got scared and tried to take off before the shit hit the fan."

Burke finally pulled his gaze from Kara. "Pretty ballsy."

"I met the woman, remember?" Varón said. "Trust me, she has balls to spare."

"Boats don't blow like that without help."

"That's where my head went, too," Varón said. "Which makes me think she was trying to run away, and it all went wrong. You wait. This is gonna turn out to be something personal between Penny Wolff and Kara Chandler."

"And there's no chance she snowed everyone?" Bleach didn't like it. "Maybe Chandler slipped away with a wad of cash and a bunch of new ID cards."

"Cops started turning up body parts this morning. She and her kid are dead."

The model shook his head. "I hope you're right and it's all personal. I'd hate to think a police investigation is going to turn up something that links Chandler to Macy's before Collado comes ashore. I've got fifty Gs riding on this delivery."

Varón stiffened. "First, let me correct your arithmetic, Burke: You've got fifty *more* Gs riding on it. Don't forget the twenty you've already made. Which means you're in this up to your baby blues. If Collado does bail out, it will mean the ring's been compromised and every one of us will be trying to catch the first plane out of here to a country without an extradition treaty. So," he leaned back a bit and aimed the rest at both men, "publicly, I want you to make sure everyone in the operation hears that Kara Chandler went off the deep end over her husband, killed Penny Wolff, and tried to run away."

They looked at him, obedient, waiting. They knew something else was coming.

"Privately," Varón said, "I have reason to believe that John Wolff *didn't* kill Andrew Chandler. Whoever did is still out there."

Varón's cohorts stared. Burke, in particular, turned to stone.

"Not Wolff?" he asked, and for the first time, Kara felt as if her presence around the table was forgotten. A pulse throbbed in Burke's temple.

Varón looked him square in the eyes. "Not Wolff."

"So we need to shake the trees and see what comes out. With*out* letting on that Wolff was innocent." Varón turned to Bleach. "Check on the Macy's contingent in Savannah. Now that the rest of the Chandler family is dead, people will talk in ways they wouldn't before." To Burke: "You track down friends of the kid—his name was Aidan— and see if there was anything his friends might have been afraid to talk about back when Chandler died. Follow up on Ms. Chandler, too—her hairdresser, her housekeeper, her girlfriends—find out what they're saying."

Bleach scoffed. "Good luck with that. She was one cool bitch. I can't see her for warm fuzzy talks with the girls."

Another squeeze of Kara's hand. "You never know. She might have confided in someone unexpected. Desperation can do strange things to a person."

Kara took a sip of her wine, hoping to cover the flush in

her cheeks. Dear God, Varón was smooth. Dangerously, fascinatingly smooth. To Burke, he added: "Don't go out of town chasing any leads. I want you close for the next couple of days in case I need an extra set of hands."

The model swiveled his gaze back to Kara. "Gladly."

Every sinew in Varón's body went rigid. "And here's something else to keep in mind, Burke, something you won't want to forget." He spoke barely above a whisper, yet every syllable came out loud and clear. "I don't share."

Kara fidgeted; his caress had become a grip, the thin bones in her hand compressing. He sat back and lifted her hand to his lips. "Sorry, baby," he said, and spread her fingers, touching his lips to the center of her palm. A stroke of his tongue sent a shot of sensation through her bones. The wine she'd been sipping—without any food in her stomach—brought a flush of heat.

Burke sneered, duly chastised, but eyes still flaring. Kara didn't know if he was upset because of thwarted lust or if it was anger that Varón had so clearly pulled rank. Either way, she made the decision not to spend any one-on-one time with Keith Burke.

As if one-on-one time with Luke Varón was any better.

Yes, it was.

Varón leaned back. "I don't have to tell either one of you that you'll be well compensated for anything you turn up."

The men took that as their dismissal and stood.

"One more thing," he said. He ran a hand down Kara's spine and around her waist, pulling her against his body. Kara wanted to rebel but didn't, and his hand slid shockingly down over her hip. "Send messages through the secure line. I'm going to be out of touch for a couple of days, until the shipment comes in." He cupped Kara's ass and looked down at her. "We won't want to be disturbed, will we, sweetheart?"

Kara managed a twitter and Varón's goons turned. Just as they left, the blond with the crew cut looked back at Varón. "Hey, you know who to talk to next, right? She's upstairs."

"Yeah," Varón said, nodding. "That's just where we're headed."

CHAPTER
27

LUKE MOVED FROM THE table and a hot poker of pain jammed into his thigh bone. He winced. He wasn't up to leaping off decks and sprinting through forests.

"Bring your wine," he said to Kara, though he noticed that she'd drunk most of the glass during his conversation with Burke and Beckett, on a completely empty stomach. He shouldn't have done that to her.

"Take your hand off me," she said through clenched teeth.

"Later. People are watching. It would be unlike me to have a beautiful woman at my side and *not* have my hands on her."

They walked out of the bar area and the moment they were out of earshot, she pulled from his grasp. "Who's Collado?" she asked.

Luke weighed his words. "He was a lieutenant for Manuel Rojàs who slipped through the cracks when the Feds and Colombian National Police busted up the cartel. He's the heir apparent for the new Atlanta ring."

"So, you work for him?"

"I like to think of us more as equals."

"But you're worried an investigation into my family would be enough to spook him, so you tell your goons to put the word out that my death is the result of a crazed wife. Thanks a lot. Never mind my reputation."

He looked down at her. In another world or another galaxy, Luke would find her chutzpah an infinite source of admiration and pleasure. In this one, he didn't dare encourage it.

"I don't give a damn about your reputation, Counselor," he said, piloting her back past the lounge and to the elevator. "I only care that Collado shows up with the shipment."

"If you're partners, why not just call him and tell him not to worry?"

A muscle ticked in Luke's jaw. "'Partners' would be too strong a word for our relationship."

She stopped, pulling her arm from his hand. "Holy shit. You're not in league with Collado." She paused, it sinking in. "You're trying to take over the cartel yourself."

Close enough. "You make it sound rather pedestrian. I assure you, it's no small feat."

She stared, her mouth unhinging, and Luke bit back a pang of sheer animal lust. He laid a finger beneath her chin and nudged her lips closed. "You're distracting me."

She snapped away and Luke gave himself a mental shake. Christ, he wished he was kidding, but he wasn't. She *was* distracting him. He'd just about flattened Keith Burke back there for the way he'd ogled her.

The porter arrived with an electronic key and slid it into the slot. The elevator doors opened.

"Enjoy your dinner, Mr. Varón," he said, and stepped back while Luke and Kara entered. She'd gone stiff as a board again. Processing the depth of his evil, no doubt.

They stepped out on the third story and Luke's nostrils twitched at the aroma of grilled pork and spices. The soft strains of classical violins played through tiny speakers in the ceiling. A couple dozen patrons speckled the room—mostly men—and he skimmed them, searching for someone who might know Kara. There was only one.

Luke took a deep breath. Baptism by fire, Kara. It would be a good test of her disguise.

On the way to their table, Luke searched the restaurant for Lacy. She sat alone at the far end of a carved mahogany bar across the back of the dining room.

"Right here, sir?" asked the host. Luke didn't recognize him.

"I think we'd rather be over there," he said, indicating the corner farthest from Lacy.

"This way."

A waitress hovered before they'd even settled into their seats. "Good evening. Welcome to Grayscale. Could I freshen your drinks?"

"I'll switch to gin and tonic," Luke said, handing off his beer bottle. "The lady's finished drinking. Just bring water with lime for both of us."

Kara opened her mouth and Luke raised a brow. Back to subservience, he warned her with his eyes.

The waitress left and Kara leaned forward on her forearms. Her breasts brushed the edge of the table on either side of the sparkling brooch on her dress. "Am I allowed to have a voice now?"

"Oh, I don't know," he said, not bothering to suppress a smile. "I sort of enjoy watching you bite your tongue. I'll wager you haven't had much practice at it."

"What are we doing here? Besides spreading rumors that I'm a crazed killer."

"First, we're eating. If you don't get something in your stomach I'm going to have a lot more to worry about than your tongue. You're surly when you're hungry. I thought you might just kick Burke in the groin a few minutes ago."

"I didn't like the way he looked at me."

Luke didn't, either. "Don't worry. He understands the hierarchy. He knows I get the first turn."

She sneered, but Luke thought there was a small dose of fear in the mix. He shifted. For some reason he wasn't wont to analyze, having her afraid of him didn't hold much appeal.

Still, it was better that way.

The waitress came back with drinks and fresh rolls. "Duck or pork?" Luke asked Kara.

"Duck," she said, and Luke held up two fingers to the waitress.

"Yes, sir," she said, and hurried away.

Luke unfolded a napkin from the rolls, and the aroma of yeast spiraled into the air. A memory hit him—eating *brötchen* at Engel's in Hopewell, Ohio. His brief visit home last year had reacquainted him with a girl he'd known in high school, Leni Engel, as well as bringing him back into the orbit of his brother, mother, and niece after too many years of distance. Just a few days there and it seemed now that every little thing was a reminder of home. He told himself he'd gone there to warn Nick that the woman he was falling for had a history. But in moments of complete honesty, Luke could admit he'd actually gone to Hopewell to heal. Rojàs was dead and Luke's work with the cartel—after more than a decade in South America and five months in what passed for jail in those circles—was finished. He'd needed a touchstone to his past.

He'd gotten it, but soon after, he'd learned that Collado was targeting Atlanta. That was all it had taken to pull Luke right back into the underworld.

"Eat," he said to Kara, diving in to the bread himself. "You need it."

She chewed through half a roll then looked at him. "Do they know?" she asked, and Luke raised his brows. "The men downstairs. Do they know you're planning to take over Collado's interest? Or do they actually believe you're working on his behalf?"

Luke smiled. "TMI, Counselor. I'd hate to save you from a killer only for you to wind up with cement shoes at the bottom of a lake."

She blanched and a stab of guilt got him.

"Relax," he said. "I just thought it would fit your image of me, that's all."

"And yet, you make a valid point. Why would you let me walk away when this is all over, knowing what I know about you?"

Luke hardened his gaze. "Because you won't become a threat to me. You know that if you do, I'll find you. And Aidan."

She peered at him, and for the first time, Luke wasn't one hundred percent sure she bought it. But his cell phone ended the conversation. It was a text from Knutson: *Call me now.*

Luke's hackles lifted. "Excuse me. I need to take care of this."

He stepped away, threading between tables to a place where he was out of the way but could still see Kara. He dialed Knutson.

"Is it Aidan?" Luke asked, surprised at the true fear in his bones.

"Aidan's fine. It's Penny Wolff. We found her. She was in a cornfield in Mississippi."

Ah, Christ.

"Just outside a town called Como, along I-fifty-five. Been there a while. The killer probably drove there Tuesday night right after Kara left Penny's house. There are tire tracks by the body, but the farmer goes in and out of there a lot, too, so they won't all belong to the unsub. And the lab's working on the photo of Penny Wolff. They've identified the wheel she was leaning against as belonging to an older model white van."

"Cause of death?"

"Strangulation by barbed wire. Just like the picture suggested."

Luke ran his hand over his head. It wasn't as if that was unexpected, but confirmation made it that much more real.

"Listen," Knutson said. "We're keeping a lid on the barbed wire—just reporting that she was strangled—but Wolff's name leaked in Mississippi. She's being connected to the Chandlers' disappearance."

Good. That would lend credibility to the rumor Luke had just started. Keep it personal rather than a cartel issue that might raise Collado's guard.

Unless the barbed wire thing got out. Luke couldn't quite imagine anyone believing Kara capable of that.

"There's more, Luke. I can't find any murders on file done by barbed wire, so we scoured through missing persons in the southeast for the past year. Nine months ago, a woman in Charlotte, North Carolina, disappeared while out walking her dog. Her name was Evelyn Camp."

The hairs on the back of Luke's neck rippled.

"She was sixty years old and supposedly was wearing

a pearl necklace. It was gone, but they found two pearls at the scene. It'll take time to get lab confirmation that they came from the same necklace Kara Chandler received, but I'm betting on it. I sent a courier with the necklace. We'll know by morning."

Luke clenched his fists. They didn't have to wait until morning: They knew now.

Knutson went on. "We know Andrew Chandler, Elisa Moran, Louie Guilford, and Penny Wolff were all tied to Kara, and indirectly, to the drug ring. But this Evelyn Camp is different. There's no connection, Luke. I mean *none*."

"Send me a picture. Kara must know her. Somehow."

"We also brought in a guy named Jay Kemp. He's the one Kara called after you first refused to help her. He says he knows nothin' about nothin' but I'd like to be sure of that."

"I'll ask."

"Do that. But mostly, find out who Evelyn Camp is. Was. The thing is, if Kara doesn't know her, then chances are good all the trophies she's been receiving are from total strangers. This may not have anything to do with Chandler and the cartel."

"Then what's it about?" Luke asked.

"Not money, not drugs, not power. Like I said, it's some asshole with his dick in his hands dreaming about Kara, that's what. Neither one of us knows what to do with that."

"So find someone who does. Bring in the BAU, someone who knows psycho-killers."

"Already done. He'll be here by morning."

CHAPTER
28

AFTER SASHA LEFT THE fire and the cops and the *FBI* behind, he drove in wide detours for a couple hours to be sure he wasn't being followed. Finally, he turned back toward the stable. Christ, what a mess. Megan had been dead since early this morning. He'd intended only to sleep for a little while before getting her buried and putting her stall together, but then he'd turned on the television and discovered Kara was dead.

Or rather, alive.

What a day.

And it wasn't over yet. The delay of tracking down Kara had turned a relatively easy task into something summarily unpleasant. Between the normal odors associated with death and whatever chemical breakdown had started on Megan's internal organs since this morning, the girl stank. Gravity had pulled her blood to the lowest points, turning her flesh blotchy and purple; she was swollen and stiff with rigor mortis and her eyes, mouth, and nostrils were crawling with flies.

Sasha cringed. All Kara's fault. Her and her fucking FBI bodyguard. Good thing Sasha hadn't gone to the nursing home this morning to bring his father here. He usually enjoyed bringing Dmitri to the stable, propping him up in his wheelchair for a firsthand view of the progress. He liked to review all he had done and watch the helpless, gape-mouthed horror in his father's eyes. He reveled in the knowledge that despite what the nurses believed, Dmitri Rodin *did* understand. He understood why his only son had tracked him down during his first week out of prison, grabbed his thick gloves and a nearby length of barbed wire, and nearly choked the life from his body. He understood why Sasha had money to burn and why he'd spent the past year and a good portion of that money reconstructing an exact replica of the Montgomerys' personal stable. He understood why Sasha kept bodies here rather than horses.

And his horror when Sasha put someone in a stall was one of Sasha's greatest joys.

But this time, he was glad Dmitri wasn't here. He didn't want his father to know the trouble Kara had caused today. He would have smirked. Others may not believe Dmitri could feel such a thing, let alone show it, but Sasha would *know*.

So leave him there in the fucking nursing home tonight. Get Megan in the ground. Kara's actions today had made the work harder, but in the end, they really hadn't changed anything. Nothing would prevent tomorrow from coming and nothing would prevent him from getting Kara to the stable. All he had to do was show her that it was ready.

So move, finish up.

Kara's truth awaited.

Luke disconnected from Knutson and the weight of the world settled on his shoulders. A serial killer, with some twisted plan for Kara. And for the moment, Luke was all that stood between them.

He closed his eyes. He'd always known the work he did was important. He'd always felt that by helping cripple a lethal organization, he was saving lives. Kids, professionals, even cops—no group of people was immune to the lure of drugs, and the Rojàs cartel—now Collado—was responsible for God-only-knows how many lives destroyed or lost.

Still, the drug war was fought at a distance, through layers of personnel and over the course of months or even years. Kara's battle was immediate. It was personal. It was about being her champion.

He forced that from his mind and came back to the table. Penny Wolff had been found and Evelyn Camp was almost certainly the owner of the pearl necklace. He had to talk to Kara about both of them, along with Jay Kemp, and he had to do it without sounding like a cop.

The guise wore on him.

He sat down across from her. "They found Penny Wolff's body," he said without preamble. "It's on the news. She was found in a cornfield in Mississippi."

Kara stared. Tears came to her eyes. "It's because I went to see her."

"It's because some freak is out there killing people, damn it. You aren't responsible for that." He sat back, reining in his emotions, trying to ignore the sheen of despair in her eyes. "Who is Jay Kemp?"

She blinked.

"I put one of my men on you after you left me in the alley. He picked up the phone after you dumped it."

She sighed. "He's a bouncer at a strip club," she said. "He's acted as an informant for me now and then."

"How much did you tell him?"

"Nothing. Just that I wanted to meet with him and had a job that would pay well. Why?"

"Because when he hears news of your death," Luke lied, "he's likely to come forward to police and tell them he'd just heard from you."

"He won't. The last time he served time was for arson by explosives. He won't want police to know he was anywhere near me."

"Okay." She was probably right. The Bureau had already taken over the investigation into the explosion and the search for the Chandlers' bodies—likely making the APD mad as hell—and reported that portions of remains had been found. Those remains wouldn't be enough to determine a cause of death, though, so for a few days, there would be speculation of murder, suicide, accident. Jay Kemp would be a fool to step up to that.

Of course, none of that had fooled the killer. Not even for a moment.

Luke leaned across the table. "How did the killer get your phone?"

Kara frowned, and Luke realized he'd changed trains of thought without her. "The tracking system. It's an easy thing to activate but he would have needed to have your phone in hand to get it going. Same with Aidan's. Once it was installed, unless you deliberately disabled the location services, it could operate without your ever knowing it."

She shook her head, looking pale and vulnerable and scared. "You're asking if my phone was ever out on my desk, or sitting in my purse, or left on a table. Or if Aidan ever lost track of his or shared his password. I can't even count how many times Aidan has misplaced his; he's a teenager. And mine? I left it at a neighborhood picnic once. I went back later and someone had found it. There was another time I took it to be repaired and left it at the store overnight. God, it could be anyone."

She was right, but Luke didn't want to point that out. She was scared enough as it was. Then she looked at him.

"How would you do it?" she asked.

"Excuse me?"

"You figured out how John Wolff's blackmail happened because you said it's what you would have done. If you wanted to activate a tracking system on a woman's phone, how would you do it?"

Luke tilted his head. "I'd flash a hundred-dollar bill and pay some kid to swipe it. If I needed a reason, I'd tell him—or her—it was because I wanted to surprise you with a message or new app." He paused, leaning back to allow the waitress to place their plates in front of them. He saw Kara glance appreciatively at the food: seared duck on a bed of puréed sweet potatoes with goat cheese, and the blueberry compote. Luke liked to cook. Had the fleeting thought that he would like to be the one to make a gourmet meal for her and put that hungry look on her face.

But he'd have to keep her alive first.

"The app we found on your phone was first activated on Memorial Day of last year," he said. "Any opportunity surrounding that date that you can remember?"

"Memorial Day?" Her cheeks went white. "Dear God, he's been watching me for over a year."

"But he's not anymore," Luke said emphatically. "I'm watching you now."

He wasn't one hundred percent sure there was any consolation in that assertion, but he liked to think so. There might have been a hint of relief in her posture.

"We hosted a Memorial Day party last year," she said. "There were over a hundred people there."

Jesus. That was probably it. "Anyone who might have a personal vendetta against you?"

"The people who come to parties are *friends*. You were better off when you asked about people I've put in jail."

"But those people would have a harder time getting their hands on your phone for a few minutes than someone you socialize with. What about hired help for the party? Caterers, housekeepers, gardeners?"

She thought about it. "I don't know. The people who *worked* the party *weren't* friends, I guess. I didn't know any of them."

She frowned at her own words. Luke tipped his head. "What are you thinking?"

"Nothing, really. It's just that I never wanted housekeepers or cooks or gardeners. It was one of the things Andrew and I argued over. We both grew up with a staff of people all around. We didn't know them; they were just *there*. I never liked it."

"So, you don't have a housekeeper? A gardener?"

"No. I take care of my own house, and yes, I'm the meanest mom around: I make Aidan mow the lawn and do laundry. But for the party, Andrew did hire help. Everything you just said: caterer, cleaning help, florist. There was a DJ and a crew that set up a tent and tables and chairs..." She set down her fork and looked at Luke over their plates. "It could have been anyone."

"Not anyone. We know it's a man. We know he has a personal vendetta against you, so it's someone you've had contact with. We know he has money and a lot of free time."

"How do we know that?" she asked.

"It takes time to have watched you for long periods, to

figure out how to get to your phone and scout someone to do it. Same with Wolff. Stealing that particular car to kill Andrew wasn't just dumb luck. The killer picked a man who had a sick baby daughter, a malleable wife, and a schedule that provided no alibi. My bet is that he took a long time searching out the perfect fall guy."

"Because that's what you would have done?"

"Common sense, not rocket science. He threw ten thousand dollars in cash at John Wolff, and if Elisa Moran had pulled through, he would have had to be ready to keep paying Penny for her silence. Not to mention whatever it cost to incite a riot inside the prison."

"He had to have help with that. We have to find out who. We need access to the police, damn it, but I can't risk bringing anyone else into this."

Luke couldn't help a wry smile. "I guess I'm expendable."

She jumped him. "You chose to put yourself in the middle of this. You broke into my house and demanded to know *why* I wanted to disappear and then kidnapped me and my son. You've made it eminently clear that you have as big a stake in finding Andrew's killer as I do. So don't you dare blame me for the fact that you—"

"You're sexy when you're angry; do you know that?" he asked. He had to put an end to her misery. It was too tempting to console her. "I came to that conclusion at the first deposition you conducted for my murder case, and you proved it again when you gave me hell in that alley. *Hot*." He leaned toward her over the table. "And now, you're even a brunette."

The fire in her eyes turned arctic. "Save it for some blushing virgin, Mr. Varón, or for one of the women who works here. I'm not impressed."

"Ouch," he said, and couldn't remember the last time

he'd wanted to kiss a woman so badly. Against every sane warning, he gave in to an impulse. "How long has it been for you?"

"Excuse me?"

"You were married in name only. So, how long has it been since a man made love to you the way a man should?"

"Not long enough."

Luke's heart sprang a leak. He wouldn't mind being the one to erase whatever bad memories she had of Andrew. Wouldn't mind that one bit.

"Can we get back to the point, please?" she asked. "A prison guard. Maybe someone on staff at the prison made a big deposit to a bank account, or bought a new car or took a vacation. Something like that." She tossed down her napkin. "Damn it, we need the police. They have no idea about the boxes I received or the text messages or even the fact that John Wolff was innocent. They don't know that Louie's death is related to Penny's. They need to know what I do."

"So call someone. You have friends in the APD. Oh, wait. There's one fewer now."

She blanched, and Luke felt cruel. But he needed for her to remember that she didn't dare come out of hiding. He needed her to confide only in him.

"Kara," he said, and just about lost his breath when she looked up. The commanding prosecutor was gone. A wounded woman looked back at him. She was alone and scared and vulnerable.

She was fucking beautiful.

"I'm not the police and I'm not your friend," Luke said. "You've made it rather clear you don't want me as your lover, though I haven't given up on that one yet. But you have to trust me. I'll find him. I can do things the police can't."

She peered at him. "Using those two gorillas downstairs?"

"Careful. Gorillas are sensitive creatures."

"Then why aren't they up here, talking to us about the case, getting the details?"

"Knutson will give them the details. Besides, they aren't allowed up here. This floor is restricted. You have to be sponsored by one of the elite to have the privilege of eating Grayson's duck. Which I notice you've quit doing. Finish up. You need the strength."

She looked flabbergasted. "Sponsored? You're a known drug cartel henchman who was charged with murder. Who the hell would sponsor you to a place like this?"

He couldn't have scripted it better. Just as she asked, the one person in the restaurant who might recognize her as Kara Chandler got up from a far table. Luke sat back, tipped a salute to him from across the room, and watched the man toss his napkin on the table and start toward them. Kara noticed, turned to see to whom Luke had waved, and sucked in a gasp.

"*He* did," Luke said.

CHAPTER
29

K ARA'S BREATH CAUGHT. A man approached their table, his eyes on Varón.

It was Gene Montiel.

Gene Montiel? Her thoughts scattered, like a dozen birds trying to find a place to light. Dear God, she'd met him. He could recognize her. But then another, even scarier thought kicked in.

Who sponsored you?

He *did.*

She swiveled her gaze back to Varón as Gene Montiel headed their way. Varón looked utterly impassive, but for a well-worn patina of arrogance. "Relax, lover. He'll expect me to introduce you."

She stared, feeling as if her heartbeat were slogging through mud. *You don't work for the new cartel. You're trying to take it over from Collado.*

Ben Archer was right: Luke Varón *was* in cahoots with Gene Montiel.

TMI, Counselor.

Varón stood, extending a hand. "Gene," he said. "Nice to see you."

Montiel smiled and they shook. Kara took a sip of her water just to keep from looking at him straight on. *Krista Carter, from Lexington, Kentucky.* Remember how you looked in the mirror—nothing like Kara Chandler. And remember where you are: The Parthenon. Not a place Kara Chandler would have ever visited. Montiel would never expect to see her here.

Andrew, of course, was a different story. Dear God, he and Montiel had probably discussed Andrew's contract with HomeAid right here in this very room, over seared duck.

Montiel nodded at Kara. Varón was quick to introduce her. "This is Krista Carter. Krista, Gene Montiel. I'm sure you've heard of him."

Kara set down her glass and shot Montiel a fatuous smile. "Sure," she said. "Wow. Nice to meet you." She wished she had some chewing gum to snap, but had to settle for twisting a short spike of her hair.

It didn't matter. Montiel gave her a barely courteous nod and went back to Varón.

"I thought you might be here last night," he said.

Varón slid his gaze to Kara. "I got waylaid last night." He gave Kara a look that left no room for further questions. She blushed and took interest in a hangnail, assessing Montiel from beneath her lashes. He was just past sixty years old, a little under six feet tall, and slightly soft around the middle. For as long as Kara could remember, he'd been wearing a neatly trimmed beard that was salt-and-pepper like his hair, and he wore round wire-frame glasses that reminded her of Franklin Delano Roosevelt. Despite his obscene wealth, he generally dressed in suits from JCPenney, but tonight he wore a button-down shirt and dress slacks.

The look of a drug lord? The prosecutor in her wanted to scream.

"I want this finished," he said to Varón, his voice low.

"Off-shore tomorrow; distribution starts Monday."

Jesus. They were talking about cocaine. Not in specific enough terms that the conversation could hold water in a court of law, but clear enough, nonetheless. As if it could be lumber or textiles or fruit.

As if an Assistant District Attorney weren't listening in.

Montiel wrung his hands. "What about Andrew Chandler's wife and son? I called one of your people and he wouldn't talk about it. He basically told me to stay out of it."

"I've got my finger on that."

"So I'm told," Montiel said, but he wasn't happy. A lack of faith in his *security officer*? Kara strained her ears, but Varón put his hand on Montiel's arm and the two men took several steps away from the table. Varón was making sure she didn't hear any more.

She tried to process it: Gene Montiel and Luke Varón in an exclusive club together, managing an international drug delivery. Ben Archer was right: The Rojàs cartel was germinating new headquarters in Atlanta. A man named Collado was the apparent head, working through Montiel, whose chief security officer was Luke Varón.

And on top of it all, Luke Varón was planning a takeover.

The conversation was over as quickly as it started. Varón and Montiel came back—Montiel looking barely mollified, although he managed a smile to Kara.

"Glad to have met you, Miss Carter," he said, and Kara said, "Yeah, you too."

And he was gone.

Varón settled his big frame back into the chair, his gaze as dark as coffee beans. A smirk lingered behind his eyes. "Congratulations, Counselor. You just snowed Gene Montiel."

Kara met his gaze dead on. "Congratulations, Mr. Varón. So did you."

His smile faded to half. "Be careful. A little knowledge is a dangerous thing."

Without Montiel's eyes on her, Kara's mind was free to put the pieces together. "Is there anyone else you're 'working' for? I mean, besides both Collado and Montiel."

Varón's gaze darkened, making him appear precisely as dangerous as he was. "You already know I'm not really partners with Collado."

"Which means you're planning what? To kill him the second he comes to shore?"

Again, that chilly curl of his lips. " 'The second he comes to shore' would be too soon. The cargo needs to move to the secondary locations first; I'll want access to that part of the network as well. Actually, I have your husband to thank for putting those routes in place. Along with Macy's, of course."

His words were like a shot of cold water to the face. "Is Macy's still alive?"

"Yes. Not to put too fine a point on it, but things would have been considerably easier for me over the past year if your husband were, too. I wouldn't have killed him, you know, even though I was ordered to."

"By Collado?"

He nodded. "He didn't trust your husband's loyalties."

She could relate to that. "And what about Montiel? Are you really working for him or are you going to kill him in the end, too?"

This time he broke into a full-fledged smile. "I could tell you that, dear, but then I'd have to kill you."

Kara wasn't amused. It shouldn't have surprised her that he was ten shades darker than she'd believed even when she'd spent weeks building a murder case against him and thought she knew every detail. There were so many layers to his character that she felt as if she never knew who she was talking to. For God's sake, he'd sold his allegiance to Frank Collado who—Kara was certain—would never live to see the rewards of his work. Varón had every intention of killing him and taking over the drug ring himself.

And Montiel? He was hovering near the deadly flame that was Luke Varón, and while Montiel was no innocent, Kara had no doubt that he may not know just how hot that flame was.

Kara swallowed. Jesus God, did she? She, too, existed in his shadow these days, and the only difference was that for now, Varón's heat was keeping her safe. The moment she stepped away from him, someone else would be waiting.

TRUTH . . . Look what you've done.

A tremor racked her body. Wasn't there a saying about going from the frying pan into the fire?

"Excuse me," she said, standing. Her knees wobbled, but she nonetheless summoned her sarcasm. "I need to go be sick now."

Varón's gaze narrowed, but he stood. "Restrooms are right over there," he said.

Kara tried to walk with reserve, but inside she wanted to sprint. She had to get away from him. She had to think. She had to call Aidan and make sure he was all right. She had to call Ben. No, she couldn't do that. What would she tell him? *Ben, don't ask any questions, but while I was faking my death to get my son away from the* real *killer of my husband, I found out that there's a shipment of cocaine coming in this week and Montiel knows... And by the way, Ben, now that I've told you, you need to watch your back and your wife's and your kids'...*

She sank back against the marble countertop in the restroom and forced herself to breathe. She pulled out her phone. For the first time, she wondered about it. *You can contact each other. Don't use them to call anyone else.*

Was this phone tapped?

She cursed, feeling like a fool. Of course it was.

She dialed anyway. Aidan answered on the second ring.

"Mom?"

A blanket of warmth wrapped around her. "Yes, honey. I just had to hear your voice."

"I'm okay. I'm in this crazy-big condo with Madelena and this other dude. Vince had to leave for a little while."

Vince.

"Mom?" he asked, and he lowered his voice. "I was thinking after we split up...Maybe we should have a code or something, a way to let each other know we're in trouble. You know? I mean, I get that Varón wants to find Dad's killer and that he needs you to help, but I still don't trust him."

Oh, Aidan, if you only knew. She closed her eyes. Aidan had been her greatest source of comfort after Andrew died, but she'd never seen this protective streak in him. Of course, she'd never been stalked by a serial killer or gone on the run with a hit man, either.

A secret code. The thought brought a sad smile to her lips and she wondered what Aidan thought he could do to help her if she ever used the code, or vice versa. But she didn't have the heart to say it.

"That's a good idea," she said. "What should it be?"

"I was thinking about that," he answered. "How about *Guapa*? Remember her?"

Guapa. Kara's favorite horse while growing up had been an Appaloosa mare named *Guapa*. The word meant 'beautiful.' When Aidan was little, she told him stories in which Guapa was the star.

Aidan had it all figured out. "If either of us ever says her name, then we know there's trouble." He paused. "I'm not sure what we do then, but... Geesh, Mom, I just want to be sure when I talk to you that I can believe you're okay."

"Me, too, honey. *Guapa* it is. God willing, neither one of us will ever have to say it." She bit back the threat of tears. "I need to go, Aidan. Varón is waiting for me."

"Okay, Mom. I love you."

"I love you more."

CHAPTER
30

L UKE MADE HIS WAY across the restaurant and to Lacy.
"Go away," she said as he came up behind her at
the bar, never looking up. "You're bad for business."

"Business is bad? Somehow I doubt it."

She spun on the stool and looked up at him. She had
thick waves of hair dyed a classic shade of red and eyes
that were a touch too blue for nature. She was built like
Marilyn Monroe, only better.

"You're deterring the paying customers, Varón."

"I'm a paying customer." He opened his jacket casually
and gave her a glimpse of green. She narrowed her eyes.

"What do you want?"

"I want to know who Andrew Chandler might have
talked about in his last weeks. There's a certain acquain-
tance of his I need to find."

Her mouth fell open. "Him again? He was ages ago."

"Then I hope you have a good memory. It's important.
Anyone whose name you'd never heard before, anyone he
might have been afraid of. Anyone—" He stopped. Kara
came toward him, her chin jutted out. She looked as if
she'd had enough of The Parthenon's subservience.

"I'd like to leave now," she said. She barely gave Lacy a glance.

"Of course, darling," he said, then reached for a ball point pen from a glass on the bar. "Lacy and I were just saying good-bye, anyway." He lifted her hand and scrawled his number across her palm. "Call me."

Lacy frowned, wiping her hand with a napkin. "What for? Jesus, Varón, we went through all this a year ago. You think I kept something from you? You were a madman; I wouldn't have dared. And I don't know any more now than I did then. Andrew stood me up for dinner that night in order to meet the dead woman—Elisa Whatever. That's all I knew then and it's all I know now. Andrew and I didn't spend a lot of our time together talking, if you know what I mean."

Luke ground his jaw. Kara looked as if she'd been slapped in the face. Goddamn it. He had to get her out of here.

He started to take her arm, then remembered Evelyn Camp. He still hadn't asked about her. "Hold on, I forgot something," he said, getting out his cell phone. He found Knutson's text and showed Camp's picture to Lacy. "Have you ever seen this woman before? Her name is Evelyn Camp."

Lacy shook her head; Kara looked completely distracted and he tipped the picture to her, too, as if just being polite and including her in the conversation. The name didn't seem to ring any bells for her. She glanced at the photo but didn't even blink.

"Evelyn Camp," he said again. "From Charleston."

"Sorry," Lacy said, and Luke pocketed the phone. So Kara didn't know her. Unless she was seeing red too much right now to recognize much of anything.

"Okay. Thanks."

He took Kara's arm and guided her out of the restaurant, her nerves crackling beneath his fingers like live wires. Christ, he wished Lacy hadn't used Andrew's name in front of her. He knew the man's affairs were no secret, but it was one thing for a wife to know about them and another for her to come face to face with one of them. Luke would have spared her that.

He kept his hand on her arm and they headed for the SUV. Kara was silent, but he knew she was ready to explode.

When they got to the Escalade, she tried the door handle before Luke hit the key fob and found it locked. She growled and pounded at the door and Luke waited it out, ready to snag her hands if she started breaking any bones, but mostly wishing she would turn into his arms, let him pull her against his chest, and allow him to soothe her.

She didn't. She smacked the window one last time, then spun on him, a plethora of emotions stirring behind the cold green eyes. Anger, hurt, shock, confusion, helplessness. And underlying it all, fear.

"I didn't mean for you to hear that," he said, and meant it.

"He was here. He stood up *that woman* in order to be with the woman who was with him when he died." She nearly vibrated with emotion, and Luke forced his hands to be still at his sides. Touching her right now would be a fool's move.

"I'm sorry," he said.

She flinched at the sound of his voice. She shook her head, as if her mind were clearing a little. "That woman—Lacy—she said you were a madman when you talked to her last year. Why?"

"I told you: John Wolff never seemed right to me for killing your husband."

She hit him with a hearty dose of sarcasm. "Oh, so you were just *passionate* about finding Andrew's killer?"

Luke didn't want to have this conversation. He lifted his hand, stroked the curve of her jaw with his thumb. "I'm a passionate man."

"Bullshit." She pulled back. "Who was Elisa Moran? Your lover?"

He punched the key fob and the lock clicked open. He started to go around the car but Kara grabbed his arm.

"Well, I'll be damned," she said, her pupils darting back and forth between Luke's eyes. "This isn't about finding Andrew's killer, is it? It's about finding Elisa Moran's."

Luke looked at her, feeling the darkness well up inside. "It's both," he said. It wasn't quite a lie, but wasn't the full truth, either. And for some reason he couldn't explain, he felt she deserved more. "Elisa was important to me, yes. But she wasn't my lover."

"Elisa." She looked shocked that she was right, as if she'd taken a stab at something in the dark and hit it dead center. Or maybe she was just shocked at the idea that Luke Varón might have cared about someone once. "Did you love her?"

Luke took a deep breath. "No. I owed her something, that's all. Now get in the car."

He reached past her and pulled the door open, but she didn't get in. "What did you owe her?" she asked. "Damn it, I want the truth."

The truth. It gnawed at Luke's soul. "I owed her my life."

"Truth."

Sasha seized Kara's face and looked down at her. The mighty Kara Montgomery was on her knees, her lips just inches away from him. "I bet you wish you chose that now, don't you?"

She glared at him, her eyes blazing. He had her now. Teenybopper wanting to show off, all because of a lame crush. A few minutes of heaven for him.

He'd take it.

"Use your hands," he said, his fingers tangled in her hair. Tentatively, she laid one hand on the side of his thigh. It barely touched him and yet scalded his skin. He wanted to feel the other hand, too, but it was on the floor, helping her balance on her knees. "Open your mouth, little girl," he said. She didn't, but her hand moved up, closer, and Sasha almost teetered with the feel of it. He closed his eyes and she rose up taller. He gripped her hair in his fists.

"Let go," she said. "Let go of my hair."

Her breath fanned the flame. It washed over him, hot and moist. Christ. She was going to do it. Five minutes of rich-bitch mouth. She's not the one for you, his father had always said. Screw you, Dad.

He groaned and relaxed his fingers in her hair, felt her left hand coming closer to his erection and felt her shift higher onto her knees and closer still, her lips right there and—

Fwshtt.

He turned to the sound and realized his mistake a second too late. The crop swung through the air toward his face. He flinched, but not soon enough, and the leather connected with his nose, the tip slapping his eye.

Sasha yelped. He staggered back with his cock bobbing. A flame burned to life behind his eyelid. He came at Kara, his eyes watering and burning, burning, and she stuck something between his feet—the crop, he realized—and his ankles tangled.

He stumbled, his legs splaying wide, and staggered sideways onto something cool and sharp, straddling it as he fell. Pain stung his groin and in the back of his mind he realized what it was and tried to stop himself, but momentum took him down. His weight sank and blinding, blood-curdling pain roared through him as tiny punctures popped his flesh.

"Aachh," he wailed, but Kara was gone, darting out the door. Guffaws and cheers of laughter exploded around her. The door to the tack room slammed closed and Sasha groaned, sucking air past his teeth, his legs astride the coil of barbed wire. Nausea roiled in his belly.

His left ball exploded in pain, and he thought he might throw up. He looked down, trying not to move. The wire had snagged his inner thigh, his testicle, his rigid penis, and there was one deep hole and scrape across his lower belly. He froze as best he could, desperate not to shift and rip himself further, and from the hallway he heard the giggles and squeals of seven birthday guests and Kara, disappearing outside to the yard.

He clenched his jaw, hissing. Fucking rich bitch and her friends. Laughing at him. Christ, he couldn't move. The barbs were like claws, pinning him in place, but the pain in his scrotum was agony. He swallowed back bile and caught his breath, then got hold of the wire, struggling to get his feet beneath him and pull his weight off the coil, growling in pain as he shifted. Finally, he was free, trails of blood like red magic marker pointing out his blunder.

Sasha sank to the floor, rolling into a fetal position and trying to contain the pain. Worse than anything that had happened on a ball field or in a fight. That bitch. She'd never intended to suck him off. It was all a lie from the moment she'd accepted the dare. She sank to her knees like she was willing, shifted her weight, and asked him to let go of her hair, and he'd been so wrapped up in the idea of Princess Kara Montgomery making him come that he hadn't considered the possibility that she'd set him up. Made him the laughingstock of the party. Would probably run to Andrew and cry rape, or worse, run to Daddy.

That was the thought that made Sasha move. The voices were gone—they'd left the stable. Sasha grimaced from the pain and hobbled over to the utility sink, found a rag and soaked it. He pressed the cool water against his thigh, groin, belly. Blood ran down the inside of his leg. His testicle was on fire.

Fuck her. Fuck Andrew. Fuck them all.

This party wasn't over.

CHAPTER
31

FROM THE PARTHENON, LUKE headed to the luxury Park Avenue condo the Bureau had set up as Varón's primary residence. He didn't want to take Kara there. For one thing, it was bugged out the wazoo—every nook and cranny, including the bedroom and bath. There had been times over the past year when more than a million dollars in cash had sat in his living room, with Beckett and Burke gathered around stacking it into bundles and divvying it up for deposit into one of Montiel's accounts. The FBI had watched and listened to every conversation, collecting the evidence that would put Collado and his men away for good.

For another thing, Luke simply didn't like the place. All sleek and modern and metal—Luke Varón's style. Lukas Mann much preferred the woodsy lodge-style house in the forest. Big windows and lots of skylights.

But that house didn't exist anymore. Some fucker had set it on fire.

Twenty minutes away from the midtown condo, Knutson called with more news.

"They found the place he put his car," he said as Luke

rolled down the highway. Kara's eyes were closed, but he doubted she was sleeping. "He axed up a bunch of tree limbs and buried it about three miles south of your house. Must have hiked in the rest of the way."

"Daylight, with a GPS," Luke said. "No problem for someone in shape."

"Right. He had the car hidden pretty well, but he wanted us to find where it had been."

"What makes you say that?"

"He left a cell phone there, the one he used to track Ms. Chandler."

Bastard. But one little pulse of hope tapped at Luke's chest. "Where was the starting point he used for the directions to my cabin?"

"Turner Field."

Luke's heart fell. The man was smart. And careful.

"That's not all. He also typed a message on the phone. It said, 'Fuck off, Feds. She's mine.'"

A blast of cold slapped Luke in the face.

"Listen, Luke. This guy's enjoying himself. Not only has he made you for a Fed, but he also sprinkled Kara's hair all over the phone. Must have taken a handful from the house."

Luke went stiff. He didn't want Kara to hear these things.

"We're tearing the phone apart," Knutson said. "Maybe we'll find something."

"You won't. The bastard knows what he's doing."

"He's a screwball. Look, the guy from Quantico is on his way. The barbed wire around Penny Wolff's throat was crazy enough to get top billing so they're sending the top guy. Someone with clout."

Meaning some psychobabble expert who would spend

his time analyzing the killer's relationship with his mother instead of catching him.

"So, let him weigh in," Luke said, being careful not to say anything on his end of the conversation that sounded like an FBI agent. "You can feed it to me."

"He's gonna want to talk to Ms. Chandler directly. The horse's mouth." Knutson paused. "Listen, Luke. Your cover is compromised. You gotta bail."

He already had, at least, sort of. "Burke knows I'm heading out for a couple of days with my hot new woman."

"Still, brass thinks you should come clean with Chandler. Bring her in tomorrow morning to brief the Quantico guy."

Luke kept his gaze aimed straight ahead. Didn't like the idea of bailing on Collado, yet if he were honest about it, he'd admit that it would be nice to have Kara Chandler look at him as one of the good guys for a change.

"I'll think about it," Luke said. "Anything on the list?" He was referring to the list of defendants Kara had prosecuted.

"Not yet. But I sent two agents to interview the wardens at Floyd, the prison where Wolff was killed. We got a list of four employees voted Most Likely to Take a Bribe. Three aren't interesting. But one bought himself a houseboat. Said an uncle died and he inherited."

Luke felt a *ping* in the back of his mind. "Why didn't this come out before?"

"He didn't bank the money until just before the boat deal—three months ago. Was smart enough to wait until the investigation went away."

"What's his name?"

"Gibson. The guy we talked to said he spends his weekends on the boat, near Red Top Mountain. I found his slip and put in a call to bring him in. I'll get someone out there—"

"I'll go," Luke said. "I'll have more influence." He meant: *A cartel hit man will be more frightening than a badge*.

"What about Kara?"

Luke thought about it. "Check with Montiel. He owns lodges all over the mountains and lake. I'll use one of those." He could feel Kara tighten at the mention of Montiel. Listening hard. "You'll have to finish up Gibson for me."

Knutson understood. "We'll take him into protective custody after you're done. That way he won't run the risk of getting strangled with barbed wire or shot by a long-range rifle."

Right. That is, if the killer still had a way of knowing what they were up to. Luke couldn't figure out how, since the bastard's tracking system was out of commission now and he hadn't been able to follow him and Kara out of the woods. Still…the guy was good.

Luke wheeled the SUV around and headed north, his blood picking up speed. It was the first lead they had. Someone who'd probably spoken to Andrew's and Elisa's killer.

Knutson said, "After I talk to Montiel, I'll send you the address of a place you can stay. And Luke, once you're there, don't forget the brooch."

Luke almost smiled. Yes, the brooch, nestled between Kara's breasts. "I'm flattered you think it will matter," he said. "Are you with Aidan?"

Kara's head spun to him. Ah, yes: Wide awake. Luke handed her the phone.

"Aidan? Aidan?" She stopped and listened, and her

entire demeanor changed. As if the sun had just broken through. "Okay, honey, good. No. I'm okay, too. I did—I had dinner. You?" Pause. "All right. I'll talk to you soon. Love you more."

Her hand fell to her lap with the phone. She tipped her head back against the seat. Luke reached over and took the phone and stuck it back in his pocket.

"He didn't say '*Guapa*?'" Luke asked.

She glared at him. "You son of a bitch."

"Guess not," he said. He wanted her to know that her phone conversations weren't private. "It was a good idea to come up with a code word. The problem is, it's the wrong word."

"What are you talking about?"

"*Guapa*. What is it? I mean, I know it's the Spanish word for 'lovely,' but what's it to you and Aidan?"

She shook her head, a combination of weariness and frustration. "My father bred racehorses. But he also built a personal stable near the house for the horses he bought me to ride. My favorite was a mare named Guapa. She died when I was fifteen, but I used to make up stories about her when Aidan was little."

Luke could see it: a young, blond-haired mama with the little strawberry-blond son on her lap, telling animated stories about a girl and her horse. "Well, that's sweet and all," he said, "but it's still not a good code word."

"Why not?"

"A code word should be something you can slip into normal conversation, something only the *right* person will understand. If you or Aidan gets in trouble and someone's listening to you—which would be the only reason you would need a secret code—you'd give yourself away throwing a word like *Guapa* in out of the blue."

"Do you have a better suggestion?"

"Yes. When one of you says 'I love you' the other answers with 'I love you more.' I've heard you do it. Is that something you always say?"

Kara thought about it. "I guess so."

"So change it just a little. 'I love you most.' 'I love you madly.' Something an eavesdropper wouldn't pick up on, but you and Aidan would."

She considered it for a moment, then said, "Okay." And a moment later, "Thank you."

Luke smiled. "Courtesy of your own personal gorilla."

"Are you going to tell me what Knutson had to say?"

Luke knew she had dissected the conversation from her end. He told her about the killer's hiding place for the car, the phone he'd left, and the message. He left out the word "Feds." He also left out the hair.

Fucking freak.

"Fuck off, she's mine," she repeated. "That message was meant for you, not me."

"Looks like I'm in," Luke agreed, and was glad for the killer's message. It pulled Luke closer. It would keep the Quantico guy from trying to shut him out.

Brass thinks you should come clean with Chandler. Bring her in and brief the Quantico guy. Knutson's words came back to him. They wanted Luke to come clean with Kara so she could communicate with them as cops. Jesus. Luke wasn't even sure he knew how to be a cop straight-out, but the thought of her dealing with this psycho while he went off to wait for Collado haunted him in ways he couldn't quite comprehend. He tried to reason it away: She was a damsel in distress, and despite years of living by an unsavory code of ethics, there was still some primi-tive, primal instinct that called a man to help a woman in need. Especially when she looked like Kara Chandler. In addition, she was strong and smart and passionate, and as a woman, it was clear she'd been neglected for far too long. Luke would question his health if he didn't want to be the one to break her fast from men—

"Was my husband screwing Elisa Moran?" she asked. Luke's train of thought screeched to a halt.

"No," he said. "It was business between them."

"What business?"

"I don't know," he lied. Some things were off the table. At least for now.

"Did he screw Lacy-redhead?"

Luke blew out a breath. "Jesus, Kara. Everyone has screwed Lacy-redhead."

"You?"

Luke blinked, and couldn't help the smile that formed from the inside out. "Why, Ms. Chandler. Do you have an interest in the status of my sex life?"

"Not if you were the last man on earth. Answer my question."

He shook his head, wondering why it mattered to him that she knew. "I haven't been with Lacy. You heard me earlier. I don't like to share, and Lacy is...generous."

That seemed enough to get her to drop the topic, but a moment later she said, "This killer knows I'm alive," she said. "He's still taunting me and he knows you're involved, and instead of being intimidated by you, he told you to fuck off."

"And?" Luke asked.

"And, nothing. That's the point: There's nothing there. I've been thinking and thinking and thinking, and I don't know what any of this means. I don't know what we're doing. I don't know what I should do next."

"Lucky you have me, then."

She looked at him, and where Luke expected to see insult, he saw something akin to relief. For half a second, he fancied that maybe she *did* feel lucky to have him.

"So, what *are* we doing next?" she asked.

"*You're* going to a motel," Luke said. "A nice little lodge, in fact. *I'm* going to talk to a guard who works at the correctional institute where Wolff died."

She straightened. "I want to go."

"No. He may be a dead end, anyway. It might be nothing."

"Bullshit. If that were the case, you'd be sending one of your gorillas to talk to him." She paused, crossing her arms over her chest. Luke might have spared a thought to wish she weren't quite so smart, except that the gesture did such nice things for her cleavage he was momentarily distracted. "How did you find him?" she asked.

"This afternoon, Knutson sent someone to talk to some prison guards at Floyd County Correctional Institute, where Wolff died. He's also been working through the list of names you gave me earlier."

She was staring at him again, studying him like a strange species of life she didn't understand. He was talking too much like a cop.

"What's the matter? Did you think Burke and Beckett were my only gorillas?" He gave a dry chuckle. "It's no surprise law enforcement can't make headway into drug cartels. You said yourself that my network is better organized, better trained, better financed, and better armed than anything the police can muster."

"Not to mention that if anyone gets in your way, they lose their kneecaps."

"Again with the kneecaps." Luke stifled a smile. "You

may not like my reasons for wanting to find your husband's killer. You may not like that in doing so, you're helping me lure in Collado. But you know I'm good."

"Louie Guilford was good, too," she said, and Luke could hear the grief in her voice. "And by this point after I went to Louie, he was dead. So was Penny Wolff."

Luke conjured up a half smile. "Worried about me?"

She looked down. He wasn't sure what she was thinking about, but he could tell the effort to lighten things up had been lost. She swallowed hard. "My son might have been killed this afternoon, if not for you. That isn't a debt that will be quickly forgotten."

An emotion Luke didn't recognize swelled in his chest. So, she owed him something now. And just how many of his sins would saving Aidan forgive? Would it forgive his having made her a widow? He hadn't been driving the car that killed Andrew, and he hadn't completed the hit. But he might as well have.

He sharpened his voice. "I'm nobody's hero, Kara. It would be unwise for you to think of me that way."

She looked at him, a wrinkle between her brows. Wisely, she changed subjects. "This guard at the prison. Do you think he knows how the riot got started?"

"Or played a role in starting it himself." He told her about Gibson buying a houseboat. Could feel her energy pick up. It was that same *ping* he'd felt.

"You have to take me with you," she said. "This is about me. I might hear something that you won't understand."

Luke's jaw hardened. "Counselor, I'm not a cop. My 'interviews' are a little different than what you're used to."

"Do I smell a tire iron and kneecaps?"

"What if you did?"

She drew a deep breath through her nose, and Luke

could feel the wheels turning. "Someone killed my husband and my friend, and is taunting me with the deaths of others. Today, he shot at my son. If this Gibson knows who did it, I'm not going to quibble about how you convince him to tell us who he is."

"Why, Counselor, I do believe I'm a bad influence on you."

CHAPTER
32

SASHA DUG. He spent all evening on it, pushing through the carefully raked layers of stall bedding, removing the rubber stall mat and sawing through the floor, then removing chunks of Georgia red clay one stubborn wedge at a time. When he finally had a hole big enough, he bullied the stiff, disgusting body of Megan to the edge and straightened.

He remembered the token just in time. He bent down and yanked a plastic barrette from the back of her head, ripping out a small tangle of hair along with it. Good enough. The hair would be a nice touch.

He rolled Megan into the hole and pushed the clay on top, replaced the flooring and the pine bedding. Tomorrow, he'd have to do something about the flies. Montgomery Manor had been pristine—kept that way by people like Sasha. He wouldn't let its replica be any different.

He put his tools away in the tack room, showered, and dressed. Looked at the cot that had served as his bed for the last several months. Jesus Christ, the three hours of sleep he'd grabbed this morning hadn't been enough and he felt like he was working through a fog of exhaustion. But there was one more thing to do before tomorrow.

He went to the storage rack across the back wall of the tack room, pulled a bucket off a shelf. Reached inside for the last nameplate.

It was wooden, the size of a license plate, and decorated with a wood-burning kit like the one Sasha had bought for himself when he was thirteen. He'd been assigned the task of making all eight nameplates for the stalls at Kara's birthday party—assigning each guest a horse—and instead of just using magic markers or paint, he'd dug out his old wood-burning kit and stayed up late every night for three days trying to make them special, burning the names into the wood in cursive letters and adding a border to each one. A couple of them, he'd had to re-do two or three times to get them looking nice enough for Kara Montgomery's birthday.

Kara hadn't noticed.

Now, the other nameplates already hung on the appropriate stall doors, their occupants long ago buried. Evelyn Camp had been the first, and now, Megan was the last.

Except for Kara, of course.

Sasha burned Megan's name onto the final nameplate, taking care with the lettering, the smell of burning wood filling his nostrils. He smiled and hung Megan's nameplate on the nail, then gave her stall a once-over and treated himself to a walk-through of the rest of the stable. Evelyn, Jessica, Anthony, Laura, Matthew, Megan. He was proud of having found them all, especially the ones with not-so-common names.

And, of course, Andrew. It was a little disappointing that Andrew's body wasn't actually buried here but frankly, at that point so early in the process Sasha simply hadn't planned it quite well enough. He hadn't predicted that Andrew would be walking with some woman the night he was struck down, and hadn't planned for a way to retrieve the body. The best he'd been able to do was get out of the car long enough to make sure Chandler wasn't going to make it and grab his sunglasses. Sending the glasses to Kara on the anniversary of Chandler's death had been a nice touch, but it had always bothered him to have that stall empty.

Recently, though, he'd decided on a way to handle that. He would put Aidan there. Had thrilled in sending Kara *that* hint.

He drew a deep breath, realizing for the first time that Kara's little stint with the FBI had changed the game irrevocably. Her kid would be under lock and key now. It would be next to impossible to get him.

Bitch. She'd fucked him over yet again. Some things never change.

He bit back a pang of anger and pulled Megan's barrette from his pocket. Kara may have forced him to alter his plans a little, but the party was still on. The truth awaited.

He boxed up the barrette and lettered the last horse-card. Not *TRUTH* like all the others. Kara's actions necessitated a change. But that was all right. Sasha might have lost the tracker; he might not know precisely where Kara was right now. But he did know how to get this gift into her hands. Courtesy of her own personal bodyguard.

Surprise, Kara. You aren't as good as you think you are.

You never were.

The Landing was a privately owned marina just outside the limits of the state park at Red Top Mountain. Knutson had sent Luke what they knew about Gibson: His name was Ronald. He was twice-divorced with one child from his second marriage. He was forty-eight years old and had been a guard at the Floyd County Correctional Institute for sixteen years, paid alimony to both wives and child support to the second. He'd rented a slip at The Landing for wet storage of his houseboat since the end of March and rumor had it that he came here every weekend. Sometimes with friends, sometimes with a woman, but most often alone. Fished. Drank. Listened to heartbreak-and-blame country music.

Luke pulled into a gravel lot, parked the SUV in the corner farthest from the security light, and got out. The air was heavy and hot and smelled of gasoline and charcoal grills, with a thin layer of algae drifting up from the water's edge.

A half dozen cars speckled the lot. Saturday night, late enough that the day boaters had already gone in. Those cars that were left belonged to the people with houseboats, or people with friends who had houseboats, out on the water for the weekend. Luke glanced to the dock where about twenty slips stood, most of them empty, with one small houseboat just now maneuvering into one of them.

Gibson.

Luke walked around to the back of the SUV, glancing around for the surveillance team Knutson would have in place. In the trees, on the water, on the trails. He didn't see anyone, but knew they were there.

He opened a hatch beneath the trunk. Kara joined him and he couldn't resist. He pulled out a tire iron and handed it to her.

"If he gives us any trouble, I'll let you do the honors," he said, deadpan.

She rolled her eyes and he pulled out a set of guns: a

Smith & Wesson 500 with a ten-and-a-half-inch barrel, a pocket-sized .22, a 45-caliber Les Baer 1911, the G18 he'd carried in the alley. In the end, he tucked the Baer into his belt and settled for a Wusthof boning knife in his hand—a knife with a narrow, seven-inch blade that could slide through a salmon like butter. A public marina wasn't a good place to start spraying bullets, even if there weren't too many civilians around right now. There would be at least two: Kara and Gibson. Gibson, he imagined, wouldn't be too much of a challenge, given what information Luke was about to lay on him. But if he had friends aboard, or if there were bystanders on one of the other boats... There had been enough killings in this thing.

He turned to Kara. The darkness concealed her expression, but he could sense the tension in her body.

He held out his free hand and she gave him back the tire iron. "Jerk," she said as he put it back in the car.

He looked down at her. "You're right that you might hear something that I won't understand. But I want you to listen, and that's all."

"I'm a prosecutor. I know how to get information out of defendants."

"You're not a prosecutor here. You're my girlfriend," he said with finality. He reached out and drew her toward him, crowding her back up against the wall of the car. "And it's time you act like it."

CHAPTER
33

H IS HEAD CAME DOWN. Kara gasped but his mouth smothered it, and she started to push back, then realized he wasn't forcing her. He eased in close, his knife hand bracing against the top of the SUV while the other came to her cheek, warm and strong as his fingers threaded into her hair and he tipped back her head to better receive his kiss. A second later, she heard voices, people climbing up the path from the dock, their laughter choking to a halt when Kara and Luke came into sight.

Act like it.

Reality struck: *It's an act.*

Her limbs loosened, her lips softened, and she gave in to the kiss. Varón slanted his mouth over hers, warm and mobile, and he pressed her against the hot metal of the SUV, marauding and suckling, the very scent and taste of him invading her senses. Frissons of sensation stirred to life at the center of her body. In the distance, the crunch of gravel changed direction—the intruders cutting a wider swath—even so, Varón didn't stop. His tongue slipped out and traced the crease of her lips, seeking entrance.

A spear of sensation shot straight between her legs.

Kara parted her lips and Varón was right there—filling her, possessing her, a tender, insistent invasion that made her knees wobble as his hand slid the length of her spine and pulled her close. She heard what might have been car doors opening and closing, then the hum of an engine coming to life, but the sounds didn't matter. Her heartbeat deepened and her nipples rose against his chest, and when she reached up to grasp his shoulders, his muscles flexed and strained beneath her fingers. A groan resonated in his throat and his free hand smoothed down the side of her rib cage, his thumb brushing the outer curve of her breast and setting loose a cyclone of sensations whirling in her belly. Sensations she hadn't felt for . . . forever.

His tongue left her mouth and he suckled her lips, then nuzzled her face to the side and trailed a path of fiery kisses down the curve of her jaw and up again. He stopped in the hollow just below her ear.

"They're gone," he whispered, his breath fanning warmth over her ear.

Kara went still. *It's an act*, her brain chanted, and embarrassment soared in. She sank back against the SUV, unsure if she could stand on her own. He'd robbed her limbs of strength and her mind of every last thread of cognition, sucked the oxygen right out of her lungs. For one, steamy moment, she'd forgotten about feeling afraid and exhausted and confused, and instead had just been *feeling*. And for one insane moment, she'd wanted to let him keep going. Keep supporting her weight, keep shielding her from the world, keep kissing her as if he wanted to swallow her whole. Even now, after his proclamation that they were once again alone, his lips still breathed kisses against her temples as if he, too, was reluctant to let it end.

"Okay," she breathed. "Then back up." She slid her

hands over his arms and laid them flat against his chest, a hot wall of iron. She managed to form a thought in spite of the craven lust that had left her feeling hollow and damp, and exerted just enough pressure that he straightened to allow an inch of space between them. His thumb grazed the corner of her mouth, his gaze snagging there.

"Good work," he murmured, and brushed his lips against her temple. "Very convincing."

She blushed deep red, grateful for the darkness. "I know how to act," she said, and he finally stepped back.

"Apparently so."

And that was that: a kiss that just about knocked her off her feet, from a murderer who held her life and her son's life in his hands.

And for a moment, she hadn't minded at all.

Kara's throat went dry. Hit man, drug dealer, kidnapper. Lover and actor. Protector. She remembered the way he'd safeguarded Aidan and, for one fleeting moment, wondered if he actually cared about keeping her safe as well.

Well, of course he did, she reminded herself. He needed her to find Elisa's killer and keep Collado coming.

Sounds drifted up from the water and she pushed that thought away. They turned and saw a figure tying off a houseboat—a thick man whose silhouette yanked the ropes tight and knotted them. Kara straightened: This was the man who might know who killed Andrew.

Varón moved back to the front of the car to close the driver's side door, and an impulse surfaced. Kara reached into the back of the SUV and grabbed the little .22, stuck it into the waistband of her panties and tugged the dress back over it. It was too heavy to hold by itself and made a bulge, but it was dark and so long as she pressed her arm against it from the outside, it would work.

The man on the dock started up the ramp. Varón came back and Kara slammed the back of the SUV closed. He took Kara's free hand.

"It's showtime again," he said.

The man from the boat came up the dock in a hurry— head down, moving fast, car keys jingling in his hands. Varón led Kara across the parking lot, started down the lane, then stopped, herding her off to the side behind a bench.

"Get down," he whispered, and hunkered down beside her. "When I go, stay here. Let me handle him."

Kara didn't argue: Varón was probably masterful at getting people to talk. And she wasn't feeling charitable enough toward Gibson to be interested in sparing him whatever Varón had in store.

Varón lifted the knife handle, weighing it, waiting. When the man hopped off the dock and onto dry land, Varón stepped into his path. Held the knife up between them.

"Christ," Gibson said, skidding to a halt. He glanced around, then lifted his hands to shoulder height. "Fuck, I don't got no money on me."

"That's all right," Varón said, his voice rich and low. "It's not your money I want."

"Come on, come on." Gibson started to whine. "Let me go. I got a call. My house got broke into. I gotta go."

"Your house is fine," Varón said. "The call was from my colleague."

Gibson blinked in surprise. So did Kara.

"What? Nothin' stolen?"

"Not that I know of. I needed for you to come ashore, that's all. I wanted to have a chat."

Now Gibson straightened and took another look around. No one else. "Who the fuck are you?"

"My name is Luke Varón. Perhaps you've heard of me."

Gibson frowned. "No."

"Well, that's okay," Varón said easily. "I'm not insulted. I'll just fill you in with a little bedtime story. Once upon a time, there was a drug cartel in South America and it came to Atlanta. Luke Varón was positioned to be its chief. Varón was an amicable fellow, so long as he got his way. But when someone crossed him, he could be...testy." He paused, running a finger along the edge of the blade. Gibson started to fidget.

Kara didn't blame him. It was impossible to reconcile the man just now talking to Gibson with the man who'd kissed her a moment before. This wasn't the man who'd set butterflies free in her belly with a stroke of his tongue, who'd reminded her what a kiss could feel like and made every fiber of her traitorous body long for more. This was the man who killed for a living and was planning to hijack a drug cartel.

"This cartel boss, Luke Varón—that's me, remember—had reason to believe a man named Ronald Gibson—that's you—had fucked around in the cartel where he didn't belong."

"I didn't," Gibson said, frantic to find an out. "I never been involved in no drug cartel, I swear."

Varón twisted his wrist and made a figure-eight in the air with the tip of the blade. "Do you know why I like this knife? It's honed to perfection." He toyed with it. "Perfectly balanced, with enough flexibility to maneuver delicate cuts. You know, like when you're removing the silverskin from a good tenderloin."

Gibson began to shake. "I'm not lying. Man, don't do this—"

Varón took one step closer. "Tell me where you got the money for that nice houseboat, Ronald. And don't give me some sad story about a rich uncle dying because the only uncle you have is a janitor at a hospital in Indianapolis, and the last I checked, he was alive. Of course, that was about an hour ago. Things could have changed."

Kara's skin tightened. Holy hell, how did he know that? *The cartels are better organized, better trained, better financed, and better armed. Not just with firearms, but apparently with computers, too.*

Even though she had known that in her head, she was daunted every time she saw it in action. With the flip of some internal switch, Varón could become an entirely new character. He could turn on the drug-lord persona and scare the devil himself back to hell. A moment later, he could turn on the hero persona and throw his body between a child and wild gunfire.

And in yet another moment, he could turn on the lover and kiss a woman's knees out from under her.

A shiver ran over Kara's skin. She licked her lips, the sensation of his kiss still lingering there. For God's sake, she had to forget it. Varón was a monster. Just ask Ronald Gibson.

Varón walked toward Gibson with measured steps. When he was barely more than an arm's length away, he stopped. "The money," he said. "The boat. And you'd better hope I like your story."

"I can't." Gibson sank to his knees.

Kara was shocked.

"You *can't*?" Varón parroted, putting voice to Kara's thoughts. "You mean you'd rather get carved up like a filet than tell me where you got the money to buy that boat?"

A sob racked Gibson. "Shit, if it's not you, it'll be him."

Kara stiffened. *Him*. Gibson knew who the killer was. He knew who killed Andrew and Louie and who'd been terrorizing her and her son.

"Who?" Varón asked. "Who paid you to stage the riot that killed John Wolff?"

Gibson hung his head. Varón circled him like a shark.

"How many inmates were in on it?"

Gibson closed his eyes.

"When was the last time you talked to him?"

"Ah, God..." Gibson whined again.

"Tell me a name, Ronald."

"Just leave me alone—"

Kara had had enough. She stepped from behind the bench. "No," she snarled, heading straight down the path to Gibson. "We won't leave you alone." She held both elbows locked in front of her, aiming the gun at his nose. Gibson looked up as if disbelieving that this could have gotten any worse; Varón looked at her over Gibson's head like a panther eyeing his next meal.

"Krista," he said, his voice a warning, but Kara kept walking. She curled her lip at Gibson.

"Varón left out part of the story," she said. "It's the part about the crazy woman who doesn't believe in giving warnings and doesn't like second chances."

"I don't know nothin' about that riot."

"Did I mention that the woman is trigger-happy?" Kara asked.

"Krista," Varón said again, then leaned down to Gibson from behind him. "Watch out. She likes kneecaps."

"It was a riot," Gibson stammered. "It's a prison. It happens."

"It was a county facility," Kara snapped. "Minimum

security. The men in Floyd are there for not paying child support and for hiding away their repos. John Wolff was there for drunk driving—an accident. He'd only been there a day and a half. You set that up. I'm not going to bother asking you to admit that because I already know that part. All I want to know is who paid you to do it."

"Ah, God." Gibson continued to shake his head. But he was weakening. Kara knew she'd overstepped known fact: She didn't know for sure that Gibson had anything to do with the riot that killed John Wolff. All she knew was that some other employee at the prison had given his name to Knutson as a possibility, and that he owned a new boat that was incongruous to his salary. But she'd seen too many lies in her career not to recognize it. It was the law of the west: Defendants lied. Witnesses lied. Informants lied. Gibson was no different. He would lie unless he thought they already had him cornered.

Or unless he thought he was about to get hurt.

Kara looked at Varón. She lowered her gun arm. "All right, darling," she said. "Go ahead and have some fun. Don't ruin your shirt."

CHAPTER
34

"WAIT," GIBSON SCREECHED, BUT Varón took Kara's cue seamlessly. He leaned down and gathered a handful of Gibson's shirt at the back. Started to hoist the man up.

"Whatever the lady wants," he said.

Gibson wailed. "Okay, okay," he said. "His name was Alexander."

Kara's heart came to a halt. *Alexander.* Adrenaline washed through her limbs. Her mind raced, trying to match the name to someone who hated her, someone who wanted to terrorize her and was willing to kill to do it. She couldn't come up with anyone. *Alexander. Alexander.*

"Was that a first name or last name?" Varón asked.

"I dunno. I swear. He just said 'Alexander.' He only said it once, when he called to tell me where to meet him. He said, 'This is Alexander,' and then we set it up."

"What did he look like?"

"Big dude. Not so tall, like you, but built wide. Like a gym freak."

"Go on."

"Light. Light hair, but army-short. Almost shaved

clean. Always wore long sleeves. I remember that. It was summer, but he was in long sleeves."

Varón's brow wrinkled. "How did you meet? How come he fingered you to do the prison riot?"

"I dunno." Gibson shrugged a little. "There ain't that many of us to choose from."

"You'd never met him before."

"No. Except he knew me. He knew my hangouts an' stuff."

"Did you ever get in touch with him?"

"No. He always found me."

"When? What times of day?"

"Different ones. Morning, night. Once at the gun range on a Sunday afternoon."

"Like he had an eye on you."

That made Gibson frown. "Yeah, sorta. He was *around*. For a while, anyway. After it was over, I never saw him again. He gave me half the money the day Wolff was transferred in. The other half he left in one of those charcoal grills at a park, the day after. Scared me to death to go pick it up."

Kara worked to even out her breathing. Varón had taken over the interview with adroit questioning that would have impressed a seasoned detective. He fired one question right after another, as quickly as Kara could think them.

The prosecutor kicked in. "How much money?" she asked. "How much was it worth to you to make sure an innocent man got killed *by accident* in a brawl?"

Gibson blinked up at her, still on his knees. He was insulted. "Wolff was a convicted criminal. I needed the money, bitch."

Varón rapped him on the side of the head with the heel of the knife.

"Aachk..." Gibson dropped back. When he rubbed his head, he found blood. "What the fu—"

"That's my woman you're talking to," Varón said. "Treat her with respect."

"The cunt has a fucking gun in my—"

This time Varón kicked him and he rolled on the ground. Kara gaped at Varón, who calmly stepped one foot over the prone body of Gibson and stood straddling him with the knife. "That's not respect. And that's the last warning you'll get."

Gibson quailed, laying back his head.

"Who was the prisoner on the inside?" Varón demanded. "Who cut Wolff?"

"A guy named Pinkham. In for drugs. Got some mental shit. He's crazy."

"How much did you pay him?"

Gibson shook his head on the ground, his mouth working on words. He didn't want to answer.

Varón touched the tip of the knife to his cheek. "And you were doing so well."

Gibson nearly choked on his own breath. "Cigarettes. That's all Pinkham wanted, I swear. I just promised him cigarettes every week until he gets out."

Kara felt sick. "You're telling me he was willing to stab a man in the throat in exchange for cigarettes?"

Gibson shrugged, as much as a man can shrug while slowly curling into a fetal position between Luke Varón's legs. "Some character of his needs them. Like some split personality shit. He *needs* them, man."

Varón cursed. "You're a real sensitive soul, you know that, Gibson?" he asked, then looked at Kara. "Any further questions?"

She swallowed. He didn't follow his question with

Counselor, but she knew that's what he was thinking. She'd taken over the interview as a DA would. Bad for her disguise, worse because Varón had told her to stay out of it.

But she couldn't think about that just now. The truth was, illogically, she was glad Varón had been there. Having him at her side gave her more courage than having the pistol in her hand. "No," she said.

"Okay, then," he said, stepping back over Gibson. He straightened and let his knife hand hang by his side. "Get up."

The man hesitated.

"I don't like to repeat myself," Varón said, his voice dangerously calm.

Gibson got up, seeming to stagger toward Varón, then—

"Fuck you." He lunged, catching Varón around the waist, pinning Varón's knife hand to his hip. Varón twisted and stumbled backward, and Gibson rode him to the ground. The two men rolled and grunted. Kara didn't dare take a shot in the darkness for fear of hitting Varón.

She didn't need to. A minute after it started, it ended: She heard the unmistakable smack of a punch against flesh and Gibson groaned. Varón climbed to his feet and dragged him up. Gibson's nose gushed blood.

"That was a stupid thing to do," Varón said, breathing hard. He held his upper arm with a hand. Kara's heart dropped to the pit of her stomach. She moved closer, angling her view with what little light there was, and her breath caught. He was cut.

"Varón?" she said.

"Not now, Krista," he growled. He never took his eyes off Gibson. A finger of panic touched her heart. She knew about Varón's temper, and Ronald Gibson was about to be at the other end of it. She adjusted her grip on the gun, wondering if she could stop Varón if he decided to exact a hit man's sort of retribution. Instead, he gave Gibson a shove toward the lake. "Walk, you asshole," he said. "Down to the water."

Gibson wavered, then took a couple of steps.

"Not to the dock," Varón said, shoving him in a different direction. "To the water."

Gibson got his feet moving and began walking, whimpering, his knees sagging like a tired six-year-old. Varón herded him down the bank, favoring his right leg, Kara noticed, then stopped and watched him walk through the sand. "Keep going," he ordered, when Gibson hesitated.

Gibson stopped at the water's edge. He was nothing more than a black shadow in the darkness, a silhouette cast by a moon that hung low in the sky above the water. Kara tensed. Dear God. She might be about to witness Varón stabbing this man in the back or putting a bullet in the back of his head.

"I didn't tell you to stop," Varón called to him. "Go on in the water. Farther."

"Varón," Kara shouted. "We need to go."

"I'll be there in a minute, darling," he called over his shoulder, his voice tight with anger. Or maybe with pain. His gait was stiff again but he followed Gibson to the lip of the lake, then watched the man wade deeper into the inky water. Gibson was nearly sobbing now.

Kara held her breath. "Luke, don't. Let him go."

Varón stood like a statue. He watched Gibson begin to tread water, then said, "Stay there for ten minutes. If you come out before then, I'll know because I have eyes all over this lake. Do you understand, Ronald?" Nothing. "I said, do you understand?"

There was a splash and a choked sound that reminded Kara more of a baby than a man.

"I'll take that as a yes."

He turned and headed back up the bank, limping slightly, but releasing his arm. A dark splotch stained his sleeve. When he came to the lane, he wrenched the gun from Kara's hand and took her by the elbow. The anger in his frame was a palpable thing, tension pouring through his fingertips. Despite the faint limp, his strides were long enough that Kara had to jog to keep up with him.

A twig snapped in the woods and she stopped. "What was that?" she asked.

He didn't break stride or bat an eye. "Nothing. Let's go."

I have eyes all over these woods. Varón's words floated through Kara's mind. *Stay there for ten minutes.*

They loaded the weapons in the back of the SUV, Kara searching the edge of the woods. For a moment after Gibson cut Varón, she'd thought she was going to be an accessory to Gibson's murder. But then Varón demonstrated restraint that didn't fit with what she knew about him. She caught him bending his right leg experimentally, saw the slight wince of pain when he used his left arm, and couldn't believe Gibson had lived through the night.

A thought popped in the back of her head like a kernel of popcorn. *Dear God.*

She picked up the keys Varón had set on the bumper. When the guns were stowed away, she held back the keys.

"I'll drive," she said.

"I'm fine," he said, reaching to take the keys.

On impulse, she stuck them behind the brooch in her cleavage. A reckless move on her part and Varón's gaze followed, then he looked into her eyes as if she'd just begun a game he was perfectly willing to play. Screw his injuries.

"Do you really want me to come after those?" he asked.

She swallowed, and their kiss came back to her in a flood of sensation. "No," she managed, but was sure that somewhere deep inside, she didn't mean it. If he bent down to her again right now, smelling of lake water and blood, she wouldn't push him away. "Your leg hurts and your arm is bleeding. I'll drive. Go get in the car."

CHAPTER
35

L UKE WOULD HAVE RATHER gone after the keys, but it was more important to get out of here. The place was swarming with Feds and Luke wasn't sure how long Gibson could tread water.

So, let her have this one.

"Go out the same way we came in," he said, climbing into the passenger seat. He spared a look at his arm. When he was rolling around with Gibson, he'd felt the blade catch his bicep, but the cut didn't hurt as much as his thigh. The bastard had landed on him just right. Between the run from the house and the fight with Gibson, it felt as if Luke's bone was in pieces again.

Kara pulled the SUV out of the parking lot and onto the lane, moving up the hill toward the main road. "What happened to your leg?" she asked.

He tipped his head back against the headrest of the passenger seat. "Took a bullet a couple of years ago. Chipped up the bone."

"Is it still there?" she asked. "The bullet."

"No," Luke said, remembering its removal only through the fog of fever and dehydration and pain: a cell in a Colombian prison, a 50-caliber bullet jammed in his femur, and Luke digging with a stick into the mass of infected, rotting flesh to try to pry out the bullet.

Collado laughing.

"But it still hurts," Kara said.

"Let's just say the surgeon's skill left something to be desired," Luke said, then noticed her turning left. "No. You want to keep going straight here."

"I think I dropped something in the parking lot. I'm going back."

Luke straightened. "Forget it. Let's go."

But she ignored him, making a U-turn and gunning the gas, hard enough to make the tires spin.

"Damn it, there's nothing you dropped that you need to get," he argued, but she picked up speed. Her knuckles tightened on the steering wheel. "What the hell—." But a second later, he knew. "Stop, Kara," he demanded, and when she didn't, he went for the wheel. She swerved, nearly fishtailing off the side of the road but holding on, and he cursed. She stepped on the gas and made it to the rise in the road they had just come over, saw figures of men dart across the road ten yards in front of her, and slammed on the brakes.

Her headlights gave shape to the silhouettes. They carried machine rifles.

She stared down the road where the figures melted into the edge of the woods and her chest rose and fell in great heaves. Luke could almost hear her heart pounding as the pieces of a puzzle fell into place in her mind... A clear-cut murder case against him that fell apart like a house of cards... A District Attorney who, without explanation, suddenly refused to file charges against Montiel in a case he'd been preparing for months... The cell phones and safe houses, the "network" that was so well-organized and well-equipped it rivaled the best police force... Even the tow truck that had blocked her from getting back to her house before he did.

And the fact that he'd protected Aidan and hadn't hurt her.

"Kara," he said, his voice low. He could feel her confusion. She'd suspected already—enough to go back and check. She might have even hoped, especially since he'd taken Aidan away. But discovering it for herself had left her in shock.

"Honey, we need to leave. Let them do their jobs."

She looked at him. Relief and shock and *hope* in her eyes. Her breaths shivered past her lips as if she were trembling with excitement.

"You're one of them?" she asked. It was almost a prayer.

Luke looked toward the lake where he knew a half dozen armed Federal agents were now moving into position to surround Ronald Gibson. He could deny it; she would expect him to, even if she came to believe it herself. And no matter how smart Kara was, he could sell the guise of Varón to her if he wanted to.

But he didn't want to. His work with Collado was over. Except for making sure nothing waylaid the shipment, then flashing his credentials to Collado and watching his face go white with shock as they hauled him off to prison, Luke was finished.

And there was a woman and a teenage boy who needed him. It was a heady sensation.

"FBI," he said, and unfastened his seat belt. "Which means, I drive."

Sasha had to get out of the tack room. The pain was intense, nausea churning in his belly, but he had to go.

What if the little bitch ran to Daddy and told him she'd been accosted by a stable hand? What if her friends put together a story about rape? He'd be tried and convicted without ever getting to tell his side: She *came to* him. *It was a game, and she knew the rules. She'd agreed to them.*

No one would ever believe that.

Fear set in. He tugged on his pants as carefully as he could, then hobbled around the tack room making sure things were back in order....Hung the crop on the wall, threw the bloody towel in the laundry basket, repositioned the coil of barbed wire to appear undisturbed. The burn in his crotch was unbearable—Christ, was the barbed wire rusty? He went back to it and looked. No, of course not. It was shiny new and pristine, like everything else at Montgomery Manor.

He glanced around the room, a grimace twisting his face. Jesus, he hurt. He could feel the moisture gathering in his pants. Blood from pinpricks of barbed wire.

He had to go. Had to get home. Find a doctor? For God's sake, what would he say? "I was trying to make Kara Montgomery suck dick and she pushed me into barbed wire."

He smothered the swell of panic unraveling in his mind, peeked out the door, and waited until there was no one between him and freedom. He bit back the pain and hobbled outside, then hit a run as best as he could until he got to his house. He ran a warm shower and stripped down. Jesus, there were five places the barbs had gone in. Felt like fucking...barbed wire.

Kara. She *did this.*

He cleaned up, forcing himself to use soap though it hurt like a bitch. Just as he turned off the water, his father's voice boomed through the bathroom door.

"Sasha! Sasha. Vystupit."

Sasha pulled back the shower curtain to grab a towel. Shit, what was his father doing he—

"Sasha," he called again, and without warning, the bathroom door flew open.

CHAPTER
36

THE DOOR TO MONTIEL'S lodge opened electronically; the key was right where Knutson had said it would be. Luke held it ajar for Kara and they stepped inside. There were a few perks to posing as a crony of Montiel; this was one of them. High ceilings with the full-length windows and the skylights Luke always wanted, an enormous stacked stone fireplace and gourmet kitchen, fluffy, high-end furnishings. He imagined the bedroom would be equally luxurious.

Wanted to take Kara upstairs and find out.

He pushed that thought away and went to the sink, stripped off his shirt and examined his arm. The cut was about four inches long but shallow, just deep enough to have soaked his sleeve with blood. He used a wet washcloth and cleaned off the worst of it, then tied a towel around his upper arm using his teeth to pull the tail tight. Rinsed his face and hands and turned back to Kara.

She stood on the opposite side of the great room, strung like the highest string of a violin. After a silent, tense drive, she was still uncertain about him, probably running through every event and conversation from the past day and night and trying to color them with the realization that she'd hired an FBI agent—not a criminal—to fake her death.

Luke walked to the edge of the great room, careful to leave the space of the area rug between them. She looked nothing like the warrior who'd gone after him in the courtroom a month ago, or the banshee who'd taken on Ronald Gibson an hour ago. She looked lost.

"What do you want to know?" Luke asked. Quietly, like a hunter trying not to spook a doe.

She lifted her face and tears shone in her eyes. "Where is Aidan?"

"Outside Dahlonega, in a Bureau safe house. Maddie—Special Agent Madelena Baez—is with him, along with an interrogator who specializes in talking to teens. He's safe, Kara. He was never in danger from me." He paused. "Neither were you."

She looked at him, and he could only imagine the confusion in her mind. He didn't know what to do to help her make sense of it. He wasn't accustomed to handling people gently or tending to their emotions. His solution to her uncertainty would be to take her upstairs and blow her mind with orgasms.

Clearly, Kara wasn't thinking of such things. She was a collection of raw nerves. Relief might be in there somewhere, but confusion and anger were, too.

"I wanted to tell you," Luke said, wondering why it mattered to him that she know. "For the first time I can remember, it bothered me to play the part."

She looked at him. "Who are you, really?"

He swallowed, surprised that his true identity was closer to the surface than he could ever remember. "Lukas Mann. I'm from a little Pennsylvania Dutch town in northern Ohio. My brother is the sheriff there and I have a passel of siblings. My mother still lives there."

"Katrin," she said, and Luke felt the tug of a smile.

"Yes."

"How long have you been Luke Varón?"

"A little over a year. He was created for me to come here. Before that, I infiltrated the Rojàs cartel in Colombia. Frank Collado is Manuel Rojàs's nephew. He was the one major player who slipped the net, and just when we thought he'd gone underground, he set up shop in Atlanta."

"Because of Andrew."

Luke shrugged. "And Montiel. His companies provided the venue for money laundering."

"What about the man who died in the warehouse fire? The one you were charged with murdering."

She was still suspicious, but Luke could see it was beginning to make sense. "He was a hit ordered by Collado—a test for me. The DEA had a bead on him. They helped us fake his death and put him in witness protection, then let Varón go to trial for murder for the sake of building credibility." He looked at her. "I'm not really a hit man, Kara."

"So you haven't killed anyone?"

He winced. "I can't say that. But I haven't killed anyone unlawfully."

She held his gaze. "Why FBI? I thought the drug war was the purview of the DEA."

Luke felt as if he was on the stand, being cross-examined. She was leaving no stone unturned. She didn't quite trust him yet. "Mostly. But the FBI handles organized crime. The Rojàs family was into more than just drugs."

"And Montiel? Ben Archer's case against him?"

"Archer was getting ready to bring indictments; we couldn't let that happen with the shipment en route. We shut him down." He cocked his head. "Which brings up an interesting point: the letter you said you have about Montiel." Her cheeks went pink. Luke smiled. There had never been a letter. "That's what I thought. Well played, Counselor."

She looked at him, unable to relax just yet. She was still uncertain, still scared.

Still so fucking beautiful.

"Andrew?" she asked.

And there it was, the heart of the issue. Luke felt a block of weariness weigh him down. "Kara, do you think we could sit down?"

Her gaze went steely. "Andrew," she demanded, still standing on the opposite side of the room. So, Luke was one of the good guys now, but he'd still worked some nefarious scheme with her husband. Who was dead.

"When Montiel got in with Collado, Andrew was a ripe target. He was in financial trouble and—" He stopped. She wasn't ready to hear about Aidan, yet. "Andrew signed on with Macy's, thinking it would solve his problems."

Luke felt as if he were the dispenser of torture. Every word he said seemed to cut a little deeper.

"Why were you ordered to kill him?"

"When the trial routes started running—smaller shipments to put all the players in place—Andrew got cold feet. He wanted out. Collado didn't trust him anymore."

A frown gathered her brow. "So you volunteered to kill him?"

"It was a little more complicated than that, but yes. Collado and I have some...unfinished business. He knows me from Colombia under my previous cover. So Luke Varón was born. Another insider made sure the pictures he saw of me were doctored enough he wouldn't recognize me, and I came on as a reputable hit man with a well-documented history."

She wrapped her arms over her midriff as if a chill had washed over her. "Did you meet Andrew?"

Luke held her gaze. "Yes."

She looked at him with sheer betrayal in her eyes.

"We marked him for an informant, and it progressed from there. Elisa wasn't his lover, Kara; she was the case agent. The night of the accident, they were nailing down the details for him to turn on Collado and come in."

"You were in custody."

"That was the story. I was actually in the same safe house where Aidan is now. Talking to Andrew and Elisa, getting the information we needed and working out a deal for him."

Kara was silent and still, but Luke could see her mind going a thousand miles an hour.

"Andrew did some bad things, Kara, but this much is fact: In the end, he decided to work for us."

"I know," she said, sounding distant. "The night he died, before he left...he was upbeat. He kissed me—for the first time in ages—and told me everything was going to work out. He said he'd screwed up, but said, 'Tonight will change everything.'" She closed her eyes, and after a long moment, looked at Luke again. "He was right."

Luke's heart sprang a leak. "I'm sorry, Kara. Jesus, I'm sorry."

For the first time since they'd entered the house, she looked at him as if she really saw him. The sheen of shock had dissipated. "It wasn't your fault. Andrew was the one who signed on to the deal. You and Elisa were offering him a way out."

"Yes," Luke said. He couldn't account for the degree of relief he felt learning she didn't blame him. He hadn't quite acknowledged how much it meant to him before.

Now, he did. He admitted deep inside that he wanted her to trust him, lean on him, *know* him.

Heady stuff.

She frowned. "So, when I contacted you, you thought it was going to be about Andrew."

"It was a helluva lot more likely than the real reason. I never dreamed a murderer had been stalking you for the past year."

Hearing it put into words seemed to take her by surprise. "Neither did I," she said, then shook her head. "So, this man who's out there now, killing people and threatening me . . . Is he connected to the drug cartel?"

"Honest to God, we don't think so anymore," Luke said, daring to take just one step closer to her. "This isn't about drugs or money. It's some psycho getting off on torturing you. All this time, I thought Andrew's death came from my end but now . . . It looks like the car accident was just the beginning of whatever this killer is doing."

"Alexander," she said, scrunching her brow. "God, I can't place it."

"You haven't had time yet. We'll figure it out. I've already got Knutson running the name."

"What about Ronald Gibson?"

"They took him into protective custody. If the poor man ever recovers from the scare you gave him tonight, they'll squeeze him."

She looked insulted. "You weren't getting anywhere with him."

Luke tried to look stern. Inside, relief poured through his veins: Her spark was coming back. "I was getting somewhere. Just not as fast as you wanted me to."

"A man like that is used to other men wanting something and pushing to get it. A crazy woman flying off the handle is different."

"No argument there."

"I didn't do anything wrong."

"Nothing wrong?" Luke asked. He started across the room, slowly closing the distance between them. "You stole a firearm from a Federal agent, disobeyed a direct order, and might have stopped Gibson from talking or gotten any one of us hurt. You were impulsive and rash and nearly out of control." He stopped right in front of her, drilling her with his gaze. "It was sexy as hell."

Her mouth unhinged and that alone pushed Luke's blood to a faster rate. The pretense was gone. She knew what he was. She didn't blame him for Andrew's death and she wasn't afraid he was going to hurt her or her child. She stood in front of him looking relieved and vulnerable and beautiful, and he wasn't the ruthless drug henchman Luke Varón anymore. He was Special Agent Luke Mann.

"I thought you were steaming mad at me," she said.

"I was steaming," he said, and couldn't help dragging a fingertip down the side of her cheek. "I was mad at first, too. But I forgot that part when you came bearing down on Gibson and I licked my lips and still tasted you there."

The rush of color in her cheeks deepened and Luke tucked his knuckle beneath her chin, letting his thumb brush her lower lip. "I'm one of the good guys, Kara," he said. "You're safe with me."

Her lip quivered beneath the pad of his thumb. Her

eyes filled with a torrent of emotion. Astonishment, skepticism, wonder. Fear, relief, hope.

Desire.

"Lukas Mann," she said as if tasting the name.

"Hopewell, Ohio. Two brothers, one sister, two loving parents. A white picket fence." He stopped. Sometimes he'd barely remembered those things himself. "I want you, Kara," he said, sliding his hands to either side of her face. "I've wanted you since the first moment I saw you."

He bent his head, his lips covering hers with all the tenderness and warmth he could muster, his hands cradling her cheeks as gently as if he were handling a butterfly. The muscles in his arms quivered with restraint and his lips played on hers, her mouth warm and supple, her body both fragile and strong at once. She kissed him back for a moment, then tipped her face toward his and let her lips fall open. Luke crushed her against his body, delving into her mouth with his tongue, drinking her in like the finest of wines. She was sweetness and heat—and an innocence that shouldn't have been there but was. Her body trembled with need and passion untapped for too long, and when he pressed her closer and felt her nipples rub the skin on his bare chest, all he could think about was being the lucky bastard who would take her places her husband never—

"Shit," he said, ripping away. The brooch had scraped his chest. His breaths came short and he set her apart from him, gazing down at that glorious cleavage. He grabbed the brooch and yanked it off the dress.

She gasped, startled. Luke bullied down the need that had his pants tight and his chest beating like a drum, and held the brooch in front of his face.

"Signing off now, Knutson," he said, never taking his eyes off Kara. "See you in the morning."

He strode to the front door. Without a shred of guilt, he hurled the brooch into the woods.

He turned back to Kara, whose shock transformed to embarrassment, then finally melted into a snicker. "I'm pretty sure you just trashed a gazillion-dollar recording device," she said, and Luke closed her into his arms.

"So sue me," he said, and bent his head.

CHAPTER
37

K ARA GIGGLED. *Giggled.* It was such a foreign sound she almost didn't recognize it. She couldn't remember the last time she had giggled. Kara's life had held its share of grief, but all in all, it wasn't unpleasant. She had a child she loved and a successful career; she had friends she enjoyed and money enough for comfort, and for the majority of her adult life, she'd had a husband who was, if not passionate, at least caring and cordial.

And yet: She couldn't remember ever giggling before. And that, in the middle of the most harrowing week she'd ever endured.

Luke stroked the side of her face with a long finger, stepping back.

"I need a shower," he said. "Can I interest you in joining me?"

Kara swallowed. Shyness flooded in. "A shower?"

"This place belongs to Gene Montiel. I'm pretty sure it has a shower."

Montiel. Money launderer for Frank Collado. The prosecutor in her made an appearance and Luke nudged up her chin with a knuckle.

"Let it go, Kara," he said. "It's an international investigation and it has nothing to do with you anymore. Or us."

Us. Warmth washed through her limbs. The idea that she was part of an *us*—and that pairing included not a dangerous drug henchman but a protective FBI agent— made her want to hand him her troubles, sink into his arms, and simply let the FBI handle it. A shameful impulse for a woman who was known for strength and chutzpah and independence. But it surfaced nonetheless.

"I don't know," she said, trying to bully down the ignoble thought. "I'm not the kind of woman who—"

"Who would indulge in a love affair?"

"I have a child."

"He's not here."

"I'm a public official."

"And I'm a Federal Agent. Sounds like a good pairing to me."

She shook her head. Everything had happened so fast she felt as if she'd been in a tornado and it had spun her and spun her and set her down with her equilibrium still reeling. She had to get her bearings back.

"I need to think," she said, and his shoulders sagged a little. He stepped back.

"Well, I need a shower." He tipped his head toward the stairs. "And I'll warn you now that I won't stay there too long knowing you're out here. So whatever thinking you're going to do, you'd better do it fast."

Sasha's father stared at the shower. "Mo bog," he said, and instead of the shock Sasha might have expected, his face twisted with disgust.

Sasha snatched the nearest towel and covered himself, but it was too late. His father slammed his hand to his forehead, like a man who'd just lost everything. A flash flood of emotions rose up in Sasha. Shock. Fear. Shame.

Rage.

His father kicked the bathroom door behind him. "It's true. You? You are the one who attacked the girl?"

Sasha's heart pounded against his rib cage. She'd told. The little bitch had told.

"I don't know what you're talking abo—"

"Do not lie to me." Before Sasha could react, his father's hand yanked the towel away. He gaped at the dark puncture wounds. "What is this?"

Sasha shoved him back and covered himself. "Get the fuck out of here. It's none of your busin—"

"It is my business. It's all of our business what you do with that girl, you understand? Your mother's business and mine." He was furious.

"What is she saying?" Sasha asked. "Kara. What did she say?"

"Nothing, at least I think nothing. I only hear the kids talking—that you maul her and she fought you. They make a pact not to tell. But they will. They are children." He glared at Sasha. "Now you talk, mo syn. Pravda. *Truth."*

Pravda. *Sasha sneered at his father. What the fuck did he care? But Sasha told him anyway and as he did, the color drained from his face.*

"Nyet, nyet," Dmitri said, and actually sank to his knees. "You have no idea what you have done."

"Stop overreacting. You said yourself; she isn't going to tell anyone. Besides, nothing happened. Fuck, I didn't hurt—"

"You don't understand. You have ruined everything."

Sasha frowned. "What are you talking about?"

His father grabbed his shoulders. "We must go. Pack a bag—only what you need. I will tell your mother." He turned away, muttering in Russian. Sasha understood most of it but didn't give a fuck. His father was acting crazy.

Screw him. Sasha knotted the towel he'd been holding and started for the door. "It was a game, you idiot. It would have been nothing, except the bitch shoved me onto a roll of bar—"

His father's hand shot out. Sasha heard the crack before he even realized what had happened, then his cheek began to burn. He touched it, shocked, and felt blood at the corner of his lip. He stared.

"What the fuck?"

His father bore down on him, eyes filled with hatred. Sasha had always known Dmitri hated him; Sasha was his father's American Dream gone wrong. The child they'd come here for was Stefan, Son of the Brilliant Mind and Great Potential, but now Stefan was dead. Sasha didn't appreciate all they had sacrificed to give their children an American education, not like Stefan had. Sasha screwed around in school and didn't study hard enough or work hard enough. He played games like baseball instead of pursuing the academics in which Stefan had shown such promise.

And it was all there now—the hatred and shame and disappointment in his child—burning in his father's eyes, vibrating in his frame. No matter that he was smart and spoke perfect English like his parents had demanded and had a talent for baseball. He was a failure.

"You don't understand," Dmitri said again through clenched teeth. "I know you don't but someday you will. Pack your things. Do not ask questions. If you come with us now—and the girl does not talk—perhaps we can still

save ourselves. If not," he said, "then you will rot in the hell of your own making and I will never spare another breath thinking of you."

Luke left Kara in the great room and climbed the stairs. He had to, otherwise he was going to be too far gone to stop. If she gave him any more—one more kiss, one more sigh, one more *look*—he would be lost.

Christ, he wanted her. He wanted to be her hero. He wanted to be her lover. And for the first time in more years than he could remember, he was a man who *could* be those things.

He walked into the spacious bedroom, groaned at the sight of the softly decorated king-sized bed, and tried to put it out of his mind. Kara needed to think—she'd told him that—and in his experience, a woman thinking too hard wasn't likely to lead to sex.

He turned his back on the bed; he had to get his head together. He unwrapped the arm. It wasn't bleeding just now, but he rooted in a cabinet until he found some gauze bandages in case it reopened. Took inventory of the rest of the drawers—clothes, toiletries, linens—and put his wallet in the nightstand drawer.

Just in case.

Then he checked in with Knutson.

"I was afraid to call you," Knutson said. "Thought you might be busy."

"From your mouth to God's ears," Luke said, then dragged himself back to business. "Is Gibson talking?"

"About a guy named Alexander. But he doesn't know much more than he told you already. You scared the living shit out of him. You and 'some crazy-ass woman with a pistol.'"

Luke smiled. "She was something."

Knutson said, "Our guy from Quantico is here; he's chomping at the bit to talk to her."

"Who is it?"

"Guy named Mike Hogan. Highly educated, good track record. Works with the BAU's elite multiple murders squad."

Luke closed his eyes. He didn't need to hear about Mike Hogan's reputation. "Does he know I'm on the case?"

"You're not 'on the case.' And all he knows is that the main target of the killer he's supposed to catch is hiding out with an undercover agent in cahoots with the DEA. He doesn't like it."

Luke cursed. Mike Hogan. It had been a long time. "Kara's beat. She's staying in hiding one more night. Tell Hogan we'll meet him in the morning."

"She gonna be any more rested then?" Knutson asked, then changed his tune. "Never mind. Listen, I've got two things for you. First, we traced the phone used to send Kara the picture of Penny Wolff. Its GPS put it somewhere near Garters' Bridge over the Chattahoochee River."

"He dumped it."

"Probably. It looks like he's never used the same phone twice. My guess is that every time he sent Kara a text over the past year, he trashed the phone right after."

"So there are a bunch of cell phones in rivers all over the place."

"The second thing is bigger: We found a missing male, thirty-four years old, in Chattanooga. His name is Anthony Fietti. His friends called him 'Tony.' He worked the eleven-to-seven shift at a refrigerator plant and got home every morning at seven twenty. Three times a week, while his wife was getting the kids ready for school, he went for a run in Eastdale Park, about a half mile from his house. One morning six months ago, he never came back from his run."

Luke straightened. Wasn't sure where this was going but knew Knutson well enough to know it was important. "And?"

"His wife's name is Gina."

Luke's pulse kicked up. "The engraved pen."

"I've got a pair of agents going to talk to the wife first thing in the morning. They'll find out if the pen was his."

It was. Luke could feel it. "Find out if they know anyone named Alexander. Find out if Tony had a coke habit, or if he knew John Wolff—"

"Luke." Knutson was frustrated. Didn't need to be told what to do. "I'll handle my end. You handle yours. I'll send you what we know about Fietti. See if Kara knew him, or why he might have been a target. If so, maybe we can get a line on who those other things belong to. Maybe figure out what this asshole Alexander is trying to do."

"He's trying to torment Kara Chandler. That's what he's trying to do."

"Then get her to name him so we can figure out why. I'd rather not get another picture like the one of Penny Wolff."

Right. God, he didn't want to lay this on Kara right now.

"Is Aidan talking?" he asked.

"Not yet," Knutson said. "Maddie's working on him, and a guy who's been debriefing him over pool cues and video games. He's been tight-lipped so far but he'll come around. He's just scared. And he's worried about his mom. He says he doesn't trust you."

Smart kid, Luke thought. He hoped when Aidan learned what Kara had, he would change his tune.

"And what about Collado?" he asked, knowing that the drug case would now roll forward without him. They didn't need him anymore. In fact, now that Kara knew who he was and her stalker had ID'd him as a Fed, he didn't dare go near that drug ring again. If anything tipped off Collado now...

"He's offshore. They're moving the load tonight, and it should be at Macy's by tomorrow." Knutson paused. "It's in the bag, Luke. You gotta let the team finish and take care of Chandler. Mike Hogan is still reading up on the case and getting up to speed, but when he saw that message on the phone from the woods, he said one thing was certain."

"And that is?"

"This killer has something specific in mind for Kara. And he's not going to let you get in his way."

CHAPTER
38

THE ALARM ON SASHA'S watch went off at midnight. He jumped to the sound of it, sat on the edge of the cot for a minute gathering his bearings, then turned on the light in the tack room. Remembered the status of his plan.

Smiled.

The stable was finished—Megan was finished, her nameplate now hanging on the final stall. Only the last gift had yet to be delivered, and Sasha knew just how to do it. Kara's bodyguard thought that by changing her appearance and taking her on the run, Sasha wouldn't have any way to send her things. Maybe even thought he would stop killing.

He was about to prove the son of a bitch wrong on both counts. He'd even had time for a couple hours of sleep first.

Now, he pulled on a fresh pair of jeans, a long-sleeved black shirt, and a pair of loafers. Looked in a mirror that hung on the back of the door: a little old for the club scene near a college, but he'd do. His hair barely showed—shaved close and blond, at that. He had a couple days of beard that softened the angles of his face. He didn't usually like to go unshaven, but his schedule these past few days had been crazy. He turned this way and that in the mirror, decided to keep it. He went to the corner of the room where he'd built a hideaway for a safe, and punched in the code. The door sprang open.

He helped himself to a few hundred-dollar bills. Didn't think he'd need that much, but occasionally, he'd found it handy to have enough change on hand to hire someone else to do a deed for him. Like getting Kara's phone in his hands a year ago to install the tracker. *That* had been a piece of cake. The kid, Aidan, had had a group of friends at their Memorial Day party, and there was one who was perfectly willing to go in on a little practical joke for the host and hostess. Only cost Sasha fifty bucks and the price of a workshirt, to allow him to look like the hired help.

He couldn't think of any reason he might need extra cash tonight, but he took four hundred dollars anyway. In case a pretty girl caught his eye...

He drove the Lexus instead of the van, parked right in front of the club where Megan had worked instead of down the back alley like he had the night before. He strode through the front doors like any other single man looking for a place to check out some ass, except that he carried an extra special tip in his pocket.

And an extra special message for Kara.

Kara closed her eyes and let Varón—*Mann*—walk away. She watched him climb the stairs to go take a shower, heard him talk on the phone for a few minutes, then heard the water start. Imagined it running down his body and found her imagination spinning out of control. *Can I interest you in joining me?*

Oh, yes.

A shiver raced through her limbs and she muttered a curse. Dear God, had it really been only twenty-four hours since she'd propositioned Luke Varón? She scrolled through events in her mind... Blowing up the boat and going to Varón's "cabin" for new identities, running from a shooter and sending Aidan with Knutson, meeting Varón's cohorts at The Parthenon and tracking down Ronald Gibson at the marina. She could hardly fathom how much had happened in the one night and one day since she'd hooked up with this man. It seemed like she'd been on the run with him half her life.

And all that time, Luke *Mann* had been protecting her, helping her, keeping Aidan safe.

FBI. She almost couldn't believe it, and yet, in some tiny corner of her mind she'd imagined and hoped and even prayed that his unwillingness to hurt her was more than a fluke. There had been times she'd wondered—the ease with which he made things happen, little touches of concern that seemed out of character, fleeting moments when she'd felt she could trust him. But it wasn't until she'd watched him field Ronald Gibson's reckless assault—fearing that she was about to witness the legendary wrath of Luke Varón—that the truth hit her, like a brick between the eyes. Varón hadn't threatened Gibson's family. He hadn't beaten him or drowned him and hadn't... well, broken any kneecaps.

That thought actually made her smile. Relief flowed into her body and loosened her limbs. He was a Federal agent. He was keeping Aidan safe.

He would keep her safe.

I want you, Kara. I've wanted you since the first moment I saw you.

She took a deep breath, looked at the stairs. She was

no sex kitten; she didn't have affairs. She had a career and a son, and until a year ago, she'd had a husband. It didn't matter that her love affair with Andrew had been short-lived; they'd married for Aidan's sake and they'd both agreed to stay that way. And it hadn't been a marriage without love: There was Aidan, and a beautiful home and two successful careers. There had been a number of good meals together and family excursions and holidays. Their marriage hadn't lacked good times.

What it had lacked, Kara knew, was *heat*. The kind of head-spinning, heart-racing heat that Luke Mann set loose in her belly with barely more than a look in his eye or the touch of his hand. Kara had always known it was missing in her marriage, but accepted it as the bed she'd made for herself one reckless night fifteen years ago. She was content to lie in it. It could have been worse. She'd had a home, stability, a child.

No heat.

Her phone vibrated and she jumped. God, it was Aidan.

"Honey?" she said, and just hearing his voice brought so much joy she nearly wept with it. Dear God, she wanted to tell him he didn't have to worry about her anymore. She wanted him to know the people surrounding him were the good guys, not the gorillas of a ruthless drug henchman. And yet, she couldn't—at least not until Mann told her to.

They chatted for a couple of minutes. He was fine. He was safe and comfortable. He was talking to one of Varón's men—giving them as much as he could remember about receiving each gift, trying to help.

He was talking to FBI agents. Thank God.

Before they signed off, Kara told him to think about the name Alexander—first name or last name, she didn't know—and felt his energy lift with the new idea. They talked about it a little more and finally, there was nothing more to say.

"Mom," he said, "you remember our code, right?"

The starch came out of her spine. They didn't need a code. "I remember," she said, "but I was thinking about it. I think we should change it to something we could use in normal conversation that no one but us would notice."

Aidan hummed. "That's a good idea. Like what?"

She told him what Varón had noticed—without attributing it to him—and Aidan was quick to latch on.

"Okay, so instead of 'I love you more,' we'll say 'I love you most.' If one of us changes it to that, then we know we're in trouble."

"Got it," Kara said, hardly able to fathom the relief she felt knowing they wouldn't need it—at least not for Varón's sake. It was as if all her bones had gone to jelly. She and Aidan weren't being guarded by outlaws. They were in the care of the FBI.

She was in the care of Special Agent Lukas Mann.

"'Night, Mom," Aidan said. "I love you."

"I know, honey," she said. "I love you more."

She disconnected, cocking her head to listen for sounds from upstairs. The water was still running. *Think fast.*

She climbed the stairs, trying to re-paint Luke Varón with the hues of Lukas Mann. The new image was enough to forgive him every harsh thing he'd done, every secret and lie. It was enough to forgive herself for melting beneath his kisses and secretly longing for more. It was enough to make her stop outside the bathroom door and slip off her shoes, shimmy from the green dress. To inch into the bathroom wearing only the lace panties, trembling with equal parts excitement and nervousness and sheer, physical lust. He'd awakened her body to cravings so long-buried she'd forgotten they existed, and awakened her mind to the reality that they were two consenting adults with no one to judge them but themselves.

I want you. I've wanted you since the first moment I saw you.

She wanted him, too.

The air hung moist and heavy, filled with steam and the spicy scent of soap. Kara's nipples tightened to peaks even as the dampness gathered on her skin. The shower filled an entire corner of the room, tiled with rustic travertine behind full-length walls and doors of textured glass. Luke stood inside.

Her breath caught. He faced away from her, his body rippling with water and shrouded by steam, his face tipped skyward in the hot spray. He looked like an Impressionist painting, and Kara found herself staring. The water pulsed down and when he rubbed his hands over his head and turned, he went still.

He looked at her. She couldn't see the details of his face—or anything else, for that matter—but she knew he was looking at her. She could feel it in the way her blood picked up speed, and in the way steam gathered and made it impossible for her lungs to fill. By small degrees, his hands lowered to his sides and he stepped toward the shower door, reaching for the handle.

She swallowed. He opened the door, water trickling down his face and lather running down the muscles of his chest and arms, over his sculpted belly and lower. Her mouth went dry. Dear God, he was beautiful. Beautiful and strong and competent and—she closed her eyes on a prayer of gratitude—safe.

I'm one of the good guys, Kara. You're safe with me.

She hooked her thumbs into the lace above her thighs,

stepping out of the panties. His eyes dipped, filled with dark, blatant hunger, then ran a lingering course back up to her eyes. His Adam's apple dipped.

"Are you sure?" he asked, his voice sounding a little stuck.

Kara looked at him. "Yes."

He reached from the shower and held out his hand. Kara laid her fingers on his warm, wet palm and he closed his hand around them.

"Thank God," he said.

The waitress Sasha chose was named Ellie. She was tall and lithe, and more outgoing than Megan. She was covering Megan's section.

"They're keeping you busy tonight," Sasha said, pulling his beer in front of him.

"We're down a waitress," she said. "A girl from the college didn't show up. My manager's about to have a heart attack."

Sasha nodded. Show no interest. Don't engage any more conversation about the missing Megan than Ellie might have with any other patron. He wouldn't want her singling him out when she went to the Feds.

Because he knew she'd go. He would make certain of it.

CHAPTER
39

A SHOWER WITH LUKE MANN was an exercise in sensuality. He stroked and massaged, lathered her nothing-hair, his hands exploring her body as if indulging in some long-awaited privilege. She stood with her back against his chest while he worshipped her breasts with his hands, kissed her neck and shoulders, then flattened his hand over her belly and pressed her back against his erection, his fingertips just grazing the apex of her thighs.

Her insides flooded. He was strength and skill and tenderness; he was energy and fervor and raw male heat, and by small degrees, the gentle ardor he began with grew more urgent, more desperate, and soon he'd pulled her from the shower. He threw a giant towel around her and clutched it in one hand, her arms pinned to her sides and his steps driving her to the bed beneath an onslaught of fiery kisses. The backs of her knees hit the mattress and he stripped away the towel and followed her into the soft cloud of a duvet. His body covered hers, his arms bearing the bulk of his weight while his lips closed over a nipple, working it into a tight bud of sensation and then paying homage to the other. Kara ran her hands over his ribs and around his back, unable to feel enough of him, reveling in the moist heat of his skin and the sensations swirling in the core of her body. His erection probed her thighs, his hands were everywhere at once, and he mouthed kisses down the side of her breast and across the shallow inlet of her belly. Kara thrilled in an onslaught of sheer sensation and he reached into his wallet in the nightstand, ripped open a condom and rolled it on, and returned to her. His hands grasped her buttocks and his hips moved, and he drove into the center of her body so deep she cried out. He took the cry into his mouth and held himself still for an instant, restraint vibrating in every sinew, then he rotated against her and currents of sensation shot to her toes. He began to move—deep, steady strokes that pushed her slowly, unwaveringly higher and higher. Pleasure spiraled around her. She clutched his back and linked her knees around his hips, and he groaned and drove into her harder and faster and when he finally sank into her that one last time, she came apart in his hands like a shattering star.

Luke came back to earth some time later, Kara's head in the crook of his shoulder and a sheen of perspiration between them. His heart had finally settled into a normal rhythm; for a while there, it had been touch and go. He thought she might have killed him.

He'd have died happy.

He put a kiss in the dark curls against his chin and ran his hand down her slender back. Christ, she felt good here. Of course, a woman usually felt good here, but this was different. Usually, this was a stage of transition: the afterglow and the requisite cuddles, serving as the bridge between their parting for the night or going another round. This stage wasn't usually part of the sex. It was the price he paid to have the sex.

With Kara, it was different. He wanted her here. He wanted to hold her and caress her and talk to her, to know her thoughts and her feelings and make sure she wanted to be here, too.

That was a first.

Then he wanted to take another shower with her and start all over again.

Her hand roved, trailing down his rib cage, exploring the little scars and marks on his torso. She brushed her fingers down his hip and came to the glossy, gnarled flesh on his thigh.

"Is it still hurting?" she asked.

"No. The heat of the shower helped. And the distraction."

She shifted, looking at it.

"What happened?" she asked. "I mean, I know it was a bullet wound, but this was more than that."

"Fifty-caliber bullet. They make big holes."

She frowned, her fingers brushing over the ragged flesh. "You said the surgeon wasn't very skilled."

"Oh, the surgeon actually has many skills. Removing bullets isn't one of them."

She scowled at him. "Don't be cryptic."

Luke took a deep breath, scooting up against the soft headboard. Kara shifted to sit beside him, cross-legged. Luke thought he just might enjoy this session of pillow talk, until she tugged the sheet over her lap and pulled it just above her breasts.

"Stop pouting," she snapped when he frowned. "This is a conversation."

He gave a mild curse and looked at his leg. It wasn't pretty. "Collado shot me."

"Collado?"

"Remember I told you he slipped through the cracks of the Rojàs takedown?"

She nodded.

"That's how he did it. In the middle of the bust, he made me for a cop but I didn't know it. I went to get him and he was waiting. He killed two DEA agents who came in right after me."

"Dear God," she said, stroking his leg with one hand, holding the knot of the sheet with the other. "You're lucky he didn't kill you."

"Oh, he wasn't interested in doing that. He had a better idea. He paid off some Colombian nationals and put me in prison. For the first week, he came to visit every day. Watched the leg get infected and swollen, stood just beyond the bars and laughed."

"God."

"Somewhere around the third or fourth day, I realized I had to get the bullet out. I was burning up with fever and wasn't very aware of what was going on, but I did know that the reason he came every day was to see me get worse. He was waiting for me to die and I didn't want to give him that pleasure. So I dug it out." He tipped his head to the scar. "This is what happens when you use a stick."

"Oh, Lukas," she whispered, brushing the scar with a feather-light touch. Hearing his name on her lips stirred something deep inside, warming him from the inside out. There was no lightning bolt from heaven, no earth-shattering moment of realization. But there was a small, niggling notion in the back of his mind that said he might want to hear her say it again tomorrow and the next day, and fifty years from now.

"How did you get out? How did you get back to the U.S.?"

"Elisa."

She stopped touching him and tipped her head. "Elisa Moran."

"Yes." Luke took her hand, stroking it with his thumb. "She wasn't my lover, Kara, and she wasn't Andrew's. She was an agent. She'd been in Colombia with me and worked like a dog to find out where Collado had taken me. Back in the States, she moved mountains between the two governments to get me out of there. It took five months."

Kara blinked. "You were in prison for five months?"

He quirked a half smile. "The history you dug up was a lot more colorful, I know. Believe me, Luke Varón was having more adventures than Lukas Mann during that time."

"The windows and skylights," she said. "Everywhere you stay. Even your cars."

He shrugged. "I like to see the sky. It's a little legacy left to me by Collado."

She shook her head and Luke could see her trying to make it all fit. "This whole thing, starting with Andrew... It's all been about getting Collado. And now you're letting him go. Because of me."

Luke looked at her. Hearing the dismissal of his life's goal put into words like that was a little daunting. But never had he been so sure of letting something go. "Frank's not so good in bed," he said. "It's a trade I'm willing to make."

"Seriously, Lu—"

"I *am* serious," he said. He leaned forward, grasping both hands. "First of all, Collado's not getting away. There are a hundred and fifty DEA and FBI agents poised in twenty-three states waiting to take him and the entire network down tomorrow or the next day—just as soon as he's on American soil and the drugs make it to their first delivery sites. The bastard is going to prison; that much is certain. They don't need me; in fact, I was already going to have to stay in hiding until all the arrests were made, anyway. Collado will recognize me.

"Second of all," he continued, "remember, this Alexander didn't *just* kill Andrew. He killed Elisa. So regardless of the fact that your stalker isn't part of the drug ring, I have good reason to want him found."

She nodded. "I'm sorry."

"And third, even if neither of those things were true, it wouldn't have mattered." He stopped, feeling his own sense of amazement over where this was going. "You had me from the moment you took your clothes off in that alley, Kara. When I realized there was something more frightening in your life than stripping down in front of Luke Varón, and when I saw how fucking courageous and determined you were, there was no way in hell I could walk away."

A breath shivered past her lips and she leaned in and kissed him. "You're quite a romantic for a ruthless hit man."

"You have no idea," he said, surprised that the observation pleased him. "But stick around and I'll show you."

Mike Hogan had dozed for an hour when his phone rang. He reached to the hotel nightstand and felt for his phone, found it without opening his eyes, and squinted to see the time. Six thirty-eight a.m.

He answered. "This better be good," he said.

A voice he didn't recognize spoke into his ear. "Is this Special Agent Mike Hogan?"

"Yes. What do you want?"

"Agent Hogan, this is Special Agent Cassie Flynn at the Atlanta FBI field office. We received a call from a concerned citizen in the middle of the night. On follow-up, we came into custody of a package and I was told to contact you."

Mike sat up. Wide awake now. "What package?"

"I'm not privy to the contents, but Special Agent Knutson told me to say 'barbed wire.'"

"I'll be right there."

CHAPTER
40

K ARA WOKE ALONE IN the big bed, the faintest strains
of sunrise lightening the room. Skylights. Luke's
story came rushing back to her...five months in a Colombian prison, digging a bullet out of his own leg in order to
survive, enduring conditions she could only imagine. And
all this during a time when, according to the research her
office had dug up, he was a different man named Luke
Varón, pushing old ladies off curbs and stealing candy
from children.

Or something like that. She drew a deep breath, his
scent lingering on the pillows and her insides pleasantly
sore from their lovemaking, and she wondered how she had
ever believed him capable of evil. Then she remembered
that not only did he have an entire Federal bureaucracy
creating supportive evidence of his evil, but he was *good*.
Damn convincing as a henchman. Just ask Ronald Gibson.

That thought brought her back. After they'd left Gibson in the lake last night, the FBI had taken him in. She
knew it was as much to keep him safe from her stalker
as anything, but she had no doubt that he'd been grilled
about the man named Alexander. A man who had some

master plan for Kara and no qualms about taking lives in order to enact it.

She threw off the covers, physically spent but her mind gearing up again. *Alexander. Alex. Al. Alec. Lex.* Could the killer be using a derivative of the name instead? She had to think. She had to find him.

She got out of bed, her nudity bringing a prickle of heat to her cheeks, and realized the only clothing she had was the green dress in a heap on the floor. Even the lovely brooch was outside, apparently recording wildlife, and the thought that Knutson would know precisely what she and Special Agent Luke Mann had done overnight brought a full-bodied blush to her skin. She tried the dresser and found lingerie and nightwear—all silk and lace—and wanted to die of shame thinking about Knutson ordering such things. It had been bad enough believing Varón's network of thugs had supplied her with clothing, but even worse knowing it was the FBI.

Your tax dollars at work.

She dragged on a pair of the lacy panties, then went to the closet, came across men's clothing first, and took the first shirt she saw. She slipped into it—a long-sleeved burgundy Oxford—buttoned it up to the second-to-top button, and folded the sleeves to her wrists. Looked in the mirror. Luke was tall; his shirt was longer than the dress she'd worn yesterday, even at the scooped-up sides. She judged it sufficient, went to the bathroom and indulged in a moment of luscious recall when she looked at the shower, then brushed her hair and teeth and studied her image in the mirror. Without makeup, she looked more like herself, but for the wispy dark hair and the exhaustion in her eyes. Even so, it was a shock to see herself looking like this. The old Kara Chandler was gone; the news would by now be confirming her death.

She closed her eyes. *Oh, Sally, I'm sorry. And Seth. When this is over, I'll bring Aidan back to you.*

Hope nudged her. For the first time since she'd realized what was happening, she had the sense that she might not be in hiding forever. She had help. She had the FBI.

She headed down the stairs, her resolve to help *Agent Mann* with the case at full throttle. The aroma of coffee touched her nostrils and she walked into the great room. Luke sat at the table in the dining area with the phone to his ear. He looked up when she came in, said "Jesus," and set down the phone.

He stood, his gaze running down her body from head to toe. She felt it like the touch of his hand and a second later, it *was* the touch of his hand, as he came to her and pulled her against his body. He kissed her slowly, possessively, thoroughly, leaving no nerve or emotion untouched. There was none of the awkwardness of waking up with one another and wondering whether the night should have happened. There was only the sense that it *had* happened and, indeed, it would be happening again.

Kara melted.

Luke ended the kiss and leaned back to look at her, plucked the collar of his own shirt at her throat. "Let me guess: Maddie stuffed the drawers full of lace and satin."

"Apparently," she said, wondering why he would know that.

"She's always taken issue with my marital status." He dropped his gaze and his eyes lingered on the buttons of his shirt—from just beneath her throat to the apex of her thighs. Kara felt as if he'd unbuttoned each one in his mind. "But if you think you're any safer in that, you'd better think again."

Kara's skin prickled. It felt... glorious.

"I was just coming down to ask for your iPad," she said. "Somewhere, there has to be an Alexander. I don't recall anyone by that name. But it's common enough that there must be several."

He nodded and dropped his hands. He took his coffee cup and headed to the kitchen, topped his off and filled a mug for her. Set both down back at the table and slid the iPad to her, then settled back into a chair in front of his laptop. "Check defendants first," he said. "Then hostile witnesses, family members, and friends of anyone you prosecuted. Also look at any defense attorneys you might have pissed off. I'm checking the websites for the APD and the DA's office. Maybe it's someone you worked with."

Kara sat down. She didn't need to be told those things; she knew how to conduct investigations. But he was a cop now, handling her case.

God, that felt good.

"Have you considered men you've dated?"

"Dated?" She pulled a face. "I've only been widowed a year and I married when I was eighteen."

"Eighteen?"

"Andrew and I knew each other as teenagers. I got pregnant."

He frowned and Kara shrugged.

"Oh, no you don't," he said, angling toward her. "You don't get to hear about my family and my enemies and my time in prison, and then brush off your own story. Spill it, lady."

"What is there to spill? You've never heard of teenage pregnancy before?"

"Sure. But I'm surprised your father let you marry so young."

"*Let* me?" Kara laughed, a sound so bitter that a split second later, she was sorry she hadn't been more guarded. *Two brothers, one sister, two loving parents. A white picket fence.* Lukas Mann wouldn't understand. He'd had the Norman Rockwell upbringing of small-town America.

His hand touched her chin and he turned her to look at him. "Kara," he said quietly. "Let me in."

She blinked. It was such a sweet, heartfelt plea that she couldn't bear to refuse him. Moreover, she realized, she didn't want to.

"My father wasn't . . . warm. I mean, I was never abused or anything like that. But I was adopted, something that I'm sure was all my mother's idea. My birth mother was a teenager and Mom got hooked up with her by the agency during the pregnancy, paid for all the medical bills and attended my birth—the whole deal. Dad wouldn't have ever said anything to me directly, but my being a girl was a big disappointment. He wanted a son, someone to take over Montgomery Manor."

"A woman can't do that?"

"This woman didn't *want* to. Montgomery Manor was a huge, sprawling ranch. Bigger than Southfork and a lot wealthier. It was cold, and all about show. My dad worked day and night to belong to that class of person. After Mom died, he didn't know what to do with me. So he built me things and bought me things."

"Like a personal stable and your own horses."

"And an Avanti and jewelry and even a wishing well. Then he put me and all my things on display. It was his way of making sure everyone would look at us and say, 'How lucky little Kara was to become a *Montgomery*.'" She scoffed. "He had no idea I used to toss stones into the well and wish we were poor. I guess I thought there would be a place for me then."

Luke's gaze dropped to her lips, lingering, then dragged up to her eyes again.

"When I wound up pregnant, he was mortified. He sent me to a 'facility' until he convinced Andrew's family that marriage was the right answer." She scoffed. "I always wondered how much that cost him—convincing the Chandlers. I figure they got special breeding privileges for years to come."

"Kara." He was angry. It took her by surprise.

"He did his best. It's just the way it was."

Luke narrowed his gaze on her. "Is that how you feel about Andrew? He did his best?"

"Andrew wasn't unkind. We were kids and we messed up. In another world, we wouldn't have ended up together. But since we did, and since we had Aidan, it seemed like staying together was the right thing to do."

Luke cursed and his disapproval of how the men in her life had treated her touched her in a place she hadn't known existed. She'd worked so hard—as a daughter, a wife, a mother, an attorney. Always trying to prove her worth, always wishing her father hadn't felt stuck with her, wishing Andrew hadn't, either.

Luke turned to face her, his gaze dark and piercing. "I would expect more from my wife," he said, and a shiver raced over her skin. She swallowed. Yes, a man like him would expect passion, not cordiality. Love, not tolerance.

Heat.

"I'm just sayin'," he added, and turned back to his laptop.

Okay. Well. Kara forced her gaze back to the iPad, trying not to appear as if the floor had just tilted. It was almost as if he was talking about the future.

But if so, he was back to business now. As if he hadn't just set her world a-quiver.

"There's a behavioral expert from Quantico who's coming to talk to you this morning," he said. "And now that you aren't suspicious of my 'resources' anymore, there are some things you need to know."

CHAPTER
41

THE REST OF THE world seeped back in and Kara's stomach flopped. Something was wrong.

Luke clicked an icon and a picture came up. "Have you ever seen this person before?"

Kara scooted her chair beside him to look. It was a man, about thirty, with dark curly hair and a trim, athletic build. The picture had been taken on a beach, the wind catching his hair.

"No," she said. "Who is it?"

"His name is Tony Fietti." He winced. *Was.*

"Was?"

"He disappeared one day while jogging, about six months ago. He just never came home. Chattanooga."

Kara didn't understand. "Luke..." she said, and was almost afraid to ask, "who is he?"

"Gina's husband."

It took a second, then it hit her.

"Oh, God," she said. The coffee came to her throat, bitter and vile. She'd forgotten about the engraving on the pen. Aidan had laughed about it. Thought it was hysterical that his mom's freaky secret admirer had sent her a gift with some other woman's name on it. *All my love, Gina*.

She closed her eyes. "I was right, wasn't I?" She forced herself to look at him. "They're all dead. Every one of those gifts belongs to someone he killed."

"I think so." He pulled out his cell phone and brought up a picture of a woman. "This is Evelyn Camp."

Kara looked, running the name through her mind. It was familiar but she didn't know—

"Wait. That's the woman you asked Lacy about."

"I was actually asking you," Luke said, "feeling you out for a reaction. I was afraid if I came right out and asked, I might come across as a cop. I just needed to know if you knew her. And you don't."

Kara shook her head. "No, I don't. But who is she?"

"The woman who owns the pearl necklace. She's been missing for nine months."

"Oh, God." She felt as if the world had gone hazy.

"Kara." Luke was in her face. "Stay with me, honey. Go back to the pen. Can you remember exactly when you got it?"

The pen, the pen. She racked her brain. "It was near Christmas. I remember it being on the front porch with a package from UPS. Only, this one wasn't wrapped in brown paper. It was…it was just like all the others, with the card attached."

"Anthony Fietti disappeared on December seventeenth."

"Chattanooga, you said?"

He nodded. "We think the killer is working within a drivable radius of Atlanta—of you. We're looking for people in that radius who've gone missing in the past year. If we can get a list of victims, we might be able to figure out a pattern, or what the killer is trying to do."

Kara felt as if the weight of the world had settled on her shoulders. "I shouldn't have run. I should have gone back to the police again after Louie."

"You did go to the police—you came to me. No one can blame you for taking dire measures to get your son out of sight, Kara. And for the record, no one will hold you liable for a faked death scheme you hatched in conjunction with the FBI. When this is over, you'll have your life back. I promise."

She looked at him, wanting with all her heart to believe him. He was so sincere and so determined that she might have come around to it, too, except that his cell phone chimed and he answered it. He listened, while his features turned hard as steel. "Okay," he said, and disconnected.

He looked at Kara. "That was Knutson. There's been another murder."

Knutson pounded on the door and Luke opened it. Mike Hogan was with him. He did a double-take.

"Ah, shit," he said when he saw Luke.

"Nice to see you, too," Luke said, offering his hand. "Here's to hoping your manners have improved since the last time."

Hogan cursed again and Knutson stepped in past him. "Okay. So we all know you two remember each other. Quantico. Big rivalry. Get over it."

Luke stepped back to make way for both of them. Mike Hogan did a three-sixty turn with his hands on his hips, taking in the luxury of Montiel's place. "I should have figured you for this kind of work," he said to Luke. "While the rest of us are out busting our balls."

Kara came down the stairs, sparing Luke a reply. She'd changed out of his shirt when Knutson called and said he was on the way, but looked no less striking in jeans and a tailored white blouse, with flat, strappy sandals. Luke saw Hogan straighten, taking in every detail.

"It's a tough job," Luke said arrogantly, "but someone's gotta do it."

"Kara, good to see you," Knutson said, greeting her.

"*Agent* Knutson," Kara said, and Knutson actually blushed.

"That would be me."

She crossed to Hogan. "And you must be the specialist from the BAU," she said, offering her hand.

Hogan gave her a glimpse of his shield on the inside of his jacket, then shook her hand and held it a beat too long. "Mike Hogan," he said. Luke drew a deep breath through his nose. Mike Hogan was the definition of what women liked—tall, muscular, dark, with a square jaw and piercing eyes. Intense. The same could have been said for Luke except that Hogan was heroic and brilliant and carried his reputation as a champion for the innocent like a halo. An agent out to make the world a better place, dissecting the sickest minds and keeping society safe, the kind of cop they make TV shows about. When Mike Hogan bedded a woman, he did it as a champion of justice. Not as a drug lord or hit man.

Just now, though, Hogan had the rumpled look of a man who'd been on a runaway train for about a week. He wore a suit barely shaken from a garment bag and a tie he might have bought at Sears. He hadn't shaved for several days and his eyes dragged dark circles beneath them. If there hadn't been such an unpleasant history between them, Luke might have spared a thought to wonder how such a charmed life had left Hogan so beat up.

But there was, so he didn't. And there had been another murder.

Luke turned to Knutson. "Who'd the fucker kill now?"

Hogan moved to the granite peninsula that separated the dining area from the kitchen, pulled out his briefcase, and opened a manila folder. Knutson went into the kitchen and opened a cooler they'd brought with them— cantaloupe, berries, muffins. Clearly, he thought they'd be here a while. He poured two coffees and handed one to Hogan, who ignored it in favor of spreading out photos.

"Her name is Megan Kessler," he said.

He pulled out a picture of a woman—young, dark-haired, a little chunky. In the photo, which had been cropped from a group picture around a table in a restaurant or bar, she smiled and held up a beer. The other shots showed an alley behind the club where she'd worked. Their locations and dates were printed in the bottom right corners. Location: 3182 Ackley Street, Canton, GA. The date: Sun 6/23. This morning.

"She disappeared the night before last, after working her shift as a waitress at The Carousel, a bar in Cherokee County."

"Someone reported her missing?" Luke asked.

"Not really," Hogan said. "She lived alone and wasn't too social. Went to college and work, and belonged to one gaming group online. That's about it. So no one noticed she was gone until she didn't show up for work last night. One of her fellow waitresses came to the Atlanta field office to report it at three this morning."

Luke frowned. "Why didn't she call the police?"

"Because those weren't her instructions," Hogan said.

"Instructions?" Kara asked.

Hogan handed a picture to her. Luke came and looked.

"What is this?" It was a picture of something in a box, but he couldn't tell what. But then Kara's breath caught.

She picked up the photo of Megan and put both pictures side by side.

"It's a barrette," she said. "Look. Megan is wearing the same one here."

Hogan nodded. "At closing time last night, the waitress at the club found that box at the cash register. The barrette was inside and there was a card." He slipped out another photo: a horse card.

Kara paled.

"Want to know what the card said inside?" Hogan asked.

" 'TRUTH,' " Luke said.

"No." He handed them the next picture, which was a shot of the inside lettering. "It said, 'Better call the FBI.' "

Luke's brain stalled, then it all came clear. "He couldn't get to Kara, so he found a way to get to me."

"You?" Kara looked stricken but it morphed to confusion. "How did he know to go to the FBI?" Her cheeks blanched. "It's just like Louie. He's still following me. He kno—"

"No, Kara," Luke said, trying to forestall the panic that threatened. "He made me for a Fed after the fire. He hung around and watched the scene until the FBI arrived. One of our agents chased him and identified himself."

Her brow furrowed and she worked through it. "That's why you didn't keep me from going back at Lake Allatoona last night. Your cover was already blown, so you didn't care."

He shrugged. "The timing was okay. There was no harm at that point in letting you in on it." He paused and looked at her. "Not to mention that lying to you was killing me."

"Moving on?" Hogan said. "Along with the barrette and the card came a photograph. It was printed on regular paper from a computer, folded up and stuffed inside the envelope."

Luke cursed. Of course there would be a picture. "Let me guess: It's a picture of Megan Kessler with ligatures around her neck and the garrote on her lap."

Hogan winced. "Sort of."

Sort of? Luke frowned and Hogan produced the photo. But he didn't set this one on the counter. He handed it to Luke instead.

Luke took it, his nerves prickling. He looked at the photo and his heart slammed into his rib cage.

Jesus, no.

CHAPTER
42

LUKE'S FEATURES TIGHTENED AND Kara saw his entire body go to steel. He started to hand the photograph back to Agent Hogan, bypassing Kara, but she said, "Give me that," and snatched it away.

Her lungs seized. Luke moved against her back.

It was a woman's body—Megan Kessler—propped up in the corner on a floor. The barrette was still in her hair and the garrote lay on her lap. Her head had been tugged back to reveal the ligature marks on her throat, and her face—

Fear sprang to Kara's breast. Megan's face wasn't visible. It was covered by a picture of Kara's.

"Oh, God," she said, but she wasn't sure whether her voice made it past her lips.

"Honey." Luke's voice was close above her shoulder, his hand on her waist. *Jesus, keep it together.* For God's sake, she was a prosecutor. She had to think. Ask questions. Dig for answers.

Her first question wasn't so brilliant. "You're sure this is Megan?"

"The other waitress confirmed that those are the

clothes she was wearing at work the night before last," Hogan said.

Knutson chimed in. "There's a team in Megan's apartment now. But we're pretty sure she never made it there after work on Friday night. It looks like she was killed in the alley behind the club, less than a block away."

"I need to see," Luke said, but Agent Hogan was quick to bat him down.

"I just came from there; forensics is doing its thing. Besides, the last thing you need right now is for some TV station to put you on the air analyzing a crime scene. Never mind that Ms. Chandler and her stalker already know you're law enforcement. My understanding is that it would be a bad time for anyone else to find out."

Luke mouthed a curse; Kara was still trying to make sense of everything. Friday night, after the club closed... Megan was being strangled to death with barbed wire in an alley while Kara was running to safety with Luke.

Coward.

"The good news," Knutson said, "is that it's a pretty good crime scene. There are signs of a struggle, scuffs, a limited number of places he could have parked without getting too much attention. Even blood," he added, "though we don't know whose. It's a crime scene that's likely to produce information; we just have to give the team time to process it. APD uniforms are canvassing the streets in that area for someone who might have seen the van or heard something. From the picture with Penny Wolff, it looks like a 2000 or 2001 Dodge Ram, white. They're running those now."

But they didn't have much more time. Kara could feel it. What was it—eleven? Eleven murders in the past year and three of them just this week? He was moving faster.

She'd read about that with serial killers. He'd hidden his actions in cryptic messages to her for months and then, this week, started being blatant. He had a plan and now that he was close to the end he was taking out anyone who got in his way. His killings would escalate and his psyche would unravel and—

"Ms. Chandler." She blinked. She hadn't been listening. Luke ran his hand down her arm as if to regain her attention. Agent Hogan said, "What we need from you now is for you to connect the victims together. If we can figure out what his plan is, we can name him and find him."

Kara felt dizzy. "I don't know."

"Damn it, listen to me," he said, advancing on her. "These victims aren't random. He's not killing blondes and he's not killing young women. They aren't all hitchhikers or hookers or gay men; they aren't all waitresses or dancers or anything else. Now, who was Megan Kessler?"

"I don't know. I've never heard of her before."

"Who was Tony Fietti?"

"I don't know."

"Who was Evelyn Cam—"

"Back off," Luke snarled, stepping in front of Kara. "She doesn't know, damn it."

They glared at each other, chest to chest. "She *does* know," Agent Hogan insisted. "Somehow, she knows. No one plans this sort of death display without a reason. She's the only one who can figure that out and by God, if she doesn't, we're going to get another picture of another body with wire marks around their neck, and since he can't get to her, he'll do someone else, maybe by the end of the day. This guy's starting to unwind. We don't have time for you to hole up in fancy cabins for a little ass while th—"

Luke sprang, and Hogan's back slammed against a wall. Knutson grabbed Luke, dragging on his shoulders, but Luke held Hogan in place with a forearm across his chest, growling words Kara couldn't understand. She called his name but he didn't seem to hear her and it wasn't until she pushed between them that he backed down.

"He's right, Luke," she said, waiting for him to take a full step back. She looked up at him. "I have to do this."

Kara turned from him, squaring her shoulders to Agent Hogan. She tried to sound strong but her voice vibrated with emotion. "If you think I know who's doing this, then help me figure it out. Help *me* help *you*. Please. I can't go on watching people die because of something I once did or said or didn't do or didn't say or—"

"Kara," Luke said, and reached out to her. She steeled her spine, refusing to give in. If she sank into his arms now, she might never come back out again. He was strength and determination and protectiveness, and although she was amazed at how much she longed for those things, she still had enough sense to know she didn't dare get used to them.

They'd had one night together. One night and a roller coaster ride trying to dodge a killer. It would be crazy for her to think there would be more than that, or to lean on him too hard.

Hogan shook his shoulders like a boxer shaking off a punch and glared at Luke. "I'm sorry," he said, surprising everyone. "That was uncalled for."

"No shit," Luke said, but Hogan let it go.

"Agent Knutson," he said, "can we set up command from here? I'm going to need some time with Ms. Chandler."

Knutson nodded. "Give me an hour."

• • •

They set out the food Agent Knutson had brought and Mike Hogan moved his briefcase and laptop to the table where Luke and Kara had already been working. Hogan looked weary and rough; Luke was calmer but still rippling with tension. There was something between him and Hogan; that was for damn sure. But Kara didn't care about that just now. Seeing her own face on the body of a girl who'd been strangled had shot terror to the marrow of her bones. She'd known this man was after her; she'd known she and Aidan were in danger. That's why she'd gone to Luke Varón in the first place. But seeing that threat in such a clear, macabre manner—seeing herself portrayed dead with the marks of barbed wire around her neck—she hadn't been prepared for that.

She tried to brush it off. Agent Hogan swore she was the one who could figure out the killer's master plan. She had to try.

Knutson moved into the other room to make some phone calls—working to bring in computers and printers and phones and whatever else setting up "command" required. Meanwhile, Hogan brought his briefcase to the table and invited Kara to sit. Luke joined them, pushing a bowl of fruit and yogurt in her direction.

"Here's what I think," Hogan said, and started laying out pictures. "The killer is working with two different groups of victims. In this group on the left are people you know or who are connected to you. Your husband and the agent he was with, Elisa Moran." He laid out a photo of each of them, alive. "John Wolff. Your friend, Detective Guilford. Penny Wolff." He laid out copies of the pictures she'd received, then paused before setting down one more. "Your son."

Kara's heart stopped.

"No, nothing's happened to him," Hogan said quickly. "Aidan is safe. I have an open line of communication with the agents guarding him. But the killer threatened him—he identified him as a target—so in the killer's mind, Aidan belongs in this group."

"Except for Penny Wolff, none of these people were killed by strangulation," Luke said.

"Right," Hogan said. "He saves his wire for the special kills. The people in the right column."

"Special?" Kara asked.

"Serial killers often favor a certain weapon," he said. "This garrote has *meaning*." Again, Hogan went into his folders. He came out with a photo of Penny Wolff—the one Kara had seen on her cell phone, except that it had been cropped and enlarged. The striped scarf lay on her lap. And the garrote.

Kara swallowed, air snagging in her throat. It was the first time she'd seen that photo in detail.

"This is a single-strand, fifteen-and-a-half gauge high-tensile barbed wire. It has tensile strength up to nine hundred fifty pounds. The barbs are five inches apart and it's a four-point wire—there are four points at each twist."

"Meaning?" Luke asked.

"It's not a common wire, and it's not easy to use. You may think of barbed wire as flexible, but most of it—the kind you see strung around cow pastures—is too stiff to handle the way he would have to handle it for murder. It wouldn't have tightened on a throat very easily."

"Gibson said Alexander was a bodybuilder," Kara said. "He's strong."

"And he'd need that strength even with this wire, especially when one considers that his victims aren't standing still and cooperating. They'd be fighting, flailing. Hard work to kill someone like this, especially when you're good with a gun. Why not just shoot?"

Kara swallowed. She couldn't let Hogan's words get to her.

"Can we trace where he purchased it?"

"People usually buy it in giant coils; it's not like it's sold by the yard. My guess is that he came across this length of wire and that's all he ever needed. He used it over and over."

"The handles," Luke said.

Hogan looked at him. "You noticed."

"Knutson and I talked about it. They're nice. Cherry, maybe, and handmade."

"Wild cherry, to be precise," Hogan said, and a memory pinched the back of Kara's mind. Wild cherry was toxic to horses. Guapa, the horse she'd told stories about when Aidan was little, had died when a fence blew down and she got trapped in a patch of wild cherry trees.

Agent Hogan went on. "Whoever made these handles worked at them. They're turned and sanded like good furniture and polished, maybe with tung oil or some other finish. They're the perfect size and shape for a large man's hands."

"Form *and* function," Luke said.

"That's the point: He takes pride in this weapon," Hogan said. "Without the bodies, we can't be sure he strangled all of these people on the right, but I'm betting he did. And what ties them together is you, Ms. Chandler. *TRUTH.*"

"I don't know what that means," Kara said.

"It means he holds you responsible for something, probably something that he believes no one else knows. And you're the only one who can figure out what it is."

CHAPTER
43

SASHA WENT TO GET his father for the day. A beautiful day, a Sunday morning—hot and clear. The day of truth for dear old Dad. Today, he would learn just how smart his son really was.

And then, he would serve as Sasha's ticket to safety.

He sauntered in through the front doors of the nursing home. Managed an insincere smile for the gaggle of nurses and a couple of orderlies who had gathered around a small TV behind the reception desk, and headed straight back to his father's room. His father sat in the wheelchair, head drooping, chair aimed toward the window as if he might be enjoying the view.

Such bullshit.

"Papa," Sasha said, walking in behind him. His father jerked at the sound of his voice and Sasha wheeled him around. "Did you have a nice night?" Dmitri's eyes bulged, lips worked, throat rasped. The dribble formed at one corner of his mouth.

Disgusting old man.

"I know I did," Sasha said. He braced his hands against the arms of the wheelchair and bent down, speaking right against his father's ear. "It's done, *nana*. I did the last one last night, just like I told you I would. Everything is ready. I can't wait to show you."

A sound came from his father's throat but it was garbled and soft. Sasha ignored it and wheeled him from the room, then went back in and got a small blue throw and tucked it around his father's scrawny knees. He added a rimmed straw hat from the small closet of clothes. Wanted to look like a caring, dutiful son taking Dad out in the sunshine.

He stopped at the front desk to sign him out—like a child being taken out of school early—and managed another smile for the receptionist, who patted his father on the shoulders and spoke in a too-loud voice.

"You have a nice day with your son, Mr. Rodin. We'll see you tonight."

No you won't, Sasha thought, but kept that comment to himself. He was too close to the end to make any foolish mistakes now. The day had finally come.

He had a party to go to.

Sarah Fogt had only worked at Mountain Ridge Nursing Home for two months. But she'd helped her mom take care of her grandfather at their house for more than ten years, so there wasn't much that grossed her out. She'd also grown up hunting with her dad and brother and she could skin a rabbit or tan a deer hide with the best of them. Sarah didn't get the heebie-jeebies easily.

But she had them now. Real bad.

Barbed wire. It was on TV. A whole bunch of the nurses and orderlies had gathered around a little TV at the front desk, watching the Sunday morning news show, freaking out at the idea that it had happened so close to home. That Penny Wolff woman had lived just an hour or so away. It had been bad enough when the news reported that she'd been abducted from her own house and that her little one-year-old girl was left behind. Even worse when they said they'd found her body in freaking Mississippi. But now, this morning, they were saying someone had strangled her with barbed wire. Sarah had never heard anything that creepy before. It made her think of that poor old Russian man in Room 144. He'd had a tragic run-in with barbed wire, or so she'd been told. She only knew about it because she was the one who bathed him on the days she worked mornings and she'd finally asked Ms. Henderson about the marks on his neck.

Henderson told her that Mr. Rodin's son had explained it—how his father had worked on a horse farm and gotten caught up in the wire once while trying to free a horse that was tangled up. The horse had spooked, panicked, and dragged Mr. Rodin for two hundred yards. By the time they'd gotten him free, he'd been without oxygen for too long.

And now, he was a vegetable. Well, that wasn't the term they used for it in the nursing home, but that's what he was. He couldn't talk or move or handle his most basic needs. He couldn't feed himself or communicate, and the only time she'd ever seen him show any sign of brain activity at all was when his son came to visit.

Like now.

His son came in the front door and through the lobby and Sarah got a little chill. She tried to chalk it up to having just been thinking about the woman Penny Wolff and then thinking about Mr. Rodin's accident, but it didn't work. True, Sarah didn't get the creeps very easily but Mr. Rodin's son managed to give them to her every time. All she had to do was check his father's vitals in the moments after a visit, and she'd find his heart rate elevated and his blood pressure in the sky, a look of sheer panic in his eyes.

She stepped back from the small crowd surrounding the TV and watched the man head down the hall, tried not to let her imagination run wild, but she couldn't help the sheet of goose bumps that rose on her skin. Ten minutes. She'd give him ten minutes and then she'd go check in on Mr. Rodin.

She didn't have to. Five minutes after the creepy man came in, he was out again, wheeling his father through the lobby. He stopped and checked him out for the day.

Sarah frowned, hearing the TV reporter's voice in the background expounding on the possibilities of someone in the Atlanta area strangling two women with barbed wire, and the weird coincidence of having a patient here who'd once experienced the same thing, even though by accident.

And then there was the look in the younger Mr. Rodin's eyes as he met her eyes over his shoulder and pushed the wheelchair through the door: *Stop me*, the look said. *I dare you*.

It was official: Sarah had the heebie-jeebies.

CHAPTER
44

A GENT HOGAN PUSHED ASIDE the first set of pictures and laid out a second.

"Here are the 'special' murders," he said to Kara. "In the order you received the packages: Evelyn Camp, nine months ago, from Charleston—a pearl necklace. Then there are two items from victims we haven't identified yet, but there's almost no chance in hell they're alive." He laid out photos the FBI had apparently taken of the woman's watch and the lady's gloves— the next two gifts Kara had received with the horse cards. "Next is Tony Fietti, six months ago from Chattanooga," he said, adding a photo of the engraved pen. She flinched; she had just learned about him this morning. "And after him is another gift we haven't yet matched to a victim." The man's tiger-eye ring.

"And now, Megan Kessler," Luke said. "She's the seventh."

Hogan added her picture along with the photo of the barrette Kara had never actually seen. It had been delivered to the FBI instead of coming to her, but it was the same story. Sending it to the FBI only showed that the killer wasn't going to be waylaid by Kara's hooking up with the authorities. In fact, he seemed to revel in it. And Photoshopping Kara's face to the body only showed that he was—

She swallowed, terror knotting in her throat. "He's finished, isn't he?" she asked. "He's coming for me now."

"When he does," Luke said, "he'll find me."

Kara tried to take comfort in that. Even so, the fear didn't go away.

Mike Hogan leaned back, his gaze on Kara. She knew he was looking for a reaction, something that suggested that seeing it all laid out like this might somehow make sense to her.

It didn't.

She touched the top picture in the right column. "Evelyn Camp," she said. "Tell me about her."

Hogan pulled out his notes. "She was a retired schoolteacher with three grown children. She was twice-divorced and lived with her twin sister. She was out walking her dog—a shih tzu." There was more, and Kara listened. She listened for anything, *anything* that might ring a bell.

Then to Tony Fietti. She'd already learned some of it from Luke and the information Agent Hogan added didn't make things any clearer.

And Megan. They didn't know a lot about her, he said; two FBI agents had been dispatched to speak with her parents this morning. Hogan had wanted to go but deemed it more important to meet Kara and start picking her brain, and it dawned on her that right now, even as they spoke, Megan's parents were being told that their daughter was missing and police didn't know where she was but it was likely she'd been strangled with—

Kara looked up. "Where are their bodies?" she asked, and looked back and forth between the two columns of pictures. "These, on the left... We have those bodies, even Penny Wolff, who was strangled like these others. But these..." She looked up and found Hogan and Luke sharing a glance. Clearly, their minds had gotten there before hers had. "He's doing something with them, isn't he?" she asked, her stomach twisting. "That's what you think."

"It's a good bet," Hogan said. "It seems unlikely to me that if he'd just dumped them the way he did Penny Wolff, that none of them have been found yet over the course of a year. And, there seems to be a delay between the times they disappear and the times he sends you the messages. Like he's doing something that takes a while and doesn't contact you until he's finished."

"Oh, God."

Luke shook his head, looking back and forth between the two sets of pictures. "Andrew is in both groups. He wasn't strangled with barbed wire and we had his body, yet Kara received a gift and a card for him and both messages: *TRUTH* with the sunglasses and *Look what you've done* with his picture—at different times."

Agent Hogan took a deep breath. "I'm not sure I can explain that, except to say that Andrew might have been so important the killer taunted you *both* ways. Andrew started it all. He was your husband. Taking him out of the picture and blaming you for his death was one hell of a way to hurt you. And then the killer hung on to Andrew's sunglasses for a whole year, apparently for the sole purpose of tormenting you."

"So it's more than just personal," Luke said. "It's sexual. He *wants* Kara."

"Maybe, but that's the problem with profiling: We look for patterns, we *live* for patterns, and sometimes, we find them where they don't exist. The bottom line is that logistics still matter to killers, sometimes more than patterns or even reasons. A serial killer who specializes in knives may use a gun now and then, or a car. A guy who kept trophies from his victims may have simply found one trophy in storage he'd forgotten about—like the sunglasses. Most of the time, at least some aspects of the killings don't follow suit and when we make too much out of a deviation, we can be led astray."

"But if that's the case," Kara said, "then there may not be a pattern here at all. He may have gone to Charleston feeling the urge to kill and Evelyn Camp just happened to be a person who walked by. Maybe it was the same in Chattanooga, with Fietti, and the same with Megan Kessler. For God's sake, the whole thing could be random."

"Does it feel random to you? Or does it feel like he's trying to tell you something?"

She quailed. He was right: Not everything fit, but there was a message here. Something Alexander wanted her to know and take the blame for. *TRUTH.*

A terrible thought niggled into her brain, the one no prosecutor dares to ponder. "A defendant," she said. "Someone I prosecuted but who wasn't guilty."

Hogan shook his head. "Mann looked into that first thing. I know that would make sense, but we can't find anyone who looks like that. And no one named Alexander."

Kara let out a breath and it felt as if all the energy went from her body. She didn't know where to start.

"Here's a list of names—common derivatives of Alexander," Hogan said, giving her the list. Alexander, Zander, Al, Alex, Lex, Lexi, Sandy . . . She'd never thought of some of them as variations of Alexander before. "There are three groups of people I'd like you to go through. Start with your cases at work—that's the biggest pool of people who may have a bone to pick with you and there are records that are fairly easy to search. Then, rack your brain in the group of people you would call family, friends, acquaintances, neighbors. I have to assume you two have already ruled out any men you've dated." Kara nodded, not looking at Luke. "Lastly, go back in your history. Think back to the places you lived before Atlanta, acquaintances in college or graduate school, like that. Tag anyone you can think of with a name related to Alexander. But especially tag anyone who fits the profile."

"The profile?" she asked.

"You're looking for someone who's physically strong and in need of control. He's smart, and is getting fulfillment by proving it. Someone with time and money. Someone around your age, give or take a few years, and probably white. Someone who may have worked on a farm or a farm supply store or anyplace he might have come in contact with barbed wire. Someone who is socially competent and probably sexually competent, but who has issues with rage—

"Who killed cats when he was little and hates his mother." Luke's hands fisted. "This is theory, damn it; that's all it is. You're asking her to find a pretend person."

"He's not pretend. And he doesn't hate his mother," Hogan said. "He hates his father."

"How do you know that?"

"He's killing both men and women, without sexual assault. That doesn't sound like mother-rage. Besides," he added, looking at Kara with those clear blue eyes, "this is someone who hates *you*. He wants you to suffer, and he's willing to spend everything he has to see that happen."

"I get that," she said. "I just don't understand why."

"That's the easy part, Kara," Hogan said. "He wants you to learn the truth."

CHAPTER
45

WE'VE GOT A PROBLEM," Knutson said, coming in from the back room where he'd been on the phone. Kara looked up. She'd searched the files of her cases for Alexanders, like Agent Hogan had asked her to. She'd found two so far, but neither was a good candidate. Luke had been working on a set of maps, both on paper and on a computer program. He looked up when Knutson came in, and Hogan came from the kitchen holding a page that curled in his hand. Fresh out of the fax machine that now sat on the peninsula.

"The farmer in Mississippi who found Penny Wolff's body sold the story to a tabloid," Knutson said. "The local newspaper picked it up. Their weekly Thursday paper came out with a special Sunday edition this morning reporting that the body Morris Sledge found was strangled with barbed wire. Sledge gave an 'exposé' detailing the marks he saw on her neck and is claiming the local sheriff's office is conspiring with Georgia officials to keep that information from the public."

"They are," Kara said. It happened all the time: Police withheld details of a crime.

"Not anymore. It's already made the morning news."

"Christ," Luke said. "The press will have a field day with this."

"Done," Knutson said. "Megan Kessler's family chimed in. They're confirming that they've been told she probably died the same way. Pretty soon the whole damn country will be up in arms over the Barbed Wire Strangler." He looked at Luke, and something passed between them that Kara thought was a warning: *Keep your head down, Varón.*

Luke cursed. He pushed back from the table and began pacing. Kara knew he felt like a caged bear: He couldn't work openly on the drug ring anymore and risk Collado recognizing him from his time in South America. And he couldn't work openly on Kara's case and risk being recognized as an FBI agent. He was trapped.

Knutson jerked his chin at Luke. "Come talk a minute?"

They stepped outside and Kara felt Hogan studying her. His intensity was akin to Luke's: powerful and concentrated, bone-deep. She spared a thought to wonder what his life must be like, day in and day out immersed in the study of the most twisted minds on earth. It seemed to have taken a toll on him.

"I'm trying," she said, feeling his gaze like the gavel of a judge. *Guilty: Murder by association.*

He came forward, holding the page from the fax machine in his hand. "See if this helps," he said, and flattened it on the table in front of her.

Kara frowned. It was a sketch, an artist's rendering of a man. Thirty-five-ish, cropped blond hair, wide cheekbones. He was muscular with wide, sloped shoulders in a long-sleeved shirt. His eyes stared at her with menace.

The drawing alone brought a shiver to her skin. "This is him?" she asked, and couldn't believe the fractured sound coming out of her throat was her voice. "Alexander?"

"Ronald Gibson agreed to sit down with an artist. He hadn't seen Alexander for almost a year, but this is what he remembers." Hogan waited, anticipation rolling off him in waves. Kara studied the picture. This was the man they were looking for. The man who'd run Andrew down in a car, killing an FBI agent at the same time. The man who'd killed Louie and Penny and who paid Ronald Gibson to set up the hit on John Wolff in prison. This was the man who'd sent Kara gifts and notes for the past year, and who had killed a twenty-two-year-old girl the night before last with his 'special' barbed wire garrote. This was the man who threatened Aidan and sent them into hiding.

This was the man who was planning to strangle her next. She would be one of his 'special' kills.

And she didn't know who the hell he was.

Tears gathered in her throat. "I don't know," she said. "I mean, there's something familiar about him but... God. I don't know."

Luke came back in the front door. He saw Kara's expression and beelined to the table.

"Fuck," he said when he realized what she was looking at. "This came from Gibson?"

Hogan nodded.

"I can't tell," Kara said. "I mean, those artists' drawings... they're always so generic. I can't tell."

Luke bent down and kissed her head. "It's okay," he said, shooting Hogan a fuck-off glare. "If you've met him, it'll come to you."

She looked up. Knutson hadn't come back. "Was that about Collado?"

"He's moving," Luke said. "He's asking to meet with Montiel and me before he gives the go ahead to move the drugs."

A stab of fear got her in the chest. She cursed herself for feeling it. She had no dibs on Luke. He had every right to finish the job he'd been working on for more than a year here in the States and long before that in Colombia. Frank Collado had shot him, put him in prison, left him to rot. Luke deserved the chance to be there for Collado's demise—especially since he was largely responsible for it.

"Okay," she said, and pushed back from the table to stand. She *was* okay. She didn't need Luke to stay with her.

But, oh, she *wanted* him to, and that realization set her heart spinning.

Get over it. There were a lot of things she'd wanted from the men in her life over the years. Acceptance from her father. Devotion from Andrew. Protection from Luke. Ironic that he was the only one who'd delivered, more so than she had ever dreamed he would. But now he had work to do. She couldn't complain: He was leaving her in good hands.

She rose up on tiptoe and kissed his cheek. "Be careful. Please," she whispered.

He blinked, then his eyes went glacial. "Be careful?" he snarled. "Where the hell do you think I'm going?"

She was taken aback. "Collado—"

"Fuck Collado." He spun away but in the same breath, spun back. Angry. "Jesus, Kara. What do you think you are to me, just another case? Because that's not what I was thinking."

Her pulse trip-hammered. *Really?*

Luke's breathing deepened. "Mike," he said without

looking up, and Agent Hogan said, "Going," and retreated into the back room. Luke continued to glare at Kara, his hands opening and closing at his sides, as if trying to keep himself from touching her.

She tried to explain. "I just thought—"

"You thought we'd play around in bed for a night and then it would be business as usual. I'm not Varón, damn it."

Something in Kara's chest fluttered. She hadn't thought of their night as playing around and then business as usual, but now, trying to justify her own assumptions, she realized it was because she hadn't *thought*, period. Like some needy, frightened, sex-deprived creature, she'd allowed herself to be swept away by Luke: his strength, his safety, his sexuality. She hadn't done it mindlessly and she wasn't sorry. But neither had she dared to view it as anything more.

"It's time to make a decision, Counselor," he said, his voice edged with emotion. "It's not about whether I chase Alexander or whether I chase Collado: I made that decision in the alley and you can't change it. I'm staying with you until this bastard with the wire is caught. You don't have any choice about that."

A windfall of relief swept through her. Her conscience tried to argue that she should be ashamed of that, but she batted it down. "Then, what decision?"

He looked at her as if trying to see to the bottom of her soul. "It's what to do after. I'll catch this killer and keep you and Aidan safe. But for the first time in my life, I can see past the end of a case. I can see who I am and what I want." His gaze dropped to her lips, then climbed to her eyes again and heated. "I'm pretty damn sure it's you."

Kara's bones melted. "It's only been . . . days—"

"It's been a lifetime." He took her shoulders, seeming

to finally lose a battle within himself not to touch her. His fingers bit in hard, his arms tight with restraint. "The first night we spoke in that alley, you claimed to know what kind of man I was. You were wrong then, and you were wrong just now, thinking I'd leave. So, you need to make a decision."

Kara's heart gave a shiver. Luke would let someone else take in Collado in order to stay with her until this was over. And maybe longer. It was a heady sensation, and strange, to be touched that she'd made him so angry. But she was touched, nonetheless. "I'm sorry," she said, and tried to pull herself together. "How about if I take it under advisement?"

Luke cursed, then swooped down, his lips crushing hers, his arms gathering her up against him so that her toes barely touched the floor. He kissed her hard, with a wealth of pent-up emotion rattling through his limbs, her spine bent back and her face tipped up to his. There was nothing tender, just an explosion of primal need that stole her breath and laid claim to something deep in her body, and when he was finished her lips felt swollen and bruised and longing for more.

And she knew she'd been delivered a message: Don't doubt him. He was here to the end.

He set her to arm's length just as the door opened behind them. Hogan cleared his throat. "Sorry," he said. "But you need to see this."

CHAPTER
46

Luke released Kara, startled by his own admission, even more rattled by her assumption that anything—even Collado—could tear him away from her. Jesus Christ, he'd made love to her for a good portion of the night, and he'd done it as Luke Mann. No bogus identity rolling her around in the sheets, no lies or ruses or false promises between them. It had been the most real night of his life and he was terrified of how much he wanted to repeat it. Again and again. Maybe indefinitely.

And it surprised him to think of Aidan: He wanted to tell Aidan who and what he was. That urge had tapped at his conscience all day, and the significance of such an impulse didn't escape notice.

He was in deep.

But none of it mattered if they didn't catch the son of a bitch named Alexander.

Luke closed his eyes, and the image of Kara's face imposed on a dead woman's body rose up to haunt him. *Fuck off, Feds. She's mine.*

No way.

Hogan paused at the door after he spoke, then came up

behind Kara. Luke might have herded him back out of the room if the look on his face hadn't stopped him.

"What is it?" Luke asked.

"I just talked to the lab serving Panola County, Mississippi. They didn't get much out of that cornfield where Penny Wolff was found, but they did get this: stonedust."

Luke frowned. "Stonedust?"

"It's crushed stone that's used in construction. As a foundation or between pavers or bricks—"

"In the middle of a cornfield?"

"Exactly. They found it in small amounts, sprinkled. The pattern based on where the wheels were makes it look like maybe it was in the van when he dragged the body out."

"We may be looking for a landscaper or construction worker, then. That would explain the bodybuilder physique."

"It doesn't explain his money or time, though," Hogan said. "He seems to have plenty of both."

"So, why would a man of leisure have stonedust in his truck?"

"Horses?" Kara asked, and they both looked at her. "Stonedust is used in horseback riding arenas."

Hogan peered at her. "Horse stalls are covered in stonedust?"

"Not the stalls, where horses sleep, but in arenas, where people ride and jump. It's harder than river sand or mulch or sawdust, so it provides a stable surface for the horses."

"Horses," Luke said, thinking it through. "You said you haven't owned a horse in a long time."

Kara shook her head. "Not since Guapa died when I was fifteen. But I know about stonedust footing. My father always insisted on six inches of it in the indoor arenas. He would have the stable hands drag it every damn day to keep it soft. Sometimes he'd actually check the depth with a ruler."

The hairs on the back of Luke's neck stood up. "What about barbed wire? Did your father use that on the ranch?"

She straightened. "Not a lot. It's frowned upon in his circles. But there was some. It was used out in the farthest pastures."

Luke looked at Mike. "You're the psycho expert. Are we looking at someone from that far back? Someone from her childhood?"

"It's a pretty fucking big grudge," Mike said. "It could have that sort of staying power. But it doesn't make sense that this whole thing started only a year ago if it's someone from your childhood. Where has he been in the meantime?"

Kara moved back to the table, picking up the artist's rendering of the man named Alexander. She studied the drawing, shaking her head in tiny movements, and Luke could see her shift gears from the people in her professional and personal lives whose names she'd been sifting through to the people she'd grown up with. He could almost see her try to superimpose images on the one in her hands.

"Who were the people in your life, Kara?" he asked. "Think about social acquaintances, people from the horse breeding world, maybe your father's circle of friends. Think about staff—you said there was a staff at the ranch. Think about people your age or just a little older—"

She gasped, then went still, staring at the man in the picture.

"Kara?" Luke said, coming to stand beside her. Hogan followed.

"There was this guy...but—" She shook her head. "This could be him. But it's been so long."

"Who was he?" Luke snapped. "Christ, Kara. Who?"

"His name was Sasha. I don't remember his last name. Something Russian. His parents were immigrants; I remember that. His father worked in the personal stable and his mother—" She paused. "I never really knew his mother but I think she worked in the kitchen. I remember a woman there who had an accent. She helped me with algebra homework once. I remember being surprised she knew it."

"What do you remember about *him*?" Mike asked.

"Her son? I didn't know him," she said, sounding distant. Mike pulled out his phone and typed something into it. "He was older than I, but not a lot. He played baseball for a while."

"An athlete, then," Luke said. *Strong.*

"I remember being surprised when I learned who his father was. He was so opposite Sasha—thin and gentle. He didn't speak much and I always thought it was because his English wasn't good, but there was a rumor that he was a genius. The kids sometimes teased about it—" She stopped, looking embarrassed. Luke recalled her saying that she hadn't liked that life, having people all around her all the time she barely knew, waiting on her. That's why she had no housekeeper and had raised Aidan to mow his own lawn.

Mike eased up beside Luke. He held out his phone and Luke looked at the screen. He'd accessed the name "Sasha." *A unisex name, orig. eastern and central Europe. Used primarily as a diminutive form of Aleksander or Aleksandra...*

Jesus Christ.

He crossed to Kara and took both her shoulders. "Sweetheart," he said, "when was the last time you saw him? What happened the last time you saw him?"

She looked up, and the look on her face almost knocked Luke back a step. The color leeched from her cheeks.

"Holy God," she said. "It's him."

CHAPTER
47

K ARA'S BLOOD ICED OVER. *Sasha.* She looked at the picture in her hands again but suddenly couldn't focus on it; it wouldn't stay still. Her hands were shaking.

"Why do you think it's him?" Luke asked. He was in her space, his fingers closing around her upper arms. "What do you remember?"

"My fifteenth birthday. He was there."

Luke winced. Agent Hogan hovered behind him. "What happened?"

She swallowed and pulled from Luke's hands, needing to move. The weight of both agents' eyes bore down on her, along with the chilling, sudden certainty that Sasha's eyes had been on her lately, too. *Sasha. Sasha.* She couldn't recall his last name, or that of his mother and father. But she remembered something he'd said to her once: He told her the reason she didn't know him was because he was invisible to her.

He was right. He'd been out there for the past year, watching her, sending her gifts, *killing people.* And she couldn't see him.

TRUTH.

"Kara," Luke said, bringing her back. She collected the memory in bits and pieces, trying to put them together.

"I had a party. It was...extravagant." Another occasion for Willis Montgomery to put his wealth on display to the world. "My father hosted this huge barbecue for a couple hundred of my closest friends," she said, not bothering to hide the sarcasm. "His friends and business associates. He hired all the makings of a carnival. There were events all weekend long, but seven of my friends were invited to stay for the whole week. They were each assigned their own horse for the week and we camped out in the stable..." She stopped, realizing that probably didn't sound very appealing to most people. "Our family stable was like a four-star hotel. We weren't exactly 'roughing it.'"

"It doesn't sound like the kind of birthday you'd like," Luke observed.

"I wanted my father to take me golfing," she said, and managed a smile. "He'd spent every Saturday for as long as I could remember at the golf course, and I always thought if I could golf, then maybe he'd want me arou—" She stopped. Tears collected in her throat. Where the hell had those come from?

She closed her eyes. *Sasha.*

"Sasha was helping his father in the stable, I guess... He'd been away from home for a year or two and had come back, and he was this sort of grown-up bad boy."

Luke's frown deepened. "Did you have a thing for him?"

"No. I didn't really even notice him. My only *thing* was for Andrew."

"Andrew was at the party?" Agent Hogan asked.

"Yes. He came every summer with his dad to breed their mares." She blushed. "That's where it all started for us, I guess."

"At a party where Sasha met Andrew."

She wrapped her arms over her torso. "Maybe," she said, closing her eyes. It all flooded in. The foolish dare, the teasing, the frightening few moments she spent in the tack room with Sasha Ro— "Rodin," she said. "That's his last name."

Hogan scooped up his laptop, opened it up on the back of a big armchair, and stood behind the chair, simultaneously listening to Kara while typing. Luke urged her on.

"You haven't said anything yet that would have caused a grudge seventeen years old."

She couldn't even fathom it. Tears sprang to her eyes because even while her brain couldn't believe it, her heart told her the shocking truth. "It was a game we were playing," she said, and everything inside her turned cold.

"A game," he repeated.

"Truth or Dare."

Sasha didn't understand. A stupid game of Truth or Dare and his father was acting crazy. On eggshells all night, waiting to see if Kara Montgomery was going to spill the beans about her stupid little game, waiting until the party had ended to go and have a private talk with Old Man Montgomery himself. That was a first. As far as Sasha knew, his father had never spoken to Willis Montgomery.

But that night, he did.

And the next day, the Rodin family left Montgomery Manor.

Nothing would ever be the same again.

CHAPTER
48

"TRUTH OR DARE," LUKE said, his blood running cold. Mike's posture stiffened, too: This was it.

"We were in the arena waiting for the horses to be saddled. Evie started the game, just killing time. But—"

She stopped and Luke could tell her mind was taking her somewhere she hadn't been in a long time. Somewhere she didn't want to go.

"It started out just killing time," Luke said. "How did it end?"

She closed her eyes and Luke couldn't tell if it was horror or shame or difficulty remembering that drew her features tight. But after a moment, she looked at him. "It ended with me hitting Sasha."

Luke hiked up his brows. "Why?"

"Andrew embarrassed me—and made me mad. He was asked in the game which one of us he wanted to be with and he chose Evie. I thought he liked me and when he chose Evie, I wanted to crawl into a hole and hide. So I did the next best thing: I took a dare on the next question, trying to show him up."

Luke's mind started going bad places. "Go on."

She walked the length of the rug and back. "They dared me to play 'Seven Minutes of Heaven' with Sasha. It's a game where—"

"I know what it is," Luke said, and his mind grew even darker.

She swallowed, looking back and forth between him and Mike, who stood listening as intently as Luke but probably with a clearer head. Hopefully. Luke's was beginning to cloud with emotion.

"I went with him into the tack room."

"Tack room?" Mike asked.

"The storage for tack—saddles, bridles, crops. It was huge, so we also stored other things there. Feeding and cleaning supplies, bags of stonedust and bedding, riding apparel—" She stopped short and her face went sheet white. "Coils of barbed wire."

Luke stopped breathing. "What the fuck happened in there, Kara?"

"He wanted me on my knees. He tried to make me—"

"Son of a bitch."

"But I didn't. I played along just long enough to catch him off guard. Then I got my hand on a riding crop and I hit him and I ran out."

"That was it?" Mike asked. "You ran away from him?"

"What do you mean, *That was it?*" Luke was furious but Mike held up a hand.

"I mean, did something else happen? Something more than a guy getting blue-balled by a cute girl?"

"I went into that tack room with him. I accepted the dare: seven minutes. I didn't think much could happen in that amount of time, and I was more interested in showing Andrew up than anything else. Until I got in there with him, I didn't realize the extent of what he thought we'd do."

"You're defending the bastard," Luke said.

"I'm not," she snapped. "I'm acknowledging that I wasn't blameless. And that I agree with Agent Hogan: It wasn't a big enough deal to make him punish me by killing people seventeen years later."

"I didn't exactly say that," Mike said. "I've known people to kill because of a perceived slight in words. I've known people to kill for a forty-dollar speed ball. Given the right circumstances, it doesn't take much."

"What are the right circumstances?" Kara asked.

"A personality disorder or some emotional hardship, probably with his father, combined with physical or emotional stresses—"

"A fucking asshole with a naïve fifteen-year-old girl in front of him," Luke injected.

Mike said, "You're a real insightful dude, you know that, Mann?"

Luke crossed to him. "What I know is that you're standing there trying to paint a picture of a personality while that personality—whatever the hell it is—is out preparing to strangle Kara with barbed wire. I don't much care *why* he wants to do it. I only care about stopping him."

"Then shut up and let Kara tell us how he's going to do it." He went back to Kara. "Was that the last time you saw Sasha Rodin?"

"Yes. His family left Montgomery Manor. We never saw them again. I always thought it was because he was afraid I might tell someone what happened that day. You know, rich man's daughter accuses employee of rape."

"And you didn't?" Luke asked, although he knew the answer. Kara would have tried to handle it on her own. God knows, her father wouldn't have been a shoulder for her to cry on.

"No. I just ran out and left Sasha there, and all the kids were waiting and giggling and wanted to know what happened, and we made a pact not to tell anyone. It would have shamed my father."

"Jesus," Luke said, and she looked at him, as if trying to make him understand.

"I was embarrassed, too. And Andrew . . . Later, he told me he'd only named Evie in the game because he was hoping to make me jealous. It became a joke. We dated for the next two years and when I became pregnant, we married."

Mike set aside the laptop and walked over to Kara. "If that was the last time you saw Sasha, something else must have happened that set him off. Something that simmered for all these years. What did he say, what did he do?"

She frowned, trying to think. "He was bitter about his life, and jealous of mine."

"What makes you say that?"

"He told me that he'd been at Montgomery Manor longer than I had and that I was probably born of someone as low a class as he was."

"I don't understand," Mike prompted.

"I was adopted. It happened when I was an infant, so it's the only home I know, but Willis and Nina Montgomery aren't my blood parents."

"And Sasha knew this?"

"Everybody knew it. My mother and father threw the party of the century the day they brought me home. The first of many."

"Okay," Mike said, and Luke kept his eyes on Kara. She was speaking of her childhood in general as if it had no lasting legacy, but he knew it must.

Kara went on, the memories now seeming to fall

into place. "Sasha told me Andrew only flirted with me because my father and his were in business together. He called me 'princess' and 'rich bitch' and referred to Andrew as Pretty Rich Boy." She stopped, seeming wearied by it all. "My friends and I put him in a position where the class system seemed alive and well. Hell, at Montgomery Manor, it *was* alive and well. My father treated the staff like lower-class citizens and if Sasha's family felt that, then maybe that's how this started."

A class issue, a crush on a rich girl. It was the stuff of dramas throughout history, but it didn't seem enough for Luke.

"Is there anyone from the party that you're still friends with?" Luke asked. "Someone who might remember more than you do?"

She thought about it. "Evie and I lost touch pretty soon after that. Gosh, I don't know where Anthony went after college." She paused, trying to think of the other people who had been there, but something she'd just said reached out and grabbed Luke by the throat.

Evie. Anthony. "Who else?" In some ways, the thought was laughable. In others—Jesus.

"Jessica Morrow was there," she said. "She Facebooked me a year or so ago, so I could probably reach her. And I think she's still in touch with Matthew. I don't know about Megan. She went to Europe after col—" She stopped, realizing what she'd just said.

"Evie," he prompted. "Was her name Evelyn?"

Her face went slack. "Anthony . . ."

Mike moved in: "Tony Fietti."

"Oh, God," Kara said.

"Who else?" Mike said, and Luke handed her a piece of paper.

"Write them down," he said, trying to keep her busy and calm. "Write down the names."

She did, her hands shaking, and gave the list to Mike. *Andrew, Evie, Anthony, Megan.* And names they hadn't heard yet: *Jessica, Matthew, Laura.*

Mike took the list, shaking his head as if he couldn't believe it. "He's killing people who were at your party—people of the same name."

"What the fuck for?" Luke asked.

"I don't know. But I can tell you this: We're gonna find out that those gloves and the tiger-eye ring and the watch you received belonged to people with these names. Evelyn's sister said they felt like they were being watched for weeks before her murder. He's identifying targets with the right name, and killing them. Collecting gifts from them to send to you." He narrowed his gaze at her and Luke couldn't help putting his arm around her. She'd gone as stiff as blown glass and looked just as fragile.

"You said it was summer when this happened—when the mares were bred," Mike said. "When is your birthday, Kara?"

Her breath hitched, and Luke could see her thinking through the past few days, which had somehow all run together.

"Today," she said, so softly Luke could hardly hear her. "June twenty-third."

CHAPTER
49

"H APPY BIRTHDAY TO YOU, *happy birthday to you…*"
Sasha sang to himself, humming when the words got tiring, which was after about ten seconds, but keeping the tune going. He wanted his father to hear.

The stable was ready. He'd scrubbed it clean, raked the stonedust in the arena, and freshened the bedding in each stall. Stuck his father's chair at the mouth of the large lobby so he could watch it all happening. He took down every nameplate and wiped it free of dust, then—making sure his father was watching—tied a balloon to each one before hanging it back on the proper stall.

"How did I do, *nana*?" he asked, turning to his father. "It looks good, yes?"

Sasha smiled. It looked more than good. It was perfect.

"An exact replica of Montgomery Manor—at least, as exact as I could remember. I spent years drawing the plans and re-drawing, calculating measurements in my head." He scoffed. Not much else to do in prison. "I got this land for a song, though the money doesn't matter, does it? There's plenty of that. I went to four different architects before I found one who was willing to recreate this exact design, then overpaid a builder to get it done in a hurry. After all, I'd already found an Evie and was anxious to get started. Well, her full name was Evelyn, but that was close enough. Just a slight derivation. Like Alexander and Sasha."

His father seemed to be struggling to breathe.

"Oh, Papa, what's the matter?" He shook his head, making a *tsk* sound. "Those nurses at the home don't think you understand anything. But you do, don't you?" He walked over to the wheelchair and crouched to his haunches, right in front of his father, using illogically tender movements to straighten the dark blue throw over his father's knees and tug his pajama collar straight. He looked up at the gaping eyes and mouth. "Your Stefan could have never done this. All that brilliance he inherited from your gene pool, and yet who's the genius now?"

He rolled his father's chair down the wide aisle to the eighth stall—the supersize one that had once housed the mare named Guapa. In the middle of the stall gaped a hole deep enough to hold a body.

"I'll bet you're wondering what I'm going to do here, aren't you, *nana*?" He strode over to the wheelchair, enjoying his father's horror. "You remember, the princess of Montgomery Manor? You told me I was a fool for wanting her, just like I was an imbecile at my school work and that baseball was the waste of a brain. You said when I tried to touch her I ruined everything." The anger started to pop in the back of his mind, little bubbles of memory that burst in his brain. He shook his head to try to scatter them. They didn't matter anymore.

"I didn't understand, did I, Papa? And you wouldn't tell me. That was part of the deal with Old Man Montgomery, wasn't it? That I couldn't know the truth." He got in Dmitri's face again. "Well, I do know the truth now. And soon, so will Kara. Tonight, she'll get an invitation she won't be able to refuse. Your cute little nurse, Sarah, will take care of that, just as soon as she goes into your room to change your bedsheets."

A throb started at the back of his skull but he smothered it. Don't let it take over. Not yet, not now, when he was so close.

He took one last look about, then spun his father's wheelchair around, wheeled him through the stall corridor, and pulled the chair upstairs, backward, one step at a time, into the viewing balcony for the arena. He turned the chair away from the arena and instead aimed his father toward the lobby and stall aisles. From there, he would be able to see everything that happened.

"There," he said, putting on the brake of the wheelchair. He straightened his father's blanket and hat, and took a step back. "I have to leave you for a little while, *nana*. There's something I need to do to make sure Kara cooperates." He pulled an iPhone from his pocket, the one belonging to Aidan. He hadn't dared to put the battery in for fear they might be looking for it. Now, it wouldn't matter if they used it to find him. He wanted them to. He expected them to.

"Enjoy the show, Papa."

CHAPTER
50

*A*LEXANDER *(S*ASHA*) R*ODIN.
    Luke studied the files. Rodin had been killing people in the area surrounding Atlanta for more than a year, and yet they couldn't find a single fucking sign of him. No driver's license, no employment, no car title, no renter's agreement or mortgage. The man had come to Atlanta and disappeared.

Busy killing people representing Kara's fifteenth birthday party. Sick bastard.

Luke forced himself to stay with the paper, learning everything he could. As soon as they had his name, the investigation seemed to put on running shoes. Mike took what Kara had told them and headed to the field office to meet with the SAC and address the task force. Luke and Kara stayed at Montiel's lodge and delved into the Rodins' history, using Bureau-backed computers that allowed Luke a level of security clearance capable of accessing almost anything. He found the elder Rodin almost right away, through immigration records: Dmitri and his wife Darya had emigrated from a village near Moscow in 1974, more than forty years ago. He was a mathematician and

she a physicist, and they'd had one son named Stefan.
Employment landed them at Montgomery Manor in '76,
where Sasha was born and where they worked as menial
laborers, despite the fact that they were both highly
educated.

They left on the night of Kara's fifteenth birthday.

Luke managed to access some school records: Stefan
was the perfect, straight-A student; Sasha struggled. Luke
made a mental note of this, but couldn't wrench sibling
rivalry into a vengeful murder spree against Kara seventeen years later. Not unless—

"Did you know his brother?" Luke asked.

She shook her head. "I didn't even know he had one."

And he hadn't, at least not by the time Kara would have
been old enough to remember. Luke kept digging and
found that Stefan Rodin had contracted spinal meningi-
tis when he was twelve. He died, leaving Sasha the only
child.

There wasn't much more of interest until Sasha turned
eighteen: He landed a minor league baseball contract.
It ended after only two years, among rumors of ill-will
between players and even accusations of assault, but there
were no charges filed. Sasha went back home to Virginia,
and a few weeks later, Kara Montgomery had a fifteenth
birthday bash.

"I don't know what happened to him after that," Kara
said, rubbing a crease between her eyes. "We never saw
them again."

But just then, the laptop dinged. Luke opened a mes-
sage from Mike at headquarters: RAPE/ASSAULT OF
MARTI DELANEY, SKOKIE, IL 1998—U.S. PENITENTIARY
AT MARION, ILLINOIS. RELEASED MAR 2012.

"Jesus," Luke said, typing as fast as his fingers would

go. He looked up the name Marti Delaney and found coverage of the stories right away. Two years after leaving Virginia—when Kara was off at "boarding school" with a swollen belly, Sasha Rodin had raped and beaten Delaney to within an inch of her life.

He clicked on a photo of the victim, taken after the trial had ended, and his heart stood still. Kara sucked in a breath.

"That could be you," Luke said. "Before Maddie re-did your hair and makeup. Jesus, Kara, that woman could be you."

She stared at it and Luke called the research office. "Get in touch with Skokie," he said. "We need to know what Sasha Rodin was doing there in 1998 and every detail you can scrounge up about the rape that put him in prison. Have someone get with prison officials. As far as I can tell, Rodin served his entire sentence, which means someone didn't want to see him paroled. Find out who. Find out why. Find out what he ate for breakfast every morning and how many times a day he peed."

He hung up, for the first time realizing how quickly things had changed. The SAC had put seven agents at Mike's disposal. Two of them were charged with finding missing persons in the past year whose first names were Matthew, Jessica, and Laura. One, a Matthew, had already been identified from police reports in Nashville, about four hours away. An agent had been sent to talk to his family and find out if he'd owned a tiger-eye ring, but no one doubted it. It was only a matter of time before the other two owners of the gifts would be discovered as missing persons as well, now that they had names to look for. Everything had changed.

It was a far cry from the speed with which things

progressed in Luke's world. In his cases, time was measured in months and years: months of creating, backing up, and memorizing a deep-cover story; months of taking baby steps to insinuate yourself into an organization, then more baby steps to pass all their tests and become integral to their operation; years of recording conversations, running deals, getting to know the players, documenting procedures, and making sure the Federal Attorneys had a record of every conversation, every dollar, every ounce, and every phone call, so no one slipped away.

Like Collado.

Luke looked at his watch: 2:08 in the afternoon. Burke had brought Gene Montiel to meet with Collado—alone—claiming Luke Varón was in the sack with a hot little number from The Parthenon and refused to be disturbed. They'd provided pictures of Luke walking with Kara on the front path of The Parthenon, his hand laid possessively on the small of her back, and more of him crowding her against the Escalade in a dark parking lot by the lake, engaged in a thoroughly convincing public display of affection. Burke complained to Collado that Varón wasn't playing fair, swearing he'd have his turn at the girl named Krista as soon as Varón resurfaced. Apparently, it had been played well: Collado settled for confirming all the deliveries through Burke and Montiel and gave the order to ship out.

The cocaine had started moving at noon today. It was on its way to fifteen stations across the southeast and Federal Agents waited, backed by local police and SWAT and canines, at every site. Frank Collado had been in a tight net of security from the moment he shook Gene Montiel's hand and stepped onto U.S. soil.

He was finished.

Hit man Luke Varón was finished.

Special Agent Lukas Mann was just beginning.

"You okay?"

Luke turned to see Kara regarding him. Yeah, he was okay. He put his hands on either side of her face and bent down, infusing his kiss with all the pent-up emotion that had gathered in his chest since Kara had summoned him to that alley. Such a short period of time, yet both of their lives had changed irrevocably. At least, Luke hoped both their lives had changed. He knew at least his had.

The front door opened and Hogan cursed. "Tell you what," he said as Luke came up from the kiss. "When this is over, I'll spring for you two to get a room."

"We had a room," Luke said. "You crashed it."

Mike slid his briefcase onto the table and opened it in one motion. "The lab worked up the photo of Megan Kessler. She was sitting on a floor of sawdust and the walls at her back were rough-hewn pine." He looked at Kara. "Sound familiar?"

"A horse stall," she said.

"He's got a stable somewhere. That's where the stone-dust in his van came from and that's where he took Megan Kessler's body. And you can bet that's where the others are."

"Oh, God." Kara wrapped her arms around herself.

"What about the maps?" Luke asked.

"I've got them right here." Mike spread them out. Luke, using a triangulation program, had entered all the locations where they knew Sasha had been. "Based on what we know, we think his home base is in this area."

The computer program had highlighted a block in yellow. It included the entire metro-Atlanta area and the areas north and northwest of the city, from Marietta to

Canton. A legend identified each mark on the map: places
he'd killed someone, places they'd found a body, places
they knew he'd visited, places where he'd made a phone
call or they'd gotten a signal from a dumped phone. Kara's
house and office had several hits; Luke's burned-up house
had one; there was the Mississippi cornfield, Penny
Wolff's house, the Floyd Correctional Institute, and the
places Gibson had said they met. Rodin had driven fairly
good distances to either find a victim or, in Penny's case,
to dispose of one, but otherwise, the north Atlanta area
was his stomping grounds.

"Jesus, he's close," Luke said, and the nape of his neck
prickled. He could *feel* him.

"When we know where the other victims came from,
this yellow area will change some. But for now, this is
what we have."

"It's a big area," Kara said.

"But now we know Megan was in a stable," Luke said.
"We can ax a lot of this by focusing on that."

"Done," Mike said. "As soon as I got this information,
I had someone start looking up stables in this yellow zone.
It's still too big an area to go door to door, but a few hours
from now, they'll have some places pinpointed."

"Someplace that's been bought or sold since he got out
of prison," Luke said.

"Right. And someplace that has an arena." He looked
at Kara. "You said stonedust isn't used in stalls."

Luke said, "What about Illinois?"

Mike put a hand on his lower back and stretched;
here was a man who spent too many hours on planes and
hunched over files. "He was supposed to be under man-
datory supervised release after he got out of prison; he
jumped. Probably typed Kara's name into a people-search

engine and headed to Atlanta. But here's the interesting thing: His father disappeared at the same time. He lived in Kentucky, where he'd picked up another job at a stable. His wife had died a couple years earlier. Sasha got released from prison and instead of participating in the release program, he disappeared. A week later, his father stopped showing up for work and quit paying rent and picking up his mail…"

"Ah, jeez," Luke said. "Number twelve."

The phone rang and they all looked at their cells. It was Mike's: the SAC. Mike put it on speaker. "Agent Hogan, we found the victim named Laura. She was a mother of two who was headed to a friend's wedding in Carrollton, Georgia. She never made it there."

"Did the watch belong to her?"

"Checking. Carrollton's only ninety minutes away; I've got the husband on his way in. But there's also a call that came into police in Alpharetta a couple hours ago, and it wound its way around to us."

"Who is it?"

"A staff member at the Mountain Ridge Nursing Home. She claims they have a patient there who might have been strangled with barbed wire."

CHAPTER
51

S ETH GUILFORD COULDN'T REMEMBER ever *wanting* to
go to his church youth group before. It met for Sunday
evening dinners when he always had homework he'd been
putting off all weekend, was led by two college students
who thought they were cool but weren't, and they usually
did something lame like plan for car washes and spaghetti
dinners or watch movies that were supposed to challenge
their faith in God. Seth didn't like planning things, didn't
like spaghetti, and had already lost his faith in God.

But tonight, he wanted to go. His dad had died on
Thursday at the ball game and his best friend and proxy-
aunt had blown up in a boat explosion the next night. His
mom did nothing but cry all the time and try to hide it
from him, and there were relatives all over the house for
the funeral, who kept patting him on the back and stu-
pidly asking if he was okay.

Aidan—the one person who would have understood
what Seth was going through—was gone.

Seth felt lost.

Guess that's what his mom had been trying to tell him
all along by making him go to church and join the youth

group. Maybe this was the kind of time when it wasn't all that lame. When your life was falling apart.

His mom didn't quiz him about it when he said he wanted to go; she just nodded and dropped him off. And to Seth's surprise, the uncool leaders of the group led everybody in a pretty cool memorial service for Seth's dad and Aidan, where everyone got to talk about why God let shit like this happen, and where they were allowed to be pissed off, and where no one even suggested they were supposed to accept these things as "God's will." He hadn't expected to, but after an hour or so, when the pizzas came, he actually felt a little better.

He was just going to the bathroom when his cell phone vibrated. His mom, probably, worried about him. He pulled the phone from his pocket and looked, and his breath caught in his chest.

Aidan.

His heartbeat tripled. *Aidan? Oh, God. It can't be, he's gone. Can it? Wait.* Seth's brain scrambled to that first day after the explosion—it was all a blur—when police were frantically dragging the lake and looking for signs of them. For a while, they'd hoped that—

He stopped himself. Get a grip. It couldn't be Aidan.

But what if it was? What if, somehow, he was alive?

Seth opened the text message, his heart in his throat.

its me—im alive. in trouble don't tell.
come to dumpster behind pool. hurry.

Agent Hogan was the official face of the investigation and the Bureau's way of showing the media they had brought in their top minds, so he went to talk to the husband of the missing Laura. Kara called the nursing home and made arrangements for her and Luke to meet with the girl who'd called in.

Sarah Fogt was a nineteen- or twenty-year-old nurse's aide with spikes of purple in bleached-white hair and a stud in her eyebrow. An older woman ushered her into the office, then crossed her arms, glaring at Kara.

"There was no reason for Sarah to notify authorities," the older woman said, pursing her lips. Kara read her tag: Ms. HENDERSON, RN, LNFA. An administrator. "Mr. Rodin's condition was not a secret."

"We want to see him," Kara said.

"Well, I'm afraid that's not possible right now. His son took him out for the day."

Kara's belly flopped.

"He just wheeled a man out the front doors?" Luke asked.

"It's not a prison, Agent Mann. Family members are encouraged to take patients out."

Dear God, Kara thought. Sasha Rodin had taken his father away. "Sarah, you said Mr. Rodin has marks on his neck that look like barbed wire."

The girl nodded. "It's creepy. And they *are* from barbed wire."

"Mr. Rodin was involved in an accident before he came here," Ms. Henderson said.

"How long before?" Kara asked.

Henderson pinched her lips. "There are confidentiality issues to consider, Ms. Chandler."

Kara glanced at Luke and he nodded: *Take it away, Counselor.* Kara closed in. "Ms. Henderson, it looks to me as if the staff of Mountain View failed to report suspected abuse and endangerment of a patient in its care. Do you know what the penalty is for that?"

"Now, wait a minute—"

Kara produced the sketch of Sasha Rodin, held it up in front of both women. "Is this the man who signed Mr. Rodin out for the day?"

Ms. Henderson looked away. Sarah seemed to shiver.

"It could be," Sarah said. "But those eyes aren't quite right."

"What was he wearing?" Kara asked.

"Jeans and a long-sleeved shirt. I've never seen him in anything else, no matter how hot it is."

"And you believe he may have harmed Mr. Rodin."

Sarah opened her mouth but Henderson cut her off. "If anyone at this nursing home believed that, we would have reported it. I told you: We've never had any reason to believe that Mr. Rodin was in danger from his son."

Sarah looked at her hands, wringing them. Luke leaned in, his voice a rumble. "You don't have to be afraid, Sarah. If anyone's job is on the line here, it's not going to be yours." He said it with a perfectly timed glance to Henderson.

Sarah swallowed. "I've just never trusted him. Whenever he came, his father's vital signs skyrocketed and he tried to speak. And the marks on his neck... It just seemed—" She shivered. "I asked about them. I heard the story. It didn't seem right. And then, this morning, when I saw the news..." She took a deep breath. "I shouldn't have waited. I should have called the police right away or stopped his son from taking him."

Luke crossed to Ms. Henderson. "I want all the records you have on Mr. Rodin, including his son's address and phone number, any insurance, records of his checks—everything." She didn't answer and he narrowed his eyes.

"Are you going to make me get a subpoena? Because I can do that, but it will put me in an even worse mood than I'm in now and that's not a pretty sight."

"It's not that," she snapped.

"Then what is it?"

"We don't have any records of insurance or financial statements. And the contact information—" She stopped and closed her eyes, and Kara recognized it: a guilty mind, trapped.

"You don't have that, either," Kara said.

"I did. But it's bogus. I tried to call him at the number he provided a couple of months ago when his father had a reaction to some medication. It wasn't a working number and the address he gave...I mapquested it. It doesn't exist."

"And you never confronted him about it?" Kara asked.

"It didn't seem necessary to pull Mr. Rodin from care just because—"

"Bullshit." Luke glared at her. "Who's paying his tab?"

"That's confiden—"

Luke bore down on her. "The man you've been in cahoots with is a cold-blooded killer. He took his father out of here today and we have every reason to believe he's planning to kill him. Now tell me the fucking truth: Where did the money come from?"

"Cash," she said, breaking. "Mr. Rodin's son paid cash. For a full year, he paid up front. The year just ended and he came to me with one more month's payment. A week ago."

Kara blinked. *One month.* She looked at Luke, who looked ready to blow.

"Did that include a little something for you?" he asked, and Henderson's face turned beet red.

Dear God. Sasha Rodin had cash, more than they'd

even imagined. Enough to leave no trail of anything. No wonder they couldn't find a record of him in Atlanta.

"We need to have a look around his room now," Kara said. "Do you have any problem with that, Ms. Henderson?"

She closed her eyes on something that might have been a prayer.

"Of course not."

Inside Room 144, the odor of stale human touched Luke's nostrils. He shut the door behind them and the second it clicked, Kara turned to him.

"Sasha's going to kill him," she said, looking at the empty bed. "He's got everyone he needs for the party except me, and Hogan said he probably hated his father. His father was there, Luke, at the party. He's going to kill him."

Nausea balled in Luke's gut. If the layer of air freshener were stripped away, the room would smell almost like a Colombian prison cell.

"Get that light," he said, suddenly claustrophobic. He hit the switch for the overhead fluorescents and Kara turned on a table lamp. The sickness eased a fraction.

They began looking around the room. It was sterile and small, with a couple of dusty knickknacks on the window ledge and a clock on the wall so the patient could watch his life tick away. A luxury Luke hadn't known during his time in a cell.

He pulled the blanket from the bed—no one had been in here since Mr. Rodin left this morning—and shook it out. Nothing. A stack of old magazines sat on the nightstand and he looked at them. They were in Russian, some sort of mathematics journals. They were from the 1990s.

Luke picked one up, remembering that Sasha's father

had a doctorate in math. He thumbed through it—puzzles and formulas and math problems, to the extent Luke could tell. His Russian was lacking.

He stopped, looking at the inside front cover. *STEFAN* was penciled in, in what appeared to be a child's handwriting. He picked up another—same thing. They had all belonged to Stefan.

He reached across the bed and handed one to Kara. "Does that look like a child's hand to you?" he asked, showing her one of the puzzles.

"Maybe," she said. She looked at another. "Yes."

Huh. He had to wonder why a man whose mind was gone kept math puzzles at his bedside that had been done by his dead son. Kara kept moving, opening and closing the nightstand drawers. She started pawing at pillows, frowned, and stopped cold.

"What is it?" Luke asked.

Kara pulled out an envelope. Her name was on the front.

"Oh, God," she said, dropping it on the bed. She backed up as if it were a bug and Luke's heart slowed. He picked up the envelope and opened it, touching it as little as possible.

On the outside of the card was one word: *DARE*. Inside, in cursive letters, it said, *It's a party!* And the details were hand-printed in the proper spaces:

When? SUNDAY, JUNE 23, 8:52 p.m.
Where? TBA
What to bring? YOURSELF. ALONE.

CHAPTER
52

T HEY CALLED MIKE, WHO met them in the parking lot
of a Waffle House.

"It's six o'clock," Mike said when Luke approached his
car.

Luke frowned. "What do you mea—" Then he remembered: Collado. Jesus. It was lift-off.

He pulled out his phone just as it vibrated in his hand.
A text from Knutson. *We're moving.*

A ribbon of satisfaction curled in his belly. It was happening. A nationwide, coordinated effort that would shut
down the entire Collado network and arrest the top two
levels of the syndicate, all in less than ten minutes' time.

It was impressive and it was his, but it didn't matter
anymore. He had other things to think about now.

Kara got out of the car and joined them—she'd been
talking to Aidan—and Mike caught them up. "Bruce
Finney confirmed that the watch you received back in the
fall belonged to his wife, Laura. He reported her missing in September when she disappeared after an aerobics
class. Carrollton police have found no sign of her."

"God," Kara said, and Luke felt the weight of yet

another person's life press down. The party guests were all dead: Megan Kessler had been the last one. But Sasha's father—God willing—could still be alive. They just had to keep him that way.

And, of course, Kara.

"Give me the card," Mike said, and Kara pulled it from her bag. She'd wrapped it in a paper towel from Dmitri Rodin's bathroom—not that fingerprints mattered. They knew who he was. As a former inmate of Federal prison, they had DNA aplenty to match to.

Mike looked at the card and cursed. "Eight fifty-two? What kind of party time is that?"

Luke had checked. "It's sundown tonight."

"Son of a bitch," Mike said beneath his breath. Then he opened his briefcase on the trunk of his car and stuck the invitation inside, exchanging it for a larger envelope of photos. He started going through them, one by one. "We've been running the yellow zone. These are aerial images of sixteen properties zoned for livestock. They all have arenas, indoors or out. We're using county deputies to drive around and check them; anything with stonedust footing will make our short list—"

"Wait," Kara said, stopping his hand. "Go back."

He slid the previous satellite image back on top. Kara touched her stomach.

"Oh, my God. That's Montgomery Manor."

"What?" Mike said.

"My home, where I grew up. This is Montgomery Manor."

Luke looked: The image showed a sprawling L-shaped complex of buildings in an open field. A completely open field—unnaturally empty. No trees, no bushes, no buildings, no crops.

"I'm telling you," she said, her voice still shaking but getting some of its strength back, "that's exactly the layout, the size. This building is the arena, and here's the lobby and the stall aisle. There are bathrooms under this roof and the tack room here, and all along this wall of the arena is a viewing balcony so people can watch the riders. And here," she said, pointing at a very small square roof, "Dear God, that's a wishing well." She looked up. "It's exactly like home."

"Where is this place?" Luke asked, and Mike held up the photo. In digital, hard-to-read letters, the address was printed in the bottom right corner: *3270 St Rt 143, Hayden, GA.*

"Hayden," Mike said. "How far away is that?"

"From here, about an hour and a half," Kara said.

Luke looked at her, seeing the wheels begin to spin in her mind. Sasha had put *TBA* for the location of the party, undoubtedly wanting to withhold that information until he was ready for her. But now, they knew in advance. Nearly three hours before he expected her, they knew where he would be at nine o'clock. Or eight fifty-two, rather.

Sick bastard.

Luke looked at Kara, saw her processing the information. The sun beat down on the parking lot, lifting tiny beads of perspiration beneath her throat, where her pulse throbbed like a piston. "No way am I letting you go up there, Kara. No way."

She looked at him, her eyes seeming to clear as she came to grips with what she'd just seen. "He knows that," she said, frowning. "After all he's done to make sure I know what he wants to do to me, there's no way he believes he can send me an invitation and I'll actually show up. And even if I did think that, he'd have to know I'd bring a slew of FBI agents with me."

"It's the dare," Hogan said. "You accepted it once before. He may be so far gone that he thinks you'll do it again."

"I don't buy it," Kara said, and something deep in Luke's chest moved. She was right. It wouldn't be as simple as Kara showing up to the party.

"If he doesn't think you'll accept a simple invitation, then he must have another way of getting you to cooperate. At least he thinks he does."

Aidan. The thought hit all of them at the same time. But she'd just hung up with him, not five minutes ago. He was fine.

"Mike," Luke said anyway, "move Aidan. Change safe houses, add guards."

Mike nodded and Kara shuddered. "They won't let Sasha get to him," Luke said. "I promise."

He could see that she was trying to believe him. "Then what do you think he'd use to get me to come?" she asked. "Why would I go to him?"

Her phone rang—the iPhone. Luke's heart jammed.

Kara dug out the phone and looked at it, holding it out among the three of them with shaking fingers. It was an unknown number. But not a text, and not a picture. Just a regular phone call.

She cleared her throat and touched it to life. "Hello?" she said.

"Aunt Kara?" A boy's voice, cracking. "It's me, Seth. Please do what he says, Aunt Kara. He's going to kill me."

CHAPTER
53

"VERY GOOD," SASHA SAID, taking the phone from the boy. He glanced up to the balcony where his father sat in the chair and hoped the old man hadn't fallen asleep while Sasha had been out getting Seth and setting up birthday surprises around the perimeter of the stable. The kid had been easy—having Aidan Chandler's phone was a boon. Seth had made his way to the Dumpster behind the neighborhood pool. Sasha rolled up and asked if he was looking for Aidan, and Seth came right up to the van.

Of course, now Sasha had to move. He only had a few more hours until Kara would come waltzing through the door.

Well, maybe not waltzing, but he had no doubt she would come. For one thing, he'd issued a dare, and Kara Montgomery was too haughty to resist that. She'd proved that seventeen years ago. But more importantly, if she didn't come, the boy was going to die. And Sasha knew she wouldn't stand for that.

It would have been better to have Aidan, but this would do. In fact, having the FBI provide him with the added challenge was...invigorating. They had called for brilliance and Sasha had risen to it.

So there, Dad.

"Move," he said to the kid, whose hands were tied behind his back. "I have a very special place for you."

Luke made the ninety minutes to Hayden, Georgia, in sixty-five. Kara had never been there before but looked it up on the way: It was a tiny little unincorporated township that had no police department and shared a sheriff with the rest of Pickens County. En route, they arranged for a local crop duster to fly the sheriff over the stable area—they didn't want to use a marked helicopter—and look for any strange activity. When Kara and Luke arrived, the sheriff reported that all was quiet. There was no sign of Sasha.

No sign of Seth.

Kara closed her eyes, trying not to picture it. *Seth.* Poor child had just lost his father and thought he'd lost Aidan, and now—

Look what you've done.

They gathered in—of all places—the local elementary school. They needed a place where they could set up computers and communications equipment that was big enough to gather area SWAT teams and deputies. Two other agents had come with Mike—the Special Agent in Charge—a man named MacGregor, and a tech specialist who would keep everyone hooked up. In addition, a half dozen Pickens County deputies gathered at the school, obsequious in their offers to help with something that would no doubt be the case of the decade: Assistant District Attorney Kara Chandler was alive. The FBI was chasing a serial killer who strangled his victims with barbed wire. A teenage boy and an elderly man were hostages.

Exciting stuff.

Kara shook that off and looked at the computer screen. The group gathered around and the tech guy said, "Hold on," and pushed some keys, and the display on the desktop appeared on a whiteboard on the wall. It was live feed of the stable, showing four different views on a four-way split screen.

"Christ," Mike said, seeing the stable closer up for the first time. "There's no place to hide. What are those fields, corn? Shouldn't corn be as high as an elephant's eye or something?"

"Not quite yet," said a deputy, "but it still—"

"He cut it," Luke said, pointing at one corner of the screen where the lay of the ground was more visible.

"We wondered about that," the deputy said, scratching his chin. "Me and Truitt rode past there a week ago and saw it bein' mowed down. All belongs to Bob Tucker. An' there was Bob, out cuttin' down his own crop a good two months before harvest."

"What do you mean?" Kara asked.

"I didn't talk straight t' Tucker, mind you, but heard in town that the owner of the stable paid him three times what he'd get at harvest to take it down now. Owner told him it was diseased an' had to go." The deputy scoffed. "No disease. That stable guy just didn't want it there."

Kara started to ask why—why would a man pay to have cornfields taken down?—when the answer came clear on the live images on the wall: Along the east side of the stable, about fifty yards out, a line of SWAT officers could be seen jogging into place around the buildings.

"He can see us coming from any direction," Luke said. "Jesus, there's not a damn thing to use for cover." He turned to MacGregor and Mike. "I don't like this. Sasha

Rodin is a marksman with long-range rifles, and he's gone to a hell of a lot of trouble to make sure he has a clean view from that stable. Kara, didn't you tell me there's a balcony along one wall of the arena?"

"Like an interior skywalk. It looks down onto the arena in one direction and the lobby and stalls in the other."

"And it has windows?"

"Facing east and west, yes. Not north and south."

MacGregor shook his head. "We can't wait until dark. I'm not risking that boy's life because we're afraid to be seen."

Agent Hogan said, "It wouldn't matter, anyway. Anything this well planned is ready for the dark. He'll have night-vision equipment."

Luke and Hogan exchanged a look; Kara tried to ignore it and think about what she was going to say to Sasha Rodin—that is, *if* they let her go in. As it was, they had agreed to get up here and get everyone into position, and then Luke had said, "We'll talk about it."

She didn't need to talk about it. If Sasha would trade Seth's life in order to talk to her, so be it. She wasn't anxious to be a martyr, but she didn't have to do this alone. She had the FBI behind her.

Resources, Varón had once said to her. *I believe they're the reason you hired me.*

Oh, yes.

"They're ready," MacGregor said to the room, and then into the microphone that jutted down from an earpiece, he said, "It's all yours, Douglas."

They watched the screen. A second passed, then two, then three, and then, the soldier at the northeast corner came up from the shorn corn. He duck-walked two yards and another came behind him, following, and—

Bgroohm.

CHAPTER
54

AN EXPLOSION BROKE THE sky. Sasha watched from the east window of the balcony, the rifle smoking in his hands. He wanted to dance with glee. Stupid SWAT team had scurried around the buildings like lines of black ants, then broke formation and started toward the stable. Surprise, motherfuckers. Two of the black ants hit the ground and army-crawled back; another hit the ground and stayed. A second later, he was dragged back into the line by his buddies, but things had changed. Suddenly the marching ants weren't so interested in coming closer anymore.

Sasha moved to the other side of the building and aimed for another land mine. He fired and it blew. No one was near that one, but he enjoyed sending his message: *You can't get to me. I can get to you.*

He smiled with the pleasure of it.

Then he called Kara.

The command room jumped in unison.

"Christ," MacGregor shouted. Flames and debris shot into the air in one of the four corners of the screen. The room filled with shock, but just when MacGregor began shouting into his headset, another explosion went off in another quadrant.

Luke stared, feeling as if his heart had turned to stone. Mike glared at the screen and along with everyone else in the room, watched and waited for more explosions.

They didn't happen.

"Get me a report," MacGregor was saying. He'd ceased shouting, but the intensity in his voice couldn't be missed. He waited, listening, and a moment later, said, "Do it," and ripped off his headset.

"We have one man down," he said. He was almost huffing. "He's not dead, but he's leaving his leg in the fucking field. From about fifty yards in, that whole field is booby trapped. They've spotted at least three more explosives, and that's just a cursory look." He cursed. "We're pulling out ten more yards—"

A phone rang. It was Kara's.

Everyone stared and she picked it up. The caller ID said *Aidan*.

"Can't be," Luke said. "Aidan doesn't have that phone anymore." An errant thought snapped like a rubber band: throwing Aidan's phone away in the woods before the house fire. In a heartbeat, Luke knew how Sasha had gotten Seth.

Mike came up beside Kara. "Put it on speaker," he said, and she did.

"Hello?"

Sasha's voice came on. "Oh, my, Kara. Look what you've done."

Kara went hard as steel. She wanted to wilt to the floor and hide her head and pray that it would end. But she'd just watched a man going to the place *she* was supposed to go and lose his leg, and the helpless horror in her breast congealed into sheer hatred.

"No," she spat into the phone, "look what *you've* done."

Luke moved closer, his hand coming to the small of her back, his strength a palpable thing.

"You think this is so brilliant," she taunted, "re-inventing my birthday party, but now you've got the whole FBI and half of Georgia's law enforcement knocking on your door. You'll never get out of this alive."

A moment of silence swelled in the air, then he chuckled. "Oh, I think I will. I have it all planned. But first, you and I have a little unfinished business. Remember, Kara? Do you remember the last birthday party I attended?"

"Where is Seth?"

"Focus, Kara."

"Where is your father?"

"Kara."

"What do you want with me?"

Silence. When he spoke again, his voice sounded strained, like she'd angered him and he was trying to control it. "Well, then," he said, "down to business. What do I want? First, I want your FBI lover to call off the hounds. All of them. They'll never get in here; the whole place is booby trapped." He paused. "Oh, wait, I probably don't have to tell you that, do I? You probably heard or saw the whole thing, holed up somewhere with your new friends."

"Go on."

"Second, I want you to come to my party. But this time, I get to make the rules."

"What rules?"

"At eight fifty-two, drive to the end of the driveway. Alone. Get out of the car and bring me the keys. Now, here's an important little tidbit, Kara: Walk straight in the middle of the driveway. I know it's a long walk on gravel, but trust me, you don't want to veer one way or the other. You've seen what happened to the little black-clad army men."

She swallowed. The entire room held its breath.

"Walk up to the main entrance of the stable and into the lobby. And, oh—did I remember to mention?—I want you naked when you do it."

Luke's body went even tighter. She looked at him: *It's not important,* she said with her eyes, but Mike was frantically shaking his finger at her. *Don't concede that.*

She swallowed. "I won't come to you naked, you bastard. You know as well as I do there are three dozen men out here."

That made him laugh. "Oh. Well, yes, I didn't think about that. Underwear, then. But no bulletproof vest, no weapons, and no wire. I want to be able to see that you're clean. Do you understand?"

She looked up at Luke. *Déjà vu.*

"Do you know what will happen if you do something different than what I've asked? And I mean, *one* little difference? Seth will die." He snickered. "Well, actually, he may die anyway, come to think of it—that depends on how well you perform. But if you change my instructions for coming in here, I can assure you he *absolutely* will die."

"Where is he?"

"Ah, Kara. You're smarter than that. If I have a nice time at your party tonight, then I'll tell you. Otherwise, I won't and he'll starve to death right where he is. Or, rather, he'll die of dehydration. I guess that would come first. Either way, he won't be going home to his mother."

"How do I know he's alive?"

"You'll have to take my word for it. Those are my instructions, Kara. Don't fuck it up."

CHAPTER
55

KARA SANK TO THE edge of the table when he hung up. Luke was there. Wrapped her up and pressed her cheek against his chest.

"You're okay," he murmured, his lips in her hair. "You were good."

Kara pulled back. "I need a car."

Luke paled.

"I have to do this," she said, and tried to ignore the true fear in his eyes. She laid a hand on his cheek, comforting him instead of the other way around. "I won't be doing it alone, right? For God's sake, Luke, look at all these resources. You figure out how you want to back me up—I trust you. But I have to do what he says."

The tech guy said, "MacGregor," and MacGregor went to look over his shoulder.

"This is yours, Hogan," he said, pointing at the laptop. "The Illinois information you were waiting for. Skyped."

Mike made a beeline to the table. "Dr. Lyons," he said, looking at the screen. "Give me one minute, let me find a place..."

He picked up the laptop and gestured for Luke and

Kara to come. Luke held out a hand to Kara and they followed Mike into the next room, where he set the laptop in front of all three of them. A middle-aged black man with a goatee looked back at them from the screen, a single gold earring winking.

"Dr. Lyons," Hogan said, "I'm here with Special Agent Lukas Mann and Assistant District Attorney Kara Chandler. She's the one who's at the center of Rodin's killing spree. This is Doctor Alvin Lyons. He's one of the psychiatrists who does group counseling at the Marion, Illinois, Penitentiary."

"Did," he corrected. "No more."

"He knew Sasha," Mike said.

Luke peered into the computer screen. "We only have a few minutes, Doctor. We don't have time to dick around with issues of confidentia—"

"Fuck confidentiality," Lyons said. "This guy is a monster."

Sasha looked at his watch: Eight thirty-three. He watched from the balcony, his father slumped in his chair ten feet behind him, dozing, smelling bad. Disgusting. But for now, Sasha would let him sleep. He'd wake him for the final round.

He left his father in the balcony facing the lobby and went downstairs. It was almost time. He'd cleaned up the tack room, making everything exactly as he remembered it: saddles here, feeding items there, articles for grooming on the third shelf, bridles and crops hung on the wall. He'd even moved out his cot, so that everything appeared just as it had seventeen years ago at Kara's party.

Except one thing: The giant coil of barbed wire was missing. He wondered if she would notice.

He went to a large basket and picked up a towel, rolled it thick and threw it around his neck, then walked over to his satchel. He pulled out the garrote, admiring it, stroking the handles as if they were the breasts of a woman, then looped it over the back of his neck like a stole. The cherry handles hung down either side of his chest and the wire nestled in the towel at the back of his neck. He ducked into the bathroom to look.

Yes. He was ready.

"I have to get ready," Kara said, putting a hand on Luke's chest. "Back off."

Luke didn't budge. He couldn't bring himself to sever contact with her. "Dr. Lyons says it's about his brother. Play that card if you can."

"She heard him, Luke, she was there," Hogan said. "And it's not about his brother."

"Jesus," Luke said. He dropped his hand from Kara's cheek. He didn't step back, but she did, clad in black lace underwear and bra, getting ready to go meet a psycho-killer whose shrink said he had class issues or maybe father issues or maybe sexual issues, but who deep inside longed for his lost brother. None of that seemed to add up for Hogan, who swore there was something they were missing. "It doesn't matter," Luke said. "Go in, get him to talk about whatever shit is in his head until he tells you where Seth is. That's the goal. And keep space between you. The only thing everyone agrees on is—"

"—that he won't shoot me from afar. He'll want to kill me up close and personal with the barbed wire garrote. I'm *special*."

Luke swore. The SWAT team was still outside—one man less, but in place, for all the good that did. They couldn't close in, not with Sasha's booby traps in place. The FBI was here, along with most of the Pickens County sheriff's department and some Atlanta police who'd accompanied MacGregor. They all knew who Sasha was and where he was and what weapons he liked; they'd learned enough of his psychology to know that somehow, Kara Chandler represented something so hateful to him that he'd go to any lengths to teach her some 'truth.'

But in the end, none of that made a damn bit of difference. She would be inside with Sasha and everyone else outside, held fifty yards out by land mines they had barely seen when it was still light and might not see at all now in the dusk.

Sasha Rodin had planned it well.

The techie said, "Here," and walked over with a hair pin. It contained a microphone. "Where do you want it?" he asked, with the tiniest smirk, and Kara rolled her eyes. She felt around in her short hair and stuck it in. They tested it, looked at the clock, and MacGregor said, "You're good to go."

They walked to the car that was waiting, dusk looming. Luke wanted nothing more than to pull her against him and shield her from the world. Instead, he fisted his hands, keeping them at his sides. "First thing when you get in there," he said, "pull him away from the west doors and windows. That's first so I have a line in. Remember, the snipers are ready. Try to get him to the east window, but be sure to be out of the wa—"

"I have to find Seth first. Don't let anyone shoot until we find Seth."

"When you get him out of the sight line of the driveway, let me know. I'll be listening to every word."

"I know."

"And I'll be inside with you as soon as I can."

"I know."

He stopped, spinning her around to him. "Kara, for God's sake. Say something other than—"

She looked up at him, her face a mixture of determination and chutzpah and utter faith in him, and Luke cursed. "On second thought, don't say anything."

He kissed her, open-mouthed and deep, her warm skin beneath his hands, her heart beating against his. A moment later he ripped himself away and touched his knuckle beneath her chin. "You can do it," he said.

He only hoped *he* could do it, too.

Kara drove to the mailbox with Luke hidden in the backseat. It was time. She angled the car so Luke would have the clearest view from a hole they had drilled through the back passenger-side door. He was to watch her walk up the drive. "If I step on a mine and blow up," she had told him, "don't step there."

He hadn't been amused.

"Here goes," she said to Luke.

"Kara—"

"Lukas Mann, I swear, if you say one more fucking thing to me I'll kill you myself."

There was a second of silence, then Luke said: "Go."

She got out, keys in hand, and began walking toward the stable. She watched her steps, barely noticing that she was barefoot on gravel, skimming the path in front of her for the little metal caps MacGregor had described to her: explosives. Some might be remotely controlled; some might detonate when they were disturbed by a footstep. But Hogan didn't really think he was that sophisticated. He thought they would need gunfire to set them off.

It didn't much matter. Sasha had already proved himself capable of that.

The bastard.

The walk was surreal, approaching a stable she'd approached a thousand times before and a thousand years ago, the sprawl of buildings looking identical to the ones she'd spent her childhood trying to make warm. She passed the wishing well Sasha had constructed and marveled at the imitation, noting that he'd forgotten to string the bucket onto the rope but that otherwise, it was just like the one at home. She imagined the interior of the stable would be equally accurate and ran through the layout yet again...where the doors were, where the windows were, what equipment was there. Dr. Lyons had predicted that Sasha would be thorough.

The sun sank below the horizon as she neared the doors, plunging dimness into darkness. She opened the stable door and stepped inside.

She winced, blinking at the white fluorescents, momentarily blinded. When she opened her eyes again, Sasha Rodin was there.

"Well, well," he said, his voice filling the lobby. "Hello, Kara."

CHAPTER
56

K ARA'S THROAT CLOGGED. SHE forced herself to take inventory: Yes, the lobby looked like it always had—the stalls branching down the aisle to the left, the arena to the right, and the various rooms along the lobby. Sasha Rodin sat on a stack of crates. He was big—bigger than she remembered—and even harsher. Fifteen years in prison can do that, she imagined, and the image of the woman he'd raped and beaten rose to mind. She *had* looked like Kara. Back when Kara was young and naïve and in love with Andrew, and hadn't entertained a passing thought about Sasha Rodin or why he and his family had left the ranch.

Apparently, he'd never stopped thinking about Kara.

Her gaze snagged on the towel around his neck. The garrote hung on top, a stole of thorns.

He got up and came toward her. "I see you dressed for the party. Good girl."

Kara swallowed. Think. *Think.* Luke was listening. She had to let him know what he was walking into. And she had to find Seth. If she couldn't do those two things, her efforts would mean nothing.

"I see you did, too," she said, finding her voice. "Nice necklace."

He laughed. "Oh, this old thing?" His fingers stroked the handles. "I made it years ago."

"For your father?"

"No, after. Doing my father wasn't planned. After I got out of prison, I found him out in a field making repairs to a fence. I thought he'd be happy to see me. He told me to go to hell. I reacted impulsively—and found my true calling in that moment. Turns out I liked the way it felt to have him hanging there between my hands in the wire. So I took the wire and worked with it, crafted these beautiful handles." His eyes bore into hers. "Every time I used it, I dreamed of what it would feel like to have *you* dangling in my hands."

Kara swallowed. Jesus God. He was sick.

He stepped a little closer. "You have no idea how difficult it was for me to wait all these months for you. Every time I killed one of your party guests, I wanted so to show you how. I wanted you to dream about our moment together along with me. But it was worth the wait. I must say, your reaction was quite unexpected."

"You mean, contacting the FBI?" she asked. "They're outside. Don't think we're alone."

"Well, I would hope they're outside. I'm going to need them in a little while. I would be foolish to think I could get out of here without their help."

She frowned, then understood. "You think that after I'm dead you can bargain with them to get out. You're dreaming."

"I don't think so. You see, I thought ahead. I have one hostage to make sure I get what I want from you. And I have a second to make sure they let me drive away. I may even demand a chopper, or something dramatic like that. I haven't decided yet."

"You have Seth. And who else? Your father?"

"Of course. You remember him, don't you?"

He looked up into the balcony and Kara followed his gaze. She swallowed. Dmitri Rodin sat in a wheelchair, slumped beneath a blanket, his shoulders clad in plaid pajamas and head covered with a brimmed straw hat—the kind the outdoor workers used to wear in the sun. She peered at him as hard as she could; she couldn't tell if he was breathing.

Let Luke know.

"You should bring your father down," she said. "It gets hot in that balcony."

"He's fine," Sasha replied. "It's the best view in the house."

"Where is Seth?"

"Oh, Kara. What kind of fool do you think I am? I know you aren't lying about all the Federal agents outside. So, why would I tell you where Seth is before I'm finished with you? I don't want them storming in here prematurely. Not all of them would make it, mind you, but they might be crazy enough to risk a few more limbs if they thought they could get to a kid."

"What do you want with me?"

Sasha began to circle her, walking a radius about ten feet away, stroking the wooden handles of his garrote and letting his eyes feast on the large amount of flesh Kara had bared. At one point he winced, almost as if a sharp pain had stabbed, and his breathing deepened. *Think bikini,* she told herself, knowing she had swimwear that showed more. Still, his leer sent shivers over her skin.

"Fine, don't tell me. I don't give a damn. But for God's

sake, what do you think this is?" she asked, gesturing to the stable. "If you wanted to bring back memories for me, you did a piss poor job of it. This is nothing like Montgomery Manor."

He snarled. "It's everything like Montgomery Manor. I ought to know. I was there for more years than you were."

She scoffed. "I'll bet you don't even have the stalls right. It didn't look right from outside."

"Oh, really?" he asked, arching a blond brow. "Let's go see. After you."

Kara closed her eyes. *Yes.*

Yes. Luke listened, still in the back of the car, and knew Kara had just given him his break. She was pulling Sasha away from the front door. Luke shifted to check the Glock in his belt, pushed the door open, and climbed out. Pulled the G18 from the floor of the backseat and jammed in the extra clip.

Dark, now. That would help. Unless he stepped a little off Kara's path and set off Sasha's idea of a booby trap.

"I'm going," he said, knowing MacGregor and Mike could hear him. At this stage of the game, they had only one path in—the one Kara had taken—but it was better than nothing. And so long as Kara kept Sasha from the west windows and door, Sasha wasn't likely to see the team start sweeping for mines at this end. All they needed was a single clean path for the SWAT team. Fifteen minutes from now, they would have it.

"Luke," Mike said into his earpiece. "Sasha isn't being sexual. She walked in there half-naked and all he can think about is his wire and the stable."

"So?"

"It's not right. He raped Marti Delaney because she

was the spitting image of Kara. And now he doesn't want her? It doesn't fit."

Luke walked slowly, carefully, eyeing the path. "I'm a little busy to be working riddles right now, Hogan. When you figure it out, let me know." He passed the wishing well that had held Kara's dreams as a child and wondered briefly if it was rigged to explode, kept his eye on his footing, and moved on. He came to the door and lowered his voice to a whisper, adjusting his grip on the G18. "Going in."

He opened the door, blinked at the lighting, and looked around. Could hear Sasha's voice faintly from the left, but couldn't see them. They'd gone down the corridor. Good girl.

You should bring your father down from there . . .

He moved to his right, toward the stairs Kara had mentioned. She'd drawn a diagram of the complex, every last detail. Looking around now, Luke could see that Sasha had it perfect.

He took the stairs two at a time into the balcony. A wheelchair sat in the middle, overlooking the lobby. An old man slouched in it.

Luke crouched low and went to the man, realizing in the back of his mind that crouching hardly mattered. The fluorescents were bright as sunshine. His nostrils twitched as he got close to the chair and his heart sank. When a person died, his bladder and bowels gave out and he could tell—

The body moved. Just a little—a raspy bit of a breath.

Dmitri Rodin was alive.

The smell was wrong.

That's what hit Kara as she walked down the wide

corridor of stalls, her heart knotting in her throat. Despite what she'd said to Sasha, the stalls were exactly what she remembered. Everything exactly the same.

Except the smell. It didn't smell of horses. Just sawdust and stonedust and straw, and maybe the scent of disinfectant. Or fly spray. But no horses. There were no animals in the stalls. They were empty.

Except—

Kara pulled up short. *MEGAN.* Her name was burned into a wooden sign in capital letters and hung on the stall door, a helium balloon attached to it. Megan, a curly-haired blonde Kara had met in the eighth grade. They'd shared the same piano teacher and become fast friends.

And now, *MEGAN*, a college student and club waitress, walking home from work...

Kara gasped. She gaped at Sasha. "In there?" she asked, and he smiled.

"It wasn't easy. You threw my timing off. First, going to Penny Wolff and Guilford. Then that thing with the boat. I very nearly didn't get Megan in the ground in time."

Kara staggered backward. She hit the wall, trying to make sense of it, her eyes skimming down the rest of the corridor and knowing what she'd find: Every stall gate was labeled. Every nameplate had a balloon. Every stall filled.

Not with horses.

By small degrees, she realized Sasha had come close to her, close enough to reach, a chuckle vibrating in his chest. "Ah, you finally got it," he said. "How does it feel, knowing they're all here? Well, all but Andrew, that is. He was the first and I wasn't quite prepared. I'd planned to take his body, but there wasn't time. And there was that other woman to deal with. All I managed to grab was his sunglasses." He took Kara by the arm and hauled her away from the wall. "But that's all right. The stall I'd planned to use for him won't remain empty forever. I've decided to put Aidan in it. Of course, you let your FBI friends ruin that, but the other boy will do almost as well. Seth."

Kara couldn't breathe. She knew Aidan was safe. But Seth..."You haven't killed Seth," she said. "You need him in order to assure my cooperation."

Sasha leaned close and whispered, "Don't you forget it." Then he smiled. "Come with me, Kara. There's a special stall I want you to see. The one Guapa used to use."

"Let go of me." Kara jerked from his hand and forced her knees to work. Luke should be in the stable by now. He was listening. He was here somewhere. "Don't touch me, you animal."

Again, Sasha chuckled. "Whatever you say. For now."

He stepped back and allowed her to walk in front of him and Kara swallowed back bile. Passing each stall where a body was buried, remembering each gift she'd gotten. She could hardly grasp it.

Sasha accompanied her down the corridor. "A shame Guapa had to get so sick and die like that, wasn't it?" he asked. "How did she die again? Something tragic, as I recall."

Kara turned to him. "How did you know that? You were gone by then."

He drilled her with those emotionless eyes. "I came back. And, oh, yes, now I remember...A fence blew down. She got into the wild cherry trees."

"You?" Kara asked.

"Who else? The fool horse was a lot like you, though. She made it hard. It wasn't enough for her to crib on the bark, so I had to make sure a little extra got into her feed." His fingers went from idly stroking the handles of his garrote to actually pulling one away from his body and regarding it with great admiration. "Wild cherry," he said. "Nasty stuff for horses. But beautiful when put to better use."

"You son of a bitch." She pulled herself together. Falling apart would get her nowhere. Even if Luke had made it inside, they still had to find Seth. She had to keep her head.

"What did you do with Seth?"

Sasha laughed. "He's down under. Where do you think? Come on, Kara, I do enjoy a good riddle. And my father would be so proud of me for engaging in one. He always thought my brother was the only one worthy of mind games." He took her arm and gave a shove. "I want to show you Guapa's stall. And if you're good, perhaps you can have your wish."

CHAPTER
57

LUKE LISTENED, HEARD KARA stumble and her voice grow weak, and his lungs stopped working. She was there and Sasha was torturing her and Luke couldn't do a fucking thing about it. They didn't know where Seth was. *Down under.* Buried already? The thought stabbed Luke in the chest. And Sasha was coming back. Luke heard the sneering voice, closer, closer, taunting Kara.

Hang in there, love. I'm here.

"Here," Sasha said. "Guapa's stall. All ready for you."

Kara looked. There was a hole several feet wide and almost as deep, the fine woodchip flooring piled high in the corner. A shovel awaiting its work.

Kara reeled. Oh, God. He couldn't have done this to Seth. In the stall meant for Andrew?

She stepped to the left of the gate, toward the lobby. She didn't know where Luke was or if he could even see her, but the closer to the lobby they were, the better chance they had. *Please, Luke.*

"So you're going to strangle me and bury me here with everyone else, is that it?" she asked.

Sasha smiled. A leering, evil smile. "Yes. But you left out the part where we finish what you started all those years ago."

"Never."

"Really, Kara? Why? Because you're not the one for me?" He whirled toward the lobby, looking across it and up to the balcony. "Do you hear that, *nana*? Papa, wake up, damn you. Are you listening? This is the girl you said was too good for me. The one I could never have. But I have her now, don't I?"

Kara looked up at the balcony. Sasha's father barely moved. She tried to rattle her brain into working. "It wasn't about being too good for you," she said. "I was a child, you were a man. I had a crush on Andrew, that's all."

Sasha looked back at Kara, his eyes glazed with hatred and something that looked almost like pain. "And for that, you ruined me?" He shook his head, as if trying to shake something off, and began to work his belt buckle. Kara swallowed. She backed up, moving away from Guapa's stall and toward the lobby, and for every step she took, he followed. "You never even knew it, did you?" he said. "How you ruined me." He was unbuckling, and Kara was backing up. He pulled his fly open and freed himself; Kara wanted to gag.

"Look at me, bitch," he said, and she tried to look everywhere but at him. He was aroused, though his face contorted in pain. Nausea balled in Kara's belly. "I said, *look at me*. Or I'll kill Seth this very minute."

Kara looked.

"Do you see? The scars. They're from you."

"No."

"Yes," he ground out, his teeth clenched. He blinked his eyes. As if something was in them. "You pushed me

into the barbed wire when you ran from the tack room.
You left me stuck and bleeding."

What? Kara reeled.

He let go of his pants, letting them hang loose. "But
don't think I'm unable to finish what we started. I am.
Marti Delaney learned that the hard way, although she
wasn't worth the years I spent in prison for having her.
Everything works, Kara."

"Then why?" she rasped. "For God's sake, I'm sorry
you got hurt. I was fifteen. You were forcing me. I didn't
mean for you to fall into barbed wire, but you just said
you're fine."

"Fine," he sneered. "You call this fine? Every fucking
time I'm hard, the scars pull and I feel you. Every time
I'm hard, I hear you and your rich little friends, laughing
at me while I bled in the tack room and while my father
blamed me for ruining everything. I felt you every time
I got in the shower at the prison where they could see,
and was the brunt of every joke. I was another inmate's
bitch for years, until after the letter. Then they started to
respect me. They knew I'd get out someday and I'd be
able to do anything. I bulked up and became the one other
prisoners were afraid of instead of the one they used for
their jollies. You know how hard it is to bulk up in prison?
No gyms, no equipment, but I did it. You should see how
many pull-ups I can do on a bunk bed, how many leg lifts
I can manage with a bench. I did it, Kara, after the letter.
The letter changed everything."

Kara's mind was a blur. "Letter? What letter?"

The rage that had seemed to have hold of him suddenly
let go, and Sasha burst out laughing. It was a maniacal
sound filled with evil, and Kara could do nothing but keep
stepping back, closer and closer to the tack wall, inching

to her right where she knew the equipment would hang. The bridles and blankets, chaps.

The crops.

He stopped laughing and looked upstairs. "Papa, did you hear? She wants to know what letter." His gaze landed on Kara, following her step for step. "The letter about my inheritance. The one *you* never got."

Kara stilled. "What are you talking about?"

"I'm talking about this," he said, gesturing to the stable. "Montgomery Manor and everything that came with it. It's mine. Your crazy father gave it to me." He stilled, looking Kara straight in the eyes. "*Our* crazy father."

Kara blinked, trying to make it all come together, and in one, sweeping thought, it did. "His anonymous donation," she said. "That was you?"

"Yes. Because I'm *his* son, *his* blood. Not you." He looked upstairs again, his body loosening up now, his gestures like those of a drunk. His pants fit again, hanging loose on his hips, his erection gone. He looked at Kara with sheer hatred. "*Sis,*" he said. "Willis Montgomery fucked my mother but wouldn't claim me. Instead, he promised my father a windfall when I turned twenty-one, so long as no one ever found out he'd been with a kitchen maid. Willis Montgomery gave you everything all your life. You, who aren't even his *blood*, and held it all back from me."

Kara couldn't believe it. She wanted to say something that might help Luke or find Seth, but she could hardly speak.

"I didn't want all that," she said, her frame shaking. "I would have given it to you."

"Bullshit," he said. "You know, I used to stand there and watch you, every fucking birthday, standing around the wishing well with your friends, tossing stones down under the bucket and I'd wonder: *What could they have to wish for? They have everything.* And there I was, not smart enough to be *my* father's son or rich enough to be *your* father's son. And not good enough for you." He straightened, seeming to get a hold of himself. "But look at me now, Kara. I'm *all* those things. Guess Old Man Montgomery finally decided to do right by me. So long as he could do it without tarnishing his image."

Kara wanted to wilt. She remembered her father's anger just before he died, when she told him she didn't want Montgomery Manor and was planning to stay in Atlanta and keep working her civil servant job. He couldn't comprehend such a decision.

In that, he wasn't all that different from Sasha.

Kara took one more step backward. *Sasha? Her brother?* "You wouldn't rape your own sister."

He laughed. "Well, I would, but it doesn't matter, because you're not my sister. You were adopted, remember? You're the one who isn't a Montgomery. But you're right; that's not what matters anymore."

"Then, what?" she asked, fear nearly choking her.

"What matters is that you know the truth. That *you're* not good enough for *me.* I want you to know that for just one moment." He glanced upstairs, as if making sure his father had heard. "Before you die."

His hands went to the handles of the garrote and he whipped it from over his shoulders. Kara backed up against the wall, her hands groping the equipment there. She thought she felt a crop but it was stuck and she wheeled around to wrench it from the wall and the wire swooped down in front of her face. She jumped, and it caught her around the chest and he tugged her back, pulling, and from nowhere came an animal roar and something crashed down from the sky.

His father—no, Luke—hit the floor. He came up and went for Sasha, grabbed him from behind, and the wire ripped into her flesh as Luke rained blows down on Sasha's arms. Sasha's grip broke and she fell to the ground. She pulled the wire from her bra and skin, it leaving deep pricks in her arms and across her upper breasts. She turned and saw Luke, wearing plaid pajamas with a blue throw tangled in his legs, pummeling Sasha with his fists, bashing him with the butt of his gun. An instant later, Hogan was on him, a line of armed agents coming in behind.

"Damn it, stop it," he yelled to Luke. "Don't kill him. Seth. *Seth*."

The words finally registered and Luke stopped, panting, his mouth hanging open like a rabid dog's. He staggered from the heap that was Sasha and his eyes lit on Kara, dipping to the bloody marks left by the wire, and he limped over to her, crushing her into his body.

Time stood still for as long as it took for Kara to realize she was safe, and for them both to catch their breaths. They parted and looked at Sasha. Mike Hogan dragged him across the floor and propped him against the wall, growling: "Tell me where the kid is, you bastard. Where is Seth?"

Sasha's head rolled against the pine wall, his face a mash of torn tissue and blood from Luke's rage. He focused on Hogan for one fraction of time and said, "Fuck you."

Hogan went for his throat and Kara said, "Wait. I know where Seth is."

Hogan looked at her, his chest rising and falling with his breathing. Luke squeezed her hand.

"He's in the well, down under the bucket that's not there." Hogan tipped his head to some of the agents behind him and they jogged out the door to go look. Kara stepped toward Sasha, her voice cold with rage. "Do I get my wish now?"

Sasha narrowed his eyes, trying to focus on her, his mouth working to form words she couldn't understand, and all the while, his hands moved, too, searching for the handles of his precious garrote on the stable floor.

"Do it," Luke said under his breath.

Sasha did. He clutched the handles and rose up, swinging the wire through the air toward Kara. Luke fired.

Sasha dropped dead.

CHAPTER
58

T HE BIG LIGHTS CAME in and the FBI cleared a path to the well. In all, Sasha had only planted seven of his homemade explosives around the property. Not an arsenal, but enough to keep the forces back when it counted.

Not anymore. The place was flooded with emergency personnel. Reporters were not far behind.

Luke showered in the stable's bathroom while EMTs tended to Dmitri Rodin. Luke had left him lying naked on the balcony floor when he took his place in the plaid pajamas and chair. Dmitri would live, such as his life was now. Luke hoped the man somehow knew that his presence in the balcony had made it possible for Luke to be there when it counted.

He tossed Dmitri's clothes in an evidence bag and pulled his own pants back over his hips, then limped out to the lobby with his shirt hanging open. The stable had been taped off into sections and little tents had sprouted up, marking evidence here and there. He walked the property. The digging would start tomorrow, and identification of the bodies was expected to be easy.

They were labeled.

Luke headed back to the elementary school where Kara and Seth had been taken.

She stood when he came through the door and Luke's heart turned to mush. He swept her into his arms, kissing her with everything he'd never given to anyone else, wanting to be no one but himself and hoping it would be enough for her and Aidan.

"Boys?" Kara said, when he finally let her go. Aidan and Seth had watched from the corner. Seth was still wrapped in a blanket, though it had been more than an hour since they pulled him out of the well. Luke figured he'd have some healing to do—and some thinking. Having an agent bring Aidan to be with him was intended to help.

The boys walked over and Luke shook both their hands. He looked at Seth. "I wasn't smelling so nice when we pulled you up," Luke said. "Glad to meet you now."

"Yeah. Uh, thanks."

"Have you talked to your mom?"

He nodded. "She's pretty confused," he said, and Kara actually laughed.

"We're going to have a heck of a story to tell her, aren't we?"

Seth nodded. He had a few scrapes and bruises, but otherwise, he was okay. Aidan studied his toes.

Luke jerked his chin to the door. "I'd like to talk to you two a minute. In private."

They looked at each other, paled a bit, then followed. Luke led them to the classroom next door and sat down, pulling a couple of munchkin-sized chairs out for the two of them. He sat down on the edge of a table and crossed his arms.

"I don't want either of you to speak," he said, "I just want you to listen." The boys swallowed. "What happened here tonight happened because a killer designed it to happen. It doesn't have anything to do with you. It didn't happen because of anything you did."

Aidan sat straighter. He looked miserable. "But I'm the reason my dad got with the cartel. I delivered a load for Raul and they blackmailed Dad with it."

"I know. But what you don't know is that you're also the reason your dad got *out* of it. He was already in cahoots with me and the FBI when he died. He was turning things around."

Aidan's shoulders slumped.

"Look at me, son," he said. Luke held his eyes. "I'm telling you, you aren't to blame for what Sasha Rodin did and you should never, ever feel responsible for that. But I'm also telling you this and you listen hard: If I ever catch either one of you trying to earn a little money or be a little cool or whatever the fuck you thought you were doing when you agreed to make a delivery for Raul Valesquez, I'll come down on you so hard you won't know what hit you. Is that clear?"

They nodded and Luke stood.

"I'm glad we understand each other."

There was a tap at the door and Kara stepped inside. "Am I interrupting?"

"No," Luke said, "we're finished."

"Okay," she said, clearly not believing him. "Because Sally's here to take the boys home."

Luke frowned. "What about you?"

"I made an appointment for you and I. Aidan, I'll be about an hour behind you, and I'll pick you up at Seth's."

The boys left—anxious to be away from Luke, he thought—and he cocked his head at Kara. "Do you mind telling me where we're going?"

"Yes, I mind," she said. "You'll see when we get there."

She pulled up to the Federal Building at one in the morning. Luke frowned, then saw Knutson standing at a side door. Luke cocked a brow to Kara.

"Just come," she said, and they walked over to Knutson.

They accompanied him down the hall and into the elevator, Knutson and Kara both smug, and by the time they got to the wing of interrogation rooms, Luke had put it together.

"You're not supposed to be here," he whispered to Kara.

"I have resources," she said, and winked at Knutson.

Knutson opened a door and gestured them into a small corridor. A half dozen Federal agents stood inside, looking through one or the other of the thick, one-way mirrors. Some wore headphones, listening in on the conversations going on in the interrogation rooms, and some milled quietly with one another. The atmosphere was light, almost celebratory. Important work going on; a landmark bust concluded.

On the right, in a room with bright lights and one table, sat Frank Collado.

Luke's muscles hardened. Collado was alone, no one talking to him. He shivered—they would have the temperature turned down low in the room—and he kept putting his head down on his forearms, then lifting it up again. Heavy chains weighted his wrists.

Knutson turned to Luke. "He's talking. He thinks he's going to deal his way out of this. Keeps laying the blame on some dude named Luke Varón." He made a dismissive little sound. "Kara thought you might want to talk to him."

Luke looked at Collado—remembered all the months he'd spent in prison at this man's hands and all the months he'd dreamed of this day. He looked down at Kara, a thousand degrees of tenderness warming his blood at the realization that she had wanted to give this to him. He cupped her cheeks and kissed her, and when he came up he said, "Naw, fuck him. Let him see me on the news."

They left, and just outside the front door, Kara stiffened.

"What is it?" he asked.

She tipped her head toward two men getting in a car. "Isn't that Montiel?"

Luke looked. "Yup. And Keith Burke."

She pulled back and looked at him. "Why aren't they—" Then she stopped. Figured it out.

"Really?" she asked. "Montiel was with you?"

"His daughter died of a drug overdose when she was twenty-two. This is something he's pretty passionate about."

She let that settle, then bristled again. "I still didn't like the way Burke looked at me."

"Well, why don't I let you take that up with his wife? She's a police officer in Roswell. And as I recall, they're about due for their second child so she'll probably be happy to give him what-for."

She shook her head and looked up at him. "How long will it be until you run out of surprises?" she asked.

Luke shrugged. "Fifty years or so, I imagine." He sobered. "Will you be around that long?"

She gazed up at him. "I'll take it under advisement. Will you stay with me while I decide?"

"How long will it take?"

"Fifty years or so."

Attorney Alayna Mann needs a fresh start. Her move from the bustle of Chicago to a remote South Carolina island marks the first step in a new life—until a walk on the beach leads to an unwelcome surprise...

Please turn this page for a preview of

Where Danger Hides.

CHAPTER
1

Thursday, October 20, 11:52 p.m.
Prince William Forest Park, Triangle, Virginia

THE SANDMAN STOOD ON the boardwalk outside an old pyrite mine, awaiting the man who was about to die. A minion, a nobody, but a risk nonetheless. As a rule, the Sandman didn't favor using minions but occasionally, it was wise to put distance between himself and a particular act. Hence, this lonely midnight appointment and the Smith & Wesson in his pocket, equipped with an Osprey ACP silencer. A mundane kill—cleanup. Not something he could take credit for in the long run. But moments from now, the risk would be ameliorated.

A movement caught his eye. The minion hiked up the path, a lanky shred of a man with nervous tics, a man who might have been mistaken for a junkie if not for the white lab coat and high-security clearance badge he sported by day. In truth, he was a brilliant medical researcher at the University of Maryland, with a wife and three teenagers, the oldest of whom had a well-developed entrepreneurial bent. His methamphetamincs business had boomed in an otherwise bleak economy.

Men who love their children are easily manipulated. Men with secrets are easily destroyed. The minion was both.

The Sandman looked around—no one, not at this hour. The minion slowed his steps for the last thirty feet, then stopped in front of the mouth of the old mine. Once, decades ago, fool's gold had been mined here.

Fitting.

"Dr. Bartholomew." The Sandman stepped out. "Do you have the pictures?"

"Christ," Bartholomew said. "Where did you come from?"

"Answer me."

"Of course I have them. That was part of the deal, wasn't it?" He squinted through the darkness, as if something didn't look quite right. The Sandman tugged his hat down an inch. "Show me," he ordered.

The little man's gaze darted around the park. He looked like a nervous ferret. "What about the money?"

"Pictures first. You didn't really think it would be otherwise, did you?"

Bartholomew cursed, then pulled a folded set of papers from beneath his coat. The Sandman took them, his heart standing still as he unfolded the pages and shed light on the photos with his cell phone. The nape of his neck prickled.

"Oh," he breathed. "The redhead." Her face was turned away, but he knew who she was. He'd offered the minion the choice of two women—one a spindle-thin brunette and this one, a curvaceous redhead. Both were hookers who worked the same block just inside the beltway. He didn't know their real names, but that didn't matter. All that mattered was that he had gotten to know their habits, established that they were competitors not friends, and identified either one as an easy mark. The only thing Bartholomew had to do was ask one of them for an hour of service and take her to a motel, knock her out with a dose of gamma-hydroxybutyrate in a drink, then move her to the cabin and bind her wrists and ankles to the bedposts in readiness for the Sandman.

Bartholomew shifted from foot to foot. He was *vibrating.* "What are you going to do with her?"

Things you can't imagine. "She's a hooker," the Sandman said. "What do you think I'm going to do with her?"

"And for that, you needed someone to give her a date-rape drug and tie her up? Leave her there for two fucking days?"

A carnal leer blossomed. "It's all the rage these days—domination and submission. You ought to try it sometime. The helplessness makes them...eager." He bent close, a man sharing a profound secret with a buddy. "It's like nothing you've ever imagined."

"Jesus God. You're a sick sonofabitch."

"And you, Doctor, a party to my madness. All because your son needs for you to pay off a judge."

Bartholomew held out his hand. "The money. Goddamn it, give me the money."

The Sandman folded the pages and tucked them inside his coat. He reached into the deep pocket, ostensibly for the money, and pulled out the .45 instead. The minion gasped and staggered back a step. Fool.

"Wait...Wha—"

Fwp. The silencer gulped down the shot, and the bullet hit him square in the chest. The minion dropped, his throat making a sucking sound, blood trickling from his open mouth.

The Sandman unscrewed the silencer and tucked the gun back into his pocket. Cleanup done. Risk ameliorated.

Now, for the redhead.

He walked past the mouth of the pyrite mine, back up the boardwalk, and out of the park, his thrift-shop running shoes pinching his feet. His left foot hurt—a hold-over from a childhood injury—and on top of that, he'd have blisters before the night was finished. But it was worth it, even hiking the two miles back to his car, which he'd left in the parking lot of an all-night Walmart. Just before he emerged from the trees, he paused—in case someone saw him getting into his car—and stripped off the booties he'd worn over his shoes. He stuffed them into his pocket, then picked at the scotch tape between his eyes until he found an edge. *Rrripp.* He tore the tape from his left eyebrow, wadded it into a ball the size of a pea, and ripped the second strip from his second eyebrow. He winced. Christ, how did women do that—pluck their eyebrows? Still, he didn't want to risk leaving something as telling as an eyebrow or footprint at a crime scene. The FBI deserved a better challenge than that.

The Sandman swung by a trash can and flicked the tiny balls of tape inside, then climbed in his car, the minion forgotten and the redhead filling his mind. He had no interest in sex with a hooker—not bound or unbound, conscious or unconscious, dead or alive. His only interest was in her body and what message he might send with it. A little taunt for the star of the FBI's Multiple Murders Unit.

A gift from the Sandman.

CHAPTER
2

Monday, November 19, 7:15 a.m.
Horseshoe Island, South Carolina

*F*ASTER.
  Alayna Mann ran, her soles pounding imprints in the sand. To her right, a giant dog loped along with his tongue lolling to one side and seawater dripping from long tufts of fur. To her left, dawn inched closer to the horizon. It wouldn't be long until the entire beach was bathed in light.
  Farther.
  Her lungs dragged in loads of salt air. She didn't know how far she'd run—three, maybe four miles north and now back again—but even with the silhouette of the beach house coming back into view and her limbs loose with exhaustion, she didn't want to stop and face the quiet solitude of the house. Out here, with the waves crashing in her ears, she couldn't hear Chelsea calling to her.
  Please...Don't let him take me...

She ran faster, panting, trying to leave the cries in the wind. She passed a rickety pier with a lantern swaying in the wind, then veered out around a mountain of craggy rocks, and by the time she cleared them, the sun had peeked over the water. The sky grew red, and Layna frowned. What was the saying? *Red sky at night, sailor's delight; red sky in the morning, sailor's take warning.*

It figured. She'd left the bitter chill of a Chicago November for the sunny beach of South Carolina, and here she was running in a dawn that would make a sailor quail.

She slowed, the coppery taste of exertion in the back of her throat. The house stood about a hundred yards ahead like a postcard photo—an isolated stretch of beach with a massive, three-story home perched just across the dune. From a distance, it looked stately and elegant, the kind of house that would sport a giant crystal chandelier in the foyer and Italian mosaic tile on the fireplace.

Up close, it was no such thing.

She slowed to a walk, her breaths coming hard. The dog seemed grateful, not bothering to sniff the beach anymore but plodding along in the surf. Layna spared a thought to wonder how long it had been since he'd been out of a cage long enough to run, then patted her leg and angled toward the house. He followed until they passed the remnants of an elaborate sandcastle someone had constructed too close to the water, the eastern-most turrets and walls now slipping into the sea one wave at a time.

Layna sighed and sank into the sand. The dog sniffed the foam around the lower edges of the castle, and she marveled at his demeanor. From the moment the attendant at the county pound had walked him into the lobby—just twenty-four hours ago—he'd seemed eager to embark on whatever journey awaited. Without knowing Layna from Adam and having no idea where she would take him. Knowing only that no matter what lay in store, it had to be better than where he'd been.

A lesson there to be sure, Layna realized, but she wasn't a dog. She couldn't forget everything she'd left behind just because there was something new to sniff. Not to mention the fact that for her, no one had stepped forward with a hundred bucks and a pocket of treats, signing on a dotted line to proclaim, "You don't have to worry about anything anymore; I'll take care of you now."

A curse passed her lips. For God's sake, that's not what she wanted.

The dog worked his way to the other side of the castle, pouncing on a wave and sneezing from the spray of saltwater. He stuck his nose back in the sand, deeper. Sneezed again.

"Come on," Layna said, getting up, but he ignored her and began to dig, throwing great hunks of wet sand into the ocean behind him. He whined in excitement.

"Hey, you." She'd have to give him a name soon. She walked around the remaining castle turrets and put her hand on his collar, trying to pull him back. He pounced in the foam, splattering Layna. "Oh, no you don't," she said, tugging at his collar. "I'll be the alpha in this relationship. Come on."

The dog lunged for the castle, pulling Layna to one knee. Icy water exploded into her face, and she tried to get her feet back under her as the dog took giant swipes at the beach with his paws, digging. He worked against the waves, going deeper every time the water receded, sticking his nose down to try to grab at whatever was there. Layna staggered to her feet, wiped the salt from her eyes, and squinted at the dent he'd managed to make in the sand.

She frowned. Something there. Another wave washed up, higher, and when the water pulled back into the sea, it left something poking from the sand—pale and smooth, like a row of sea-washed pebbles. A finger of worry tapped at Layna's mind but she bent closer, the dog scooping giant divots of wet sand behind him. He unearthed two more pebbles, white on one side and dark red on the other—

Horror struck. Layna staggered back. Oh God, oh God, oh God. She forced herself to wait through another wave, but her breaths went shallow. In the next moment, the foam took a layer of sand and left five rounded pebbles lined up, large-to-small.

Toes.

Layna screamed. She stumbled backward, and the dog began to bark, as if proud she finally got it. He dove at the toes in between every surge of water, engaging in a strange sort of tug-of-war with the sea. The waves kept coming, each one a few inches higher than the last, each dragging another batch of sand from the castle walls and leaving pools of foam swirling in the grooves and—yes . . . a woman's foot lodged in the sand.

Layna hugged her waist, fighting back the urge to vomit. She turned around and around, searching for any other human. Too remote, too early; there was no one. Beach houses spotted the shore, but each sat on ten or twenty acres of land with nothing but sand and dune grass in between. The ominous red dawn stretched along the horizon, but even in the houses that Layna could see, the lights weren't yet on.

Phone.

She tamped down the panic and patted her arm band, her phone tucked in a Velcro pouch. She ripped it out and dialed 911. Her voice sounded hysterical in her ears.

"There's a woman," she gasped, the dog still trying to get ahead of the tide. "Buried in the sand."

"A woman in the sand?" the voice repeated, sounding undaunted.

"Yes." Layna's heart pounded like a piston.

"Is she breathing?"

"No." Of course she wasn't. Wait. Maybe—"I don't know. I can't see her."

And yet, even as she said it, a larger wave came up and swept away a big enough batch of sand that even the dog backed up, and in the space of five seconds, another foot came into view.

Layna tasted bile. She looked up at the houses again, trying to remember the address of this one. Hibiscus Drive. That was it. Three-seventeen Hibiscus Drive Northeast.

She spat the address at the 911 operator, trying to get her heart to beat evenly again, and in some distant corner of her mind, she heard the operator command her to stay on the line until police arrived. She dropped her hand to her side, her fingers barely holding on to the phone, and with the other hand she took the dog's collar, watching in utter helplessness as the woman's feet came into full view between waves. Painted toenails, a toe-ring on the second toe of her left foot, a butterfly tattoo on her right ankle.

Oh, God.

The 911 operator's disembodied voice came from the phone in her hand, but Layna couldn't bring herself to listen. She looked at the horizon, feeling the inexorable power of the sea—stripping a woman's body of sand, yet at the same time, burying it in rising water. By the time police got here, the woman would likely be knee-deep under water. Or floating freely. That thought brought the nausea up, and Layna hobbled to the water's edge and threw up, her stomach heaving on the emptiness there. When it passed, she rinsed her face and wiped it off with the sweatshirt tied around her waist, then held the dog again and watched another wave pull back into the sea and reveal a knee.

She remembered the phone and put it back to her ear. "I'm here," she said, and let the woman on the other end of the phone try to soothe her. A car had been dispatched; police were on their way. *Was Layna hurt?* No. *Was there anyone else around?* No. And the famous admonition for every crime scene: *Don't touch anything.*

Layna might have laughed at that if it hadn't been so tragic. There would be nothing for police to see. The ocean was taking care of that.

The lawyer in her surfaced. This was a crime scene. Most likely a secondary one, but a crime scene nonetheless. And in a few moments, there would be nothing left.

Against orders, she disconnected from the 911 operator, her brain beginning to function again. She ordered the dog to stay back—the urgency in her voice actually causing him to do it—and touched the camera icon on her cell phone. Frantic, she began snapping pictures, catching the still-erect portion of the castle and then the lumps and gullies of what had once been the eastern walls, shooting photos between waves, from one side and then the other, trying to get every angle and imprint in her mind with an image of what the castle had originally looked like. She moved around the top of it, the upper walls still mostly intact, hoping she might catch a footprint or hand print, maybe a—

She stopped. In the brightening light, something came into view in the uppermost portion of the castle, where the sand was piled deepest. She lowered the camera and bent down. It was a funnel, plastic, buried with the wide-opening up. She reached for it, knowing not to compromise anything about the scene but also knowing that within moments, the scene would be leveled anyway. Police wouldn't get here in time to see this. She looked at the two cone-topped sand turrets that were left and realized that whoever made the castle had left the plastic funnel here.

Fingerprints?

Layna's heart kicked up again, and she snapped several more pictures, then stepped into the soupy sand and grasped the funnel. She pulled, freeing it from the sand, but it seemed to pull back. It wouldn't come loose. She wiggled it, shaking off more sand, then realized it wasn't just a funnel. A tube was attached to the base, duct tape wound around the narrow end of the funnel and sealing it to the tube, which ran beneath the sand.

She frowned and in one terrible instant, reality struck. "No," she breathed, and at the same time, her fingers sprang open and the funnel fell to the beach. Layna swayed, dizzy with horror, and a wave surged in and tossed the funnel in foam. *Is she breathing?* the 911 operator had asked.

Oh, God.

Layna tossed her phone up to dry sand and grabbed the funnel, sinking to her knees, holding it up high. She dug into the sand like the dog and a moment later, he was there, too, digging in glee. She tried to match his energy— harder, deeper, with sobs trembling on her lips and shards of shell cutting her hands. She groaned, forcing her fingers deep into the soaked beach even as the waves kept coming, chilling her to the bone. She freed a few inches of the tube and jammed it under her arm to keep it out of the water, but the beach became moister and heavier with every wave. Sand hit her in the face and clung to the tears on her cheeks, grains flying into mouth and making her cough, and she gagged and grunted as the waves came higher and washed sand and water back into every dent she made. She got a few inches down, then a wave washed in, over and over again. She wailed and cursed the sea. *Is she breathing?* In minutes, both sand and water would pour down the tube into the mouth of the woman beneath. She moved lower toward the woman's feet, where the sand wasn't as deep, and dug harder, deeper, her arms numb and right hand bleeding, scraping at the sand until her nails ripped across something.

A thigh. Layna bit back nausea. Tears mixed with sea water on her cheeks and the dog barked. The ocean lapped at her knees, inches deep now, and something grasped her shoulders, and she screamed and tried to shrug it off, but voices shouted over the waves and other hands began to dig and she was lifted up, the tube falling from beneath her arm, and someone dragging her up the beach and dropping her to dry sand.

"Stop it, lady," a voice said, pinning her arms to her sides. "Stop it."

"She's under there," Layna gasped, coughing. "There's a woman."

"I know. We'll get her."

"She may be alive. There's a tube and funnel. She can still breathe."

"Funnel?"

The man went still. He straightened and watched one

of the uniforms pick up the plastic funnel, the connected tube attached but disappearing into ever-deepening water.

"Jesus Christ," he said, deep in his chest. Another man handed the dog off to Layna, then jogged back to the castle site. Layna turned and looked to see who had pulled her away—a uniformed officer in his fifties, emblems and bars on his jacket. His face was the color of rice paper, and he stared at the two men who'd taken over the digging as best they could with their hands, one of them shouting, "We need shovels, we need shovels!" even as he dropped to his knees in the surf and dug deeper. Two more officers arrived, and the man holding Layna reached out and snagged one of them.

"Call the FBI," he said, his voice choked. "Ask for Mike Hogan."

"The FBI?" asked the cop. "What the hell, Elliott?"

The man named Elliott swallowed, still sheet-white. He bent toward the cop and spoke just above the rumbling waves. "Tell him it's the Sandman."

THE DISH

Where Authors Give You the Inside Scoop

♥ ♥ ♥ ♥ ♥ ♥ ♥ ♥ ♥ ♥ ♥ ♥ ♥ ♥ ♥ ♥ ♥

From the desk of Marilyn Pappano

Dear Reader,

One of the pluses of writing the Tallgrass series was one I didn't anticipate until I was neck-deep in the process, but it's been a great one: unearthing old memories. Our Navy career was filled with laugh-out-loud moments, but there were also plenty of the laugh-or-you'll-cry moments, too. We did a lot of laughing. Most of our tears were reserved for later.

Like our very first move to South Carolina, when the movers lost our furniture for weeks, and the day after it was finally delivered, my husband got orders to Alabama. On our second move, the delivery guys perfected their truck-unloading routine: three boxes into the apartment, one box into the front of their truck. (Fortunately, Bob had perfected his watch-the-unloaders routine and recovered it all.)

For our first apartment move-out inspection, we had scrubbed ourselves to nubbins all through the night. The manager did the walk-through, commented on how impeccably clean everything was, and offered me the paperwork to sign. I signed it, turned around to hand it to her, and walked into the low-hanging chandelier where the dining table used to sit, breaking a bulb with my head. Silently she took back the papers, thumbed through to the deduction sheet, and charged us sixty cents for a new bulb.

There's something about being told my Oklahoma accent is funny by multi-generation Americans with accents so heavy that I just guessed at the context of our conversations. Or hearing our two-year-old Oklahoma-born son, home for Christmas, proudly singing, "Jaaan-gle baaaa-ulllz! Jaaan-gle baaaa-ulllz! Jaaan-gle *alllll* the waaay-uh!"

Bob and I still trade stories. *Remember when we did that self-move to San Diego and the brakes went out on the rental truck in 5:00 traffic in Memphis at the start of a holiday weekend? Remember that pumpkin pie on the first Thanksgiving we couldn't go home—the one I forgot to put the spices in? Remember dropping the kiddo off at the base day care while we got groceries and having to pay the grand sum of fifty cents two hours later? How about when you had to report to the commanding general for joint-service duty at Fort Gordon and we couldn't find your Dixie cup anywhere in the truck crammed with boxes—and at an Army post, no less, that didn't stock Navy uniforms?*

Sea life was great. We watched ships leaving and, months later, come home again. On one homecoming, the kiddo and I watched Daddy's ship run aground. We learned that all sailors look alike when they're dressed in the same uniform and seen from a distance. We spied submarines stealthing out of their bases and toured warships—American, British, French, Canadian—and even got to board one of our own nuclear subs for a private look around.

The Navy gave us a lot to remember and a lot to learn. (Example: all those birthdays and anniversaries

Bob missed didn't mean a thing. It was the fact that he came home that mattered.) I still have a few dried petals from the flowers given to me by the command each time Bob reenlisted, as well the ones I got when he retired. We have a flag, like the one each of the widows in Tallgrass received, and a display box of medals and ribbons, but filled with much happier memories.

I can't wait to see which old *remember when* the next book in this series brings us! I hope you love reading A MAN TO ON HOLD TO as much as I loved writing it.

Sincerely,

Marilyn Pappano

MarilynPappano.com
Twitter @MarilynPappano
Facebook.com/MarilynPappanoFanPage

♥ ♥ ♥ ♥ ♥ ♥ ♥ ♥ ♥ ♥ ♥ ♥ ♥ ♥ ♥

From the desk of Jaime Rush

Dear Reader,

Much has been written about angels. When I realized that angels would be part of my mythology and hidden world, I knew I needed to make mine different. I didn't want to use the religious mythos or pair them with demons. Many authors have done a fantastic job of this already.

In fact, I felt this way about my world in general. I started with the concept that a confluence of nature and the energy in the Bermuda Triangle had allowed gods and angels to take human form. They procreated with the humans living on the island and were eventually sent back to their plane of existence. But I didn't want to draw on Greek, Roman, or Atlantean mythology, so I made up my own pantheon of gods. I narrowed them down to three different types: Dragons, sorcerers, and angels. Their progeny continue to live in the area of the Triangle, tethered there by their need to be near their energy source.

My angels come from this pantheon, without the constraints of traditional religious roles. They were sent down to the island to police the wayward gods, but succumbed to human temptation. And their progeny pay the price. I'm afraid my angels' descendents, called Caidos, suffer terribly for their fathers' sins. This was not something I contrived; these concepts often just come to me as the truths of my stories.

Caidos are preternaturally beautiful, drawing the desire of those who see them. But desire, their own and others', causes them physical pain. As do the emotions of all but their own kind. They guard their secret, for their lives depend on it. To keep pain at bay, they isolate themselves from the world and shut down their sexuality. Which, of course, makes it all the more fun when they are thrown together with women they find attractive. Pleasure and pain is a fine line, and Kasabian treads it in a different way than other Caidos. Then again, he is different, harboring a dark secret that compounds his sense of isolation.

Perhaps it was slightly sadistic to pair him with a woman who holds the essence of the goddess of sensuality.

Kye is his greatest temptation, but she may also be his salvation. He needs to form a bond with the woman who can release his dark shadow. I don't make it easy on Kye, either. She must lose everything to find her soul. I love to dig deep into my characters' psyches and mine their darkest shadows. Only then can they come into the light.

And isn't that something we all can learn? To face our shadows so that we can walk in the light? That's what I love most about writing: that readers, too, can take the journey of self discovery, self love, right along with my characters. They face their demons and come out on the other end having survived.

We all have magic in our imaginations. Mine has always contained murder, mayhem, and romance. Feel free to wander through the madness of my mind any time. A good place to start is my website, www.jaimerush .com, or that of my romantic suspense alter ego, www .tinawainscott.com.

Jaime Rush

♥ ♥ ♥ ♥ ♥ ♥ ♥ ♥ ♥ ♥ ♥ ♥ ♥ ♥ ♥

From the desk of Kate Brady

Dear Reader,

People ask me all the time, "What do you like about writing romantic suspense?" It's a great question, and it always seems like sort of a copout to say, "Everything!" But it's true. Writing novels is the greatest job in the world. And romantic suspense, in particular, allows my favorite elements to exist in a single story: adventure, danger, thrills, chills, romance, and the gratifying knowledge that good will triumph over evil and love will win the day.

Weaving all those elements together is, for me, a labor of love. I love being able to work with something straight from my own mind, without having to footnote and document sources all the time. (In my other career—academia—they frown upon letting the voices in my head do the writing!) I love the flexibility of where and when I can indulge myself in a story—the deck, the kitchen island, the car, the beach, and any number of recliners are my favorite "offices." I love seeing the stories unfold, being surprised by the twists and turns they take, and ultimately coming across them in their finished forms on the bookstore shelves. I love hearing from readers and being privy to their take on the story line or a character. I love meeting other writers and hobnobbing with the huge network of readers and writers out there who still love romantic suspense.

And I *love* getting to know new characters. I don't create these people; they already exist when a story begins and it becomes my job to reveal them. I just go along for the ride as they play out their roles, and I'm repeatedly surprised and delighted by what they prove to be. And it never fails: I always fall in love.

Luke Mann, the hero in WHERE EVIL WAITS, was one of the most intriguing characters I have met and he turned out to be one of my all-time favorites. He first appeared in his brother's book, *Where Angels Rest*, so I knew his hometown, his upbringing, his parents, and his siblings. But Luke himself came to me shrouded in shadows. I couldn't wait to write his story; he was dark and fascinating and intense (not to mention gorgeous) and I knew from the start that his adventure would be a whirlwind ride. When I put him in an alley with his soon-to-be heroine, Kara Chandler—who shocked both Luke and me with a boldness I hadn't expected—I fell in love with both of them. From that point on, WHERE EVIL WAITS was off and running, as Luke and Kara tried to elude and capture a killer as twisted and dangerous as the barbed wire that was his trademark.

The time Luke and Kara spend together is brief, but jam-packed with action, heat, and, ultimately, affection. I hope you enjoy reading their story as much as I enjoyed writing it!

Happy Reading!

Kate Brady

♥ ♥ ♥ ♥ ♥ ♥ ♥ ♥ ♥ ♥ ♥ ♥ ♥ ♥ ♥ ♥ ♥

From the desk of Amanda Scott

Dear Reader,

The plot of THE WARRIOR'S BRIDE, set in the fourteenth-century Scottish Highlands near Loch Lomond, grew from a law pertaining to abduction that must have seemed logical to its ancient Celtic lawmakers.

I have little doubt that they intended that law to protect women.

However, I grew up in a family descended from a long line of lawyers, including my father, my grandfather, and two of the latter's great-grandfathers, one of whom was the first Supreme Court justice for the state of Arkansas (an arrangement made by his brother, the first senator from Missouri, who also named Arkansas—so just a little nepotism there). My brother is a judge. His son and one of our cousins are defense attorneys. So, as you might imagine, laws and the history of law have stirred many a dinner-table conversation throughout my life.

When I was young, I spent countless summer hours traveling with my paternal grandmother and grandfather in their car, listening to him tell stories as he drove. Once, when I pointed out brown cows on a hillside, he said, "Well, they're brown on this side, anyhow."

That was my first lesson in looking at both sides of any argument, and it has served me well in my profession. This is by no means the first time I've met a law that sowed the seeds for an entire book.

Women, as we all know, are unpredictable creatures who have often taken matters into their own hands in ways of which men—especially in olden times—have disapproved. Thanks to our unpredictability, many laws that men have made to "protect" us have had the opposite effect.

The heroine of THE WARRIOR'S BRIDE is the lady Muriella MacFarlan, whose father, Andrew, is the rightful chief of Clan Farlan. A traitorous cousin has usurped Andrew's chiefdom and murdered his sons, so Andrew means to win his chiefdom back by marrying his daughters to warriors from powerful clans, who will help him.

Muriella, however, intends *never* to marry. I based her character on Clotho, youngest of the three Fates and the one who is responsible for spinning the thread of life. So Murie is a spinner of threads, yarns...and stories.

Blessed with a flawless memory, Muriella aspires to be a *seanachie*, responsible for passing the tales of Highland folklore and history on to future generations. She has already developed a reputation for her storytelling and takes that responsibility seriously.

She seeks truth in her tales of historical events. However, in her personal life, Murie enjoys a more flexible notion of truth. She doesn't lie, exactly. She spins.

Enter blunt-spoken warrior Robert MacAulay, a man of honor with a clear sense of honor, duty, and truth. Rob also has a vision that, at least for the near future, does not include marriage. Nor does he approve of truth-spinning.

Consequently, sparks fly between the two of them even *before* Murie runs afoul of the crazy law. I think you will enjoy THE WARRIOR'S BRIDE.

Meantime, *Suas Alba!*

Sincerely,

Amanda Scott

www.amandascottauthor.com

♥ ♥ ♥ ♥ ♥ ♥ ♥ ♥ ♥ ♥ ♥ ♥ ♥ ♥ ♥ ♥

From the desk of Mimi Jean Pamfiloff

Dear People Pets—Oops, sorry—I meant, Dear Readers,

Ever wonder what's like to be God of the Sun, Ruler of the House of Gods, and the only deity against procreation with humans (an act against nature)?

Nah. Me neither. I want to know what it's like to be his girlfriend. After all, how many guys house the power of the sun inside their seven-foot frames? And that hair. Long thick ribbons of sun-streaked caramel. And those muscles. Not an ounce of fat to be found on that insanely ripped body. As for the...eh-hem, the *performance* part, well, I'd like to know all about that, too.

Actually, so would Penelope. Especially after spending the evening with him, sipping champagne in his hotel room, and then waking up buck naked. Yes. In his bed. And yes, he's naked, too. Yeah, she'd love to remember what happened. He wouldn't mind, either.

But it seems that the only one who might know anything is Cimil, Goddess of the Underworld, instigator of all things naughty, and she's nowhere to be found. I guess Kinich and Penelope will have to figure this out for themselves. So what will be the consequence of breaking these "rules" of nature Kinich fears so much? Perhaps the price will be Penelope's life. But perhaps, just maybe, the price will be his...

Happy Reading!

Mimi

♥ ♥ ♥ ♥ ♥ ♥ ♥ ♥ ♥ ♥ ♥ ♥ ♥ ♥ ♥

From the desk of Shannon Richard

Dear Reader,

I knew how Brendan and Paige were going to meet from the very start. It was the first scene that played out in my mind. Paige was going to be having a very bad day on top of a very bad couple of months. Her Jeep breaks down in the middle of nowhere Florida, during a sweltering day, and she was to call someone for help. It's when she's at her lowest that she meets the love of her life; she just doesn't know it at the time. As for Brendan, he isn't expecting anyone like Paige to come along. Not now, not ever. But he knows pretty quickly that he has feelings for her, and that they're serious feelings.

Paige can be a little sassy, and Brendan can be a little cocky, so during their first encounter sparks are flying all over the place. Things start to get hot quickly, and it has very little to do with summer in the South (which is hot and miserable, I can tell you from over twenty years of experience). But at the end of the day, and no matter the confrontation, Brendan is Paige's white knight. He comes to her rescue in more ways than one.

The inspiration behind Brendan is a very laid-back Southern guy. He's easygoing (for the most part) and charming. He hasn't been one for long-term serious relationships, but when it comes to Paige he jumps right on in. There's just something about a guy who knows exactly what he wants, who meets the girl and doesn't hesitate. Yeah, it makes me swoon more than just a little. I hoped that readers would appreciate that aspect of him. The diving in headfirst and not looking back, and Brendan doesn't look back.

As for Paige, she's dealing with a lot and is more than a little scared about getting involved with another guy. Her wounds are too fresh and deep from her recent heartbreak. Brendan knows all about pain and suffering. Instead of turning his back on her, he steps up to the plate. He helps Paige heal, helps her get a job and friends, helps her find a place in the little town of Mirabelle. It just so happens that her place is right next to his.

So yes, Brendan is this big, tough, alpha man who comes to the rescue of the damsel in distress. But Paige isn't exactly a weak little thing. No, she's pretty strong herself. It's part of that strength that Brendan is so drawn to. He loves her passion and how fierce she is. But really, he just loves her.

I'm a fan of the happily ever after. Always have been, always will be. I love my characters; they're part of me. They might exist in black and white on the page, but to me they're real. At the end of the day, I just want them to be happy.

Cheers,

ShannonRichard.net
Twitter @Shan_Richard
Facebook.com/ShannonNRichard